David Butler is a popular writer for the stage and television whose many successes include EDWARD VII, DISRAELI and LILLIE. More recently he has written the bestselling novel, LUSITANIA.

Keith Miles was born and brought up in Wales and went on to read History at Oxford. He has written plays for television, radio and the stage and contributed to many series. He has ublished several novels, most recently, the MEET AGAIN based on LW utler.
MARCO PO and this noveliza ts an already esta avid *Butler* and

David Butler and Keith Miles

Marco Polo

Based on the screenplay by David Butler, Vincenzo Labella and Giuliano Montaldo

Futura/Jade
Macdonald & Co
London & Sydney

A Futura/Jade Book

First published in Great Britain in 1982 by
Futura Publications, a Division of
Macdonald & Co (Publishers) Ltd

ISBN 0 7088 2221 5

Filmset, printed and bound in Great Britain by
Hazell Watson & Viney Ltd, Aylesbury, Bucks

Futura Publications
A Division of Macdonald & Co (Publishers) Ltd
Maxwell House
74 Worship Street
London EC2A 2EN

Emperors and kings, dukes and marquises, counts, knights and townsfolk, and all people who wish to know the various races of men and the peculiarities of the various regions of the world, take this book and have it read to you. Here you will find all the great wonders and curiosities of Greater Armenia and Persia, of the Tartars and of India, and of many other territories. Our book will relate them to you plainly in due order, as they were related by Messer Marco Polo, a wise and noble citizen of Venice, who has seen them with his own eyes.

The Travels of Marco Polo (1298)

Prologue

Night came like death itself.

Mist shrouded the whole fleet, and the galleys could see nothing more of each other than the occasional position light, casting its spectral glow for a few seconds before disappearing again. Though the wind was too low to do more than tease the sails, its touch was clammy and its whisper unsettling. The blue waters of the Adriatic were colourless now, cold and lifeless. Voices sounded eerie in the stillness and the laughter of men below deck seemed strangely hollow and unreal. The vessels themselves sighed and groaned like spirits in torment, their tall masts pointing despairingly upwards, their rigging skeletal, their proud flags limp.

The cloaked figure on the quarterdeck of one of the leading galleys was motionless, leaning against the bulwark, gazing out into the moonlit sky. When two men came from the covered bridge and stepped on to the deck with heavy feet, he did not even hear them, nor did he stir when their lantern found him. The men, whose beautifully-made leather armour marked them out as officers, exchanged a glance and then crossed over to the silent figure.

One of them cleared his throat. 'Captain . . .' There was no response. The officer raised his voice. 'Captain Polo!'

Marco Polo shifted and looked round inquiringly.

'It's the eleventh hour, sir. Our turn for guard duty. You should get some rest, sir.'

'The sea is as flat as a plate,' said the other officer, 'and the mist is rising all the time. We are in safe waters.'

Marco Polo shook his head. Beard bleached by sun and brine, skin hardened by travel, he had the weathered look of a man who has lived a life of adventure in the open air.

His face was handsome, his startlingly clear blue eyes shrewd and alert. He was of a good height, his body honed down to a lean hardness, as supple and agile as a boy, although he had just passed forty. He drew his woollen cloak more tightly round him against the dank air. A long and close acquaintance with danger had given him an instinctive awareness of its presence. 'I don't like this calm,' he said. 'It suits the light galleys of the Genoese fleet.' He glanced up at the sails, hanging limply from their yards. 'Ours are too heavy. With no wind they won't even answer the rudder. We'll have to use the oars.'

'With your permission, Captain Polo,' reminded one of the officers. 'You know that the Admiral has ordered the fleet not to break formation.'

'We should not change our position until we can see our way clear,' warned the other man.

Marco narrowed his eyes to peer into the gathering mist. He caught a glimpse of a stern light on a neighbouring vessel; then it was lost. Once again he felt the prickling sense of danger. 'Soon we'll be sailing blind. May St Mark protect us!'

As if in answer, the flag atop the main mast was disturbed by a freshening breeze and unfurled enough to display the symbol of the Republic of Venice – the glorious lion of St Mark.

'There's a west wind blowing up, sir,' reassured one of the men.

'If we can't see – neither can they!' added his companion. 'We shouldn't be far off Curzola.'

A long silence followed. It was broken by the sound of the hatch door opening behind them. A shaft of light cut into the gloom and a voice called to one of the officers, 'Alvise! Alvise!'

But before Alvise could swing round to answer, there was a tremendous crash and the galley tilted sharply to one side as if it had just struck submerged rocks. Yells were heard from below as men came scrambling up on deck to see what had happened. Suddenly, above the clamour and confusion, a new and terrifying sound rang out, a rousing battle cry that came from hundreds of throats and seemed to fill the whole sea.

'For Genoa and St George! Genoa and St George!'

With the advantage of surprise and superior numbers, the Genoese sailors surged aboard the Venetian galley which they had rammed so effectively. Grappling irons bit into the wood of the bulwark. The officer standing by Marco coughed and slumped to his knees, dead, even as he plucked at the shaft of the arrow which had smacked into his throat above his silver gorget. More arrows came whistling out of the darkness, scything through the Venetian seamen as they clambered from the hatches. Then the decks were alive with clashing pikes, thrusting swords and daggers as the two sides closed in a death struggle.

Marco and Alvise were at the very heart of the battle. A small group of Venetians rushed to form a protective wall around their captain, but two of them fell at once to enemy steel and a third was clubbed to the deck at Marco's feet. As a grinning Genoese raised his mace again, Marco stabbed up under his chainmail corselet. The man doubled over with a bubbling scream.

Both sides were now fighting with skill and savagery, and the decks were awash with blood. Howls of pain and cries for mercy could be heard above the clash of weapons, but no quarter was given. In the ferocious battle between the two old enemies, lungs and stomachs were ripped open, limbs hacked off, heads severed from bodies. Some were trampled to death, others hurled overboard into the sea. One man fell from the rigging to be impaled on a pike, which held him for one long, quivering second and then snapped under his weight.

Marco sensed that the boarding party had the upper hand, and it made him struggle more desperately. Using sword and dagger, he lunged, thrust and parried, clearing a space round the wounded Alvise and the Venetians who had come to his side. He felt the galley list even more, and water came bursting over the bulwarks. He knew that his vessel was lost, but he was determined not to surrender. He felt a searing pain in his left shoulder as a sword-point cut through his armour, then dispatched his assailant with a thrust that took steel clean through the man's neck.

More water was pouring across the decks now and adding to the Venetian terror. A jubilant cry from above made Marco look up in time to see a nimble Genoese sailor tear down the lion banner from the main mast and throw it into the sea. Victorious cheers went up to signal that the galley had been taken. St Mark had been humbled by St George.

Though he continued to fight bravely, Marco's resistance was short-lived. Hopelessly outnumbered, he was forced back against the sterncastle. All around him lay the dead and wounded bodies of his men. He still fought with the rage of defeat, although he had lost his dagger and his arm was numb with pain, until a heavy spar thrown from the side smashed into his forehead and he fell into the darkness of oblivion.

How long he remained unconscious he did not know, but when his eyes finally opened he found himself stretched out on bare boards slick with bilge scum in the hold of the Genoese galley. He heard moaning and muttering all round him. He tried to crane his neck to look around at the dozens of other prisoners, but the pain in his head and shoulder made him wince. There was another dull ache in his right hand, from a gash he had received in the battle. Both wounds had been bound with rough, dirty cloth, but he had clearly lost a lot of blood and was very weak. All that he could do was to lie there and endure the warm stink of his companions, gazing up at the iron grille above that admitted a fierce column of light. Soon he lapsed back into sleep.

A tumultuous welcome greeted the galleys of St George as they arrived in triumph at their home port of Genoa, towing the captured Venetian vessels stern foremost and with banners trailing. Weak and downcast, Marco and his fellow-prisoners were herded up on deck as their craft sailed past the Molo Vecchio, the vast breakwater that was being built to provide safe harbourage for the commune's mighty fleet of war galleys and merchantmen. Though still frail and unsteady, Marco managed to push his way through to take a first look at the city.

Genoa was breathtaking. Even Marco, who had gazed on so many wondrous sights, was impressed by what he saw. Rising high above the city were majestic, cloud-capped mountains, dressed in a robe of olive trees, which hung in rich, green folds and which lent an air of opulence to the whole prospect. Nestling against the hem of this striking natural garment was Genoa itself, its marble palaces glinting in the sun, its cathedral reaching towards heaven, its houses, towers and spires giving the effect of the most delicate embroidery.

'Come on! Move along there!'

The fairytale exploded the moment that Marco and the others were driven ashore by the guards and through the jeering crowd on the quayside. What had looked so enchanting from the sea was dirty, noisy, ugly and haphazard at close quarters. As the prisoners were taken up interminable flights of steps twisting between high buildings, they found themselves in narrow streets that shut out virtually all light.

The climb took its toll of Marco's remaining strength and he stumbled to the ground. Another prisoner knelt beside him.

'Messer Marco!' Though limping himself, the man tried to lift the prostrate figure. 'Captain . . . Captain!'

Marco revived enough to recognize Giovanni, one of the archers from his galley. A guard came pushing through the prisoners to see why the column had stopped. When he saw Marco he gestured with his pike. 'Pick him up and get moving!'

Marco was helped to his feet, but moments later he pitched forward again. Another prisoner grabbed his left arm to support him, and Marco screamed out in pain as the gash in his shoulder opened again.

'Careful!' warned Giovanni. 'He's wounded.'

Feverish as well as exhausted, Marco leant against Giovanni. His legs refused to obey him, and Giovanni had to take his full weight, gasping as he did so. After a few steps, Giovanni turned imploringly to the guard. 'Help him, I beg you. He needs water. He's burning with fever.'

'Everyone has fever,' replied the guard.

'But this is Captain Polo! Marco Polo. He's a Venetian nobleman!'

The guard shrugged. 'Keep moving,' he ordered.

'You have no pity!' accused Giovanni.

'You Venetians killed two of my brothers, so don't talk pity to me. Now, move!' He prodded Marco roughly in the back with the butt of his pike, pushing him forward.

Leaning heavily on the younger man, Marco dragged himself painfully along until they reached the gates of the prison. He took a last look at the small patch of open sky that was still visible, and was then thrust inside by the guard.

Though his rank entitled him to better treatment, Marco was thrown into a large, dank cell with a mass of other Venetians. It was overcrowded, with only a few filthy palliasses to sleep on. These were soon taken by the fittest, while the rest lay on a scattering of dirty straw on the stone floor. Once a day there was watery gruel and stale bread to eat.

Giovanni, who had elected himself the personal servant of his captain, soon discovered that he had to act as a bodyguard as well.

'That's enough! Break it up! Break it up!'

Genoese guards unlocked the cell door and came rushing in to stop what sounded like a small riot. Two prisoners were wrestling fiercely on the ground, egged on by the others, who were shouting and kicking at the smaller of the two as they rolled over. When the guards waded into the uproar, lashing out with their clubs at whoever was nearest, the prisoners moved quickly to the walls of the cell, pretending to have had nothing to do with the disturbance. Giovanni, who had been grappling with a man much bigger and stronger than himself, was panting as he got unsteadily to his feet.

Footsteps were heard coming down the stone passage-way and all eyes turned to the door as Arnolfo, the Prison Commander, strode in. He was an elegant man dressed in exquisitely chased armour, with the grace and bearing of an aristocrat. He looked around with cool disdain at the scene which confronted him, his nostrils contracting at the stench of sickness and stale urine. He spoke calmly but with chilling effectiveness, looking slowly and menacingly around the prisoners, who were now cowering away from him. 'You will tell me who began this disgraceful brawl. Otherwise, every tenth man will be hanged.' There was an agonizing silence as each prisoner weighed the commander's words.

After a minute's silence Arnolfo ran out of patience. 'Very well.'

He signalled to a guard, who stepped forward to grab a first victim for the gallows. Losing his nerve, the big, glowering man who had fought Giovanni pointed at the figure on the floor. 'It was him! He started it!'

Arnolfo glanced around questioningly at the others. None of them dared to speak, because the big man had already established his ascendancy as the bully in the cell. Arnolfo took their silence as consent. 'Bring him!' he snapped.

Two guards bent down to pick up Marco from the straw. He was limp and unprotesting in their hands, his eyes unfocussed, his whole body streaming with sweat.

'Can't you see, sir?' pleaded Giovanni. 'He's wounded, and he has the fever. He can hardly move. The others attacked him. I tried to defend him, but . . .'

Giovanni's bruised appearance showed that he had been getting the worst of the fight. Seeing that Marco was quite harmless, Arnolfo nodded and the guards lowered their burden to the floor again. The Prison Commander appraised the Venetians.

'Why did you accuse him? What has he done?'

'He's a troublemaker!' retorted the bully.

'It's all because of his lying, sir,' argued another man.

'All those stories he goes on about,' said a gaunt man in ragged clothes. 'You should hear them, sir!'

'Blasphemies!' the bully agreed. 'That's what they are! He's the son of Satan. He tries to make us believe stories of priests that fly, of a dust that explodes, of gods and dragons. He takes advantage of our ignorance!'

'What are these stories?' asked Arnolfo.

'He's only remembering his travels, sir,' explained Giovanni. 'He's a Venetian merchant, commander of a galley. He tells of many strange things, things that are difficult to understand. But only because he has the fever, sir. He's delirious – he doesn't know what he's saying.'

'The commander of a galley?' Arnolfo's interest had been aroused. 'And who are you? His servant?'

'One of many, sir,' said Giovanni, lying readily. 'He's a nobleman, sir. His family is very rich. They'd pay a fine ransom for him.'

'Rich, you say?' Arnolfo studied the sick man at his feet. 'Well, we certainly don't want him to die before we can collect that ransom. We'll put him in the tower, in the same cell as that other storyteller.' He looked at Giovanni. 'Take his feet.'

'Yes sir!' Giovanni could not obey quickly enough.

Arnolfo crossed over to the three prisoners who had spoken out against Marco. 'So you would betray one of your commanders to save your own miserable necks,' he said with contempt. Turning to a guard, he gestured scornfully at the bully and his two companions. 'Whip them. Thirty . . . no, *fifty* lashes!' He strode out.

After the conditions they had endured so far, the cell to which Marco and Giovanni were conducted was almost comfortable. It was dry and clean, with a small barred window that afforded a view of the sky, a chair, a table, two stools, and two truckle beds.

As the guards slammed shut and bolted the thick nail-studded door, the cell's other occupant rose quickly and helped Giovanni to lay Marco on one of the beds.

The fever which had dogged Marco was now tightening its hold. By nightfall he was delirious, threshing wildly, babbling continuously and alternating between bouts of copious sweating and fits of shivering. For days Giovanni nursed him, now wiping him with a damp cloth, now covering him with every possible source of warmth, even the woven floor mat, talking gently and encouragingly to him, although there were times when Marco struck weakly at him, pushing him away in what seemed like terror. All through the night, Giovanni knelt beside him, listening for the faint stir of his breath, gazing in the pale glimmer of moonlight at the plain crucifix on the wall above him.

From far away, Marco heard the sound of trickling water and his head turned slowly towards it. It was as if he was looking through a clouded glass, which gradually cleared. He was on the edge of a tiny, enclosed garden, formal and pretty, the paths of raked pebbles and the carefully-placed flowering shrubs drawing the eye to a small fountain in the shape of twin pagodas. Water spilled musically from the tops of the pagodas into the marble base, where long-finned goldfish swam indolently. Seated by the fountain was a slender girl, wearing an ankle-length rose skirt with a silken lavender overtunic, gathered by a wide sash. Her dark hair was upswept. She was beautiful, her skin a warm ivory, her eyes delicately aslant over her high cheekbones. She looked up and, as if recognizing him, smiled shyly. He knew her. He was sure he could remember her, but as he tried to say her name, the image blurred and he saw that he was in a stone cell bright with sunlight from its one window. He was nearly naked. A man was kneeling on a mat near him, wringing out a cloth into a bowl of water.

The trickling sound. Slowly he recognized the blunt features of young Giovanni, the archer. 'Where . . . Where are we?' he croaked.

Giovanni dropped the cloth and spun round. 'Messer Polo!'

'Where are we?' Marco repeated.

'Genoa. In prison,' Giovanni told him. He peered closely at him, relieved to see that Marco even managed a smile. 'Your fever's broken,' Giovanni whispered. 'You're going to get well.'

'He should drink some water,' a quiet voice said from the other side of the room.

Peering past Giovanni, Marco made out a table, on which lay a few scrolls of parchment and an illuminated prayerbook. A man was standing at the table, pouring a beaker of water. He was wearing a brown, faded monk's habit and looked older than Marco and shorter, balding. The old robe he was wearing was looped over a belt, which bisected a notable stomach. 'Who are you?' he murmured.

The man passed the beaker to Giovanni. 'All questions will be answered when you have drunk the water and slept some more,' he promised, his voice reassuring.

Soon the effort of talking and remembering had been too much and Marco's eyes had closed again, but this time in a deep and restoring sleep.

It was night again when he awoke. The man in the monk's habit was seated at the table, reading by a stub of candle. Giovanni came to Marco and helped him to sit up slightly.

'Now you can eat.' He laid something by Marco's side.

Marco was surprised to see a dish of milk and a peeled orange. 'From the Genoese?' he asked wonderingly.

'From the good Captain of the Guard,' Giovanni admitted with a grin. 'I'm afraid I led him to believe that you are very rich.'

'In misfortune,' Marco said quietly.

'Just the opposite, I'd say.' The man at the table turned and Marco saw again the mobile, intelligent face and the bright, humorous eyes. 'I've never met anyone more fortunate. You were badly wounded and eaten up with fever. You should thank the Lord for giving you a heart of iron.'

Marco was puzzled and touched his shoulder carefully. 'I don't understand,' he said. 'My wound has healed.'

'And so it should have. You've been here nearly five weeks.' Marco gazed at him, shaken. 'You are lucky to be so strong, my friend. There are ten thousand of you Venetians in here. Over half are dead or dying of the plague. So you are doubly lucky to have been sent to join me up in the tower.'

Marco closed his eyes. He was still weak and tears came easily at the thought of the fate of his comrades. 'You'll forgive me, sir,' he said, 'but who are you?'

The man smiled. 'My name is Rustichello. Amadeo Rustichello, of Pisa. Captured in the first of these Trade Wars.'

'Are you a monk?' Marco asked.

'Bless you, my son,' Rustichello intoned solemnly, then chuckled. 'No. A prisoner like yourself. By profession I am a writer of romances, tales of courtly love and knightly adventure.' He gave a mock bow. 'When my own clothes wore out, the kindly friar who came to hear my confession presented me with his own second-best robe.' He sniffed at his arm. 'I'm afraid that now it has more the odour of wine than of sanctity.'

His infectious, irreverent laugh made the others smile.

'Eat now and sleep some more, sir,' Giovanni insisted. 'Time enough for talking when you're really well.'

Marco slept the clock round and all the next night. When he woke, his head was clear and he was strong enough to sit up by himself. Rustichello was writing at the table. He laid down his pen and nodded approvingly. 'That's better. I hope you realize how much you owe to your servant.'

'Not my servant,' Marco said, looking over to Giovanni. 'My friend.'

Giovanni flushed with pleasure. He hardly knew where to look and muttered his thanks, bobbing his head.

'Better still,' Rustichello chuckled. 'As friends we shall have more chance of surviving in this Genoese pesthouse. And we can talk more freely.'

'There's a lot I want to ask you,' Marco said.

'And I you, my dear sir,' Rustichello assured him. 'Oh, indeed. A great deal. I could scarcely control my patience until you had recovered.'

'What are our chances of release?' Marco asked. 'Or of escaping?'

Rustichello's mouth pursed regretfully. 'None. Very few have been released, and no one has escaped successfully. It's a sure way to death. I should know. I've seen many attempts.'

'How long have you been here?' Marco asked.

'Nine years,' Rustichello shrugged. 'Or maybe ten. I've a suspicion I may have mislaid one.'

It was a fearsome thought, and Giovanni shivered, crossing himself. 'Ten years . . .' he whispered.

'I have no money to pay a ransom,' the older man explained philosophically. 'But the Genoese treat me well enough in return for a few tales of battle and enchanted princes. Now they expect the same from you, friend Marco.'

Marco did not follow him. 'From *me*?'

'Were you not sent up here for causing such an uproar with your tales?'

'I'm no romancer,' Marco said. 'I only tell what I recall of my travels. I'm a plain merchant-venturer.'

'Come now,' Rustichello beamed. 'No need for modesty. I listened to you in your fever and you babbled things a hundred times more intriguing and extraordinary than any of *my* stories.'

'That's true, sir,' Giovanni chuckled. 'Such wonderful inventions!'

'But they were not inventions,' Marco told him seriously. 'I have been to those places.'

Rustichello was dumbfounded for a moment. Giovanni's jaw dropped in surprise, then he grinned; obviously Marco was trying to fool them. The older man scratched his bald patch and leaned in closer to Marco. 'But no man of the West, of Europe, has ever journeyed to the lands of darkness and returned.'

'I have,' Marco said simply.

In the silence, Giovanni looked from his captain to the writer of romances and back. 'Then it's all true, sir?' Giovanni's eyes widened. 'Everything you said was *true*?'

'How long were you there?' asked Rustichello.

'For twice as long as you've been here. I left when I was still a boy.'

'And how much do you remember of what you've seen and heard?' Rustichello's eagerness was showing.

'Everything,' Marco sighed. 'I am cursed with a memory that will not let me forget one day of my life.'

Rustichello clapped his hands in delight. 'Then you must tell me the story of your life, your travels and your adventures! You *have* seen wonders?'

'Many.'

'Would you like to hear your Captain's adventures, too, Giovanni?'

'About kings and foreign lands? They make my head spin. If Master Polo has no objection . . .'

Marco hesitated, embarrassed. To tell it truly, holding nothing back, would be like a confession. And there were things he preferred not to remember. 'But I should have to talk for days and days . . .'

'We have endless days ahead of us, friend Marco,' Rustichello said. 'Years, perhaps.'

It was a sobering thought and it helped Marco to come to a decision. He looked from one to the other, then made an effort to concentrate. There were so many details to remember and so many events to describe. If it were to be told, he wanted to make sure that it was all in the right order, not a dry tale nor a storyteller's fantasy, but fairly and truly set forth.

The beginning? he thought. The beginning was Venice, La Serenissima, the Most Serene Republic, Bride of the Adriatic. Venice, under its elected Doge and Council of Elders, had made itself the foremost trading port in the known world. Every day brought ships to its teeming docks from all over the Mediterranean and Africa, from as far as England and the Baltic. Its fleets carried the Crusader armies to fight the Moslem Saracens in Syria and Palestine. Its treasury enriched by commercial treaties and conquest, it has grown almost within living memory from a township of wooden houses to a city-state of mansions and palaces, with nearly a hundred thousand inhabitants, fine churches, schools and monasteries. Nothing grander or more superb could exist on the face of the earth, he had once thought. But that was before he had seen what he had seen.

Giovanni was waiting, puzzled by his silence. Rustichello had sat again at the table and was trimming the point of his quill. He dipped it in the inkhorn and looked up expectantly.

Marco breathed in slowly, clearing his mind. 'Know then,' he began, 'I was born some forty years ago in Venice, in the year of our Lord, twelve hundred and fifty-four . . .'

Chapter One

With shrieks of joy and cries of despair, an ancient Venetian game was being played on one of the wider canals by a dozen young boys. The Cane Fight combined laughter with terror. Armed with long bamboo poles and standing aboard two light boats, the rival teams did their best to knock each other into the water and out of the game.

One boy in particular was excelling himself. Short, dark, tousled and smiling, he was showing remarkable agility and concentration for someone who was barely eight years old, when a shout from the bank of the canal caught his attention.

'Marco! Marco! Everyone's been looking for you! Father says you have to come home!'

Marco saw his cousin shouting to him. He was distracted for only a second, but it proved fatal. Caught off his guard, he was sent headfirst into the water, causing the biggest splash yet, as well as great mirth in the enemy boat.

Soaking wet and covered in mud, Marco hauled himself on to the bank and started to trot home. A summons from his uncle was never a good thing and he knew that he would probably get a beating for the state he was in. When he reached the brick and wood house, the familiar figure was waiting for him in the doorway. Uncle Zane was a stoutly-built man of middle years with a short brown beard, uneven teeth and a constant frown which made him always seem worried. He clicked his teeth with impatience as he watched his nephew approach, and raised his hand when Marco came within a yard of him. The boy flinched automatically, but his uncle only wanted to take him by the arm.

'Your Aunt Flora and I have been searching everywhere

for you for the past hour! Your mother . . .' Uncle Zane's voice trailed away. He cleared his throat and started again. 'Your mother was . . . taken ill.' Marco stared at him with sudden fear. 'It happened two hours ago. She called first for you, then for your aunt.'

A pinched, careworn woman, his Aunt Flora, came out on to the balcony above them. 'And about time!' she said crossly. 'Come along, boy. You're nearly too late.'

With a hand on Marco's shoulder, his uncle led him into the dark, damp house and up the steep staircase. Aunt Flora was waiting by the door of the main bedroom. She was about to go in with Marco, but Zane put his hand out, stopping her. Marco went in alone.

The bedroom was long and high-ceilinged. Above the wooden panelling, the plaster was painted with fishing and hunting scenes, separated by scrolls of flowers and sea creatures. On a chest in the far corner stood an ikon of a narrow-eyed Byzantine Madonna and Child, flanked by the smaller figures of St Mark and St Theodore. Although it was mid-afternoon, the curtains were drawn across the windows overlooking the canal, and the room was lit dimly by candles.

A woman was lying on the fourposter bed, her dark hair loose and tangled on the pillow, so still that Marco held his breath as he tiptoed closer. Her hands lay motionless on the brocade coverlet. Her eyes were closed, her face pale and haggard, but not even the ravages of her wasting illness could erase all traces of her beauty.

As Marco watched her silently, afraid to move, her dry lips parted and he gasped in relief. Her eyes flickered open and she saw him beside her. 'The Lord be praised, my son,' she whispered. 'I thought I had to go without seeing you.' The thin hand nearest him stirred and he held it, surprised at how cold it was. 'I've called for you so much.'

Marco felt guilty. He had been playing without a thought of her. His mother had been sick before, often, yet never like this. 'I was – I was with my friends,' he stammered.

It was difficult for his mother to speak. Her weakness was growing, but she found the strength to smile. 'You are . . . just like your father.' Marco smiled back. 'This house is too small for you. Venice, too . . . perhaps.'

Her voice was as tender as ever, although the struggle for breath made it little more than a dry whisper. Marco took comfort. Whenever she had been ill before she had always recovered. This time would be no different. The sprawling, old house was too much for her to manage on her own, since she had had to let the servants go. The money his father had sent was almost all spent, he knew. He made up his mind to help more. He reached out timidly and caressed her forehead with his free hand. She murmured and laid her cheek against his wrist.

'You look so like him, so like my Niccolo,' she whispered. 'But he's tall . . . with big hands. He'd lift you up like a . . . like a feather. I've done all I could for you, before this sickness made it so hard. You need him.'

'When *will* he come home, mother?'

Her eyes closed briefly in a spasm of pain. When they opened, she made herself smile again. 'One day. He will . . . You'll see,' she promised. 'And everyone in Venice will do him honour. "Welcome back, Messer Polo. How rich you are, Messer Polo. Will you join the Council, Messer Polo? . . ." ' Marco laughed. It was a game they had often played to cheer themselves up. 'He'll have presents for you – for everyone. You'll be so proud of him.'

She made an effort to lift her head from the pillow, looking round for something. Marco understood at once. On the great, painted marriage chest by the bed was a group of strange objects, wooden, ivory and stone figures of animals, men in outlandish clothes, of devil masks and heathen gods. Under one of them, Marco's favourite, a small jade statuette of a naked, dancing Persian girl, was a folded letter. He slipped the letter out from under it and turned back to the bed.

His mother nodded faintly. 'Yes,' she panted. 'Read it.'

He unfolded the single sheet of parchment. It had been

read and reread so often that the folds had cracked and the paper was brittle. He took his mother's hand in his again and began to read aloud. ' "My dearest wife. This is to let you know that I am well, although when you receive this, I shall be farther away than any man has yet been from those he loves and his native land. I shall not talk of how successful our trading has been, since to tell it would beggar belief. We rode all day yesterday and the day before across a burning desert and came at last to this city, which seems to be made all of fountains and palaces with roofs of gold." ' Marco looked at his mother. Her eyes were closed as she listened. He knew the letter so well that he did not need to see the words, and he went on from memory, ' "I know you are missing me, as I think of you often and pray to Our Blessed Lady that you are well, and our child who will by now be in your arms. Strange not to know whether it is a boy or girl. I would I were home with you. But a Venetian is born to travel—" '

Marco broke off. He could no longer hear his mother's soft, panted breathing. The lines of her face had somehow been smoothed away and she seemed many years younger. Her hand lay heavily in his and he pressed it in sudden fear, but there was no response. The tears he had been fighting back could no longer be checked and he called to her desperately, promising never to leave her alone as his father had done, if only she would speak to him. He could not make her hear.

His only true companion, the maker and sharer of his dreams was gone.

He was still kneeling at her side, sobbing convulsively, when the door opened and white-haired Father Anselmo, the parish priest, came in with Aunt Flora. Two older women followed them, and Uncle Zane. At a glance from Father Anselmo, Zane drew Marco to his feet and led him out. The boy stumbled, blind with tears. Behind him, the priest had begun to pray and the women wailed in the ritual keening of mourning.

*

The black funeral barge was heading for the cemetery island of San Michele. A black velvet cloth embroidered with silver thread had been draped over the coffin, hiding the crude carpentry and bestowing some dignity on Marco's mother as she made her final journey. Marco himself, pale, solemn, and feeling completely alone, stood in the prow. Uncle Zane, Aunt Flora and the other members of the family were huddled together in the stern. A bell began to toll, its sad message hanging in the still air.

Marco gazed back towards the bank where a small group of mourners had gathered to show their respect. Among them, his face drawn and serious, was his best friend, Giulio. He raised his hand a fraction as if to wave goodbye, and then shyly, almost furtively, made a sign of the cross. The gesture was an important one to Marco. He turned back to look down at the coffin and felt the full weight of his grief.

Sunshine gilded Venice on the following day and a fresh breeze blew through its lagoon and canals. As one phase of Marco Polo's life had ended, a new one began with dramatic suddenness, when Uncle Zane, Aunt Flora, their three sons and daughter, moved into the Polo house. As porters brought in the furniture from the large gondola, and the children raced around the house laughing and exploring, Marco tried to get something clear in his mind.

'This is *my* house now, isn't it, Uncle Zane? Now that my mother's dead?'

'In a manner of speaking,' conceded his uncle.

'But it's mine. Till my father comes home.'

'*If* he comes home,' muttered Aunt Flora; then she became brisk. 'It's a big house and we'll fit in very comfortably here. You can't be left on your own, so we are moving in to look after you.'

'Aunt Flora will take your mother's place now,' explained Uncle Zane. 'She'll take good care of you, Marco, you'll see. Just as she took care of your mother.'

'And God knows how I suffered and sacrificed for her!' added his wife, seizing on her cue. 'With my own house as well to look after! As for that brother of mine who's been gone eight years now and wasn't even here when his son was born – well, I ask myself why he had to get married just before leaving – *and* to a woman in such delicate health!'

Marco Polo stared sadly into the flames of the little fire. Things were going to be very different from now, and he was not at all sure that any of the changes would benefit him. He did not have to wait long for his first real shock.

'What are you doing, Aunt Flora?'

It was the afternoon of the same day, and he had wandered up to his mother's bedroom to find the shutters flung wide open and the bed itself being stripped.

'I'm letting some fresh air in. Chasing the smell of sickness out.'

Aunt Flora picked up the heavy, embroidered coverlet and admired it with a proprietary eye. Now that all the bedding and hangings had been removed, the fourposter looked bare, exposed, almost indecent.

Marco was hurt; it seemed almost like sacrilege. 'I don't want anything in my mother's room touched.'

'*You* don't want!' she snorted. 'Your uncle and I are having this room, so it will be how *I* want it.'

'Where am I to sleep?'

'Downstairs with your cousins,' she replied. 'Your poor mother said: "Flora, he's in your care and protection." Easy to say that, but what have we been given in exchange? She didn't leave a penny either to your uncle or to me.'

Looking around the room, her eye lighted on the ornaments that stood on the chest, mementoes of Niccolo Polo's travels, each one treasured by his wife and son. Aunt Flora grabbed an Indian idol and a Moroccan amulet and strode to the window. 'These things are going out!'

'No,' pleaded Marco, standing in her way. 'They're the presents my father sent home from Constantinople.'

'Pagan idols, witchcraft! They've no place in a Christian

household!' With cruel deliberation, she flung them one by one into the canal, Marco powerless to stop her. 'Ashamed! My brother should be ashamed of himself – if he hasn't already been called to the Lord's justice, with the weight of all his sins on his soul.'

'My father has gone to make his fortune – for my mother and me! When he returns . . .'

'There is no fortune for those who lose their way among infidels,' she announced, crossing herself. Her own children had now come rushing in to see what all the noise was about, and they listened to her with mouths open. 'Tartars, Mongols . . . cruel and barbarous people, sons of the Devil! Perhaps your father is lost down there, among the savages, where the light of the sun never shines. On the very edge of the world where a body can slip over into emptiness.'

Before Aunt Flora could prevent him, Marco had snatched his precious jade statuette and clutched it protectively to his chest. 'My father is *alive*. He'll come back, you'll see.'

'Never!'

'He will, he will!' shouted Marco, tears now streaming down his cheeks. 'He *must* come back!'

Before she could stop him, Marco had raced from the room, down the stairs and out into the street, still clutching the precious memento. His aunt's voice pursued him vengefully until he was at last out of earshot.

St Mark's Square was its usual hectic conglomeration of noise, colour, bustle, excitement and hard bargaining. From his privileged position atop one of the columns, St Theodore, former patron saint of the city, now an imposing stone figure standing on a crocodile, looked down on a scene that resembled nothing so much as a never-ending fair.

Uncle Zane was far too accustomed to it all to be distracted in any way. For him Venice had always been like this: a thriving, cosmopolitan marketplace. Ignoring the din, he clinched his latest sale and summoned his assistant.

'Marco!' The tall, handsome youth of seventeen was at his side in a second. 'Help Messer Alessandro to load his purchase on the boat.'

'What did you say the material is called?' asked the customer, whose rich robes proclaimed a man of some wealth. 'Ormesine?'

'That's right. Made in Hormuz, a city in Persia. It's only just arrived.' Zane clicked his fingers at his nephew. 'Pick it up!'

Marco lifted up the heavy bolt of cloth and followed the client in the direction of the Riva Degli Schiavoni. The crowd was milling all around them and the man, though absurdly fat, had difficulty forcing his way through. Some monks pushed past on their way to the Basilica; then a butcher, bent double under a huge side of beef, obstructed them; a fishseller whose basket was brimming with red mullet and silver cod was a further hindrance. But the customer's biggest problem came in the form of a sturdy, open-faced, good-natured youth elbowing his way towards them with real urgency.

'Marco! Marco!'

'What is it, Giulio?'

'Over there! Hurry!'

'Get a move on!' ordered the fat man, angrily. 'I've wasted enough time already.'

'Forgive me, sir. I have to go now.'

Marco thrust the cloth into the arms of the astonished man and disappeared into the throng with Giulio. They soon came to a knot of people who had gathered to hear a group of sailors. Giulio pushed a couple of boys aside to make room for Marco and himself. The sailors, sitting on bales and barrels, were passing a flask of wine amongst themselves and trading stories. An old sailor with a leathery, pleasantly ugly face was holding forth.

'. . . Men with heads of dogs and eagles that can lift

elephants into the air! But I can tell you, I've never met women more gentle and more . . . welcoming.'

'Welcomed you with open arms, did they?' asked a younger sailor, and the crowd laughed.

'That they did,' chuckled the old salt. 'And the men, mind you, not jealous, not a bit. Though if you so much as touched a camel, they'd split you open. *Zt!*' He made a graphic gesture. 'Just like that. And throw your guts to the dogs. There was one time in Persia . . .'

'You've been to Persia?' asked Marco, hanging on the man's every word. 'Whereabouts?'

'I got as far as Tabriz. I've seen the Mongols.' A ripple of interest not unmixed with fear went through the crowd. 'From a distance, I mean. There were thousands of them – and twice as many horses. Each man had two. The sailors told us they were off to teach someone a lesson. We decided to get out of there quick.'

An even older soldier, more grizzled and almost toothless, now took up the story. 'You don't know how lucky you are here in Venice. You don't know what *he* had in mind.'

'Who?' wondered Giulio. 'The Great Mongol?'

The grizzled sailor nodded. 'Genghis Khan, the terror of the world. The whole world, that's what he was after. Every mortal, God-made part of it. He swept like an avalanche through Persia, Hungary, Poland, Germany – and he was on his way here!'

'Saints preserve us!' exclaimed a querulous merchant.

'They must have. For just as he turned south, towards us, God struck him dead. And all the Mongols went riding back to where they come from to choose their new leader. But if he *hadn't* been struck down . . .' The grizzled sailor paused and spat into the air for effect. 'He'd be here now, as sure as thunder follows lightning. Venice, Rome, Naples and then on to France, Spain, England. Nothing could have stopped him. There would have been terrible massacres and butchery . . .'

'But why?' The merchant was trembling. 'How can they behave with such cruelty?'

'For the fun of it, sir. War's a sport to them.'

Marco now addressed the old sailor who had been speaking when he had first arrived. 'Your pardon, sir,' he said, shyly. 'During your travels, did you . . . did you ever meet or hear of my father, Niccolo Polo? A merchant travelling with his brother, Matteo?'

'The world is a big place, son. When did he leave?'

'About sixteen years ago.'

'Where for?'

'The Far East. They wanted to cross Persia.'

The old sailor shook his head. 'No. Never met them. Mind you, I hardly set foot in Persia. One look at those Mongols was enough for me. If your father ended up among those devils . . .' He nodded towards a morose-looking individual in the garb of a blacksmith. 'Ask him. He knows about the Mongols.'

'Spawned in the depths of hell,' said the blacksmith grimly. 'I should know. I lived under them once.'

'Under their rule? Where?' asked the merchant.

'Dalmatia, when Genghis Khan's army swept up to the borders of Venice.'

'Why weren't you killed?' wondered the merchant.

'Because we didn't fight them. If you fight back, they don't stop till everyone's dead – men, women and children. And their heads piled up in a mound where their houses used to be.'

'That's their way,' agreed the grizzled sailor. 'Mounds of heads.'

'And they've no pity for their own either,' said the blacksmith. 'Anyone who steps out of line – chop, off go their hands and feet – chop, off go their heads! Luckily, they needed me because I was good with horses. They treated me all right – till the day they left.' Bitterness soured his features. 'They wanted something to remember us by – so they took our right ears. The ears of every man and boy. Hundreds and thousands of them. They filled baskets with them and took them home as trophies. If you don't believe me . . .'

He removed a greasy, leather cap and pushed back his hair. All that was left of his right ear was a lump of twisted and discoloured scar tissue.

'Marco! Marco!' Uncle Zane sounded as if he was in a mood to cut off both of his nephew's ears. 'Marco! Come at once!'

Reluctantly, Marco got up and made his way back.

Sunset found Marco and Giulio at an abandoned boathouse. While helping to repair an old boat, Marco and Giulio repeated to other friends the stories they had heard from the sailors in the Square that morning. Most of the others listened with amused scepticism, but one of them, a quiet, sensitive boy named Bartolomeo, sketched with charcoal on a wooden tablet, following intently.

'When I listen to sailors' stories,' confided Marco, 'I feel as though I can't breathe. Venice is like a prison. People think that this – the Square, the lagoon – is everything that's worth knowing. But there's a whole world out there beyond the horizon. A huge, wide world as vast as the sky. My father's seen it.'

'Who knows where your father is now?' mocked one of his friends. 'Perhaps he's married again and changed his name.'

'His father will come back all right,' affirmed Giulio, loyal as ever.

'Meanwhile, Marco keeps building this boat,' the mocker went on.

Marco flushed angrily. 'You'll never understand, will you? Building a boat is like opening a door on to that big world. The boat is the key to escape from the prison.'

The others remained silent for a few moments. Then Bartolomeo brought the wooden tablet across to show Marco what he had been drawing. 'Just like that sailor told you. Here are the men with heads of dogs . . . and these are the eagles lifting elephants.' One of the boys laughed at his imagination. Bartolomeo shook his head. 'If I've drawn them, it means they exist,' he said, partly to support and comfort Marco. His sketches were fantastical yet somehow strangely real. Everyone crowded round to admire his work and Giulio told him that he had eyes in his fingertips. Encouraged by the praise, Bartolomeo led them to the far wall, a blazing torch in his hand to dispel the shadows.

When his friends saw what he had done, they gasped in astonishment. Painted on the wall in bold colours was a large fresco which, though naive and limited in some ways, was nevertheless rich in imagination. Part of the fresco had been inspired by Marco's tales. Mythical beasts and griffins, chimeras and salamanders jostled with strange humans. What Marco noticed first was the towering figure of a warrior in weird armour and headdress. The scowling warrior was standing on a rocky reef and held a scimitar high as if threatening the sea itself.

'Who's that?' asked Marco.

'Jingle Khan,' said Bartolomeo proudly. 'He's reached the very edge of the world and he's angry because there are no more lands to conquer. But look here . . .' He moved the torch to light another area of the fresco. Beyond the sea, on a thin green stretch of coastline, he had painted two tiny figures beside a miniature castle. 'Those two are Messer Niccolo Polo and his brother. They have travelled beyond Mongolia and they're laughing.'

His friends were so appreciative that in patting him on the back, they knocked the torch from his hand and plunged the fresco, the beasts and Marco's father back into darkness.

Marco Polo continued to dream his dreams of escape from Venice, and to keep them from his sly uncle and his scolding aunt. Then one morning an entirely new element entered his dreams. A girl waited at the door of his uncle's shop one day, while her old nursemaid bought some fine muslin. He learnt nothing about her except that her name was Caterina, yet he found he could not forget her.

Two days later, he was at his stall as usual, straightening a pile of cut cloth that was in danger of toppling over, when his uncle ordered him off to buy some fish. Needing no further excuse to leave the shop, he set off across the Square towards the stalls of the fish fryers. It was then that he saw her again.

Caterina was perhaps fifteen, certainly no older, just entering the first flower of womanhood. Her face was heartshaped, its features elfin with dark, lustrous eyes and smooth, shining hair that fell unbound to her shoulders and beyond, held in place around the smooth forehead by a silver band. The litheness of her movements suggested an agile body beneath her costly robe, and she seemed to be at once sophisticated and untamed – a well-educated Venetian maiden, but with a streak of wildness about her.

Marco's eyes met hers for a long second and he was startled, seeming to see a flicker of recognition. Then she vanished into the crowd with her nursemaid, a thin, wiry, watchful female, trotting at her heels.

Marco was still in a daze when he reached the fish fryer and placed his order. The man dipped a wooden spoon into his pot and scooped out three sizzling codfish, which he wrapped in vine leaves before handing them over. Marco paid him, turned towards the Square, and found that the girl was now behind him in the queue. The fish fryer was explaining to her that he had just sold the last of his cod. Marco decided quickly. This was his chance. He bowed shyly to the girl and offered her his own fish. Though the nursemaid immediately refused, the girl thanked him for his gift and replied with a curtsey. Forced to accept, the nursemaid now tried to hurry her charge away, reminding her that she had wanted to stroll to the church of Santa Luca. But the girl held her ground until she had learnt Marco's name and thanked him once more.

'I've changed my mind,' she told her maid. 'I want to go home. We can walk to Santa Luca tomorrow after vespers.'

It was minutes before Marco realized that she had given him an important message. Not even the anger of Uncle Zane when he returned emptyhanded could quench his excitement. He thought of nothing but meeting her the next day at the appointed hour.

When the time finally came, Marco approached the old Byzantine church cautiously and his heart leapt to see her there already, seated on the top step of the portico. She was alone and gave him a warm smile of welcome. He sat beside her, his heart pounding.

'I wasn't sure if you'd understood,' she said. 'But here you are.'

'You knew I would come?' he asked.

'Your eyes told me you liked me. You do, don't you?'

There was a directness about her which disconcerted Marco. He could only nod. 'Yes . . . I do.'

'Well, that's settled then,' she laughed.

He glanced round involuntarily at the arched doors of the church which were not wholly closed. From inside came the soft chanting of the monks at their evening mass.

'You don't have to worry about my old nurse,' she told him. 'She's visiting the cemetery. I told her I was going home. We have hours yet.' She smiled to him, rising, and he rose with her, watching her as her arms went round the slender, fluted pillar beside her, as if hugging it. He stepped towards her but she swung away, spinning round the pillar with one hand, leaning back, her dark hair with its hints of copper flying loose. It was oddly pagan, and somehow disturbing against the background of the monks' voices. She was laughing quietly, whether with him or at him he could not tell, but he laughed too, following her as she swung from column to column round the semicircular portico. At the far end, she spun back to come face to face with him, looking up at him, only inches away. A perfume swept round him, light and fragrant like spring flowers, then she was gone, jumping down lightly on to the grass of the forecourt. When he jumped down beside her, she took his hand and they walked round the tiny baptistry to reach the bank of the narrow canal which curved behind the church.

They were beyond the outskirts of the city in a green and pretty landscape with trees and flowering bushes by the water. As they walked along, the attraction between them held him silent, but it provoked her into all the questions he wished to ask: How old are you? Where do you live? Where were you taught? Do you have any brothers and sisters? Marco found himself speaking to her more freely and openly than he did to anyone except Giulio. Each new thing he learnt about her he treasured, storing it away to be savoured when he was alone. He discovered that she was an only child like him, and lived in Silversmiths' Court with her mother.

'Is that your shop in the market?' she asked.

'No, it's my uncle's.' He stopped. 'How do you know about it? Oh, of course. You saw me that day.'

'I'd seen you before. Often.' She smiled at his surprise. 'Did you think you'd noticed me first? I've seen you many times. At your stall.'

'When? How could I have missed seeing *you*?'

Caterina laughed, walking on. 'You were busy with your cloth.'

'That's only to please my uncle,' Marco told her. 'I don't want to spend my life running a stall in the market.'

She glanced at him. 'Why not? It's a fine trade. You could become rich . . . and respected.'

'Maybe,' Marco agreed. 'But I want to travel, like my father.'

Caterina paused, watching the shifting flicker of light on the surface of the canal. 'So why aren't you with your father?'

'I've never known him,' he told her. 'He left before I was born. He's travelled far, farther than any other merchant in the whole of Venice.'

'Do you hear from him?'

Marco frowned. 'Not for . . . not for many years. But look – he sent this with other things to my mother just before she died.' He took out the little jade figurine of the dancer and handed it to her.

'It's beautiful,' Caterina breathed. She held it up against the sun, marvelling at its translucence. 'Where does it come from?'

'I don't know.' Marco paused. The statuette was his most precious possession, yet it was all he had to offer. 'You can keep it, if you like.'

Caterina looked at him quickly. She sensed how important it was to him. It was like a commitment between them. Instead of answering, she raised the figure to her lips and kissed it. The happiness in Marco's smile was almost tangible and she smiled back, turning away from him to sit on the canal bank. She kicked off her shoes and slipped her bare feet into the water, holding up the statuette to let the light gleam through it.

Marco stood watching her. She had drawn her long blue dress up to above her knees, showing the beginning of her slim, naked thighs. She seemed quite unconscious of the effect it created, yet Marco had never seen anything more lovely. He had talked and walked with girls before, some of them flirtatious and giggly, but he had not responded. With his friends he had seen the harlots at the lower windows of their houses by the main canals, smiling and calling to the men who passed in their gondolas, easing back the fur-trimmed wraps from their shoulders to show their powdered and scented bodies. Although he always looked away, he had been excited – but never as much as now. As Caterina splashed her feet gently in the water, the dress slid farther along her smooth thighs. She reminded him somehow of the little jade figurine, free of inhibitions and unaware of her own loveliness. Suddenly she jumped up, shaking down her skirt and set off along the bank, barefoot.

Marco picked up her shoes and followed her, catching her up. 'You never said if you agreed with me,' he reminded her. 'Do you think I'm right to wait for my father?'

The canal was winding now through open country. On the opposite bank were the trees and wall of an enclosed orchard, part of the monastery of St Anthony. Caterina paused to pick a cluster of little white star-shaped flowers and smelt them. 'If you feel it inside you – in your blood – then you are right.'

Marco flushed. One thing he certainly felt in his blood was a strong desire to see Caterina again. He slowed to a stop, wondering how to ask when they could next meet. But she was not looking at him. She was listening to the bell of the monastery which had begun to toll. Unconsciously, he had also been counting the beats. 'It's late. We'll have to head home.'

Caterina turned with him. 'I don't like to go home,' she said quietly.

Marco was concerned. 'Are they unkind to you?'

She was serious again. 'No. Not like your aunt. My mother's very pretty, very gentle. But I'm always alone at night. She locks my room.' Marco did not understand and there were questions he wanted to ask, but Caterina suddenly announced, 'I'm hungry.'

Ahead of them, a wooden plank spanned the canal as a makeshift bridge. On the opposite bank baskets of apples and pears lay invitingly on the grass under the wall of the monastery orchard. To Marco's amazement, Caterina lifted the hem of her dress, sped over the plank, snatched up two ripe pears and flitted back to him. As she threw one across to him, Marco became aware of two monks glaring angrily over the wall. 'What are you doing?' one of them shouted. 'Those pears belong to St Anthony!'

For answer, Caterina bit into her pear, laughing, taunting them.

Marco was shocked by her boldness, yet could not help laughing with her when the monks began to splutter and shake their fists. 'Blasphemy! Blasphemy!' the monk shouted. The other was pointing at them. 'I know you! I know you, Marco Polo! You'll answer for this!' Caterina put her shoes on, took Marco's hand and they ran off together along the towpath.

He saw her back to the city, but she would not let him come farther with her than the side of St Mark's Basilica, although it was growing dark. She had meant it, however: she wanted to see him again, whenever it could be managed.

When he got home that evening, his mind was still racing. He was too preoccupied to spot the danger signs when he came in. Zane was sitting silent by the fire and Aunt Flora at her place at the table with Marco's supper waiting for him, cold. The monks had been there before him and his aunt flew into a rage, ridding herself of a whole catalogue of complaints about his behaviour and sinfulness and lack of consideration for her, to which thieving was now added.

'It was only two pears,' Marco said.

'That doesn't make it right,' Zane rumbled.

'It's theft from Holy Church! Sacrilege!' Flora shrilled. 'And disporting yourself with that shameless, indecent hussy!'

'You don't know anything about her!' Marco protested. 'We did nothing wrong.'

'They saw you – the monks saw you and that slut!'

'You've no right to speak of her like that!' Marco blazed.

'How dare you answer me back?' his aunt screamed. 'Saints defend us – the strumpet has bewitched him. Zane! Zane, beat it out of him!'

His uncle lumbered up from his chair and Marco swung to face him, his fists doubling. He had taken many beatings from his aunt and uncle over the years, but this time it was totally unjust. Zane was moving towards him, but hesitated, seeing his determination. Marco had grown and, if he had decided to resist, punishing him single-handed might not be an easy matter. 'Now, Flora,' Zane muttered, 'perhaps we're being a bit hard on the boy.'

'It's the only way!' she insisted. 'We've only saved him from the devil by whipping the evil out of him. Flog him!'

Zane still hesitated. Marco meanwhile waited tensely, his teeth slightly bared, his fists clenched at his waist. Aunt Flora was gaping, unable to believe what was happening. The moment ended when Marco turned and walked stiff-legged to the inner door. As he climbed the stairs, he heard his aunt's shrill voice, alternately sobbing that he was lost to the tribe of Satan for ever, and railing at her husband for neglecting his duty as head of the family.

The next weeks were difficult. Uncle Zane was awkward and silent at the shop and Marco was unable to respond to his clumsy attempts to patch things up. At home, Aunt Flora maintained a bitter, injured silence. Marco's cousins were encouraged to avoid him as much as possible and loudly commanded to beg for God's mercy for him in their prayers.

Yet in some respects, it was the happiest period of Marco's life. Knowing Caterina had awakened new feelings in him. They were often together and, although they did not talk of love, they shared everything, including all his hopes and dreams of travel. He showed her the boathouse and the skiff, now nearly complete. She marvelled at it, and over Bartolomeo's frescoes which she traced reverently with her fingers as though the weird creatures spoke to her. Bartolomeo was enchanted with her. The only disappointment was Giulio, who jealously accused Marco of not working so eagerly on their boat. Yet Marco could not help it: Caterina was everything to him. However, there were still parts of her life and of her thoughts which she refused to disclose to him. Marco noticed that sometimes, even when she seemed most carefree, she would grow silent, her expression tinged with sadness. But when he asked what troubled her she simply laughed, laying her fingers on his lips.

He had not given up his quest for news of his father and

uncle. One afternoon in early April, he had gone to the quayside after work as usual to question the crews of any newly docked ships. A carrack from the Levant was tied up, unloading a rich cargo of cloths and spices. The mate had answered him with a brusque shake of the head. As Marco still lingered, watching the carrack, he had seen a man come down the gangplank, a prosperous merchant with something of the east in his dress. As he reached the quay, he glanced towards Marco and smiled. Marco's heart lurched. The man looked just as Marco had always known his father would look. For a moment Marco almost believed it *was* his father; but no – the merchant went directly past without even a glance.

That evening he stayed in his room, not speaking to the cousin who shared it with him, refusing to come down to supper. Brooding, alone, Marco had reached one of the lowest points of his belief in himself and in his destiny. He felt alien, not only among this family, but in Venice. The city seemed more of a prison than ever. He needed to retain his belief in his father's return, which was as vital to him as his faith in the Virgin and the Holy Trinity. Yet what if he came too late? Marco could live and die and never have set a foot beyond the confines of the Most Serene Republic; never have been for more than a day outside Venice's protective girdle of sea and lagoon and marshes. Only his mother had ever fully understood how he felt. Until Caterina.

All at once he needed to be with her, to see her and be comforted by her. Caterina seemed to catch his thoughts even before they were spoken. He had opened her eyes to a world outside Venice, its infinite, unknown possibilities, and her quick imagination now outstripped his own, her practical streak adding colour and elements of her own which made the dream more real. He knew she was always at home in the evening, always alone. Her mother, Monna Fiammetta, was very protective, a widow. He had not met her nor been to the house, but it was time he did. Surely she would at least allow him to see Caterina for a few minutes?

It had been raining and the night was dark when he slipped out of the pantry door into the *ramo*, the side alley linking up with the lanes behind the house. He had changed into clean hose and his best doublet, a dark russet with gold work at the collar and slashed at the lower sleeves to show the frill of his lawn shirt. He was glad he had worn his calf boots, for the cobbled, poorly-lit streets were slippery with refuse and animal and human droppings, and his feet kept sliding off the stepping-stones to squelch ankle-deep in the stinking mud.

Through a tangle of narrow, twisting alleys, the houses dark and shuttered, he came at last to the *campiello* off which was Silversmiths' Court. He looked round the small open square, but saw no one to ask. From the side, he heard the sound of music and headed towards it. A gateway in the wall led to an open courtyard. It was paved and dry, with an ancient, gnarled apricot tree in one corner and an arbour walk of vine beyond the stone horsetrough. Although half-filled with shifting phantoms of mist, there were lights at the windows round the courtyard. Bursts of laughter came from the windows and the music of pipes and lutes was louder. There was a welcoming warmth in the courtyard, and Marco began to smile.

A blazing torch hung in a sconce inside the gateway. As he stepped forward into its light, a huge, hulking figure moved out of the shadows to block his path. Marco stopped short. The gatekeeper was frighteningly ugly and more than a little drunk. 'Where do you think you're going?' he growled.

Marco had no reason to be afraid. 'Is this Silversmiths' Court?' he asked.

'What if it is?'

'I'm trying to find Monna Fiammetta,' Marco said. 'I believe she lives here.'

The gatekeeper grunted. 'Come calling, have you?' he

chuckled. 'Well, you look respectable enough. Go on, then, on the fourth landing. And wipe your boots.'

Marco thanked him, cleaned most of the mud off his boots on the iron scraper and hurried up the steep stairs. There was only one door on the fourth landing, of polished oak with a richly carved lintel. He rapped with the knocker in the shape of a dolphin and checked his appearance, combing his hair quickly with his fingers and pulling up his collar. He was about to knock again, when the door opened an inch. There was someone watching him. The light of lamps and candles inside shone brightly through the crack. After a moment, a voice drawled, 'What have we here?' And the door opened wider.

A woman was standing in the doorway, tall and strikingly beautiful. She was dressed in a lounging wrap of heavy gold silk, wide-sleeved and trimmed with ermine. On her feet she wore pointed, brocade slippers. She was full-fleshed, voluptuous, her face made up, her cheeks rouged, her wide mouth gleaming red. Her eyes were outlined in kohl, the upper lids painted green. Her eyebrows were plucked bare, as was her hairline, to give a fashionable high forehead round which her hair was combed up and out in a tawny mane, falling to below her shoulders and threaded with ropes of tiny pearls. Round her neck was a pendant of rubies, and a single drop pearl nestled in the cleft of her deep bosom. The hallway behind her was lined with colourful tapestries and lit by a many-branched candelabra set on an inlaid ivory table. It was much grander than Marco had imagined.

'Well?' the woman smiled.

Marco found his voice and bowed. 'I'm looking for Monna Fiammetta's house.'

'You've found it.' The voice was a caress.

Marco found the woman's slightly quizzical smile unsettling. 'Could I . . . could I, please, speak to her?'

The woman's laugh was low, in her throat. 'You *are* speaking to her. I am Monna Fiammetta. In the flesh.' Her tongue touched her lips and she pouted provocatively.

'Is the flesh to your liking?' She laughed again, posing for him, amused by his awkwardness. She was holding the wrap closed with one hand at her bust, and she now let it fall open. Under it she wore only a short cambric shift, ending at mid-thigh, and yellow stockings gartered under her knees. The shift was little more than a film over her perfumed body. It hung from the tips of her swelling breasts, and as she moved her shoulders enticingly, the plump mounds quivered and the large aureoles of her nipples showed above the gathered material. 'Of course, it's not cheap,' she said softly. 'Three ducats, even to you, handsome. In advance.'

Marco swallowed. 'I – I think there's a mistake,' he stammered. 'I wanted Caterina.'

'Caterina?'

'I came for her.'

Monna Fiammetta's face was blank with disbelief. 'You . . . ?' Suddenly she twitched the wrap shut around her. 'You filth!' she hissed. Her mouth twisted with fury and she screamed, 'Giuseppe! Giuseppe, get up here!'

Marco backed away from her, conscious of having made a terrible mistake. He could hear the gatekeeper beginning to charge up the stairs. Caterina's mother was reaching for him, her fingers clawing. He evaded her and started down the stairs, while she screeched obscenities after him. '*Maledet! Stramaledeto! Fiol d'un can!*'

He reached the second landing at the same moment as Giuseppe. The massive gatekeeper was swaying, clutching a wine flask in one hand. 'What've you been up to?' he roared, catching sight of Marco. He lurched forward to intercept him, fumbling for the knife at his belt. Marco's agility saved him. When the man grabbed at him, he ducked and dodged round him, racing on down the stairs. The wine flask smashed against the wall behind him. 'Come back here, you little rat!' Giuseppe shouted.

With Monna Fiammetta screaming curses at him from an upper window, Marco ran out into the courtyard and through the gate, slipping and stumbling on the wet paving stones.

'You look as if you'd seen a ghost,' Bartolomeo said, as Marco arrived panting at the boathouse.

Marco's clothes were sodden. He was silent and still shocked. He knew now the reason for Caterina's silence about her mother and reluctance to talk about her home life. It horrified him. Even if Caterina had not yet joined her mother's profession, the thought of her future made him want to be sick.

Noticing that he was shivering, Giulio led him to the fire. 'You're wet through. Here, come and dry off a bit by the fire.'

Bartolomeo had stopped his painting, concerned. Giulio glanced at him and back. 'What's up?' he asked.

Marco had not meant to tell them, but he could not prevent himself. It all came spilling out. When he finished, there was a silence. Bartolomeo came to crouch beside him.

'Won't you see her any more?' Giulio asked.

Marco shook his head. 'I don't know.'

'Oh, come on!' Bartolomeo snorted. 'So her mother's a whore – half the women in Venice are on the game. Doesn't mean your Caterina takes after her.'

'I suppose not,' Marco admitted.

'Mind you,' Bartolomeo chuckled. 'There'll be the devil to pay when your Aunt Flora finds out.' Marco smiled wryly, imagining his aunt's scandalized face. Bartolomeo's words had helped him come to a decision.

He looked across the fire at Giulio. 'We must finish the boat. I want it ready.'

Sunday morning was bright and clear and nearly the whole population thronged the Square as the bells of St Mark's summoned the faithful to second mass. Dressed in their finest silks and velvets and furs, with an air of studied respectability in marked contrast to the jocularity and quarrelsome chaffering of weekdays, the citizens of Venice, high and low, streamed towards the great Basilica with its five domes. Friends and neighbours greeted one another outside the main porch, divided by three sculptured arches.

Marco strolled with his cousins behind his aunt and uncle. As they paused to bow to the head of Zane's guild, Marco looked over their heads to the mosaics on the cathedral's golden façade and up from them to the four superb horses of gilt bronze, seized at the capture of Constantinople and placed here in triumph above the portico. *Constantinople* . . . One day, he would travel to Constantinople himself, to trace his father and uncle, rescue them if need be from the dungeons of the Tartars. He promised to make a special prayer to the Madonna and to San Marco and Saint Theodore, beseeching their help and promising to dedicate himself to their service. He hurried to keep up with the others who were moving on.

The crowd surging round the front of the church itself began to split apart, making an avenue for the elders of the city, leading members of the Senate and their families, who had chosen the moment when they could appear to maximum effect and win the buzzed, respectful acclaim of their people. Displaying their piety, the Senators scattered alms to the horde of beggars crouching by the bases of the arches, legless and armless veterans of the city's wars of conquest, scrofulous, ragged children scrambling for the coins with the blind and maimed and diseased. In their long robes, silk mantles and hooded caps, the Senators passed into the nave of the Basilica. The cries of the beggars and the applause of the crowd followed them.

Aunt Flora, resplendent in her best dress, distributed gracious smiles to all those around her. There was a faint stir of hostility among the crowd and she nudged her husband. Uncle Zane turned to see what had caused so many frowns.

Moving in procession, a small group of elderly servants were heading towards them, each man wearing ornate, pretentious livery. Behind the servants, dressed in a gorgeous, loose, full-bodied gown came Monna Fiammetta. She walked imperiously, the skirt of her gown lifted to show her fine ankles and her ten-inch, stilt-like shoes. She was made up more modestly now, carrying a silver-bound missal, but Aunt Flora hissed at the sight of her. At her side was Caterina, her long hair gathered in a net of silver thread, her lovely, clear face set off by the exquisite simplicity of her high-waisted dress.

More hisses came from the women as she passed, but nothing could have made Marco turn away. All the doubts he had had about her vanished as he looked at Caterina, her beauty and simplicity so different from her mother's arrogant gaudiness. She had seen him and stopped to return his smile. An audible whisper of scandal went around the crowd. Monna Fiammetta glanced at Marco contemptuously and ordered her daughter to follow her, but the girl did not move until her mother took her arm and led her firmly on.

'What's got into you, boy?' Zane muttered worriedly.

Guiseppe was lumbering up, his gaudy clothes tight round his massive bulk. The crowd fell silent as he planted himself in front of Marco, raising his huge fist. His voice was coarse and loud enough for all to hear. 'This is the second time I'm telling you – and it had better be the last. Keep away from her!'

The procession continued, Caterina walking beside her mother, her eyes lowered. Marco was left standing under the furious stare of his Aunt Flora.

'Shame!' she hissed. 'You've brought shame on us!'

Days rolled past. Marco's misery deepened and his desire to escape from Venice grew stronger and stronger. Every minute of his free time was spent on the boat, and at last it was finished. Launched by moonlight, it stole out of a side canal into the lagoon. Marco stood at the stern, working a broad-bladed oar as a sweep, and Caterina sat in the shelter of the prow on a pile of old nets and sailcloth.

After bribing her nurse to unlock her door, she had crept out of the house to meet him. He had said it was important, but until they reached the boathouse, she had no idea that this was the night he meant to begin their journey. She was excited, but troubled.

'Where are we going?' she asked.

'To the coast of Dalmatia.' Marco worked the tiller with his knee, steering the skiff in a curve that would carry them round the tiny, cypress-crowned island of San Michele.

'In *this* little boat?'

'Don't worry,' Marco told her. 'We'll make it. We'll find a ship there bound for Greece. And then, Alexandropolis or even Constantinople.' *Ave Maria, stella maris, protege nos*, he prayed silently. He knew he was taking a considerable risk, attempting to cross the Adriatic by dead reckoning, and each stage of the journey would be just as difficult. But he could not wait any longer. All would depend on luck and the favour of the Madonna . . . He spoke confidently to reassure Caterina.

'If I'd realized we were going so far, I'd have brought some more clothes. And maybe something to eat,' she teased.

He was stung. 'Are you laughing at me?'

Her smile faded. 'Are you really serious about this?'

'Of course. It's our chance to get away.' He could see that she was uncertain. 'Don't you want to be with me?'

'You know I do,' she said softly. 'I'm just sad to be leaving Venice.'

'You should be happy,' he said. All that meanness and suspicion . . . We'll find my father and he'll help us. We'll never go back.'

His confidence and enthusiasm comforted her, but a light wind was blowing up and she shivered, crossing her arms on her breast. 'It's hundreds of miles, isn't it?' she said. 'Are you going to row all the way?'

'I'll only have to steer,' he laughed. 'Look . . .' They were now beyond San Michele and into deeper water. He shipped the oar, slotted the single mast into its housing and hoisted the square sail.

In the bright moonlight, Caterina could see that it was a patchwork of odd pieces sewn together. She bit her lip to prevent herself laughing. 'If I'd known what your sail was like, I'd have given you a sheet.'

'It'll hold,' he promised. 'Giulio and I spent days stitching it.'

He was standing looking down at her. It was the first time they had ever been really alone without fear of interruption. She eased back until she was lying on her elbows. 'What now?' she asked.

Marco had a plan worked out. It would be dangerous to sail far at night before the skiff was properly tested. They would steer for one of the farther islands and anchor in its lee. Any hunt for them would concentrate on the mainland and no search party would scour the lagoon until daylight. At dawn they would slip out through the exit to the sea at Porto di Albiola among the early morning fishing boats.

'And until then,' Caterina said softly, 'at least we're here, together.'

Marco tied off the tiller and came to sit beside her. They were both silent, both slightly nervous. The wind which had begun to flutter the sail blew some strands of hair across her face. As she smoothed them back, her eyes gleamed up at him. 'You're so beautiful,' he whispered. He could just make out her smile as she touched his cheek. He took her in his arms.

His kiss was tender, but after a moment she pressed harder against him, her mouth opening under his. The closeness and warmth of her slim body roused him instantly and she could feel it. He tried to draw away, but her arms clung to him and she whimpered in her throat. 'Marco . . . Marco . . .'

Marco felt lightheaded. It was as if his whole life had only been leading him to this moment, at once ecstatic and fearful. Caterina was trembling just as he was. She was kissing his eyelids, his nose, his mouth. He knew he should pull back from her before it was too late, but she caught his right arm and pulled it round, twisting until his hand lay on the faint swell of her breast. His fingers closed on the soft shape underneath and she gasped, her lips tightening.

He raised his head, gazing down at her, afraid he had hurt her. But she was smiling. 'Yes . . . Yes,' she breathed, and she begged him to hurry, not to be gentle. Her body in the moonlight was even more perfect than he had imagined, slender and delicate. She cried out once, but it was not a cry of pain.

The disaster came just before dawn.

Asleep in each other's arms, Marco and Caterina were both unconscious of the increased rocking of the boat as the wind got up. The patchwork sail bellied and strained and one of its seams began to part. The gap grew steadily wider, weakening the surrounding patches, until the wind changed direction suddenly in a violent squall. There was a wrenching, tearing sound and Marco came awake to see the remnants of the sail fly away in tatters. He scrambled for the stern as the skiff lurched, but the rope holding the tiller snapped and the little boat spun round crazily before overturning. Caterina screamed as they were pitched overboard into the choppy water.

When he reached the surface, he searched frantically in the darkness and driving waves until he found her. Helping her, he swam with her to the wallowing, upturned hull, where they could cling to the ridges in the planking. In the coldness of the water it was their only hope.

By the time the squall blew over, they were too numb even to speak. Caterina's dress was weighing her down and Marco was supporting her with one arm, craning his neck for a sight of any other vessel as the surface brightened with the rising of the sun. When a small sailing boat emerged from the morning mists and came to investigate the overturned skiff, he had barely strength to call to it.

*

One of the fishermen took Caterina home. It would be too risky for Marco, she insisted. His clothes were nearly dry, but he was bedraggled and subdued when he reached his own home. He cursed himself for a stupid fool. Caterina had not said it, but he was only too aware that after all his boasting his grand odyssey had ended before they had even left the lagoon. He could not let himself think what they would both now have to face from their families. Perhaps it was the Madonna punishing him for what had taken place between Caterina and him, so soon after he had besought Her protection.

He stiffened. His Aunt Flora was standing in the stone archway to their house with its frieze of carved rosettes. He nearly turned away, but she had seen him. 'Marco!' she frowned. 'Where have you been all night?' She gestured sharply. 'Come in, boy.'

Marco followed her down the passage. 'I – I was trying out my boat,' he said. 'I had an accident.'

He followed her into the kitchen, expecting her to turn and scold him. But she was silent. Uncle Zane was standing by the hearth. There were two strangers with him, men in their forties, their clothes rough and worn. One was seated at the table. He was lean, very tanned, with handsome, well-defined features; eyes as blue as Marco's. The other man, in the chair by the fire, was more squarely built, physically more powerful, serious, with a blunt nose and a greying, close-cut beard. Aware of the strangers watching him, Marco was more embarrassed than ever by his sodden appearance.

Zane shifted his feet and coughed. 'Well, Marco . . .' he began. 'It appears your . . . your father's come home.'

For a heartstopping moment, Marco could not believe it. Then he took a step towards the smiling man at the table.

'No, I'm your Uncle Matteo,' the man said. 'This is your father.'

Marco turned to the bearded man by the fire, who was rising. An undemonstrative man, Niccolo Polo was unsure what to say or do, but Marco caught his breath and ran forward, throwing himself into his father's arms, clasping him, burying his face in his shoulder. Niccolo patted his head awkwardly, looking at the others for help.

Within a few hours, Marco was very attached to his Uncle Matteo, a friendly, likeable man with a ready laugh. The awkwardness with his father continued, but Marco was sensible enough to realize that they probably needed time to get to know each other. For years he had thought of little else but this meeting, while his father had had many other, more important things on his mind. The main disappointment was that to all his questions about their travels and adventures, his father only answered, 'Later, boy. Later.'

It was easy to see why people had always spoken with respect of Niccolo Polo. The elder of the two brothers was clearly the leader, shrewd, intelligent, with a born power of command – but not an easy man to charm or to cheat.

One of the first results of their homecoming was the transformation in the house. Marco grinned as he heard the tramp of Uncle Zane's and Aunt Flora's feet above him; they were now moving out of the main bedroom, to make way for the master of the house. When they came down later, Zane and his sons were carrying bundles and boxes, and Marco had a chance to see another side of his father.

'What's this?' Niccolo asked.

'Well, you're home now,' Flora said tightly. 'Obviously we're not needed any more . . .'

Niccolo and Matteo glanced at each other quickly. They knew their sister. 'Come, come, Flora,' Niccolo said. 'You've taken care of this place and my boy for ten years. It can't have been easy, but you've done a good job. This is your home, too. Besides, Matteo and I need someone to run it for us. We couldn't do without you.' Flora sniffed. 'Here. I've something for you.'

All morning, bales and crates and chests had been

carried from the quayside and stacked in the house. He threw open the top of one of the largest chests. It was packed with bolts of the finest silks and linens, exquisite cottons and a delicate, transparent gauze which even Zane had never seen before. 'I meant them for my poor wife,' Niccolo explained. 'But . . . I want you to have them, Flora. You and your girl.' Flora and her daughter Giacomina marvelled and exclaimed over the rich materials.

'Where are they from?' Marco asked.

'Persia and China,' his father told him.

'China?' Marco wondered.

'What you call Cathay,' Matteo explained.

Marco stared at him. Cathay? They had actually been there? It really existed? The land of Prester John?

Matteo had taken a doeskin bag from another box. He undid the drawstring and poured the contents on to the table, a glittering cascade of precious stones, rubies, emeralds and diamonds, topaz and amethysts. As they spilled, sparkling, on to the dark wood, the whole family crowded round, gaping. Matteo chuckled. 'I want you each to take one, any one you choose.' Each stone was worth a fortune in Venetian ducats, and they hesitated. 'Don't worry. We've plenty more,' he said.

Later in the day, Marco went to find Giulio and Bartolomeo. They were shaken to hear of his mishap with the boat, and that Caterina had been with him. 'Better pray she doesn't give you away,' Bartolomeo said. 'Or that her mother wants it kept quiet,' Giulio added. Yet more than anything, they wondered at the strange way that Marco's prayers had been answered. If the boat had not capsized, Marco might never have met his father. It would have been a cruel irony if he had fled from Venice at the very hour that Niccolo Polo had returned.

Marco brought his two friends home to meet his father and his uncle, and to Aunt Flora's annoyance, Niccolo invited the boys to supper. Giulio worked in the meat market and could not stay, but Bartolomeo accepted gladly. He had brought a folder of his drawings with him and asked Matteo's opinion of them.

Niccolo had much to ask Marco and questioned him about his life and interests and schooling. 'And your mother,' he asked at last, 'did she talk to you about me?'

'Every day. She was ill for a long time. She always hoped to hear from you.'

Niccolo grunted. 'Well, I'm not much of a one for writing, except invoices and bills of sale.' He refilled his wineglass. 'Still, it was a shock to hear that she had died. She was a good woman.'

'He says you told him how to draw these, Marco,' Matteo interrupted. 'Remarkable.'

'Sir,' Bartolomeo asked Niccolo politely, 'is it true what the sailors say – there are men with heads like dogs, who speak like us, but bark when they're angry?'

'I can't say I ever saw any, boy.'

Matteo could see that Marco was disappointed with his father's reply, and quickly cushioned it. 'I'm sure I did once. I couldn't see them too clearly, but, oh, how they barked!' He chuckled and passed a drawing over. 'What about this one, Niccolo?'

His brother studied the tablet, which showed a woman, naked but for light hair like a monkey's, leaning forward so that her ten breasts dangled close to the ground. Niccolo did his best not to laugh.

'That's a Mongol woman,' Bartolomeo explained earnestly. 'They have so many children that nature has given them lots of breasts like sows or bitches, in order to feed them all.'

'The sailors told you about them, too?' asked Niccolo. 'No, I don't think I ever came across a woman like that.'

'You'd have remembered if you had,' Matteo said drily. The two brothers laughed quietly to each other.

Marco felt almost excluded. 'How far did you go? How many miles?'

'It's difficult to reckon in miles. But it took us three years to get there and more years to return.'

'To get where?'

'The court of the Great Khan.'

'Genghis?' Bartolomeo gasped.

'No, no,' said Matteo. 'Genghis is dead and buried. His grandson, Kublai. He's emperor of more people than there are fleas in Venice – and that's millions!' The boys laughed as he scratched himself. 'He rules over the whole of China, Persia and part of India.'

'The priests taught us that no-one lives in the lands of darkness,' Marco said. 'Only beasts and evil spirits.'

'Since they've never been there, how do they know?'

Marco smiled. 'For years I've dreamt of places like Cathay, which you call China. But what is it really like?'

'A country like any other,' said Matteo, 'only bigger and richer than you or anybody else can possibly imagine.'

'Mother said that you had gone to make your fortunes.'

'And so we did,' his father shrugged. 'Although we had to leave most of it behind.'

Matteo nodded. 'The Khan wanted to make sure that we'd go back. Still, we didn't come empty-handed, even though half of it was stolen from us on the journey home.'

'You see, Marco,' explained his father, 'we're not exactly what we seem. We may have left as simple merchants, but we've returned as ambassadors from the Great Khan to the Senate and Doge of Venice.'

Chapter Two

'Friendship – with a barbarian?'

Disdain and disbelief showed in the face of the Bishop Patriarch. Old, proud and deeply prejudiced, he looked disdainfully at the Polo brothers, who stood in the Council Chamber of the Venetian Senate, dressed now as gentlemen of rank and distinction. Some of the Senators murmured in agreement. Although some were sceptical and some antagonistic, all listened intently to the answer.

'The days of Genghis Khan are long over, my Lord Bishop,' Niccolo explained courteously, 'except, it seems, in the imagination of Europe. His successor, Kublai, is a man of peace – cultured and tolerant.'

'Yet you say he has conquered more territory than his grandfather,' noted the Doge, Lorenzo Tiepolo, seated beside the Patriarch. 'Three times as much, in fact.'

'It is true, my Lord. But now his only wish is for trade and the ties of friendship.'

'Pah!' snorted the Patriarch. 'Everyone knows that the Mongols are a race of murderous savages.'

'Yet on our way back, it was only when we reached so-called "civilization" that we were robbed,' Niccolo told them. 'Before that, we had travelled thousands of miles armed with nothing more than the passport given to us by the Khan when he appointed us his ambassadors.'

From the folds of his robe, he took out a tablet of gold, some twelve inches long and three inches wide. The Doge received it from him and examined the inscription which, in a language he could not identify, carried the Great Khan's order to supply the bearer with all necessary food, shelter and transport animals, on pain of death.

After weighing the tablet in his hand, the Doge passed it on without comment to the Senators. Niccolo and Matteo watched in silence as the grave rulers of Venice studied the curious object.

'But it's gold!' exclaimed one of the Senators. 'Pure gold!'

Many of his colleagues were equally impressed, though none could decipher the Mongol and Chinese characters, or recognize the Khan's seal that had been stamped at the bottom. The Doge turned back to the two brothers.

'You said your main interest was trade?'

'We are merchants, my lord,' explained Niccolo.

'The advantages to Venice, to us all, through an agreement between your Serene Highness and the Khan were obvious,' Matteo pointed out.

'To your master too, no doubt,' sneered a plump Senator. 'But what does he have that would interest us Venetians?'

Matteo looked the man in the eyes. 'Mountains of gold, silver, diamonds, lapis lazuli, seas filled with pearls, silks, spices and precious furs.'

The speech clearly won some respect from the Council, which was much more easily persuaded by commercial facts than by talk about ties of friendship. Niccolo quickly pressed home their momentary advantage.

'We have discussed it fully with his Ministers. In two to three years, we could open a trade route from Venice to the heart of the empire that could carry a constant stream of priceless goods. Our noble city could become the storehouse of Europe.'

The old Bishop Patriarch was alarmed by the growing number of Senators who seemed to see merit and profits in the Polos' mission. His voice cut across the buzz of interest. 'Trade on such a scale with the Infidel would inevitably lead to widespread corruption and the perversion of our Christian souls.'

'We have dwelt among them for many years, my Lord Bishop,' replied Niccolo, 'yet our faith is firm and unaltered.'

'So you say.' There was a hint of menace in the old

man's piercing eyes. 'Yet I find it suspicious that this approach has been made by your master at this time.'

'Why so, sir?' asked Matteo, innocently.

The Patriarch's voice rose. 'Far from thinking of trade, in Europe many Kings, many Princes of the Church, are calling for a Holy Crusade to rid the world forever of the Mongol scourge!' Some of the Senators muttered eagerly in agreement. 'Soon your master will tremble as he faces the Soldiers of the Cross!'

'My Lord Bishop,' said Matteo, seriously, 'the Mongol Empire is ten times greater than the Empire of Alexander. It stretches from Russia and Persia, through India to the furthest shores of China. All Italy is the size of one of its smallest provinces.'

A shocked silence fell on the Senate. Matteo's warning was all the more effective for its quietness.

Niccolo reinforced it. 'If attacked, the Khan would put millions of men in the field. We tremble for Venice, and for Europe, if its leaders choose to provoke his anger.'

'*Portae inferi non praevalebunt*,' muttered the Patriarch, uneasily. 'The gateways to Hell will not prevail.'

'Be that as it may,' the Doge said soothingly, 'the first concern of our Republic is the salvation of souls, as you know well, Patriarch. But – we are not here to discuss a new Crusade. Let us try to examine more closely what the brothers Polo report to us.' He rose from his chair and crossed over to them. 'As you say, you are both merchants, so you are unaware of the diplomatic obstacles involved. Even as to trade, I see great practical difficulties. Not least the shipment of huge sums of gold over the distances you speak of.'

'But huge sums change hands every day throughout China,' replied Niccolo. 'In the form of paper money.'

'*Paper money?*'

The very notion caused laughter and derision. Niccolo took some Mongol banknotes from his pouch and gave them to the Doge, who had never seen anything like them before. They were made of yellow paper with Chinese characters and pictograms showing the value. Each note bore the Khan's seal stamped in red. One of the notes had been passed to the plump Senator, who weighed it dubiously in his hand. 'And this is the coin we are supposed to trade for?' he sneered.

'It's not the paper, sir, but the value it represents.'

'Which is precisely *nothing!* At any moment, your Khan could refuse to honour it.'

'It's a question of trust!' Niccolo was offended.

'Trust an infidel?'

Before Niccolo could reply, the Senator had taken a gold coin from his pocket and dropped it on to the table. Its chink brought smiles of approval from the others. The Senator then held it over a candle until it blackened in the flame. With a quick wipe on his sleeve, he restored the lustre. When he held one of the banknotes in the flame, however, it was consumed at once and ended up in ashes on the floor. He ground his foot into the charred remains and acknowledged the mild applause. He looked triumphantly at Niccolo, as if challenging him to answer.

Niccolo was quietly contemptuous. 'You have just burned the equivalent of twenty pounds of silver. Congratulations.'

The Senator's jaw dropped and there were gasps as he gazed down at the smear of ash by his foot.

'I must repeat,' said the Bishop Patriarch, 'that Holy Church is totally opposed to any treaty, or dealings, with the enemies of the only true God.'

'But Kublai Khan is most anxious to learn more of Christianity, my Lord Bishop,' announced Niccolo, to a stir of surprise.

'He wishes to convert to the true faith?' Incredulity made the old man's voice falter.

'Not precisely, my Lord. He has studied the doctrines of Mohammed and of Buddha. He now wants to study the Testaments.'

'All religions interest him equally,' added Matteo.

'The sure sign of a barbarian!' the Patriarch snorted.

'Our commission is not only to Venice, but also to his Holiness the Pope,' said Niccolo. 'The Khan has asked the Pope to send back a hundred learned doctors of the Church. He wishes to call a great debate. If our champions win, it will prove to him that ours is the true religion.'

There was a growing hubbub in the chamber.

'And if they do not win?' the Doge asked.

'It's a trick,' protested the Patriarch. 'A trick to confound the representatives of Christ! To make a mockery of them! To force them to abjure their faith! It is the Devil's scheme to exterminate the Church!'

An angry roar greeted the speech and Matteo had to shout above it to make himself heard. 'But if the Holy Father gives his consent?'

'That is impossible,' retorted the Patriarch, sardonically. 'There is no Pope in Rome. For three years the Convention of Cardinals has been trying to choose a successor to his late Holiness.'

Niccolo and Matteo stared at him blankly. 'So . . . what can we do?' Niccolo asked.

'You must wait,' advised the Doge. 'And your master, the Khan, must wait – as we all do. We shall use this time to consider. With God's help – and St Mark's.'

When Marco hurried home after work to hear what had happened, his father and uncle were still angry. Niccolo was pacing. 'That fools like that are in command of the State!'

'The Cardinals sound no better,' Matteo agreed. 'Three years to elect a Pope? . . .'

'Perhaps if you warned them about the other religions?' Marco suggested. 'You said millions believe in them and follow them. If you explained—'

'What do I care about heathen religions!' Niccolo exclaimed irritably.

'But you lived there for years,' Marco said. It was no

use. 'Of course. You saw nothing, except your account books.'

'You watch your tongue, boy,' Niccolo growled. 'Or you'll get the back of my hand!'

Marco was silent. His father was very different from how he had imagined. Worst of all, neither of the brothers seemed to have paid much attention to the marvels they had seen, and none at all to the customs and people and histories of the strange lands they had passed through – except in so far as they affected their trading schemes. To his surprise, he heard his father call to Uncle Matteo to hurry and pack. 'Where are you going?' he asked.

'To Viterbo,' Matteo told him. 'Where the Conclave of Cardinals is meeting. We must be there to arrange an audience with the new Pope as soon as one's chosen.'

'I'll come with you,' Marco said eagerly.

'No, you will not,' Niccolo grunted.

'But now we've found each other, wherever you go, I go,' Marco said.

'I don't know where you got *that* idea.' Niccolo could see that Marco was hurt, and softened his tone. 'In any case, you have work to do here. Zane needs you to help in his shop.'

It was long weeks before the brothers returned, and when they did they were more irritable than ever. The trip to Viterbo had been a waste of time. The conclave was still completely divided. Groups of Cardinals, either bribed or under threat, would vote only for candidates approved by the King of France or his rival, the Holy Roman Emperor, while other candidates tried to promote their own election to the Holy See. All those years of travelling from the other side of the world and there was no one to whom the brothers could deliver their embassy.

'Nothing but a farce,' Niccolo kept muttering. 'A shameful farce.'

Two days later, however, a message arrived, brought by

a state official who would not even give his name, summoning the brothers to the Doge's Palace and warning them that if they did not obey the conditions to the last detail, telling no one of the summons and arriving in secret, the meeting would be cancelled.

A building of stunning magnificence, the Palace adjoined St Mark's Basilica and shared with it the honour of being the spiritual and physical heart of the city. Why the brothers had been invited there, they did not know, but plainly it was a matter of some urgency. As they were shown into the spacious Council Chamber, the bells of St Mark's were tolling the second hour of the morning.

Branched candelabra created pools of light around the room, and the Doge himself was waiting. He began by apologizing both for the circumstances of the meeting and for the attitude of the Bishop Patriarch at the meeting of the Senate.

'I understand the Patriarch, as you must try to understand him. The only true religion is subject to continuous threats. I share his fears. Yet the weight of my responsibility is even heavier. Venice has countless friends – but enemies, too. And to defend it, we need funds. What you reported to us has made me think deeply. If the Khan's offer of peace is to be considered, and if this peace will bring gain and wealth to the Republic, then we cannot refuse it. But first, my friends . . . I want the full truth from you. The Truth before God.'

The Doge's manner was impressive. Tall, ascetic, dignified, Lorenzo Tiepolo had brought intelligence and industry to his onerous duties ever since he had first been installed as Doge four years earlier in 1268. Niccolo and Matteo knew that they were in the presence of a remarkable man, and as they poured their story out to him, they withheld nothing.

'The Patriarch must believe us!' protested Matteo. 'The

Great Khan could help the Pope regain possession of the Holy Sepulchre of Christ.'

The Doge stopped and looked at him intently. 'Be careful, Messer Polo. We Venetians took up the cross and fought in the Holy Lands. The Doges Vitale and Domenico Michiel, Ordelafo Talier, led the Venetian Crusade into battle against the Saracens, and paid their tribute to the Holy Cause with blood.' As he began to pace the Chamber, his voice became confidential. 'Yet Venice has never denied her mercantile instinct. We still sell weapons and armour to those same Saracens, and from them we buy spices, cloth and precious metals. The question of alliances is an enormous one – and difficult. All I can say is this: return to your Khan and tell him that Venice is willing to shake the hand he holds out to us. Our Republic wishes to keep its independence from the Church. However, my friends, do not forget that you are Christians.'

'The Great Khan respects our religion,' Niccolo assured him. 'He is anxious to approach the Pope.'

'Yet the Conclave of Viterbo shows no sign of reaching a decision, as you have just seen,' the Doge reminded them.

'Then you advise us to wait?' asked Niccolo.

'No. You must go back to your Khan.' Niccolo was about to argue, but the Doge stopped him. 'Where would you make for first?'

'Acre, on the coast of Galilee.'

The Doge smiled. 'There is a godly man in Acre, Teobaldo Visconti from Piacenza, the papal representative in the Holy Land.'

'We met him on our journey home,' Matteo said.

'A fortunate meeting,' the Doge nodded. 'Take my greetings to him. He will help you.'

'Forgive me, my Lord,' Niccolo said, hesitating. 'I . . . I fear the anger of the Great Kublai when he sees us return without the wise men he is expecting from the Pope. Would it not be more sensible to . . . delay our departure?'

'No!' Lorenzo Tiepolo spoke firmly and frankly. 'The

Saracens grow in strength, while the princes of Europe cannot agree on another Crusade. Whatever is done must be done quickly, before the Holy Land and the eastern Mediterranean falls into Saracen hands. Go now. Go with God. For Venice and St Mark.'

The brothers kissed the Doge's hand, bowed and went down the steps. He did not move until they were out of sight.

In less than a week, the ship the Polo brothers had chartered was tied up at the Riva Degli Schiavoni, the quay for Dalmatia. Supervised by Matteo, a stream of dockers and sailors loaded livestock and foodstuffs and the rest of the cargo with which they would trade on the way. Marco watched as Niccolo chose new servants for the journey. Two had already been hired and a third was sent to join them, an older, steady man, a widowed seaman named Agostino. Niccolo told the others he would not take anyone else whose experience was all on ships, since much of the route would be overland. One of them stepped forward. 'Jacopo, sir,' he said, touching his forehead. 'I've made three trips to the Levant, but I was reared in the country. I know horses and mules, prefer them to ships any day. And I can cook. I'm a hard worker. Ask anyone. You won't go wrong if you take me.'

Niccolo ran his eyes over him. Jacopo was fleshy and smooth-faced, but a few months on the road would get the fat off. 'Very well,' Niccolo said, 'you're hired But you'd better be prepared for hard work. This is no pleasure trip.' He turned to the others. 'Sorry. That's all.'

Marco saw the man called Jacopo grin to himself at his own cleverness, then touch his forehead again ingratiatingly and move to join the group of hired servants.

Marco moved to join his father. There was something that had to be settled 'You didn't need that last man, father,' he said. 'I can work with horses, too.'

'You?'

'I'm coming with you,' Marco said. 'That's understood.'

'Not by me,' Niccolo told him flatly. This was a moment he had tried to put off as long as possible. The boy was romantic and still wet behind the ears, yet he disliked hurting him.

Marco refused to believe his father meant it. Since nothing had been said, he had managed to convince himself that he would be going too. 'But surely I'm coming with you!'

'I'll hear no more of that!' Niccolo growled. 'I'll make ample provision for you at home. All right, you don't want to be a merchant. You can be a scholar, a lawyer, a priest – whatever you're best suited for. But as to coming with us, it's out of the question.'

'Why?' Marco asked, stricken. All those years of waiting and praying for his father's return, only to be rejected . . . It was too cruel.

'Because you're not fit to make the journey,' Niccolo told him bluntly. 'You're too young.'

'I'm nearly nineteen!'

Niccolo controlled his irritation and tried to speak more reasonably. 'I'm sorry, but it takes a special kind of discipline to travel those distances, a discipline you just don't have.'

'I could learn,' Marco insisted.

Niccolo swung away in exasperation. 'Tell him, Matteo.'

Matteo had heard and was upset for his nephew. He had warned Niccolo to prepare the boy for it more carefully. 'Listen to your father,' he advised quietly. 'The journey is dangerous – so many different races, customs, laws and languages. Be happy to stay here and learn a good, safe trade from your Uncle Zane. You're a Venetian.'

'But a Venetian is born to travel,' Marco answered. 'You said so yourself, father.'

'When?'

'In the only letter you ever wrote to my mother. When I was a child, she read it to me over and over again, until it fell to pieces.'

The mention of his wife and the hurt in Marco's eyes made Niccolo uncomfortable. 'Well . . . I may have said something of the sort.' It was not a conversation to hold in public. He saw the new servants watching them and, gesturing to them to come with him, strode off down the gangplank. Marco and Matteo followed.

At home later that day Marco desperately tried to make one final appeal. As Niccolo came downstairs, carrying a bundle of swords, Marco seized his arm imploringly. 'Don't you see? . . . All my life I've dreamt of being with you. I've wondered where you were, how you lived, what you were doing. When they told me that you were dead, I didn't believe them. I always knew you'd come back for me. Don't leave me behind now, I beg you!'

Niccolo's head was bent and he was motionless. What he had to say was very hard for him. 'Marco . . .' he began. 'You've been alone since you lost your mother. I understand. If I could . . . The fault is not yours. It's in me. I knew I had a child, of course, but until I came back to Venice I didn't know I had a son. I didn't know you. I'm just not used to being a father.'

Matteo joined them. 'Take my word, Marco,' he added gently, 'it is better for you to stay here.'

Marco had tried and could do no more. He had just turned to go up to his room, when he heard shouting outside. There was a crash and a voice roared, 'I said, get out of my way!' The inner door flew open and a man burst in. It was Giuseppe, the doorkeeper from Monna Fiammetta's, raging and dangerous.

Marco froze. For weeks he had had no word of Caterina, could get no message to her. He had heard nothing of her since that night on the lagoon.

Giuseppe had caught sight of him and started for him. 'There you are, you little rat! Sneaking off, are you?'

Niccolo was between them. He drew one of the swords quickly from its scabbard and rested its point on the table top. 'You will take not one more step in my house, my friend,' he said calmly, 'without my permission.'

Giuseppe's hand flew to the knife at his belt, but when Matteo closed in beside Niccolo, he paused. The bearded man looked as if he might know how to use that sword. 'So you're Messer Polo, are you?' he sneered. 'Well, you needn't think you can save him. I'm her father. Caterina's father.'

'Whose?' Niccolo asked blankly.

Marco was horrified. '*You're* her father? I don't believe it!'

'What's this all about?' Matteo demanded.

'Him!' Giuseppe snarled. 'He tried to run away with my Caterina – spent the night with her. He's dishonoured her!'

'Is this true?' Niccolo asked.

Marco could not look at his father. 'I – I—'

'See? He can't deny it!' Giuseppe cut in. 'She tried to protect him, wouldn't tell us who it was. But I beat her black and blue – locked her in the cellar with the pigs until she gave us his name.'

'You'd no right to touch her!' Marco said hotly.

'Hold your tongue!' his father ordered.

'I'll have him up before the Courts – and the Church!' Giuseppe promised.

'That would only cause scandal,' Niccolo said quietly. 'I'm sure we can settle it.'

'There's one way,' Giuseppe insisted. 'He can marry her!'

Marco opened his mouth, but his father snapped, 'I told you to be quiet!' Niccolo laid the sword down and nodded to Giuseppe. 'Yes, that's one way.'

He glanced at Matteo, who took his cue and asked reasonably, 'If they're married, how big a dowry would she bring?' As he expected, the question threw Giuseppe. He went on, 'No girl comes to her husband empty-handed.'

'That's not the way of it!' Giuseppe blustered. 'Monna Fiammetta wants a good price for her daughter . . . She's been keeping her safe – till she could arrange a good marriage. Now he's ruined her, she wants compensation!'

'I see,' Niccolo nodded. 'So it's just a question of how much. We'll need a day or two to think about it.'

Marco wondered at his father's matter-of-factness. It seemed his whole future was being decided like a business transaction.

'Don't try to put me off!' Giuseppe warned. 'I'll go to the Senate, if I have to.'

'No call for that,' Niccolo said. 'We all want to avoid trouble, I'm sure. Here—' There were some small bags of money on the table. He tossed one of them to Giuseppe.

Giuseppe weighed it in his palm. 'It's not enough.'

'It's only to show we're willing to talk,' Niccolo smiled. 'Now, if you'll excuse me – I want to speak to my son.'

'If it was me, I'd have his guts on a plate,' Giuseppe said venomously, then stormed out.

When Giuseppe had gone, Marco could feel his father and uncle looking at him. 'It – it wasn't the way he made it sound,' he began.

'It never is,' Matteo murmured, amused.

'Caterina and I—'

'I don't want to hear about it!' his father snapped. 'It's unthinkable that a son of mine should marry into a family like that.' He had started to pace. 'I knew it . . . I knew I couldn't get out of it.'

'It was my fault,' Marco said. 'Any blame that—'

'In a minute,' Matteo drawled, 'you'll have me believing you're as big a fool as your father does.' Marco looked at him. 'Don't you understand yet? You're coming to Palestine with us.'

Marco's stomach lurched.

'Yes, it's the only way,' Niccolo agreed gruffly. 'The trip to Acre will take four to five weeks. Then we have some business there, so you won't be home for about six months. By then, all this'll have blown over.'

Marco was bewildered, torn between his feelings for Caterina and excitement at his father's decision. Matteo winked to him and he found himself smiling.

His father noticed the smile and scowled. 'You're only

coming as far as Acre, you realize? Not a step beyond! Now, go and pack.'

As soon as he could get away, Marco ran to the boathouse where Giulio, Bartolomeo and other friends had gathered. Even though he was only going as far as Acre, it was farther than any of them had ever been and any one of them would have given ten years of his life to see the famous Crusader citadel, its name resounding in the tales of the Holy Wars to free Jerusalem from the followers of Mohammed.

Marco could tell that Giulio was disappointed not to be coming with him, as they had planned for so long. 'Don't worry, Giulio,' he said. 'Think about building another boat instead. When I come back, we'll set off together, I promise.'

Guilio smiled, not wanting his sadness to spoil his friend's moment of triumph.

'You'll have to go to St Mark's,' Bartolomeo reminded Marco. 'To give thanks to all those saints you've been bothering.'

Marco had not forgotten; but he had another, secret reason for going to the Basilica. After a long wait in the shadow of the porch, his patience was finally rewarded. Amongst a group of old women arriving for confession was Caterina's nursemaid. She tried to avoid him, nervously, but his youth and earnestness won her over and she agreed to take a message for him.

Early next morning, before even the stalls in the Square were open, Marco was waiting. The pearly light of dawn threw the shadows of the twin pillars past the portico of the Doge's Palace. The bell of St Mark's began to toll, slowly and regularly, and a few early worshippers appeared from the dark mouths of the alleyways, heading for the cathedral. Among them were Caterina and her nurse.

The nurse was more nervous than ever, terrified of them being seen. 'Only two minutes, now,' she cautioned.

Marco led Caterina into the space between two shuttered

stalls. She wore a dark green dress of wool brocade, wide-sleeved and high to the throat, and over it a mantle of white linen. Her hair was no longer loose, but was looped back in a silver net. She was even lovelier than he remembered, smiling at him with a hint of shyness. In spite of the nurse watching, he wanted to hold her, but when he touched her arms, she winced. Her body was still tender from the beatings her father had given her.

'He should have beaten me, instead,' Marco reproved himself bitterly. 'It was my fault, that night.'

'It was no fault of yours,' she told him. 'It was what I wanted.' She paused. 'And now you're leaving Venice.'

'But not you!' he swore. 'You're coming with me.'

Caterina smiled. 'What does your father think about that?'

'I can hide you on board, until we're under sail,' Marco said. 'I'm not leaving you.'

Caterina shook her head. 'You've left me already. Or maybe it's me who's drawn away from you. You think I am like you, Marco,' she went on quietly. 'But I am not.'

'But we planned everything together . . . We had the same dream.'

'I said things,' Caterina told him softly. 'But inside me, I did not believe them. You really *see* the things you dream. When you talked to me, for a moment I seemed to see them, too.' The bell was now sounding again, calling the faithful to first Mass. The nursemaid coughed to attract Caterina's attention and began to move off. 'I must go, Marco. One day—'

'Tomorrow!' he urged. 'Come with me.' He caught her hand and raised it, pressing it to his lips. 'We belong together. Come with me.'

Caterina could not tear her eyes from his. She felt again the warmth of her need for him, which had once made her blind to everything else. Her face was tilting towards his, when she stopped herself. 'I would be . . . a burden to you. I'm not even sure what I feel for you.'

'I *know* what you feel,' Marco insisted.

Caterina bit her lip. She pulled her hand away from his and shook her head again, forcing herself to be practical. 'Feelings are not everything. My mother has other plans for me. I will not become like her. She wants me to marry a man with some position in life, a rich man, who will take care of me, not one who is always away from home, always travelling.'

Her nursemaid called to her and she turned to leave.

'Caterina, wait!' Marco pleaded. 'My father is only taking me as far as the Holy Land. Then he'll ship me back home. We'll see each other again soon!'

'You won't leave him,' she said quietly. 'You'll try to follow him, until your shoes crack and your feet bleed. If he really sent you home to Venice, it would break your heart, Marco.' She smiled to him for a last time and hurried to catch up her nurse.

Marco watched her leave. He tried to call after her, but the words died on his lips. He felt an almost unbearable sense of loss. He could not begin to explain or understand the change in her, nor the stirring sense of relief inside himself that she had set him free.

Caterina was reaching the portico of St Mark's, a step or two behind her nurse. She knew that he would still be watching her and fought the instinct to run back to him. She had accepted that her mother was right, yet she could no longer hold back her tears and sobbed, veiling her face with her mantle as she disappeared into the hushed Basilica.

Marco was still trying to work out his conflicting emotions when he arrived home. The sense of loss was no less acute, yet he could not stop thinking that tomorrow . . . *Tomorrow . . .*

As he stepped inside, he heard a voice he recognized. It was Giulio's. His friend was normally softspoken, but to his surprise the voice was loud with indignation. In the living-room, he saw Giulio facing his father and uncle. He was wearing his black Sunday tunic with the white band at the neck, as if dressed for an important occasion.

Niccolo glanced at Marco as he came in. 'This insolent pup claims that he owned the boat you sank in the lagoon!'

'It wasn't just a boat. It was all I had,' Giulio stressed.

'You lent it to him as a friend, at your own risk,' Matteo pointed out.

'But he sank it – and I have the right to compensation,' Giulio insisted.

What had got into him? Marco wondered. Giulio was the gentlest and quietest of his friends, the last to thrust himself forward or to behave like this.

'Compensation?' Matteo repeated, with distaste. 'Such as?'

'A place on *your* boat,' Giulio said quickly. 'To work for you.'

Matteo and Niccolo understood at the same moment as Marco. Matteo chuckled. 'So you want to join us on our journey, is that it?'

Niccolo was not so amused. 'Has Marco told you he's coming no farther than Acre?'

'If we decide to take you,' Matteo said, 'you will have to come with us all the way.'

'Yes, sir,' Giulio acknowledged.

'Very well, then,' Matteo decided. 'A trip to the end of the world in exchange for a boat that finished at the bottom of the sea.' He chuckled and held out his hand. 'You're hired.'

Giulio shook his hand warmly. 'Thank you, Messer Matteo.' He bowed respectfully to Niccolo and left before they could change their minds. As he passed Marco, he winked and smiled. Marco laughed and followed him out.

'I wonder if Marco's young friend will still thank us a year from now?' Niccolo said drily.

Matteo tapped his forehead. 'If he's as useful as he's smart, we've made a good bargain.'

*

Marco could never recall very clearly the day they left Venice. He seemed to remember rain and a chill wind that pierced his cloak as he stood on the stern deck, watching the city recede. Through the rain he could hardly make out the loggia of the Doge's Palace, and soon the towers and spires of the chief buildings, even the cupolas of St Mark's, were lost to sight. He could remember Bartolomeo hugging him and waving up to Giulio, who was with the other servants, lashing down the movables on the deck, since the Captain had forecast rough seas. And to his astonishment, Aunt Flora kissing him and bursting into tears as he said goodbye. He had half-expected to see Caterina at the quayside and half-feared that Giuseppe would come searching for him. But neither of them appeared, and only a few friends and members of their family paid any attention to the two-masted, deep-bellied cargo vessel of the Polo brothers with its proud Lion Banner floating above their own house flag, as it pushed off from its dock and turned its prow towards the Adriatic.

The first few days were also a blank in Marco's mind. He was miserably sick, yet he took comfort from the fact that so were all the servants and some of the crew.

At last, the bad weather began to improve and he woke one morning to find that the pitching motion had lessened and that his head was clear. The sun had broken through the clouds and when he came out on deck, he braced himself, sucking in lungfuls of fresh, sweet air. He saw Giulio standing amidships at the rail, watching something, and moved to join him. Off to port was their first distinct sight of the rocky coast of Dalmatia, the first land they had seen that was not Venice. They grinned to each other and Marco punched Giulio on the shoulder, wanting to hug him.

They sailed on, with frequent stops, down the Dalmatian coast to Corfu and Ulysses' island of Ithaca, past the Grecian Peloponnese to Crete and Famagusta in Cyprus, where they moored for a week. While the Polo brothers renewed trade contacts and sought news of events in the

Near East, Marco and Giulio explored. Everywhere they looked there were things to delight and fascinate them and Giulio marvelled at how Marco could remember so much of what they had seen. Already in his own mind, islands and ports and buildings were beginning to be mixed up, while Marco could describe whole towns he had totally forgotten.

Marco enjoyed each day moment by moment, noting down facts and figures about each place they visited on pieces of parchment which he had bought specially for the purpose. He refused to think of the end of his journey, when they reached Palestine, and stifled any feeling of jealousy that Giulio would be going on. At least he would have seen the Holy Land.

Standing with Giulio one day, watching his father check the accounts, he heard the cry of '*Land ho!*' from the crow's nest, and running forward to the prow, they saw in the distance a shadowy, low-lying coastline. His father and uncle came up to join them and watched as a white glimmer of houses became visible. 'Look – look, Giulio!' Marco breathed.

'St John of Acre,' Matteo said.

'We'll be landing in a few hours,' Niccolo added. He jerked his thumb at Giulio. 'You! Get back with the others. There's work to be done.'

Giulio hurried to help the other servants, who had begun to pack the Polos' travelling baggage under the direction of the dependable Agostino. Marco could not take his eyes from the approaching walled city, where individual buildings had begun to stand out. 'Will there be Crusaders there?' he asked.

'Well, of course,' Matteo told him. 'They're still holding out here against the Saracens. It's the only Christian port left in North Africa.'

'And remember – that's as far as you're coming with us,' Niccolo said.

The harbour of Acre was dominated by a vast stone gateway in the fortified walls. While his father and uncle supervised the unloading of their goods, Marco gazed up at the gate flanked by massive towers, where armed guards kept a constant watch for Saracen galleys. Crusader pennons fluttered from the battlements and a huge flag, marked with a Cross, unfurled lazily in the breeze.

When at last they joined the stream of sailors, merchants, townspeople and Syrians heading for the gate, Marco's heart was beating fast and his mouth was dry. His eyes were everywhere, taking it all in, afraid to miss the smallest detail. A Crusader Guard signed to them, and his father identified the group. 'Niccolo and Matteo Polo, merchants from Venice – my son, Marco, and our servants. We have business with the Papal Legate.'

They were waved on through into the city itself, where Marco's senses were assaulted at once by a whole new series of sights and sounds and smells. The narrow streets of bleached stone were crowded with people, priests, soldiers and monks, Arabs, Jews, Turks and Nubians in every variety of national costume. The uproar was deafening: hammers clinking, shouts of greeting in many languages, laughter, the squawking of chickens, voices squabbling, arguing, the wailing, tinny music of unknown instruments and vendors' cries, mixed with the bleat of sheep and the clamorous braying of donkeys. The smell was overpowering, a pungent blend of spices and open sewers, cooking, perfume and urine. There were emaciated beggars, their running sores clustered with flies, begging for alms; winesellers with casks on their backs and trays of tiny cups round their necks; and hedge priests, half-crazed, preaching a new Crusade at corners, though no one paused to listen.

Niccolo led them to the side past a small bazaar with colourful booths of carpets and metalware, fruit and pottery.

'Where are we going, father?' Marco asked.

'To the merchants' quarter, to find lodgings,' Niccolo said. 'We'll stay there until we can arrange safe conduct to Jerusalem.'

'Jerusalem?' Marco exclaimed.

'Now don't start again, boy!' his father growled. 'Are you never satisfied?' Marco had stopped. 'Come along! As soon as we've found somewhere to stay, we must arrange an audience with the Legate.'

The Papal Legate's mansion was not the most imposing in Acre, but certainly the busiest. It was filled every day with a noisy throng of suppliants in search of his help, advice or blessing. 'We need all three,' Matteo muttered, as he waited in the long, inner gallery with his brother and Marco.

Marco, who was present very much on sufferance, had dressed with some care in a clean, white shirt and tan hose with a loose tunic of dark blue linen over them. Teobaldo of Piacenza was a famous name. A soldier-priest, he had come to Palestine as Chaplain to King Edward of England on the last Crusade and made such an impression by his capability and intelligence that he had been chosen as the Pope's representative. Now that the kings had gone and the Saracens had reconquered most of the Holy Land, he was virtual ruler of the city and territory of Acre, the last bastion of Crusader power. Niccolo and Matteo had paid their respects to him and told him of their mission on their way home, and today their application for an audience had been granted immediately.

There was a stir of hope among the people waiting in the gallery. A secretary monk had come from the guarded, inner doors. He beckoned to the Polos.

The room they entered was broad and spacious, with arched, wooden beams and tall, deep-set windows. In an apse, under a great tapestry of a Byzantine Christ in Majesty, stood a dais with an ecclesiastical throne for the Papal Legate's use on formal occasions. Painted armorial shields were the only other decoration on the stone walls of the audience chamber.

The Legate, Teobaldo, was a sparely built, austere man

in his fifties. His appearance at first surprised Marco. Unlike the monks and friars of his household, he was almost indistinguishable from a simple soldier, wearing light chainmail and a Crusader's tunic, with a plain silver cross hanging from a chain round his neck. Yet his stillness and air of quiet authority were impressive. He frowned as he listened to Niccolo's report of their failure in Italy. 'So your mission achieved nothing?'

'Not with the Senate of Venice, Lord Legate,' Niccolo replied. 'The Patriarch did nothing but curse the Mongols.'

Teobaldo did not hide his disbelief. 'The establishment of communications, the opening of a trade route between Europe and the Empire of the East? I thought they, of all people, would seize such a golden offer!'

'Because the Great Khan Kublai is a Mongol,' said Matteo, 'they did not trust his word, my lord.'

'Even though the opportunities it would have given for trade were almost incalculable,' added Niccolo.

'Not only for trade, Messer Polo.' Niccolo and Matteo did not understand, but Marco nodded. The Legate smiled to him. 'So you agree, young Master Marco?'

Niccolo glanced sharply at Marco, warning him to watch his tongue.

'It would . . . give us a chance to learn more about them, my Lord,' Marco said, hesitantly. 'And for them to learn more of us.'

'And why would that be desirable?'

'We have been taught to fear and hate the Mongols – as men fear that which is strange. Hate comes from ignorance.'

'Exactly, exactly!' agreed the Legate, pleased. 'And we are dealing here with many races so strange to us that they might as well be living on the moon. How many opportunities have been missed through distrust and fear! We should clear roads, build bridges, open doors – not just for trade, but for ideas, new thoughts, the slow, irresistible spread of the truth.' He spoke with total conviction. Marco's eyes were shining and Teobaldo nodded to him.

'All those millions of souls, eh, Marco? But I could not expect the Patriarch of the Most Serene Republic to think of them. They are too far away for him.'

'That's a fact, my lord.' Niccolo's voice grew bitter at the memory. 'The Senators laughed at us. First, we must find the Pope, they said! But we can wait no longer. We promised to return to the Khan, and we must not break faith with him.'

Teobaldo was impressed. 'He must be a remarkable man to inspire such loyalty.' He turned to Niccolo. 'I shall give you a letter for the Great Khan, explaining that your mission failed through no fault of your own. It may help. It may also convince him that not all of us in the West are blind to the gesture he has made. That might encourage him to try again when we have elected a Pope at last. Now, you mentioned that the Great Khan seeks two things. What are they?'

'First, we were to ask his Holiness to send back with us a hundred Doctors of the Church, learned in all the arts.'

'To instruct him in the faith?' the Legate asked, surprised.

'Not exactly. Provided they obey the laws, all religions are permitted in his empire. Moslems, Buddhists, Jews and many others.'

'Remarkable! Of which is he?'

Niccolo hesitated. 'Of all, and none. He gives equal honour to all beliefs in his search for the one best able to help him govern. What he had heard of our faith made him wish to learn more.'

Marco saw that Teobaldo had become completely still, listening.

Matteo took over. 'He asked for the hundred wise and holy men so that he could see with his own eyes if their prayers and arguments would be proof against the magic of the heathen priests.'

'Do you realize the opportunity we risk losing?' said the Legate with quiet intensity. 'A Christian world, stretching from Ireland to the farthest shores of China – and all thrown away for lack of a Pope!' He pondered for a moment, then sighed. 'And what was your other commission?'

'To bring back some of the oil that burns in the Church of the Holy Sepulchre in Jerusalem,' explained Niccolo. 'The Khan has been told that the oil is sacred, a powerful talisman.'

'And so it is – or can be. For some, it has worked the miracle of healing. Yet only through great faith. To the Khan, I fear, it will be of small value. Still, no doubt you want my help to reach Jerusalem. It is a dangerous journey. We hold Acre, but the Saracens have the Holy City and most of Palestine. We live, as you see, in a state of armed truce.' He considered, then nodded. 'Very well – return at noon tomorrow.' He addressed his secretary. 'Make out three safe conducts for Messers Niccolo, Matteo and Marco Polo and their servants so that they may reach Jerusalem.'

Marco tensed, but his father said quickly, 'Your pardon, my lord – we need only two. My son is to remain in Acre with merchant friends of mine, waiting for the ship that will take him back to Venice.'

Marco was about to protest, but checked himself and lowered his head. Teobaldo had noticed his excitement, and now his bitter disappointment. A glance at Niccolo, stolid, not looking at his son, told him everything. His voice became coldly reproving. 'Have you so little care for your son's soul? Has he come to the Holy Land merely to buy and sell?' Marco's body was rigid as the Legate's gaze shifted to him. 'With the Saracens in possession of Jerusalem, we have had to fight hard for the right of pilgrims to enter it. Everyone who does so is a soldier of the Cross. Is it the journey you fear, young man? Or have you no wish to make the pilgrimage? No wish to pray on the Hill of Golgotha, to tread in the steps of Our Lord?'

The injustice of it made Marco stammer. 'It . . . It is what I wish more . . . more than anything in the world!'

'Very well, then!' the Legate said sternly, and looked

again at Niccolo. 'Let me hear no more talk of his remaining in Acre. A safe conduct for Niccolo, Matteo and *Marco* Polo.' He turned away, dismissing them.

Shaken, Niccolo and Matteo bowed low, but as Marco began to bow, Teobaldo Visconti glanced back and Marco could have sworn the Legate gave him the very faintest of smiles.

Disillusion set in early. Marco soon learned that the Holy Land, which had been so golden in his dreams, had a pitiless sun that beat down unrelentingly and an equally fierce wind that lashed any exposed portions of skin with driving sand and grit. He discovered the agony of saddle sores and was nauseated when his father ordered him to attend to the lumpish Jacopo, who had developed a kind of nervous dysentery through fear of being attacked by Saracens or bandits. Yet Marco would not give his father the satisfaction of hearing him complain. Looking after Jacopo, grooming the packhorses, standing double watch at night – these were his father's way of breaking him to his will, of proving that he was right not to take him on the longer journey. Marco refused to break. Giulio was finding it a struggle, too, and Marco was helped to survive by sharing the hardships with his friend.

It was not all misery. Although as Christians they rode at all times under threat of attack in this hostile country, there were valleys of cool shade and green grass, with pools to bathe in and water the horses. In the last hour before sunset, a mauve light and gentle shadows partly veiled the harsh landscape and a soft wind blew from the hills, and as they knelt for their evening prayer, Marco could feel in his heart the timeless beauty of this land which for untold ages men had called Holy. Once they caught the heart-stirring sight of a troop of Crusader cavalry, helmets gleaming, pennons a-flutter on the bright tips of their lances, horses and men proudly carrying the sign of the Cross into the heart of enemy territory. They were singing as they rode, harnesses jingling, white cloaks with red crosses streaming behind them. Marco saw Giulio clasp his hands as he watched them, and followed his thought exactly. It was just so, as boys, they had dreamed of serving the True Church against its enemies.

That was the day his father announced they would reach the Holy City in three more marches. It cheered everyone.

For the remainder of the journey Matteo rode beside Marco. He had to admit a grudging respect for his nephew, who bore hardship without complaint. Not like three of their servants, including Jacopo, who would bolt if they were ever given the opportunity. Agostino had been detailed to keep an eye on them.

They were riding up the first slope of a line of low hills, with higher peaks beyond, and Marco was watching a Bedouin herdboy guarding a small, scattered herd of goats. Below him were the few black tents and fires of a nomad camp. Women tended the fires and some children were playing. A few ragged men squatted in the shade, while their sheep grazed in the sparse scrub. It was a quiet, pastoral scene, like something from the days of Abraham. The herdboy waved shyly, and Marco and Giulio waved back. They were surprised when Niccolo led them higher, away from the camp, and Matteo told them the people were Bedouin.

'Saracens?' Marco asked.

'You could say so,' Matteo smiled. 'But they're shepherds. They travel wherever there's grazing for their herds.'

The sun was dipping towards the horizon and Niccolo called back, 'We'll camp in the next valley. Make a start again at dawn.'

As they rode on, they heard the sound of a scream behind them and looked round quickly. The Bedouin women were snatching up their children and running for the tents, as a troop of Crusaders rode swiftly towards the camp. Marco watched, uncomprehending, and then his mouth opened as the Crusaders' lances swept down and their warcry roared out: '*Dex Veult! Dex Veult!*'

The Bedouin shepherds, holding only their herding sticks, ran forward to stand between the cavalry and their camp and were cut down without even disturbing the charge. The Crusader captain, wielding a huge battleaxe, sliced the head off one of them in a single, sideways slash. Then the horses were among the tents. Two women were trampled by their hooves at once, one of them carrying a child.

Marco was pleading silently, horror-struck, 'No . . . *No . . . No* . . .' Giulio had closed his eyes tightly and was praying. They saw an old Bedouin, grey-bearded, hobble forward, his arms raised in appeal. He was speared through the chest. There was no real fighting. Anyone who moved or ran was impaled by lances or had his skull split open by the Captain's axe. Marco's horror increased when he saw that the Crusaders were laughing. It was a massacre with no hint of mercy.

Crusaders stabbed at the fires with their lances, taking up burning wood which they hurled on to the tents. Others were slaughtering the few gaunt animals. One woman was rolled over a fire and her clothes set alight. She went rolling on over the sandy ground, screaming and beating at herself to put out the flames, tearing at her burning robe. As the terrified children fled from the blazing tents, they were trapped in a circle of horses where the Crusaders' lances goaded them to try to escape, when they were cut down.

Giulio was weeping. Jacopo vomited over the side of his horse. 'Move on! Move on!' Niccolo was urging. Matteo grabbed Marco's bridle and forced him to move, but Marco could not turn his head from the slaughter. The woman with the smouldering robe had torn it off and, naked, had run for the rocks at the bottom of the slope to hide. Four or five Crusaders had caught up with her, thrown her on her back and were now taking turns to rape her.

Marco wrenched his horse's head round to ride down and try to stop them, but Matteo had a tight grip on his bridle. 'No, boy! No!' he ordered. 'They'd only gut you!' The small cavalcade started up the slope away from the horror, but Marco knew he would never forget it, never wipe out the filth of it, nor his disillusionment. 'It's a religious war,' Matteo told him gruffly. 'If you didn't know what that means, you do now. And think of it – I could tell you stories of what peasants like those have done to our pilgrims that would turn your stomach.'

The party of Venetians travelled on, subdued, anxious now only to reach their destination. Marco could not even discuss with Giulio the horror they had witnessed. It had burnt itself too deeply into him. He withdrew into himself and was not roused from it until two days later, in the early morning, when his father pointed out to him a low mudbrick house, poor and undistinguished, by the side of the dusty road. 'That means we're nearly there,' Niccolo said.

'What does?'

'The House of Lazarus,' Matteo said. 'Over there. Lazarus, the brother of Martha and Mary. The man Our Lord brought back from the grave. That was his house.'

Marco crossed himself automatically, as did the others. He felt an immediate sense of reverence. What those Crusaders had done had been committed by men, fallible men. It did not affect the unshakable strength of his faith. Looking back, he saw that an Arab woman and her small boy had come to the door of the house and were watching them curiously. The child held his hand out, stabbing two fingers towards the Christian group in an obvious sign to ward off the Evil Eye. Only a few days ago, Marco would have resented it. Now he thought he understood.

That evening, they climbed up through an olive grove on foot, leading their tired horses, and came out into a more open space. Ahead of them, white in the moonlight, were mighty walls with towers and domes beyond them. There was an eerie stillness, broken only by the tolling of a bell far away in the city. They had reached Jerusalem the Holy.

They were all eager to enter the city, but Niccolo reminded them that the Mamelukes were in command here; no one was allowed in or out after sunset and no Christians permitted on the streets during the hours of dark. As they made camp, Marco sat silent, gazing at the walls. 'What's the matter?' his father muttered impatiently. 'We haven't had a word out of you for days. Here we are, where you wanted to be. I thought you'd be pleased.'

'I am. I'm grateful, father,' Marco said quietly. 'But I cannot stop thinking of those people we saw butchered. And of the devils who cut them down.'

'Devils?' Matteo came over to them. 'They were just men, Marco, like you and me. I'm afraid it can be a painful business, losing your youthful illusions.' He glanced round. 'Still, it's a strange conversation to be having here.'

'Why?' Marco asked.

'This olive grove. Where we are,' Matteo explained. 'It used to be known as the Garden of Gethsemane.'

Next morning, Marco awoke at cock crow to find the others already up, repacking the horses. He heard his father tell Agostino that the servants were to wait outside the East Gate. Only the Polos would enter the city. He saw Giulio's flush of disappointment and asked, 'Can't Giulio come with us, father?'

'It costs too much,' Niccolo answered brusquely. 'Two ounces of gold each to pass through the gates. Here – put this on.' He handed Marco a length of blue cloth. 'Wind it round your head like a turban. It's one of the rules.'

'Blue for Christians. The Jews wear yellow,' Matteo said. 'Remember – here we're the infidels.'

The world which had appeared so safe and sane in Venice was a tortuous place.

In the hubbub of the City of David, the area by the Wailing Wall was strangely calm. Marco paused with Niccolo and Matteo to watch the Jews in their yellow turbans praying in front of all that remained of their great Temple, some bowing, others weeping, some silently impassioned. Their fervour was evident, yet not a sound could be heard. His father and uncle looked at it as a curiosity, but Marco was unexpectedly moved. In Venice the Jews formed a private, secretive community, tolerated because they handled the distasteful business of money-lending, which was forbidden to Christians. He had never before thought of them having a genuine religion, a belief which could affect them so profoundly.

He was still musing when they came to the Via Dolorosa, the twisting street up which the Son of God had carried his heavy Cross to the hill of Golgotha. As Marco felt the stones of the street under his soles and realized where he was walking, his eyes filled with tears. If the massacre had put doubts in his mind, they were swept away now. He walked as if rapt, hardly seeing the crowds of pilgrims and traders or hearing the hawkers shouting their wares, selling souvenirs and religious trinkets to the credulous. An Arab dragoman fell in beside them, offering to show them the room of the Last Supper and the tree where Judas hanged himself. Niccolo sent him off. Like Marco, perhaps influenced by him, Matteo and he had begun to feel awe at the thought of approaching the holiest of places.

At last they came to the Church of the Holy Sepulchre, a haven from the clamour of the streets outside. By the dim light they saw the small sepulchre itself, sheathed in white marble and with a single, low door. Beside the door, the stone which covered it was also sheathed in marble, three holes left in it to show the original rough stone. Pilgrims were queueing up to kiss the stone through the holes, before moving on and dropping a coin into the hands of a waiting monk.

Niccolo, Matteo and Marco approached and stopped to peer into the small cave, eight foot square, with its raised marble platform along the north wall. No light was admitted to the cave but the single, beautiful lamp that hung over the tomb platform bathed it in a gentle radiance. All three of them were moved by what they saw.

'This is the stone that closed the entrance,' said Matteo.

'That's the tomb itself,' muttered Niccolo. 'And the lamp.'

'The Tomb of Our Lord!' Marco whispered.

An old Georgian monk who had been watching them with growing suspicion shuffled across and warned them that they could not go inside without special permission. Niccolo told him that they had come to fetch some of the sacred oil from the lamp in the sepulchre.

'There's none to spare,' the monk declared.

'We have credentials!' Matteo assured him. 'A letter from the Papal Legate, the Archdeacon Teobaldo.'

Niccolo handed the letter to the monk who examined it suspiciously. 'That's the Archdeacon's seal,' Niccolo swore. 'It's genuine.'

'I don't doubt it,' came the surly reply. 'It's easy enough for him to say give away the oil. Give it away! But it's scarce. We use only the purest.'

'We're only asking for a little,' said Matteo.

'That's what they all say. There's not enough. Every pilgrim wants some to cure his boils or bad leg – or to sell at a profit when he gets home.' The emphasis on the last phrase was cunning.

Niccolo understood. 'Naturally, we should wish to leave some alms for the Church, Father,' he said, and placed a few coins in the monk's hand. When the hand remained outstretched, he added more coins, until finally the monk was satisfied and shuffled off towards a niche in the side wall.

Niccolo shrugged. 'He's right, after all. The monks need oil. They should be allowed to sell it.'

Matteo laughed quietly. 'For a few drops of oil, the monks can buy themselves a dozen bottles of wine.'

'But what does a greedy monk matter?' Marco asked. He had never felt such religious certainty. 'The Lord Jesus died for his sins as well as ours.'

His uncle was brought up short by his earnestness. 'You

are right, Marco,' he apologized sincerely. 'You make me feel ashamed. *Mea culpa.*'

Marco and Matteo knelt and crossed themselves, bending their heads in prayer before the door of the Sepulchre. Behind them, the monk handed a small glass phial of oil to Niccolo, who placed it carefully in his pouch, then made the sign of the cross and knelt beside his brother and son.

An hour later they had passed through the East Gate and were back outside the Holy City. It was not easy, however, to locate the rest of their party, since they were now at the point of departure for most of the camel trains and, quite apart from the commotion of hundreds of camels, donkeys and mules, the area was teeming with Bedouin cameldrivers and herdsmen, Syrian traders, Turkish, Egyptian and Jewish merchants and their retainers. There were makeshift coffeehouses and caravanserais, but the Polos' servants had been warned to stay away from them, as they were reserved for Mohammedans. Sensibly, Agostino had set up camp beyond the sprawl of tents, tethering the horses and packmules to a clump of thorntrees. A fire was lit and Jacopo had everything ready to prepare a meal.

'We might as well eat now,' Niccolo decided. 'We won't want to stop again before nightfall.'

Before the meal, Niccolo carefully transferred the phial of oil from his pouch to a silver casket. He knew there were some in the throng outside the gate who would commit almost any crime to acquire it. Their lives would also be in danger from the many Mohammedan fanatics if they were suspected of carrying such a powerful Christian talisman.

'So far, so good,' Matteo said.

'So far,' Niccolo grunted. 'The problem is, what do we do about *him*?' He nodded towards Marco.

'We're only fifty miles or so from Joppa,' Matteo said. 'We could sail to Acre from there.'

'We'd waste days – weeks, maybe,' Niccolo objected impatiently. 'And he'd never get there on his own.'

Marco had heard, and with a glance at Giulio, he seized his chance. 'Why do I have to?' he asked. 'Now I've come as far as this, why not let me stay with you?' He continued less hesitantly, 'I'd be no trouble! And there are many ways I could help.'

It was a request Niccolo had been expecting for days. 'How many times do I have to tell you?' he snapped. 'It's not possible.' Ending the matter, he turned to stow the small silver casket containing the Holy Oil in his saddle pack.

But Marco had taken all he could. He spoke directly to his father, intensely. 'Why don't you admit it? You just don't want me. All those years I waited for you to come back for me – I should have understood.'

Niccolo was stung and about to reply angrily, but bit back the words. There was more than a little truth in what his son had said.

Marco saw his uncle gesture to him warningly. He already regretted having let his hurt and bitterness show so openly. 'Forgive me. But surely I haven't been a burden to you?'

Matteo was sorry for the boy, and also for his brother who could not take the final step of accepting his son. 'Marco, listen,' he said soothingly. 'I know it seems heartless to you, but don't you realize that compared to the distance we still have to cover, what we've done so far is a Sunday morning's stroll to the Rialto. We won't reach the Khan's court this year – nor the next. Perhaps not even the year after.'

Niccolo saw a way to finish the argument cleanly. 'That's the truth,' he declared. 'And there's danger every league of the road. I'll not risk my son's life.'

Marco raised his head. 'What you're saying is that I'll never see you again.'

'No, no,' Niccolo said gruffly. 'We'll be back sooner or later.'

'Well, *you* expect to return safely. Why couldn't *I*?'

'For pity's sake!' Niccolo roared. He smashed his fist on to his knee and started up. Marco rose to face him, and it seemed as though Niccolo would strike him.

'Wait, Niccolo! Wait,' Matteo pleaded, urgently. 'I have a suggestion.' Niccolo's heavy fists were still clenched, but he nodded. 'We don't want to waste time going back on our tracks. Marco is burning to see more of the world. I say, let him come with us.' Niccolo glared at him and Matteo explained, 'Only as far as the Levant. We can cross the mountains and head due north-east into Lower Armenia. We'll pass the port of Lajas. We'll have Marco's company till then, and he can sail home to Venice from there.'

There was a tense pause while Niccolo considered. 'Would that satisfy you?' he asked curtly.

Marco's voice was just as flat. '. . . Yes, father.'

'Very well.' Niccolo shrugged as though the whole business had been trifling and sat again to close his saddle pack. He did not address another word either to Matteo or his son.

They sat in silence as they ate the goat stew which Jacopo had prepared. Undependable and workshy as he was, he was nonetheless a gifted cook who could turn even these stringy lumps of flesh into something palatable. Marco found that he was ravenously hungry. He sat beside Giulio, whose irrepressible smile witnessed his delight at the change of plan. However, Marco knew better than to smile.

Just as he was finishing his meal he heard his father call softly, 'Agostino!'

Agostino nudged the two servants beside him and they rose, moving back to stand guard by the packhorses. Two men were approaching the fire from the side of the caravanserai. They were tall, wearing pilgrim cloaks. A third stood watching farther off.

'That's close enough,' Niccolo said, and the men stopped. Their cloaks were dusty, their faces burnt dark by long exposure to the sun. They stood erect, their shoulders braced, and as one of them shifted his booted feet, Marco saw the blunt tip of a scabbard peep from under the hem of his cloak. Giulio had spotted it too, and whistled soundlessly between his teeth, their old signal. Marco nodded. What manner of pilgrims held themselves like soldiers and wore Crusader swords?

'We are looking for the Polo brothers of Venice,' one of them said.

'That's us,' Matteo told him.

The man stepped closer, lowering his voice. 'I bring an order from the Legate Teobaldo Visconti. You are to return at once to Acre.'

'*Acre?*' Niccolo repeated, shaken. 'But how can we? We're headed east!'

'There is nothing more I can tell you,' the messenger said. 'That is the Legate's order. An escort is waiting for you at Bethany.'

There was no disputing it. 'What now?' Niccolo muttered to Matteo, fuming. 'Are we never to get away?'

When the group arrived back in Acre, they were conducted immediately to the Legate's mansion, where their escort left them again in the gallery anteroom to the audience chamber. This time it was even more crowded with dignitaries and suppliants than before.

'Nothing moves slower than priests,' Niccolo complained. 'We must reach the Khan without delay, he says. And what does he do? Brings us all the way back!'

Yet it was only minutes before the Crusader officer appeared again from the audience chamber and beckoned to them. There was a murmur of protest as Niccolo, Matteo and Marco, still in their sweat-stained travelling clothes, were passed in by the guards at the main entrance.

The great hall was empty, apart from two monks at a lectern to one side, chanting softly in unison. Teobaldo was seated in a carved chair at the foot of the dais. A huge, dramatic painting of the militant Christ seemed to loom over him. He was sunk in thought and made no movement as they advanced towards him uncertainly, made timid by his stillness and by the echoing rise and fall of the monks' plainsong.

Reaching the Legate's chair, they hesitated and bowed. He did not acknowledge them. Niccolo coughed. 'We came, as you ordered, my lord,' he said.

Teobaldo looked up, becoming aware of them for the first time. He raised his hand in greeting. 'I am grateful, Messer Polo. And to you, Messer Matteo. And . . .' he smiled, 'to Master Marco. I take it your visit to the Holy Sepulchre was successful?'

'Completely, my lord,' replied Niccolo. 'By now, we'd have made a good start on our journey . . .'

'—If I had not summoned you back, you mean.' The thought seemed to amuse him. 'You really have no idea why?'

'None, my lord.'

'I must ask you to return the letter I gave you for the Emperor Kublai.'

Niccolo did not hide his reluctance. 'If you say so . . .'

'I must give you a new one.' All three were puzzled and Teobaldo went on, serious now. 'Circumstances change, my friends. Men are sometimes plucked by fate from humble stations and raised to heights of which they have never dreamed. Sustain me with your prayers. When you left here, I was Teobaldo of Piacenza, Legate of Palestine. Since then, word has come that the Conclave of Cardinals has finally reached a decision and has chosen me, unworthy as I am, as the new Pope of Rome.'

His three listeners were stunned by the news. Marco fell to his knees in front of the new Bishop of Rome and Head of the Holy Church.

The chamber was a plain, stone-walled room, partly relieved by ikons and an ivory crucifix on one wall and lit by candles and torches in wall brackets. A large, carved wooden coffer stood along one wall. The three of them sat at the trestle table, eating their supper of chicken, bread, dates and figs. A map was spread out in front of Niccolo, whose index finger traced the route they were to take by land from Acre to the port of Lajas and on to Inner Armenia.

Matteo filled his brother's goblet with wine. 'I'm still afraid I might wake up,' he confessed.

'If you say "The Lord's ways are Infinite," once more, I'll throw the rest of this chicken at you,' warned Niccolo.

'Well, they are, they are . . .'

The brothers laughed softly together, but Marco did not hear them. He was lost in his thoughts, reflecting on all that had happened in such a short time, still emotionally uplifted by the ceremony they had just attended, in which Teobaldo had accepted his election as Supreme Pontiff. In an intensely moving ritual Teobaldo had also declared that from henceforth he wished to take the name Gregory, in honour of Pope Gregory VII, who had brought back so much strength to the Church.

One of the two doors suddenly opened and priestly attendants brought in a number of items which they set on the coffer in silence before leaving again. Bemused, Niccolo stared at the jewelled ikon, the richly chased golden vessel and the crystal goblet and ewer. Then the other door opened and Pope Gregory came in, followed by two Dominican friars. Marco, who rose and bowed at once, noticed that the Pope was now wearing his Crusader tunic, although he still wore the papal ring he had donned during the ceremony. Niccolo and Matteo hurried to show respect by rising, also. Relaxed and friendly, the Pope told them to be seated.

'My secretary is copying out letters for you to take to the Great Khan,' Teobaldo said, and gestured towards the coffer. 'These are gifts I have chosen for you to present to him. We cannot hope to match the Khan in riches, but at least we can impress him with the best of our craftsmanship – from the goldsmiths of Florence, and the glass-makers of Venice.' He sat down beside Marco and smiled. 'We must not leave out Venice, eh, Marco?' His tone was almost familiar now. 'Well, tell me, my young friend, did Jerusalem live up to your expectations?'

'Much more, in some ways, your Holiness. Much less, in others.'

'Indeed?' Marco's intelligence and natural honesty appealed to the new Pope and he waited for him to continue.

'I . . . I have never felt so humble, nor so close to the presence of our Lord.' Gregory nodded, obviously pleased. 'And yet . . . I have never felt so angry.'

'Angry? Why was that?'

'Foolishness, your Holiness,' interrupted Niccolo. 'He's an inexperienced boy . . .'

'Let me be the judge of that, Niccolo . . . Well?'

Marco ignored the warning glance from his father and explained. 'I was angry with the Saracens, who make people pay to enter the city, which should be free to all who come to worship.' He paused. 'I was angry with some of the pilgrims whose only thought was to buy trinkets and fake relics.' Gregory nodded again. 'But what angered me most was to see soldiers of the Cross killing women and children without mercy.'

One of the Dominicans gasped out loud and Niccolo jumped to his feet. 'Forgive my son, your Holiness!'

'There is nothing to forgive,' Gregory said gently. 'I have often felt the same feelings myself. I hated the weapons I carried.' He became more businesslike. 'Now – you have the gifts and the oil. Soon you will have my letters also. The Great Khan asked as well for a hundred wise and holy priests. There are not so many to be spared and . . . I doubt if I could find them in any case. After all, our Lord only found twelve – and one of those betrayed Him.' He paused, with a slight smile, and glanced at the Dominicans. 'But you will not go alone. I have chosen two pious and learned men to accompany you, both of the Order of the Blessed Saint Dominic.'

He introduced Brother Nicholas of Vicenza, a noted theologian, a stout, assertive and self-important man who bowed curtly to Niccolo and Matteo, but ignored Marco. Brother William of Tripoli was introduced next. William had studied the Koran and the doctrines of Mohammed, and was older and more ascetic, thin-faced; but there was a gentle quality about him that appealed to Marco. Unlike his colleague, William included the youngest of the Polos when he bowed his greetings.

Suddenly a great roar from outside broke in on them: '*We want the Pope! We want the Pope!*'

Undisturbed, Gregory continued. 'Brother Nicholas and Brother William have the power to grant absolution, and to ordain priests and bishops in my name. They are the rocks on which our Church in the East shall be founded.'

'In the prayer that we may prove worthy,' William said.

'And in the knowledge that our way is the way of martyrs,' Nicholas added piously.

'Do not be in too great a hurry to join that Blessed Band,' warned the Pontiff. 'I want my letters to reach the Khan's eyes and my words to sing in his ears.'

'*The Pope! The Pope! Where is our Pope?*'

The demands from an evidently sizeable crowd grew louder and more insistent, and soon the secretary came scurrying in. 'Holy Father, the Crusaders ask you to show yourself to them. They want your blessing.'

'Later, later . . .'

'But there are so many of them, and they've waited for hours.'

'The labours of my new task are beginning,' Gregory sighed. He smiled and rose, signalling to everyone to come with him.

They followed him through the door, along a corridor and into the Audience Chamber itself, which was lit by torches and packed with armed Crusaders. The din subsided as the Pope appeared, but the respectful hush soon gave way to fresh shouts of acclamation. When Gregory raised his arms to confer the blessing, the Crusaders beat their swords on their shields with enthusiasm.

Afterwards, with the Polos and the two friars still at his

heels, Gregory led the way back to the private apartments and at once picked up the thread of their conversation.

'The first and most important purpose of your mission is to assure us the allegiance, or at least the neutrality, of the Mongols. Without the fear of the Mongol threat, it will be easier for us to plan for the liberation of the Holy Sepulchre.'

'With your permission, Your Holiness,' Matteo said worriedly, 'you entrust us with a responsibility too great for us. We are only plain merchants.'

'The Great Khan trusts you. You are the link between us. The three of you are the proof of my sincerity.'

Marco straightened in shock and looked to his father, hoping he would confirm the Pope's assumption that he would be taken on the journey. Niccolo dashed his hopes by whispering sternly, '*Our agreement, Marco.*'

'Where are you headed next?' Gregory asked, realizing the situation once again.

'To the port of Lajas, Your Holiness,' Niccolo answered, 'on the way to Armenia. We were about to set off when Your Holiness called us to return.'

'It is a safe port, with more frequent ships sailing for Venice,' Matteo said. 'We have many friends there who would be ready to welcome Marco on board and take him home.'

'But surely you would not leave him behind? One more will increase the chances that at least one of you will reach your destination.'

A determined man, Niccolo did not accept easily having his decisions overruled. 'Is it your command that we take him with us, Your Holiness?' he asked thickly.

Marco held his breath as the Pope answered mildly, 'I have no right to decree how a father should deal with his son. Let us say, it is my *wish*.'

Before his brother could protest, Matteo said hurriedly, 'Your Holiness, your wish is command enough.' He bowed, forcing Niccolo to bow too. Marco's eyes closed for a second.

As they were taking their leave, Marco knelt and kissed the ring on the Pope's right hand in gratitude. Gregory blessed him and smiled, saying just loud enough for him to hear, 'When engaged in a campaign, Marco, it is sometimes advisable to conquer only one city at a time.' Marco understood.

And so it was that when the small band of travellers struck out into Armenia, Marco was one of their number. On the long, taxing journey from Acre to Lajas, he proved himself a useful and durable member of the group, and Matteo was more and more impressed with his nephew's stamina and good humour. Even Niccolo had to admit that his son had courage. At the port of Lajas, they heard the alarming news that Armenia had been invaded by the feared Bibars and his Saracen host, who had swept through the country, destroying everything in their path; plainly they could be expected to have no mercy for any Christian merchants or friars. The two suspect servants deserted, and only Agostino prevented the cowardly Jacopo from sneaking off too. A difficult decision had to be reached, whether to risk going on or to wait, perhaps for months. Marco was the one most ready to push on, and his determination heartened the others.

Slowly and warily they journeyed into Armenia, keeping to the least-used paths through the rocky terrain. One morning at first light, they rose to take part in a service of Holy Communion, celebrated by the officious Brother Nicholas, assisted by Brother William. A simple crucifix and a strip of fringed cloth had turned a boulder into an altar and the Polos, together with their three remaining servants, knelt before it.

Matteo's attention was distracted by a distant sound. 'Niccolo, look!' he hissed, pointing to a party of fast-riding horsemen crossing the plain behind them.

Niccolo rose cautiously to his feet. The horsemen had seen the smoke of their small fire and were heading for the camp. Quickly, he told Nicholas to hide the crucifix and the missal, warned the servants to stay by the horses and called Marco to his side.

In a panic, Jacopo reached for the sword by his pack saddle.

'No, you imbecile!' snarled Niccolo. 'One hostile move by any one of us and we're finished!'

Matteo had caught sight of the spiked helmets. 'They look like Saracens.'

The horsemen were approaching at full gallop, sending up a cloud of dust and fanning out in battle order. When they reached the camp, they slowed abruptly, rearing their mounts a few yards from the travellers. Their leader was a fierce and hawk-faced Sheikh. Niccolo stepped forward and raised his right hand. '*Neharkum sa'id*,' he said in Arabic. 'May your day be prosperous!'

'May your day be prosperous and blessed,' replied the Sheikh, surprised to hear his own tongue. 'Where are you from?'

'We are Italians. Merchants.'

The Sheikh nodded, but one of his men, looking extremely fierce, came to growl something to his leader. The other Saracens put their hands to their sword hilts. Brother Nicholas had uncovered the crucifix again. Fearing that his last hour had come, he prayed silently, impassioned, his arms and eyes raised towards heaven. The Sheikh's glare was hard and angry. For a moment, their lives were in the balance. Giulio instinctively drew closer to Marco. It seemed as if the Sheikh would order his men to cut the little group to ribbons; but instead, he suddenly gave a sharp order, swung his horse round and galloped off, his men trailing after him.

'All saints be praised!' cried William.

Marco had seen how the friar's ostentatious display had offended the Mohammedans. He could not believe he was still alive. 'Why didn't they attack us?'

'Because he had answered my greeting,' Niccolo said quietly. 'He could not kill us after wishing us a good day.'

'You, on your feet!' Matteo shouted to the kneeling Brother Nicholas.

'Beware of sacrilege, my son!' warned William. 'He is praying.'

'You heard me!' Matteo was fuming. 'Get up!'

Startled by the hand on his shoulder, Nicholas opened his eyes, looked around and saw that the Saracens had ridden away. There was ecstasy in his voice. 'They've gone?'

'No thanks to you! Your foolishness nearly got us all killed. It was a miracle that the Sheikh managed to restrain them.'

'God answered my prayers!'

'Listen, Sir Priest,' said Matteo, jabbing a finger at him for emphasis. 'The Pope himself advised us to be careful. If you're looking for martyrdom, then you're going against his orders.'

'O, ye of faint heart! I am not afraid to praise my Lord in the shadow of death.'

'Then you don't understand,' Niccolo snapped. 'If you persist in offending every pagan we meet, we won't survive the first fifty miles! Is that clear?'

Brother Nicholas was shaken and turned to his colleague for support. 'I think . . . perhaps they are right, brother,' advised William nervously.

'I will not hide my faith,' Brother Nicholas muttered, but he took the crucifix up quickly and wrapped it in the altar cloth.

Agostino had climbed a rock to watch the departing horsemen. 'Will the Saracens come back, master?' he asked.

'They might,' said Niccolo. 'Those horsemen could be a patrol reconnoitering Armenian territory for a larger force to attack the warriors of the Khan. It's a day's ride to the next village. We'll spend the night there. We know the people. They're hospitable.'

They rode on across the barren landscape, pausing only to rest the horses and eat a frugal meal. It was nightfall when they came at last to the village, which was no more than a scattering of mudbrick huts. Niccolo's confidence that they would be given a warm welcome was soon proved to be quite unfounded. Carrying torches and shouting threats, the villagers ran out to chase the visitors away. A few sticks were thrown and dogs set on the horses.

'So much for Armenian hospitality!' Matteo commented drily.

'We'll try the next village,' decided his brother.

But the same story was repeated at the next village, and at the next again. Spurned and attacked wherever they sought food and shelter, they avoided settlements altogether and struggled on for days across the desert. A vicious, burning wind hit them, sapping their strength, and the shortage of water became critical.

Niccolo forced them on, consulting a faded map from time to time, and plotting a course towards an oasis. Behind him rode Brother Nicholas and Brother William, weary, aching, breathing with difficulty, and sweating so profusely in the chafing heat that they seemed to be glistening. Of the servants, the plump Jacopo was suffering the most, though both Giulio and Agostino were in constant discomfort. Marco was bearing up well under the strain.

'What's wrong, Uncle Matteo? Why does everyone drive us away?' he asked, wincing at the pain of his cracked lips.

'I wish I knew, Marco.'

'They all seem frightened of something.'

When the wind dropped at last, they dismounted to rest the animals, and trudged along on foot, leading their horses and mules, who were now frothing yellow at the mouth. Brother Nicholas was limping, his breathing erratic, and Jacopo could barely stumble along, holding on to the stirrups of his mule.

They were climbing a rise with Niccolo leading, when he lurched to a stop. 'I knew it!' he called out through cracked lips. 'I knew we could find it!'

They had come over the rise to see a clump of palm

trees in the distance and the brick walls round the mouths of wells. Almost delirious with joy, they hurried down the slope, but Niccolo brought them to a ragged halt. Ahead of him, sitting beside the larger of the two wells and wrapped in a burnoose, was an Arab. He seemed to have fallen into a heavy slumber, but his long spear was stuck into the sand within easy reach.

'A Saracen!' Niccolo whispered. 'Wait here.'

While the servants took shelter with their mules behind a sand dune, Niccolo crawled forward until he reached the oasis. Seeing that the guard was alone, he got up cautiously and addressed him. '*Salam aleikum.*'

The Arab did not stir and the others crept closer, their desperation overcoming their fear. Niccolo went right up to the man, raising his voice. '*Moya-water.* We need water.'

Marco had been moving stealthily towards the well, but suddenly he stopped, scenting a strange, sweetish odour. Matteo had noticed it too, and was disturbed. Brother Nicholas, unable to wait any longer, stumbled forward towards the guard, crying out, 'In the name of God! Water, water . . .'

Grabbing the shoulder of the seated figure, he shook him violently to rouse him, but the Arab simply toppled over, rolling on to his back on the sand. Nicholas started back in horror. Inside the burnoose was a skeleton covered in the merest shreds of rotting flesh, and alive with buzzing flies.

'*Sancta Maria, Mater Dei!*' muttered William, crossing himself.

'Don't drink it!' warned Niccolo as Jacopo picked up a battered drinking gourd and lumbered towards the well.

Matteo reached the servant in time to dash the gourd from his hands. Jacopo collapsed to the ground and began to weep.

Marco was hypnotized by the corpse. 'How did he die?'

'Maybe the plague?' William suggested with a shiver.

'Or poisoned wells,' said Matteo.

Progress became slower than ever, and they had to drag

their parched animals along behind them. Marco was feeling near exhaustion himself now, but rallied when he saw that Giulio was in a far worse state at the rear of the column. He dropped back to walk alongside his friend, who was breathing stertorously and staggering badly.

'Giulio!' whispered Marco, concerned.

'I'm not well. I ache all over,' Giulio said weakly.

'Don't show it,' Marco warned.

'I'm afraid. I don't think I can make it. This is . . . so different from how we thought it would be, Marco.'

'Climb up in the saddle. I'll lead the mule. My father says that we'll soon find water. Here, lean on me. And don't talk. Save your strength.'

Leading the mule with one hand and his own horse with the other, Marco walked beside his friend to watch over him. Giulio grasped the saddle girth of his animal to support himself.

They had not journeyed much further when Niccolo gave the order to halt. Out of the heat haze, a solitary horseman had come speeding towards the caravan, head bent low over his horse's neck. Niccolo brought his group together for safety and Marco made sure that he was shielding the exhausted and panting Giulio.

When the rider spotted them ahead of him, he slowed his mount to a canter and straightened in the saddle. Marco was now able to see him more clearly and was fascinated. The man was unlike anyone he had ever encountered before. Squat and powerfully built, the rider had a flat nose, slanting eyes and dark, weathered skin. He wore a leather cap topped with an iron spike, and his clothes were of fur and tanned leather. On his back was a small round wicker shield and a quiver of arrows. Guiding his horse with his legs, he took the deeply curved bow from his shoulder and fitted an arrow swiftly to its string in case of attack. Marco was astonished at the feat of horsemanship this manoeuvre required, and was struck by the man's proud, warlike, barbaric appearance. He looked questioningly at his uncle.

'A Mongol courier,' Matteo said.

'A Mongol? Here?' Nicholas was puzzled.

Greatly relieved, Niccolo strode towards the rider and greeted him in the Mongol tongue. The man brought his horse to a halt and watched the merchant carefully. From under his shirt Niccolo took the golden tablet that had been given to him by the Khan as his passport. Its effect on the Mongol was immediate. Marco watched, incredulous, as the rider dismounted, knelt before Niccolo and prostrated himself so that his forehead touched the ground, his arms spread wide.

Matteo joined his brother and the two of them spoke at length with the courier. The man got up and pointed in the direction that they were heading, speaking with urgency. Marco and the others were mystified when the Mongol pointed ahead, then moved his arm from side to side in a wide arc. The discussion ended. Niccolo clapped the Mongol gratefully on the shoulder and the man stepped back and bowed. He leapt into the saddle, raised his right arm in salute and galloped away.

Over the group's excited questions, Niccolo ordered, 'Quickly now! We must keep going.'

'But what did he say?' Marco asked.

'Was it the plague?' William demanded nervously. 'Is it spreading?'

'Those rumours we heard in Lajas were true,' Niccolo said shortly. 'There's a war. The Sultan of Egypt has now invaded Armenia in force and is trying to push the Mongols south into Persia. Matteo—' Taking his brother aside, he unrolled the map, spread it on the ground and they began to study it. The others watched in silence, tense and anxious, as Niccolo's stick traced the route by which they had travelled so far.

'And where are we now?' William asked.

'Somewhere around here. Not far from the Persian border.'

'In other words, right in the middle of the war.' Brother

Nicholas was trembling with dismay. 'What do you intend to do?'

'We have no choice,' Matteo told him. 'We must go on and find a passage towards Persia. Now we really do need your prayers.'

Fearful that the Saracen hordes might come over a hill at any time and conscious of being caught up in a war between two ferocious enemies, the caravan started out again. Parched and blistered by the heat, they passed over rough, stony ground for some miles until they came to the dry, rocky bed of a stream that had run through the arid landscape a long time ago. The animals had trouble picking their way over the hard, cracked ground and they had to proceed with great care. There was no escape from the sun. Giulio was now too ill to walk at all and Marco helped him on to his mule, leading it by the reins for him as his friend lolled and swayed. Every movement was an effort for Marco himself, and he had to drive himself on.

Towards evening, they climbed to the ridge of yet another hill and halted at the top. The scene which met their gaze was so horrifying that only exhaustion prevented the whole group from running away in terror. The bodies of men and horses covered the entire valley. Armour lay shattered, standards torn, weapons abandoned. Swarms of flies feasted on the dead and carrion vultures had long since claimed their share of the funeral banquet. Brother Nicholas was seized with a fit of coughing as the stench hit his nostrils. Brother William prayed convulsively. As the others sank to their knees, Marco helped Giulio from his mule and crouched beside him, beaten at last, knowing that without water they could not survive one more day.

As Marco gazed down at the grotesque carpet of blood and mangled corpses, a crazy idea came to him. He rose unsteadily and broke into a stumbling run towards the battlefield. His father and uncle yelled hoarsely for him to come back, but he did not listen. He hunted frantically through the heaped bodies until he saw a canteen still hanging from the saddle of a horse. When he grabbed it, he found it empty, but there was another nearby, almost full. He held it up in triumph, shaking it.

'Water! Water!'

Now the others overcame their superstitious fear and scrambled down the hillside, searching for other canteens amongst the carnage, drinking, laughing, pouring water over their heads. Brother Nicholas tore a flask from a corpse, paused when he saw its ravaged features, but put the vessel to his lips and swallowed the contents greedily. Niccolo poured water into two concave shields for the mules and horses, and shouted to the others not to waste what they found.

Before darkness fell, they put as much distance as they could between themselves and the hideous carnage in the valley. Fearing that the Saracens responsible for the massacre might still be in the vicinity, they were especially vigilant. Niccolo eventually stopped the caravan near a rocky ledge. He posted Agostino as lookout and called Jacopo to him. 'Build a fire over there, under that overhang, so that no flame or smoke can be seen.'

'Excuse me, Messer Polo,' interrupted Brother Nicholas firmly. 'For days now we've been going on, halting, changing direction – and you haven't told us what is happening, nor what your plans are.'

Niccolo was unpacking his baggage and merely shrugged. Surprised to hear the friar speak so aggressively, Matteo and Marco drew near to listen.

Brother William was more blunt. 'We are already in lands controlled by the Khan, you tell us, and yet we hide, we avoid the caravan routes. *Why?*'

Matteo could see that his brother was about to lose his temper. 'Please,' he said, conciliatory. 'Have faith in us. We don't want to run any risks, either for ourselves, or for you. If we're to keep you safe, we have to be careful.'

'This is the last night stop,' declared Niccolo. 'From tomorrow we will rest by day and travel at night until we reach safer territory. Sleep in peace and . . . leave us to sleep in peace as well.'

The Dominicans were still unhappy, but the argument was over. Marco helped Giulio over to where Jacopo was building a campfire and settled him down, then took out parchments, pen and inkhorn to write his notes by the light of the fire. Huddled on the rock above them, Agostino kept watch.

Niccolo came over to look at Giulio. The youth was clearly in the grip of a fever, flushed and sweating, his head tossing from side to side. 'How are you, boy?' Niccolo asked, concerned.

At his voice, Giulio started, but somehow found the strength to lie. 'Better, sir,' he stammered. 'It's b-better without the sun . . . without the sun . . .' His whole body was trembling.

Niccolo was about to say something, but saw Marco watching him anxiously. He walked away with a gesture of irritation. He lay down on the pallet beside his brother's and spoke quietly. 'He's too young. He won't make it. We should never have brought him, Matteo. Nor my son.'

'What else could we do?'

Niccolo was about to reply when a warning hiss from Agostino made him break off. As everyone began to get up, he ordered sharply, 'Down! Stay down. And keep still!' In the silence that followed, they heard the faint neighing of horses and the clink of harness. At a sudden thought, Niccolo crawled over to the two friars. 'Quick!' he demanded. 'The Pope's letter and the other things. And the crucifix!'

The friars slept with a pack containing the Pope's gifts between them. Frightened, they handed it over at once with the crucifix rolled in its altar cloth. Taking the Khan's gold tablet from around his neck, Niccolo beckoned to Marco, who crawled over to him. 'Here!' he whispered. 'Hide them in that crevice and cover them with sand.'

Marco slithered off and buried the objects as quickly as he could. He was only just in time. The distant noises became a steady drumming of hooves as the horsemen came surging out of the night. Jacopo scrambled on all fours to cower beside the two friars for protection. Agostino jumped down to try to reach the horses, but it was already too late. Riders were circling the camp.

Scattering sand over the opening of the small crevice, Marco saw his father and uncle throw down their swords. Giulio had pulled himself to his feet and staggered to stand in front of Marco in an irrational attempt to protect him. 'No, Giulio!' Marco shouted, but a lance sliced through the air and cut Giulio down, sending blood pouring from a wound in his side. The whole camp was suddenly overrun by trampling horses and grim Saracen cavalry. Resistance was impossible and the members of the little caravan backed against the rocks, holding their arms wide for mercy.

The prison cell in Tabriz was large and dark and airless. Marco and Brother William carried Giulio in and placed him gently on the filthy straw pallet on the floor. Niccolo was limping badly and Matteo helped him to sit down. Jacopo crouched in a corner, weeping. Agostino leant against a wall, wiping blood from his forehead. Brother Nicholas was on his knees, praying in silence.

Marco knelt anxiously beside Giulio, who was holding a pad of blood-soaked cloth against his side. When Marco spoke to him, his eyes opened, but it was as though he could not see. 'Giulio!' Marco urged. 'It's me. I won't leave you. But help me . . . you can make it. You've got to!'

Giulio recognized him and tried to smile. Marco held him, supporting him under the shoulders. He could hardly hear his friend's voice. 'I'm sorry,' Giulio whispered. 'I can't . . . Can't . . .' His strength was ebbing, the cloth unable to stem the flow of blood from his wound.

'Don't try to talk,' Marco said. 'I'll look after you.' Giulio smiled again and clasped his hand, his eyes closing. His body all at once seemed slack and Marco started to ease him down. He could no longer hear his friend's panted breathing. The realization was almost unbearable. 'He's . . . he's dying,' he faltered. 'Giulio's dying!'

The others gathered around, but it was too late. When Brother William tried to lift Giulio's head, it fell back heavily and blood trickled from the corner of his mouth. The Dominican crossed himself and began to intone softly, '*Requiescat in pace. In paradisum perducant te angeli, Julium filium Christi . . .*'

Marco looked down at the pale figure and slowly released his hand. He felt lost. Giulio had been a very special friend for so many years. He had come on this journey because of Marco and had lost his life trying to protect him, as he had fought for him so often when they were boys.

Marco turned away, his chest heaving as he wept. He was facing a small, oblong slit in the wall and he bit his lip, staring. He was being watched by two very dark, deep-set eyes.

In the tower cell in Genoa prison, shadows were lengthening across the room. Marco Polo sat silent, staring at his hand, remembering that last handclasp with Giulio. He had been so absorbed in telling his story that he had not touched the thin soup that had been brought.

'And what happened then?' asked Rustichello.

'I grew up.' Marco lowered his hand.

Giovanni shifted uncomfortably. The story was fascinating, but it had been more serious than he expected.

'Well, you must have got away from Tabriz somehow, or you wouldn't be here,' Rustichello smiled, trying to lighten the atmosphere.

'So – how did you escape?' Giovanni asked eagerly. 'Did you break out, or bribe a guard? Tell us.'

But Marco had told them enough for one day. He had awakened memories that were as fresh and painful as the day his oldest friend had died. 'Another time,' he said, and picked up his bowl of soup.

'Marco!' Rustichello protested.

Marco looked at them. He could not blame them for not understanding. He laid down the soup. 'I'll tell you . . . another time,' he said. He lay back on the bed and closed his eyes.

Chapter Three

Demented cries rang through the prison and brought them quickly to the door of their cell. They peered through the tiny grating in time to see a gaunt, bearded man shake off the two guards who flanked him and run screaming down the stone steps. Recaptured almost immediately, the man was dragged off down the corridor, shrieking wildly.

Rustichello breathed out slowly and turned away. 'I know that man,' he said bitterly. 'He's from Pisa, like me. In this place, madness grows like mould on the walls. For ten years we've been shut away here and Pisa has forgotten us. War has humiliated her, but she's still too proud to sign a peace treaty.'

Captain Marco Polo shuddered. 'If I have to spend ten years here, I'll go mad, too.'

'Perhaps I'm mad already,' Rustichello said wrily, 'and just haven't realized it.'

Quite unexpectedly, Giovanni did a somersault in the middle of the cell. 'That doesn't worry me,' he laughed. 'My mother used to tell me I've been mad ever since I was born.'

His clowning momentarily distracted his two companions from their thoughts.

'And she was right, too,' Rustichello chuckled. He sat down at the table and began to sharpen his quill pen. He looked over at Marco. 'You were telling us about Tabriz – about the death of your friend, Giulio . . .'

'Yes,' sighed Marco, sitting beside him. 'He died of fever in my arms . . . It was then that I first saw the Mongols. They were very different from the all-conquering warriors my father had always talked about.'

The stub of candle that was flickering between them began to splutter. Rustichello was disappointed.

'*Ite missa est*,' he sighed. 'We'll continue tomorrow. When I can see to write.'

Quick as a flash, Giovanni pulled a lump of crudely moulded wax from beneath his mattress. He fixed the wick, then lit it from the dying flame. 'I've been saving the candle ends, Master Rustichello,' he grinned, very pleased with himself.

'So even you can be useful sometimes, Giovanni,' said the writer, delighted that they would be able to continue.

Marco Polo looked at the unpredictable young man who had been an archer on his galley and smiled. Giovanni was the salt of the earth. But as his thoughts turned once more to Giulio, the smile faded slowly away.

In the prison cell at Tabriz, Marco had no tears left to shed and sat numbly against the wall, comforted by Agostino. Niccolo and Matteo stood in silence, watching as the two friars, having fashioned a crucifix from some pieces of rough wood, placed it between Giulio's fingers and knelt in prayer over him.

'*Animam suam perducant ad Te Domine . . .*'

'*. . . In sempiterna iustitia tua . . .*'

Without warning, the door burst open and Moslem guards shouted, ordering them out. Brother William hastily slipped the crucifix from the dead boy's hands and hid it under the straw. Marco, the last to leave, paused to look one last time at his dead friend before a turbaned guard grabbed his shoulder and pulled him out.

After the half-light of the cell, the afternoon sun was blinding and they had to cover their eyes, clinging to one another for support. When they were able to take stock of their surroundings, they found themselves facing a scene of sheer horror.

They were in a huge, fortified enclosure which had been turned into a prison camp. Low-built, white-painted barracks encircled it, beneath walls of mud and straw, baked to the hardness of stone by the merciless sun.

Scattered across it were uncountable wooden cages crowded with prisoners, wounded and starving, tortured by the sun and by the burning wind which whipped up the fine clay dust, adding to their torment.

The Saracen guards drove the Polos' group forward with the butts of their lances.

As they passed the first of the cages, Matteo glanced at it furtively and stopped still, gazing in dismay at the prisoners. 'Oh, great God,' he muttered. 'They're Mongols . . .'

They were the first Mongols Marco had seen, apart from the desert courier. But unlike him, these were not proud and warlike. They were listless, parched with thirst, slumped in defeat.

'We shall die . . . die . . .' Brother Nicholas was moaning, 'with no hope of a glorious end. No one will know what became of us!'

The guards barked at them angrily, shoving them on.

Marco scarcely heard Jacopo's snivelling or the mumbled complaints of the friars, who were loudly blaming his father for their present plight. All round them was the evidence of mass execution. The bodies of prisoners lay heaped against the walls, shot full of arrows. Others had been crucified, and there were long rows of Mongol bodies hanging from gibbets. Drums were beating, loudly and rhythmically. The pounding, the guttural, incomprehensible shouts of the guards, the dryness of his mouth and throat and the stench of blood in the hot air made his head swim. At least Giulio had been saved this savagery.

Many of the cages were empty and others were systematically being cleared by the guards, who herded the prisoners in long lines towards each of the four corners of the enclosure. Guards ringed each corner and within each circle, half-glimpsed through the haze, performing their duties with the thoroughness of experts, stood a group of Saracen executioners. To the loud, regular pounding of the drums, they were raising their scimitars high into the air and bringing them down with such timing and precision that several Mongol heads rolled in the dust simultaneously. Hundreds of prisoners had already bowed before them, and the ground was now littered with their remains. The spurting of the blood, the sickening crack as the blades sliced through bone and the sadistic enjoyment of the guards made it a scene straight from hell.

But the most terrifying thing of all was that Marco and the others were being herded towards one of the death lines as if they were about to join it themselves.

Brother Nicholas crossed himself continually. 'We'll be slaughtered like animals! So these, Messer Polo, are the invincible Mongols you lied about! You lied to us as you lied to the Pope!'

'Keep quiet!' hissed Niccolo. 'And remember – we are merchants. Only merchants.'

'We are envoys of His Holiness,' William insisted. 'We are anointed priests!'

'If they find *that* out, we shan't last a minute!' Matteo warned, then winced as the scimitars whistled through the air again.

To their surprise and relief, they found themselves pushed on past the grim line of victims and into a simple, low-ceilinged hut. Even here, the thin mud walls could not keep out the sounds of slaughter in the courtyard. The furnishings were sparse. Spread out on a long table were some objects covered with a white cloth.

An exceptionally tall and imposing figure was seated on a cushioned dais against the far wall, his strong tanned features totally impassive. A senior Saracen officer, he was armed and white-robed, his turban topped by the glittering spike of a concealed helmet. As soon as Marco caught sight of his deep-set eyes, he recognized the man who had been watching him through the slit in the wall of the cell.

When he saw the pitcher of water, Jacopo, tortured with thirst, fell to his knees imploringly. To the surprise of all, the tall man rose and picked up the vessel. He handed it to Niccolo, who first helped Jacopo to drink and then sipped the water himself. The pitcher was passed around them all. The last to drink was Marco. He took a mouthful, then hesitantly returned the pitcher to the Saracen, repeating the ritualistic gesture of the invitation to drink. Though the man's lips were dry and chapped, he put the vessel down untouched.

Brother William bowed and offered his greetings in Arabic, but the man ignored him completely and addressed himself to the merchants. His voice was low and resonant, his Italian perfect.

'You are Messers Niccolo and Matteo Polo from Venice?'

'We are, sir,' answered Niccolo, amazed. He bowed. 'I am Niccolo Polo . . . my brother, Matteo . . . my son, Marco. We and our servants are travelling with these gentlemen.'

The man's eyes flicked to the two friars briefly. 'I am Ali Ben Yussouf. The Sultan Bibars has conferred on me the command of this region.'

'You'll forgive our surprise, sir,' said Niccolo, 'to hear you speak our own language.'

'Why should I not, since it was the first that I learned? You are puzzled. Let me explain. Until ten years ago my name was Lorenzo Rizzo. I was born in Ragusa.'

'In Dalmatia?' Niccolo was even more surprised.

'We were born by the same sea, Messer Polo. I was a fisherman. Then, one day, we were attacked by Moslem pirates. I was wounded and would certainly have drowned had I not been kept afloat by one of my companions. We were captured and taken to Tripoli. There we were sold as slaves.'

'Then you are a Christian?' asked Brother Nicholas hopefully.

'No. I'm a Moslem. I was fortunate enough to have a kind and enlightened master who taught me the way of the Prophet, whose name be praised.'

Nicholas was appalled. 'You became a Moslem to escape from slavery?'

'No, I became a True Believer, because I believe that

the way of Mohammed is both the true continuation and the fulfilment of the teaching of Moses and Jesus, the two great prophets who preceded him. He is the seal of the prophets, the ultimate.'

Marco was intrigued. 'Is that why you refused to drink with us? Because we're Christians?'

'Hold your tongue!' his father muttered sharply.

Ben Yussouf smiled. 'No. I did not drink because this is the month of Ramadan, when we Moslems celebrate the revelation of the Holy Book, the Koran. From sunrise to sunset, no food or water may touch our lips.'

'How can you, born a Christian, lend yourself to the horror we saw outside?' demanded William indignantly. 'Our Lord gave his life for men – but you, following Mohammed, destroy life in the name of God.'

Ben Yussouf's lips tightened with anger. Seizing the friar's arm, he dragged him over to a window and forced him to look out on a group of Arab women in white mourning robes, surrounded by crowds of children, receiving food served to them in wooden bowls. 'Those women, those children – they have no more tears,' he said gratingly. 'How many of those people have your Crusaders massacred in the name of Christ? In order to conquer the city of Jerusalem, sacred to us all, not only to Christians!'

He hurled Brother William across the room with terrifying force and swung round on the others. Ben Yussouf waited for his anger to subside, then swept the cloth from the table. There were gasps of shock and fear as he revealed all the objects they had tried to conceal at the moment of their capture. Opening the silver casket, Ben Yussouf brought out the phial of Holy Oil and held it up to the light.

Brother William was lying on the floor and raised himself to his knees. 'Have a care! This is the oil from the lamp that burns on the Tomb of Our Lord . . .'

'Which you are carrying to Kublai Khan, the Mongol Emperor,' Ben Yussouf said flatly. Niccolo and Matteo were tense. He was amused by their shocked expressions.

'The golden passport told me that you were envoys. And your names are in the letters which you are taking from the Pope.' He put the phial back on the table and surveyed the other objects. 'There you see your superstition. In our mosques you will not find one single idol, but you have filled your churches with images that degrade the figure of God – and you worship those images. You have made a divine thing of this oil – just as you have divided God, the Supreme, the Indivisible, into three.' He paused, then proclaimed, 'There is no God but Allah, and Mohammed is his prophet!'

'Christians believe otherwise,' Brother Nicholas muttered.

'As you well know!' Ben Yussouf accused. 'You and your friend here are Christian priests. The rest of you are servants of the Mongol Khan. According to the law, you deserve to die!'

He strode to the door. Jacopo sank to his knees, moaning. The others stood frozen with horror. They could hear the work of the scimitars continuing relentlessly in the courtyard outside. Ben Yussouf had stopped. He turned slowly and his voice was calm. 'I cannot go back on my word. The man who saved my life was a Venetian. The debt I owe him, I now repay through you. I vowed to pay for my life by saving others.' He waited for a moment, seeing their incredulity. 'I have already given order for your horses and possessions to be returned to you. You are free to return to Palestine.'

It was true, then. Niccolo glanced at Matteo and stepped forward. 'We thank you, sir,' he said, 'with all our hearts. But we must not insult your generosity with dishonesty. We have also made a vow – we have to go on.'

'Ahead lies the road to the East, but there you will find only death and desolation. You will never live to reach the Great Khan.'

'To go back is just as dangerous,' Matteo pointed out. 'War is everywhere.'

'Yesterday we exchanged a group of Crusaders for some

of our warriors held prisoner. If you ride fast to the West, you will catch them and be able to travel under their protection.'

'The Saints be praised!' Nicholas cried.

'Amen!' added William.

'We are grateful to you, sir,' Niccolo said firmly. 'But we have given our word to the Pope.'

Ali Ben Yussouf drew himself up to his full height. He had withdrawn again behind his proud mask. 'I have given *my* word to set you free, but do not presume on my patience. Go back to Acre, to your Pope; tell him that his dream of an alliance with the Mongols is madness. Tell him you have seen their invincible army humbled and defeated. His only hope, the only certainty of universal peace, lies in the understanding that one Father, Abraham, unites us all – whether we be Christian, Jew or Moslem!' He pointed to the table. 'Take your belongings and go.'

While the others hurried to do so, Marco approached the Saracen. He hesitated as he looked up into the dark, impassive eyes, yet he had no fear of being refused as he made his request. 'You have spared our lives, but . . . I have one last favour to ask. I have a friend who died in our cell. He was like a brother to me. Allow us to bury him and place on his grave the sign of our faith.'

They camped that night in some old ruins, huddled up against a crumbling wall for protection against the wind, and aching with fatigue. Tempers were frayed and the argument which had been simmering broke out when Brother William said that their capture had been a sign that their journey was not meant to succeed. 'You lied to us, Niccolo Polo,' he muttered.

'We have seen the truth with our own eyes,' Brother Nicholas agreed. 'Your Mongols are defeated.'

Niccolo raised his head wearily and stared at the priests in contempt. They were not worth the effort of a reply.

'You don't understand,' Matteo told them, trying to

reason with them. 'What we have seen means nothing! One lost battle is nothing more than a scratch to the mighty body of the Mongol Empire. The Great Khan probably isn't even aware of what's happening here. To him, Ben Yussouf's whole army is of no more matter than a grain of sand.'

'Did you not listen to the words of the renegade?' Nicholas asked impatiently. 'We have no hope of ever reaching your Khan.'

Marco was troubled. To him, the duty placed on them by Pope Gregory was something which could never be set aside, even in the jaws of death. 'You are priests,' he urged with spirit. 'It is unthinkable that either of you should break your oath to the Holy Father. He himself sent us on this mission and we are sworn to complete it.'

'Don't prattle to us of a mission, boy!' William retorted. 'It is easy to read the heart of you Polos. What drives you on is your merchant's greed. Brother Nicholas and I have decided. We are returning to Acre to tell his Holiness that the Mongol Empire, such as it is, has fallen. And that what you told him was lies!'

Niccolo lunged forward angrily, and Marco was just in time to catch his father's arm. He had to hold Niccolo tightly to prevent him from striking the priest, who flinched back in alarm. Niccolo threw Marco's hand from his arm and sat back, scowling at the two friars. 'You swore an oath – to bring the word of God to those dark lands – you and that fat oaf, who longs to be a martyr, but runs from his own shadow. I am ashamed I ever honoured you.'

'You are mistaken in us,' William said with dignity. 'We would both die gladly for the sake of Our Lord Jesus, if it would advance His Kingdom by one fraction of an inch.'

Brother Nicholas had flushed. 'When we took our vows to follow Christ, we knew we had to be prepared to accept martyrdom if it would serve the cause of the Lord. But the Lord would not forgive us for throwing our lives away to no purpose!'

Jacopo, who had been listening intently, suddenly broke

in, 'Listen to them, Messer Polo! They're learned men. They know what's best. When you met Teobaldo, he was just a Crusader – now he's a Pope. One day we might meet one of these priests again – and he could be a Cardinal.'

'Hold your tongue, you fool!' ordered Niccolo, pushing him aside. He drew his sword and stood over the two friars. 'We are going forward and you are coming with us, even if it means I have to drag you by your ears and tie you both to the saddle!' He gave the sword to Agostino. 'Stand guard over them till dawn.'

The priests had gazed as if hypnotized at the point of the sword as it swung from one to the other. They were relieved when it was handed to Agostino and were not disposed to argue any further.

Agostino awoke with a start, sprang to his feet and looked around in agitation. He had dozed off. It was dawn, and Brother Nicholas of Vicenza and Brother William of Tripoli were nowhere to be seen. Agostino roused the others. Niccolo grabbed the sword from his servant and searched the ruins, but found no one.

'Well, we're free of their company at least,' said Matteo, trying to be philosophical. 'They'll never reach Acre. Their throats will be cut long before.'

Alarm gripped Niccolo. 'The Pope's letter! The Holy oil!'

'They're still here,' Marco told him, pointing to a bundle by his side. 'Thc oil, the letter and the crucifix. I kept them with me.'

Just then, Jacopo came hobbling from behind the wall, pulling up his breech cloth. He was agitated. 'Master! Look there!' he shouted. He pointed a shaking finger towards the eastern horizon. Great columns of flame were starting to lick the dawn sky as a whole village blazed, another casualty of the pitiless war. Even as they watched, a second fire broke out, half a mile to the right of the first, lighting up the plain all around with its ferocity. Marco did not need to be told what it signified. The atrocities were directly in their path. To continue the journey east would be to walk into the gates of hell. He swallowed as flames and thick, black smoke towered up from a third village, dreading what must have happened to the inhabitants.

Niccolo had snatched the map out of his saddlebag. He unrolled it, studying it. 'There's only one thing for it,' he decided quickly. 'We'll have to turn south towards Persia and make for Hormuz. Here . . . on the Gulf.'

'Take the sea route?' Matteo was astounded.

'Find another way if you can. It's the long way round, but we have no choice. From Hormuz we can sail to India and China . . .'

Marco could not suppress a start of excitement.

With the all-consuming war now raging to the north and east and west of them, they turned south and picked up the age-old caravan trail to Persia. The sands became more golden, the dunes more undulating, the sense of being trapped less overwhelming. They still sweltered in the great furnace-heat of the sun, but they were beginning to feel safer now, and even had friendly greetings from the occasional passing caravan.

From Saveh, where they marvelled at the burning oil wells, they headed south across desert plains, plagued not only by the sun but also the constant, goading sting of mosquitoes and flies. The horses, too, were tormented by the insects swarming around their eyes and nostrils. After passing Kashan and Isfahan, they took the trail that led to the fine, old, Moslem city of Yazd, a busy commercial centre. Marco was especially impressed by the silken fabric named after the city – *yazdi* – and wondered what Uncle Zane would have thought of it. How far away Venice seemed . . . He had difficulty even remembering Caterina's face. The thought of her did not pain him any more.

Beyond Jazd lay another great plain that took seven days

to cross, with only three inhabited places where the traveller could shelter. Along the route they rode through many groves of date-palms and saw abundant wild game; Marco developed a pleasure in hunting and was soon skilled at catching partridge and quail. One afternoon he even caught a glimpse of the famed wild asses, noble beasts who could run at speed all day and survive on the barest of nourishment.

They continued on through the mountains of the Kerman region, where the temperatures were freezing at night and the wind cut through the valleys and passes like a Saracen scimitar. They pressed on, down the escarpment and into the huge plain of white sand that led to the sea.

After the barren mountains the terrain looked more inviting, but they soon found the going harder than ever. Slipping and slithering on the yielding sand, they stumbled on foot, dragging their horses behind them. On the third day, Marco was out in front, trudging up the slope of a high dune, thinking of the sea and the ship that would carry them to India and Cathay. The dune seemed endless, but finally he reached its summit. For a moment he was not aware of it, then he stood still, gazing at the horizon, where a gleaming white-walled city shimmered beside a blue cobalt sea.

Matteo came up behind him and gripped his shoulders. 'It's Hormuz, Marco . . .' he panted. 'Hormuz at last!'

Entranced by the sight of the city from a distance, they were despondent when they saw it at close quarters. Hormuz was dirty and squalid, its houses were streaked and stained, its tortuous streets and alleys running with filth. The visitors were puzzled to find few people about, and those that were seemed to be wandering in a dream. A funereal air hung over the whole place.

Niccolo Polo led his caravan down a twisting lane and paused as a weird procession came towards them. A drummer was beating out a mournful tattoo and the sad-faced people at his heels were chanting something between a psalm and a lament. Most of them were dressed in white or torn, grey robes, and none looked at the strangers as they filed past. Marco began to notice the braziers burning outside many of the doors, and the resinous fumes caught in his throat. Then another procession came, preceded by a drummer, and the Polos pressed against the walls to let it pass. In the centre was a man who held up what appeared to be a bundle of rags in the air. When the bundle went by, Marco saw the dead limbs of a small child dangling from it.

Hurrying away from the drumming and the birdsong chanting, the travellers came out of the noisome alleyways into the bright, sunlit streets above the harbour. The air was healthier here, the houses cleaner and more attractive, with pleasant roof terraces and small balconies with pots of herbs and plants. But the people they saw still looked strained and anxious, and they could still smell the acrid smoke rising from the braziers they had left behind.

They turned a corner and came to an inn, a whitewashed building of two storeys, with blue painted doors and windows. As they entered hesitantly, the man who had been lounging on a bench smoking a hookah got up and smiled readily. The innkeeper was a stoutish, bearded man of middle years with bright, restless eyes and expressive hands. 'This way, sirs,' he beckoned. 'Here you will find food, drink and a safe bed for the night. I bid you welcome, in Allah's name.'

Niccolo signed to the others to put down their baggage. 'What is happening in your city?' he asked.

'People in mourning everywhere,' Matteo probed. 'Like a city of ghosts.'

Ignoring their questions, the innkeeper called, 'Zorah! *Zorah* – we have guests!', placed his hookah on the floor and, busying himself to hide his agitation, wiped the top of the table and waved his guests to seats.

A girl appeared at the door, a true desert maiden, with a lean, agile body, a dusky skin and gleaming white teeth. Her dark hair, under a small skullcap, was long and loose. She wore cotton trousers under a calf-length skirt and embroidered bodice which moulded her breasts, which were surprisingly full for her slim shape. Marco was struck by her at once. As she served him wine and gave him a shy smile, Jacopo grinned and winked to Agostino.

The innkeeper was speaking to Niccolo and Matteo. 'The Arab ships, you know, are full of rats as big as dogs. They let the cargoes rot in the holds. It's all their fault, they brought the infection to the city.' He qualified his slip quickly. 'Of course, it's confined to one or two quarters only. You saw the braziers? We're dealing with it. We're purifying the air, and the infected houses are immediately boarded up.'

'Infection!' Niccolo was instantly alert.

'Is it what's called the Black Plague?' asked Matteo, tensing.

The innkeeper did his best to put their minds at rest, but he was obviously trying to reassure himself as much as them. 'It's still not certain. It seems to be just bellyache and vomiting. As you can see, it's not here, the infection – may Allah protect us! Only healthy people can come into this part of the city. That's why we have only two guests at the moment. One has just gone out and the other drank too much wine and has taken to his bed.'

'We shall not be staying long,' Niccolo said. 'Just as long as it takes to find a boat to transport us to India.'

Interest flickered in their host's eyes. 'A boat? I think I can help you there. The best in Hormuz is owned by a cousin of mine – Abdelatiff.'

'Where can we find him?' Niccolo asked.

The innkeeper scratched his stomach. 'Ah – well, I can get a message to him. You could meet him tomorrow.'

'Why not before?' Matteo asked.

'There's a curfew.' The innkeeper nodded to the windows. Outside, the light was changing as the sun made its abrupt descent. There was no twilight so far south. In a few minutes it would be dark. 'No one's allowed out without special permission, between sunrise and sunset.'

'Very well,' Niccolo decided, after a pause. He glanced

round the main room of the inn whith its arched windows, open fireplace, scrubbed wooden tables and benches. It looked clean and comfortable enough. 'Thank you. We'll need rooms and we could do with something to eat.'

'If you'd like to see the rooms?' the innkeeper suggested.

'I'll take care of it,' Matteo said, and signed to Agostino and Jacopo. The two servants picked up some of the bundles and boxes and followed him and the innkeeper up the stairs.

Marco felt too tired to go with them. He sat and watched his father and saw with concern that Niccolo looked near exhaustion as well. It was hardly surprising. He had to think and plan for all of them. Frequently, it was only his will that kept them going. Marco wanted to say something to his father, to show that he understood and was ready to help, but he did not know how to say it. In any case, his father would be sure to reject the attempt. He was not a man to admit weakness or a need for affection.

Marco looked up. The girl, Zorah, was standing near him with the earthenware flask. She made to pour more wine for him, but he waved his hand. 'Don't you like it?' she asked. 'It's made from dates.'

So as not to offend her, he lifted his beaker. 'Oh, yes. It's very good.' He sipped some of the wine and coughed at its raw bite. 'Strong. Spicy.'

Zorah smiled, intrigued by him. 'You speak our language very well.'

'I've been trying to learn it,' he told her. 'And Arabic and Mongol.' Another skill Marco had discovered in himself was an ability to pick up languages quickly.

'Are you a scholar?' she asked.

'No,' Marco laughed. 'I suppose you'd call me a merchant. I just like to understand what people are saying.'

'We've hardly seen any foreign merchants for months, because of the sickness,' the girl pouted, then smiled coquettishly. 'How long are you staying?'

'We've only come here to hire a ship,' he explained.

'I hope you're lucky,' Zorah said. 'Most of the trading

captains left weeks ago. The harbour's nearly empty.' The innkeeper was coming back down. She smiled to Marco, a quick smile that said she liked him, and moved away.

Matteo reported that the sleeping quarters were adequate. If, as the innkeeper swore, the infection had not touched this part of the city, they were safe enough and their departure could be arranged, hopefully, in a few days. Marco crossed to join his father and uncle.

'*Nigra sum, sed formosa*,' Matteo quoted, ironically. 'I am black, but comely, O ye daughters of Jerusalem . . .'

'Finished your flirting, have you?' Niccolo asked.

'I wasn't flirting,' Marco told them. Zorah was undeniably attractive, but he respected women too much to trifle with them or think of them as casual objects of pleasure. 'She said there are hardly any ships left here.'

'If you're prepared to spend the money, you can always get what you want.' Niccolo shrugged. 'What else were you talking about?'

'Nothing much. I just liked talking to her.'

Niccolo frowned. 'I've told you before. Don't get mixed up with the natives – especially with their women.'

'If I don't talk to people, how can I make sense of it all?' Marco protested. He could tell that his father and uncle were puzzled. 'That's why I wanted so much to come with you. There's so much to see, and to learn. Every day, new things.'

'What things?' Niccolo queried.

'About the world. How it is fashioned and what it contains. The way people live, what they believe in, what they think.'

'What they think?' Matteo repeated.

Marco smiled. 'Don't you keep wondering about that?'

'We've enough to do, just to stay alive,' his father said, and the two brothers turned to each other, dismissing his childishness from their minds.

Somewhere around midnight, Marco rose silently from his

corner of the room he shared with the rest of the party. The heat had dropped after sunset, but it was still stifling. He was wearing only his breech cloth and shirt, which was sticking to him. The chafing of sweat and grit in every crevice of his body and the whine of the mosquitoes had kept him awake, listening to the snoring of the two older men. He remembered a rickety, wooden ladder at the end of the passage and climbed it, coming out, as he had hoped, on to the flat roof of the inn.

The night air was not much cooler, but there was a whisper of breeze from the sea and he lifted his face to it, sucking it in through his open mouth. Above him in the inky blackness, the constellations were frozen in their eternal patterns, brighter than he had ever seen them. It was awesome gazing up at that void. What was it? he wondered. What *were* those stars? And the moon? . . . He shook his head. There were enough mysteries here on earth. More than enough. A whole lifetime was scarcely sufficient to begin to fathom them.

He had come on this journey as an act of faith, believing what his father and uncle had told him, although the most learned priests maintained that beyond the reach of Christendom lay only howling darkness. A hundred times already, his father had been proved right and the priests wrong. Yet how vast was the world, in truth? Was there really nothing beyond the empire of the Great Khan, as his father had said, only the unending waters of the ocean? Or did it continue as it did now, mountains and plains and valleys stretching on to eternity?

He had to be practical, he scolded himself, sensible. His imagination had so often betrayed him. He must deal only in what he could vouch for, and keep sharp in his mind all that he had seen – all he would see. He had set out to discover the world, but it would be useless if he could not remember it. His father and uncle had lived among wonders, yet could not describe them; their only real memory was of buying and selling. Even there his memory was better than theirs; he could remind them, when they had forgotten, of the true price of muslin in the city where it was produced, Mosul – or how many days exactly it took from Kaisariah to Sevasta. And there were other things. He could remember his first glimpse of the shining snows of Mount Ararat. Their guides had told them that here was the final resting place of the Ark after it saved Noah from the Flood – that it was buried in the everlasting ice on its summit. Sometimes, they said, when the lower snows melted and the surrounding plain became green with lush grass, the Ark was revealed again, perfectly preserved. For all the two days it had taken to ride round the base of the mighty mountain, he had gazed at the topmost peaks until his eyes ached. Once he had thought for a moment he saw something, a shape, but he could not swear to it. Yet all the time, his father and uncle had slouched over their horses' ears, talking of nothing but the silks and carpets to be bought in Tiflis.

All at once, his senses snapped back to the present. There had been a noise to the side, faint but distinct. The sound of a splash. He ran his tongue over his dry lips. Was there water up here? Many of these houses had cisterns on their roofs, doing double duty as reserve tanks and cooling the rooms underneath. He was standing in shadow, and moved round the low wall behind him into brighter moonlight. He could make out the brick-built cistern, large and square, the height of his chest. The small splash could have been made by a night bird, or by a rat. He moved forward cautiously.

'Don't come any nearer!' a girl's voice said.

He stopped, surprised. The voice was Zorah's, but he could not see her. 'Where are you?' he asked the darkness.

After a pause the voice came again. 'Oh, it's you. I thought it was one of the old ones.'

There was another splash. He moved nearer the cistern, and there he saw her. She was standing in the water up to her shoulders. The surface was so dark that he could not make out what she was wearing. 'What are you doing?' he asked, his voice low like hers.

'I come up here often,' she said, smiling, her teeth white in the moonlight. 'Whenever I can't sleep, I come up here.'

'You stay here all night?'

'No, silly!' She laughed quietly at the thought. 'A lot of people do the same here. Sometimes it's the only way to get cool.' She shook her wet hair and the ruffled surface of the water was shot with silver. 'I was just going to come out.'

'I'll give you a hand,' Marco offered.

'No, you won't,' she said positively. 'You'll turn round – and you're not to look.'

Marco suddenly understood. There was a length of cloth like a towel lying over the lip of the cistern. He could feel himself blushing and stepped quickly away, turning his back to her. He could hear her laughing and a rippling sound as she waded to the side; a louder splash, and a patter of water as she climbed out. He squatted, looking out at the night, waiting. At last he risked a glance round. Her back was to him and she was shaking out the cloth. She was naked, her body gleaming as though oiled, the moist tendrils of her hair clustered on her shoulders. Her figure was slim but shapely, tapering to a tiny waist above full haunches, with long, sleek legs. He looked away, aware of a hot rush of desire. He was ashamed of himself. He felt not love, as he had for Caterina, but sheer, brute lust. He knew that Uncle Matteo sometimes visited the wineshops with their attached brothels in the cities they passed through. He was not sure about his father. But he had schooled himself not to think of such things, to subdue the flesh. He was here as an emissary, however insignificant, of the Holy Father and the Apostolic Church. He heard her padding towards him on her bare feet and wished fervently that he had not strayed from his room.

She sat beside him, the bolt of cloth folded round her like a wrapper. She tucked it more securely round herself, leaving her legs bare from the knees down. Somehow she looked so natural and companionable that he felt even more ashamed of his thoughts. He smiled to her.

'What's your name?' she asked. He told her and laughed quietly with her when she found it difficult to pronounce. 'Tell me about where you come from.' He told her about Venice and she marvelled at the idea of a city built on water. 'With all those people, one day it must sink,' she decided.

He laughed, relaxing with her. She was the first person of his own age he had talked to in all the months since Giulio died.

'The man, the strong one – he's your father, isn't he?' she said. 'He must be happy, having you with him. My father's a sailor.'

'Where is he now?' Marco asked.

'We haven't heard from him for nearly two years.' Her voice was sad. 'He sailed with a shipload of pilgrims for Mecca. Some say they were lost at sea. His other two wives have left to marry again. My mother refuses to believe he is dead or to accept my uncle, my father's brother, as her husband. She's determined to wait. It's hard for her and – for us, her children. You don't know how hard.'

Marco felt a sudden rush of sympathy for her. 'My mother died waiting for my father to come back.' She was looking at him with new understanding, her eyes enormous in the moonlight. He looked away at the shadowy outline of the other lower roofs. In the distance, a voice was wailing, the lament rising and falling. 'So that's why you – you work in the inn,' he said. 'And that man, the innkeeper, he isn't—?'

'My father?' Zorah's smile changed to a scowl. 'No, nor my husband. Nor anything else, the fat pig!'

Marco was still trying to work out something. 'You said your father had two other wives?'

'Yes,' she said.

'Oh – you see, my religion forbids that. One man, one woman, that's the law.'

'Really?' she laughed. He could feel her watching him again, studying his profile. 'Well, naturally it's always like that for a while . . . But the Koran, our sacred book, teaches us that to love a man is a woman's duty. And that a man's heart can find room for many loves.'

Marco shifted. Her voice had been like a caress. Did she really believe what she had said?

She reached out and her slim hand touched his face, then slid down to lie on his uncovered chest over his heart. 'You're burning,' she said softly.

Marco's throat was tight. He had controlled his reaction earlier, but now he felt the stirring in his loins begin again. Her fingers trailed across his chest, over the film of perspiration.

'You'll never sleep like that,' she whispered. 'You're not used to the heat like we are. Why don't you go into the water and cool down?'

Marco snatched at the suggestion. In another moment, he would have been unable to keep his hands from her. He could smell the warm, womanly freshness of her body. The wrapper she wore was unbelted, baring her legs nearly to the tops of her thighs. He pushed himself to his feet. 'I – I think I shall,' he said. 'I can't stand this heat any more.' She smiled.

He left her and went quickly to the cistern. Round the corner from her, he pulled off his shirt and breech cloth. She was still sitting, looking out over the sleeping town. He eased himself carefully over the edge of the cistern, biting back a gasp at the unexpected coldness of the water, which came up to the middle of his chest. He lowered himself and rose, repeating it, cupping handfuls of water over his face and hair. Luxuriating in it, he smoothed his palms over his abdomen and thighs, cleansing himself of the dust of days.

He heard her quiet laugh, and turned.

She was sitting on the lip of the cistern, her feet in the water. The cloth wrapper hung at her shoulders and she pushed it back, letting it fall behind her. She was naked, smiling to him, wanting him to admire her. Her breasts hung free, their nipples darkly risen. There was light enough for him to see that her loins were unshaded, depilated. She smiled at what she could read in his eyes.

She tilted her pelvis and slipped down into the water, silently. He stood motionless as she came towards him, closer and closer, until her full breasts brushed his chest. Her hands touched his arms and slid up them, until they rested on his shoulders. He bent his face towards her. They kissed suddenly, fiercely, and he braced himself, taking her weight as her legs swung up and locked themselves round his hips.

The next morning, at breakfast, Matteo was amused to notice that Zorah had not spoken to, not even glanced at, Marco. 'Your little friend is disappointed in you,' he murmured. 'Probably expected you to go to her room last night.' Jacopo sniggered.

'That's enough of that,' Niccolo said, impatient to be moving. 'Landlord, you said this cousin of yours is waiting for us?'

The innkeeper bustled forward. 'Yes, sir. Ready and waiting.'

Behind his back, Zorah at last gave Marco a fleeting smile. Marco realized that her only purpose in ignoring him had been to allay any suspicions the innkeeper might have. They had not parted until the first streaks of dawn, and had agreed to meet again this night. Her smile was a reminder of shared pleasures.

'From here all streets lead down to the harbour,' the innkeeper was saying. 'Eh – you can't miss it. The first to the left, go down the alley to the right, then left again, and—' He thought of something much simpler. 'Zorah! You show them.'

'Jacopo, you'll stay here and look after the baggage,' Niccolo said, rising. 'Agostino, you come with us.'

They had slept later than they had intended and the sun was already high. Walking in front with Marco, Zorah led them by the shortest route to the harbour. 'I wish I could stay with you today,' she whispered.

'Why don't you?' he suggested.

'He'd skin me alive!' Her laugh was cut off when they heard the sound of loud, angry voices from farther down the alley. A woman's screaming pierced through it.

Turning the corner, they saw three men nailing planks across the door of a house just ahead of them. The people in the house were struggling to get out, but a guard thrust them back with a spear, jabbing at the hands reaching out through the planks. They heard children crying inside. The woman was screaming, 'Don't leave me here! Don't leave me to die!'

'Mother of God!' Agostino muttered, crossing himself.

The men finished boarding up the door, then one of them daubed a large cross on it with whitewash.

'It *is* the plague,' Niccolo said.

'We must get away from here,' Zorah urged. 'Come!'

She led them back towards a narrow side-alley. They had to stand back. A turbaned man was coming towards them, walking slowly and unsteadily. As he passed Agostino, he stumbled and clutched at him to stop himself falling. Agostino tried to hold him up, but the man's legs gave way and he collapsed to the ground. Marco stooped to help Agostino, who was trying to lift the man.

'Don't touch him!' Niccolo shouted.

The man was lying still. His face was discoloured and livid sores covered one cheek. They backed from him, horrified. Agostino was staring at his hands, which he held stiffly in front of him.

'You'd better wash them at once,' Matteo advised. Agostino nodded bleakly, knowing only too well what might happen otherwise.

'Then find the names of the provision merchants,' Niccolo ordered. 'And meet us back at the inn.'

They hurried away from him down the alleyway. At the end of it, Zorah headed into a dark underpassage from which they emerged into sunlight again. The harbour was directly below them. They were very few boats left in the once-thriving port and those they saw were in a deplorable condition, their sails torn, their planking loose and warped.

The best of them was the medium-sized trading ship belonging to Abdelatiff, the innkeeper's cousin, a high-prowed vessel with one mast. Eager to agree terms, he told them that he had made many ocean crossings in it and was planning to leave in four days for Fuchow. Matteo's inspection, however, revealed that it would not survive a single voyage even to the west coast of India, far less carry them to China. In the manner of most Persian coastal shipping, its timbers were not nailed, but bored and sewn together with twine caulked with fish glue. In the storms of the Indian Ocean, they would burst apart. The ship's captain pleaded with them to reconsider, almost weeping in his desperation to get away. Matteo shook his head regretfully. 'However much time it might save us, it's not worth the risk.'

Meanwhile Marco had seen smoke drifting over the harbour from boats moored out in the water. They were on fire, and men stood in rowing-boats round them, throwing oil on to the flames.

'They're burning their own ships,' Marco blurted. 'Why?'

'They must be full of rats,' his father told him.

Matteo shivered. 'Filthy creatures . . .'

'We leave this cemetery as fast as we can,' Niccolo decided. He looked at Zorah.

'Yes,' she nodded. 'I'll help you to pack and I'll show you the shortest and safest way out of Hormuz.'

They hurried from the harbour and back to the inn. By the time they arrived, they were almost running. On their way they had seen more houses being boarded up, whole families imprisoned in them because one of them had the plague, or was suspected of having it. Bells were ringing in every quarter and muezzins called to the faithful to pray for deliverance. No one answered cries for help. Those who collapsed in the streets were flung on to pestcarts to be burned with the dead. The plague had the city in its grip.

Jacopo was waiting at the door of the inn. When he saw them, he waved frantically. He was shaking. 'Quick!' he shouted. 'Come quickly!'

They ran after him into the main room. Halfway down the stairs lay the body of one of the guests, his eyes open, dilated, a yellow foam covering his mouth.

'Who is he?' Niccolo demanded.

'A Syrian merchant,' Zorah told him, trembling. 'He had a room upstairs.'

'I heard cries . . .' Jacopo was weeping. 'I heard cries and went to help him . . . but I didn't touch him! I swear I didn't. He fell . . . and he hasn't moved since.'

'Where's Agostino?' Matteo asked him.

'Not back yet.'

'*Zorah . . . water!*'

The hoarse cry came from the far corner of the room, where the innkeeper lay sprawled against a wall. His face was white and waxen, with purple blotches all over it. His breathing was very laboured. He tried to lift a hand, but it would not move. Zorah started towards him, but Marco caught her arm. 'Don't go near him!'

Picking up a ladle, he dipped it into a crock and held the water to the man's lips to give him some relief, taking care to stand well away.

'We must leave at once!' Niccolo said, urgently. 'Gather up the baggage! Hurry!'

Matteo, Marco and Jacopo rushed upstairs with him to collect their belongings, avoiding the corpse on the steps. When they got to the rooms, they had just begun to pack when an agonizing scream from below halted them. Marco dashed back down to the main room.

Zorah's hand was over her mouth. 'The door!' She was quivering.

Violent hammer blows made the door-frame shake. Marco hurled himself at the wood, but he was already too late. Even when the others came to help him, their combined pushing and battering could not budge the door.

'They've boarded us in!' yelled Jacopo hysterically. 'We'll die like rats in here!'

They backed away from the doorway, dazed by the realization of what awaited them. Zorah was sobbing uncontrollably. Niccolo and Matteo stood helpless. Execution in the prison camp at Tabriz would have been a kinder end than this.

It was Marco who roused himself and tried to take action. The windows on the ground floor were mere chinks, but the one upstairs might be big enough for a man to squeeze through.

No sooner had he reached the room than he saw that it was hopeless: an iron bar had been set into the stone, bisecting the space. Looking down into the street, he saw a guard posted outside the inn, armed with a lance, ready to prevent any attempts at escape. He thought of the roof, but there was no means of lowering themselves from it without being seen. They were completely trapped.

He returned to the main room. His father and uncle had checked the rear door, but that too had been nailed up and guarded. Jacopo was sitting on the floor, hugging himself and moaning.

Zorah's sobbing brought Marco out of his daze. He held her, drawing her close. 'Don't cry,' he said, comforting her. 'My father will think of something. We shall get out somehow.'

She shook her head, and Marco saw that she was staring beyond him at the innkeeper, who was now hardly breathing. 'He's dying too . . .'

'He has come to the bridge,' Zorah said.

'The bridge?'

Her tone was hushed. 'My grandmother told me. When you die, you go to a place where there is a deep abyss, a deep, deep ravine with a bridge over it. On the other side is a shining angel to welcome you to the kingdom of happiness that they call paradise. If your heart is pure, the bridge grows wider and wider as you cross. But if you have been evil, the bridge gets narrower and narrower, until it is as thin as a thread.' She indicated the innkeeper who had now stopped breathing. He lied to you. The plague was already in this house, but he would not let me tell you. Now the bridge is ahead of him . . .'

The two of them stared at the dying man with superstitious fear, seeing the same gruesome fate in store for themselves.

'Stand back!' The shout came from outside, startling them.

Niccolo leapt to his feet. Suddenly there was a loud crash at the door. Drawing his sword, he hauled Jacopo up. Marco was rising with Zorah and Matteo closed in beside them. They waited tensely. Loud, rending sounds were heard as the boards were torn away from outside. When the door finally swung open, they were astonished to see only one man facing them.

'Agostino!' Marco almost laughed with relief.

Agostino, sweating and panting, stood on the threshold, his hands held out as if to beg forgiveness. They saw the blood on them and looked beyond him to the crumpled figure of the guard who had been stationed outside. The killing of the guard was the first and only act of violence in his gentle life, and Agostino was plainly tormented by remorse. Yet when he had returned to the inn and found them all boarded up, he had had no choice.

Marco hugged him in gratitude, then turned to Zorah. 'You must lead us out of here,' he told her.

Seizing the bags that were most essential to them, they followed the girl out into the silent, deserted street. Zorah led them swiftly but cautiously through a maze of alleys, where fortunately night was falling, providing dark shadows in which to crouch and hide. At one point she halted them with a raised arm and made them press back into a low doorway. A wooden cart was clattering towards them, dragged by men with blazing torches. The stench of decay rose from the grisly load it carried, and none of them dared to look as the heaped corpses were trundled past them. As soon as the cart turned the corner, Zorah checked the street, beckoned to Marco and set off again.

The heavy luggage slowed them down, but they struggled on, slipping past guards and corpse collectors, knowing what would happen to them if they were caught within the city walls. Shouts and running feet not far behind them announced that their escape had been discovered. They hurried on down more narrow streets with the sounds of pursuit spreading around them. In one side-alley, Zorah stopped at a house with stone steps up the side of it. Motioning them into the shadows, Zorah crouched on the bottom steps and sent out a high-pitched yelp like the call of some desert animal. A door opened above them. In the light that spilled out, a woman appeared. After some whispered words, Zorah waved to them and they scurried up after her, through the doorway. Marco had a brief glimpse of a crowd of children inside the room. Zorah was tugging at his arm and they ran up to the flat roof of the house.

They continued their flight over the rooftops, guided by Zorah, who was as lithe as a cat. More than once they had to lie flat as guards charged past in the street below, but at last they came to a thick stone wall. They could go no farther.

'Here you leave Hormuz,' said Zorah. 'Beyond the wall the ground rises and it's easy to jump down. If you go straight on, you'll come to the oasis where the caravans stop.'

Matteo signalled to the servants. They threw their bundles over the wall and helped each other to climb over. As ever, Niccolo thought of the practicalities. 'We need horses.'

'You can get them at the oasis,' Zorah told him.

'Thank you – for everything.' Niccolo took some coins from his pouch, but she refused them. He nodded to her and clambered up on to the wall. Matteo followed him.

Marco was left alone with Zorah. He hesitated, conscious that they would never have escaped without her help and courage. 'Come with us,' he said, taking her hand.

'No, I – I can't,' she said, although she seemed tempted. 'My mother – you saw her back there – she needs me. Though I cannot go to her until I know that I haven't caught the sickness. You must hurry.' She tried to get her tongue around the unfamiliar name. 'Goodbye . . . *Ma – Marco.*'

She slipped her hand from Marco's. Her cheek touched his and she was gone into the night. He had not known she was crying until he felt on his cheek the moisture of her tears.

Niccolo Polo opened the mouth of the animal and studied its teeth. A lifetime of travel had made him an expert judge of horses and he liked to buy the best. The horse dealer, a big, bold-faced Persian, stood beside him. Several other horses were in a nearby pen. It had been a long and exhausting trudge from Hormuz to the oasis, and Niccolo was determined to secure the best transport. The merchant in him made him equally determined to do so at the best price. He glanced around at the animals. 'Keep your prices low, dealer – you are short of customers.'

'And you are short of a horse,' smiled the man.

'Our animals were stolen. Perhaps we shall find them amongst these.'

'Look if you want to,' the Persian chuckled. He became serious. 'Where are you heading?'

'East. We planned to take the sea route from Hormuz, but – well, we changed our minds. We want to go back to Kerman, across the Rudbar Plain. Then we turn north.'

'You plan to cross that plain on your own, friend?'

'We know the country. We passed through it on our way west.'

'What about the Karaunas?' the dealer asked anxiously.

'Karaunas?' asked Matteo, joining them. Like Niccolo, he had caught the hint of fear in the man's voice.

'Desert bandits. They have the power to make fog rise when they wish to attack. They spring out at you like demons. Those who travel alone are doomed.'

'We came that way before,' said Matteo. 'We saw no Karaunas.'

'A miracle, then,' the dealer asserted. 'Next time—'

'Do you want to sell horses or not?' demanded Niccolo.

'Of course! Twenty pieces a horse.'

'Ten.'

'Fifteen,' the dealer countered.

'Ten!' repeated Niccolo with an air of finality.

While his father was bargaining with the dealer, Marco rested in the shade of some palm trees with their two servants. He heard Agostino groaning and looked round to see him bent over, holding his stomach, sweat dripping from him. 'What is it, Agostino?'

'I have fire inside. My head's bursting.'

'It's fatigue, I'm sure. Let me see.' He examined the man's face and eyes carefully. 'Press under your armpits. Does it hurt?'

'No . . . I want to . . . throw up.'

'It's only a matter of emptying your stomach,' Marco said reassuringly. 'Go behind those bushes. You'll feel better afterwards.' Agostino staggered off.

When Niccolo came up with the new horses for Jacopo to load, he asked where Agostino was. Marco told him that he had a stomach ache, but that it was nothing serious. Only when he had a moment alone with Matteo did he let his concern show. 'Agostino is ill, Uncle Matteo – very ill. I'm worried.'

The farther they rode across the plain of Rudbar, the worse Agostino became. But although he was feverish, Niccolo refused to stop and rest in such hostile country, driving them on until they caught up with a small caravan heading for Kerman. The camelmaster and merchants welcomed them. The Karaunas, the camelmaster told them, were not imaginary. They were a tribe of Tartar-Indian half-breeds, vicious bandits, who infested this area. He was glad to have the Polos join him for added safety.

Niccolo fretted at the caravan's slower pace, but could see it was better for Agostino. During the night, however, his fever increased and Marco rode by him all the next day to watch over him. They were skirting the shore of a shallow lake when they noticed a light mist rising, like gauze blown by the wind.

'Do I smell fog?' Matteo asked Niccolo uneasily.

'Close up!' Niccolo ordered. The group bunched more tightly together behind the caravan.

It was none too soon. The mist descended, wrapping itself round the caravan and growing thicker, until it had turned into a fog so dense they could scarcely see one another. They had lost all sight of the caravan. Niccolo produced a coil of rope. He tied one end to his saddle and handed the rope to Matteo. 'Pass it on to the others. We mustn't get separated.'

The rope was tied to each of their saddles, linking them in a chain. Marco was last in the line. As he fastened the rope, his horse whinnied and reared, nearly unseating him. It had been disturbed by a party of spectral riders passing swiftly by on their left. As Marco peered towards them, terrifying screams and yells rang out suddenly in the fog, coming from all round them.

'Karaunas!' Matteo shouted.

Instinctively, the whole group had reined in, but Niccolo called to them, 'We have to get out of this fog before those devils attack us!'

It was too late. Even as they jolted forward, the inhuman cries of the bandits echoed through the mist and four of them came charging towards them, swinging their scimitars. They had not expected the group to be ready for them and in the first rush, Niccolo despatched one with a single, slashing cut. Matteo unsaddled another. They could hear screams and the clash of weapons as the rest of the caravan was set upon. It was every man for himself. 'Let's go!' Niccolo shouted.

Spurring his horse, pulling Matteo and the others behind him, he charged into the fogbank, determined to find a way out. But the Karaunas came after them in force and soon they were being harried on all sides. Jacopo was screeching, hacking about himself in terror. Marco parried the stroke of a bandit's sword as the man raced past. He saw Agostino swaying dangerously in his saddle and grabbed him with one hand, parrying again as his attacker circled back. The Karauna, snarling and bearded, whirled swiftly, his scimitar ready to slice down, but the point of Marco's sword took him through the throat and he toppled from his horse.

The attack had briefly been beaten off, but Matteo had been slashed in the hand and Niccolo nursed a slight wound in his right shoulder. Agostino had slumped over his horse's neck, unable even to defend himself. As Marco panted, his sword poised, alert for any movement in the fog, he realized that no sound was coming from the rest of the caravan. Sudden howls of triumph could be heard coming from the bandits and, as they came hunting for the Polos, Niccolo led his group to the right.

They galloped blindly and for a moment it seemed as though they had won clear. Then all at once the savage whooping of the Karaunas sounded closer, directly in front of them. They swerved to the side and stopped, determined to fight to the last. Unnoticed by anyone, Agostino straightened laboriously and slipped the knot of the rope that attached him to the others. Gathering all his strength, he drew his sword and spurred his horse off into the fog at an angle. Within seconds he was swallowed up, the cries with which he attracted the attention of the Karaunas mingling with their screams of rage as they discovered that he had distracted them from the rest of the group.

Marco felt the rope tauten on his saddle and realized that his father had begun to move again. He rode forward, puzzled to find no sign of Agostino. The ground was rising and before long the fog grew thinner. Yet still he could not see him. In another moment, they broke out into hazy sunlight and halted, throwing off the rope that still linked them together.

'Agostino's gone!' Marco shouted. None of the other three even looked at him. He moved closer to Matteo. 'Don't you see? Agostino's gone!'

'Yes,' Matteo said.

'What do you mean, yes?' Marco demanded. 'We must search for him – help him!'

The others were looking at him now. 'It would do no good,' Matteo said, his voice level. 'He's dead by this time. Don't you understand? He gave his life for us.' Marco was staring at him. 'He was dying, anyway. And it was better than dying of the plague!'

'Keep moving!' Niccolo ordered.

Marco's head was reeling. First Giulio. Now Agostino . . . It was an effort for him to urge his horse on. Dimly he heard yelps from behind him as some of the Karaunas came galloping out of the fog. With their screaming coming closer, his horse needed no spur and he raced after the others.

It was a near-run thing, a crazy dash over the lower slopes of the foothills, but it ended unexpectedly. From the whooping and yells, Marco knew the bandits were gaining on them and was afraid to risk a look round. Yet as he raced down one of the long declines, the sounds of pursuit became fainter. He glanced back. The Karaunas had stopped and were milling in fury, shaking their fists. He looked ahead and saw in front of him the walls of a small, fortified township.

The Karaunas had given up the chase and ridden away, but Niccolo and his group did not slow down until they were within bowshot of the walls. Lookouts and archers on the towers were waving to them, and the high wooden gates were opening.

As they rode up, a man came out to meet them and they

halted in front of him. He was quite old and he held himself with dignity, the headman of the township. He raised his hand in greeting to Niccolo. 'We saw,' he said. 'You were fortunate to escape. *Salam Aleikum.*'

'*Aleikum salam,*' Niccolo replied. 'We ask for your protection and shelter for the night.'

The headman nodded, considering. 'You travel alone?' he asked.

'We were with a caravan bound for Kerman. But I'm afraid its drivers and everyone with it have been butchered by now.'

The headman nodded again. 'Where did you join the caravan?'

'I was advised to catch up with it,' Niccolo said, 'when we left Hormuz.'

The headman drew back. 'Then I am sorry for you,' he said quietly. 'You must keep away from us.' He gestured to the archers on the walls and turned back to the gates.

Marco had dismounted. Dizzy, he stared at his father, trying to understand what was happening. Niccolo was protesting, 'You promised to help us!'

'Keep away!' the headman repeated. He turned in the gates, which had already closed to a crack. 'May Allah have mercy on you.' He stepped back into the citadel.

The Polos and Jacopo waited irresolutely. Even Niccolo seemed crushed for once, unwilling to leave, yet knowing it was useless to stay. As they waited for him to make a move, three women came from the town. Two set down bowls of fruit and pitchers of water, then hurried back inside. The third, a stooped, old woman with a seamed face, came forward cautiously until she was level with Marco's horse. They saw that the bowl she carried was filled with a red liquid. She dipped her finger in it and smeared the horse's forehead. It whickered and tossed its mane. In silence, she daubed the foreheads of the other three horses and left without a word.

'What was she doing?' Marco whispered. 'What is that?'

'Blood,' Matteo told him. 'To drive away evil demons. And call on the good spirits to aid us.'

Arriving at a rocky incline, they dismounted to lead their horses over the treacherous surface. Flurries of stones were dislodged and went cascading down the mountainside. Niccolo, seemingly tireless, led the way. Jacopo, gasping with every step, followed. Matteo, too, was weary; but it was Marco who was feeling the strain most. When he tripped and staggered, Matteo had to catch him to prevent him from falling. 'You're tired, boy,' he said, halting. 'Niccolo!'

'Why have we stopped?'

'We need to catch our breath.'

About to protest, Niccolo shrugged instead and moved off to sit alone. Unwilling to admit his fatigue to the others, he looked ahead to plot the remainder of the ascent. Jacopo took care of the horses and Matteo helped his nephew to lower himself down in the shade of a rock.

'Bring us some water, Jacopo,' Matteo asked.

'We only have two skins left, sir – and this one is almost empty,' he reported. He passed the goatskin to Matteo, who put it to Marco's mouth. Marco took a mouthful gratefully, then let his uncle drink. Jacopo, parched himself, watched them sullenly.

'Let's hope we find a well soon,' said Matteo. 'Everything is dried up around here.' He picked up a handful of dark grey stones. 'And yet the Old Man of the Mountain's paradise used to be just behind here.'

Marco looked behind them, but saw only a sheer wall of grey rock. 'Paradise?'

'It was a wonderful garden with green lawns, flowers and trees laden with succulent fruit. And water – lots and lots of water. In the midst of all this was the castle of the Old Man of the Mountains.'

'Who was he?' Marco had settled back, his head resting on his arms.

'Alaudin, the leader of the Assassins.'

'Assassins?' Marco repeated the strange word.

'Users of hashish,' Matteo explained. 'Young warriors whose obedience the Old Man made sure of by visits to his pleasure garden. The girls there were as beautiful as the Houris in Mohammed's paradise. The warriors were offered a drug, hashish, which intoxicated and exalted them. After a while they were enslaved by it and by the garden's countless delights. But the Old Man made them pay a price: when it was time, he sent them on missions of death, to murder anyone who refused to acknowledge his sovereignty. And all the young warriors obeyed him, anxious only to return to that paradise in the mountains. They made the name of Assassins feared from Cairo to Khorasan. Then Hulaga Khan, the Great Kublai's brother, destroyed the Old Man's power. All that's left is a few burnt stones. The garden of paradise has completely vanished.'

Niccolo roused himself, deciding they had rested long enough. 'All right! On your feet,' he told them.

But as Marco was helped up by his uncle, he found that his vision was blurred; it was as if he was still caught in the fog with the Karaunas. He wiped his arm across his eyes, but still could not see properly. As soon as Matteo withdrew his arm, he reeled and fell heavily to the ground.

Niccolo hurried across to look at his son and immediately saw the fever in his face. Together the two brothers carried Marco back to the shade of the rock and laid him down gently. Niccolo summoned Jacopo, who came scuttling over with a flaccid leather bottle. But when it was tilted over Marco's lips, not a single drop of water came out. Matteo hurled the bottle away and Niccolo turned on Jacopo in fury. 'You treacherous dog! You've drunk the only water that was left!' He seized his whip.

'It wasn't me, master!' Jacopo cried, trying vainly to escape as Niccolo beat him. 'The bottle was torn . . . the water leaked out . . . I didn't touch it . . .'

Only a low cry from Marco saved the servant. Niccolo bent down to his son, and saw his features twist in terror.

The sun had beaten down brutally on to Marco's upturned face, dazzling his eyes. His head had fallen to the side and he was gazing at a jagged rock. Slowly, an enormous, bright-scaled serpent took shape before him, rearing up from the rock to strike at him. Weakly, he tried to stretch out his arms to push it away . . .

Niccolo caught his son's hands as they jerked and rose. He looked where Marco had been looking, but saw only a harmless green lizard basking on a stone. He felt Marco's forehead. It was like a furnace. His whole body was sweating, burning up with fever.

Marco was not conscious of his father kneeling over him, shading him, his uncle watching. His eyes had closed and he was slipping away into blessed coolness. He was swimming . . . swimming in the limpid water of the lagoon at Venice. Behind him, he could hear a voice calling him. 'Marco! Wait for me!' It was Giulio's voice. Marco smiled and swam on, buoyant, carefree. Then he heard a strangled cry. He looked round and all he could see was an arm clutching at the air before it sank. 'Giulio!' he shouted, and began to swim back frantically. But there were waves obstructing him, bearing him back. Where had they come from? And rearing on the crest of one of the waves was the monstrous serpent, its curved fangs glistening. He screamed.

And found himself lying in a boat. His boat, and Giulio's. It was drifting in mist and Caterina lay next to him on a pile of nets. She smiled to him. 'My dearest . . .' she whispered. 'Come to me . . . Come to me . . .' As he leaned over her, her face shimmered and altered, and he was bending over Zorah. She was naked and smiling, writhing softly. Her arms were round him. As he kissed her, he realized that her face was white, deathly white, covered with plague sores. Her arms tightened and he fought to get away from her . . .

Niccolo held Marco down as he struggled, racked by fever. The boy was moaning, his eyes rolling. It shocked Niccolo. Suddenly, he was afraid of losing him. He could not understand the rush of panic he felt. They had never been close – he had set his mind and his heart against it. Yet suddenly, he was afraid. His own son was suffering and there was nothing he could do for him. No way to save him. Unless he had water soon, it would be too late. And there was only one source within reach. The Dry Tree. There they would find a well with plenty of water for him, plenty for everyone. But they had to get there. And get there soon.

Together Niccolo and Matteo lifted the inert figure on to his horse, then mounted up themselves. When they had gone a few yards, Niccolo looked back at Jacopo, who was still cowering on the ground. The servant got up and joined them quickly, less afraid of Niccolo than of being left behind.

They came down from the keen air of the mountains to a flat, desolate plain that seemed to stretch forever. There were no tracks, and only Niccolo's instinct guided them. The immense emptiness of the place was oppressive. Marco had somehow stayed on his horse, but was virtually hanging around its neck, flies crawling over his mouth and eyes. Once again, the sun was his worst enemy. Anxious and parched themselves, Niccolo and Matteo stumbled slowly on until they saw in the distance the great tree that they had been seeking. Their relief was immeasurable, although they would not reach it before sunset.

'Let's pray to God that well isn't dry,' said Matteo. 'Or poisoned.' He glanced at Marco. 'I fear for him, Niccolo.'

'There has to be water – a well full of water!'

'So long as it isn't the plague, we can save him,' Matteo promised.

'It's not the plague! It can't be the plague!' Niccolo muttered, trying to convince himself. 'It's only a fever.'

'God protect us all!' whispered his brother.

They came at last to the extraordinary tree that stood by itself in the vast loneliness of the plain. The Dry Tree was of massive size and girth, its trunk knotted with age, its gnarled branches drooping, its leaves and berries the colour of bright copper. It was said to mark the place where Alexander the Great had fought with Darius, King of Persia, and many other legends had grown up around it.

It was evening when the travellers arrived, and to their relief they found that the well had abundant clear water. They refreshed themselves gratefully, and wooden bowls were unpacked and filled so that the horses could slake their thirst as well. Marco was laid under the boughs of the Dry Tree on a pile of sacks. When he had sipped his fill, his face was bathed by the attentive and concerned Matteo. Riven by the fever, Marco drifted off into troubled sleep.

Exhaustion claimed them all very quickly and they slumbered on the ground. A slight breeze blew across the plain, rustling the leaves of the tree, which made a slightly metallic sound. Marco's sleep was fitful. At one point he sat bolt upright, reaching out in front of him as if he had seen someone there. Then he closed his heavy eyes and sank back to the ground, his head rolling from side to side, lost in a world of dream that was frighteningly vivid. The nightmare seemed to be his only reality.

The ivory-and-gold gate of the garden opened soundlessly in front of him and he passed through into the paradise beyond. Green lawns, thick, flowering bushes and trees laden with enamelled fruit stood all round him. Water played from a marble fountain, surrounded by white doves and pink turtledoves. Marco was in the garden of Alaudin's castle, an honoured guest in a place of enchantment and wonder. The castle itself, fronted by a great carpet of emerald-green grass, was weird and insubstantial, as if it had been cut out of paper and set against a painted sky. But it had the brightness and intricacy of a Persian miniature and he gazed at it with awe.

Two young men were flanking him, but as the three of them walked deeper into the lush garden, they were met by beautiful girls with slender figures and graceful movements who came flitting towards them. The veils that fluttered around their perfumed bodies seemed to create a music of their own – the soft lilt of lutes and rebecks. The girls stretched out their arms to offer him flowers, fruit and golden-crusted loaves of bread. Their laughter echoed like the tinkling of crystal.

As the girls encircled him and moved in harmony, they were joined by more dancers, and then by more again, until the whole garden was filled with their sweetness and beauty. Marco moved to their rhythm, caught up in the ecstasy of their movements, following them round and round until they suddenly halted and froze like statues. The circle broke and the statues fanned out.

Recovering from his surprise, Marco found himself standing in front of the Old Man of the Mountain, a noble, majestic and striking figure with a flowing white beard and rich, jewelled robes. Young warriors dressed in white stood all around him, each holding a long, sharp-bladed sword. The Old Man's eyes were mesmeric, his voice young and fresh.

'I have been waiting for you, Marco. For you, I have the most important mission of all.' He handed Marco a golden-bladed dagger that gleamed in the sun. 'To rid the world of its greatest enemy – the Pope of Rome. You will go to him, and my mind will guide your hand.'

A girl came forward and offered Marco a golden cup in which a thick, red liquid shimmered. He saw his reflection encircled by the rim, and raised the cup to his lips.

The next second he was watching the precious chalice being raised in the ritual gesture of offertory, containing the red wine that symbolized the blood of Christ. The girl and the garden and the castle and the Old Man of the Mountains had vanished and he was in the Church of the Holy Sepulchre in Jerusalem. A low liturgical chant echoed, yet he could see nobody there but the Pope himself, standing before the altar with the chalice raised, dressed in his long, red pluvial.

As if guided by an unseen hand, Marco moved forward silently through an avenue of columns. A cloud of incense rose from the censer on the altar steps and he inhaled the pungent odour as he passed. The Pope had knelt before the altar now, his back towards the assassin's dagger. Marco raised the weapon to strike and held it poised above his victim. Then the Pope turned around to look up at him and he saw that he was staring into the face of his own father . . .

He awoke with a stifled cry beneath the Dry Tree. 'No! *No!*' he panted. Glancing wildly around, he saw the sleeping figure of his father a short distance away and began to crawl towards him. His strength had gone and he could barely manage to inch along the ground, but he did not give up. The little journey he was making that night beneath the cover of the mighty tree was one of the most important of his life. Niccolo Polo heard the panting and felt the presence of someone alongside him. He opened his eyes, saw his son and reached out impulsively to clasp him to his chest. It was a moment of love and tenderness that brought tears of joy to them both.

Marco Polo had found his father at last.

Chapter Four

It was cold in the cell and Rustichello wore his spare shirt draped like a shawl round his shoulders. He laid aside his pen, rubbed the fingers of his right hand to relieve the cramp, then read through what he had so painstakingly written. Something troubled him, an incompleteness in the narrative.

'I don't understand. You said that you were in a wide desert plain, in the middle of which was what you call the Dry Tree. You said that not one blade of grass was in sight. And now you talk of Badash – of a Garden of Eden – hills, meadows, water. For once, there must be a gap in your memory.'

Marco was lying on his low bed. It was some time before he realized that Rustichello was waiting for a reply, and when he spoke it was almost absent-mindedly. 'Not Badash – Badakhshan. My father decided to take me there. I was ill for a long time, so ill it seemed I might never recover, but he said that the air there had the power to bring the dead back to life.' Marco got up and went to the table. Taking up the quill and turning over the parchment on which Rustichello had been writing, he traced a few quick lines, then added a cross. 'Look. We were here – under the Dry Tree. From this point, after marching for ten days, one reaches the eastern end of the plain. I have not forgotten anything, I promise you.' He sketched in more detail on the map. 'Following the great river Oxus, here, one reaches the high plain they call Badakhshan, in the northern part of Afghanistan. To me it *was* paradise. My father was right. The air was so pure up there, that the flames of our fires gave less heat. They were not red, but pale blue – and water took an age to boil.'

'Please, Master Marco! Wait!' interrupted Giovanni,

who sat huddled under his blanket. 'Captain Arnolfo said that he wants to be here himself when you tell the rest of your stories.' Giovanni saw the tales as a bargaining counter. 'He promised to bring us wine, fresh bread, maybe even fish.'

'The Captain will read Marco's tales when I have written them,' insisted Rustichello, anxious not to halt the flow of Marco's memories.

'Begging your pardon, Master Rustichello. But, if I may say so, it's not the same as when Master Marco tells them.'

The writer almost threw the inkwell at him. 'This creature! Why did you have to bring him along with you?'

'If it weren't for him,' Marco smiled, 'you wouldn't be listening to me now.'

Giovanni basked in the compliment. Rustichello was keen to hear more about paradise. 'So how long did you stay in Bada . . . ?'

'Badakhshan. Six or seven months. Long enough for me to recover my strength and for my father to teach me Mongol, Tibetan and Chinese – at least, enough to say "Good day" and "I'm hungry".'

The key was heard in the lock and the cell door swung open. Ducking under the low lintel, Captain Arnolfo, commander of the prison, came in. 'How's the fairytale workshop going?' he asked.

'We've arrived in paradise!' Giovanni told him.

'Captain,' Rustichello sighed, 'I would like so much to make hell a present of this madman. But could you at least move him to another cell?'

Arnolfo smiled, put his head out of the door and gave an order. A guard entered at once with a basket covered with a small white cloth. Before the astonished eyes of the three prisoners, the cloth was removed to reveal a wine-jug, a loaf of bread, fruit and three fishes. Marco and Rustichello looked in astonishment at Giovanni, who was almost preening himself, enjoying his success. Arnolfo took the basket and put it down on the table next to the map of

Badakhshan that Marco Polo had drawn on the faded parchment.

It was late summer. Crystal-clear peaks speared an azure sky above a mountain range whose splendour stretched for mile after mile. Rich and verdant pastures reached high up the gradients before shading into dark, craggy rock. The air was keen and invigorating.

Hidden behind a large boulder with an arrow fitted to his bow, Marco waited for the animal to come within range. It was a strange-looking beast, a cross between a deer and a ram, with the former's lithe grace and the latter's curling horns. Seeing it trot down the mountainside towards him, Marco stepped out with his bowstring taut, but something stopped him from releasing it. Hunter and prey simply stared at each other, as if transfixed by the same curious emotion.

'Marco! Marco!'

Matteo's call echoed around the valley and broke the spell. The animal bounded off swiftly. Marco turned away. Further down the slope, on a path winding up from the Afghan village where they had lived during their long stay in Badakhshan, stood his Uncle Matteo. A herd of horses and mules were grazing behind him, attended by a few Tibetans. As soon as he saw his father haggling with one of the herdsmen, Marco realized that their idyllic stay in the region was over.

'Come on down!' Matteo called, hands cupped around his mouth. 'The Tibetan guides say the passes will soon be closed. We must leave before the blizzards start. It's now or never!'

Marco was torn. He did not want to leave the wild beauty of Badakhshan, yet he had the explorer's questing urge to seek out the new. He sent his arrow climbing high into the sky, and made his way down the slope towards the others.

*

Led by two Tibetan guides, the caravan crawled its way along the snowbound passes of the Hindu Kush. They had left all trace of vegetation behind. Marco was standing up well to the ordeal of the trek, the cold, invigorating mountain air completing his recovery from the fever that had tortured him beneath the Dry Tree. Like the others, he was dressed in the furs of a shepherd, and was gazing, enthralled, at the immense panorama of mountain peaks all around them.

'Incredible to think that Alexander the Great crossed this pass with his army,' Matteo panted. 'On his great horse, Bucephalus.'

Marco had heard the local tales too. 'They say that all the horses here are descended from him.'

'Let's hope they're right,' Niccolo said drily. 'I ended up paying far too much for these scrawny beasts.'

Marco laughed. His father's good humour made the difficult journeys so much easier to bear. It was as if Niccolo Polo, in finding his son that night a year ago beneath the Dry Tree, had also rediscovered a happiness in himself. He could still be stern and authoritative when need be, but he had certainly mellowed since the early days of their travelling together.

Soon the caravan was pushing on across a huge, snow-covered plateau, where icy winds shrieked their displeasure at the intruders. Snowdrifts were a constant hazard, the horses slipping and shying, sometimes having to be dragged. Only the mules seemed to have sureness of foot, plodding on without urging. For men and beasts the cold was a terrible trial.

'Move your arms, Jacopo. Like this,' Niccolo instructed.

They had pitched camp on a white slope in the lee of some overhanging rocks. Because the fire could not warm them, Niccolo was showing the shivering servant how to clap himself with his arms. 'Stand up, man,' he ordered. 'Stamp your feet.'

'I can't, master,' said Jacopo through chattering teeth. 'It's so cold. Even the fire's got no heat in it.'

'We're very high up,' Marco reminded him.

'If you think *this* is high up or cold,' his father warned, 'wait until we reach the peaks of Pamir.'

He pointed ahead to mountains so immeasurably high their summits were lost in the clouds.

'How far are they?' asked Marco.

'Fifteen or twenty days' journey.'

Matteo joined them, his expression serious. 'The guides say we'll have to leave the horses.'

'What!' Niccolo was furious.

'The climb is too steep for them from here on. They'll never manage it, they say.'

'I should have realized when they sold them to us at such a good price,' Niccolo growled. 'The thieves!'

'No!' Matteo restrained his brother from crossing to argue with the Tibetan guides. 'They say if we free the horses, they'll round them up on the way back and keep them in lieu of pay. But tell me, brother, why did you insist on having horses, when they warned you to take only mules?'

Niccolo sat back and bit his tongue. For once his instinct had been wrong. He had to take the blame for the situation in which they now found themselves.

Next day the horses were released and the travellers pressed on with mules only. Temperatures fell even lower and the wind lashed at them with a thousand invisible whips. For hours they inched along a treacherous ledge clinging to the side of an icebound gorge. Stones loosened by the hooves of the mules plunged into the bottomless abyss below. Marco saw Jacopo fall behind and shouted encouragement to him to keep up, but the impact of his voice in the rarefied atmosphere caused a flurry of snow to shower down from the slope. One of the guides spun round and motioned him to keep silent.

Eventually, they reached the other side of the pass and came out into an open area where freezing winds lashed them with even greater fury. To their right was a large conical stone shrine on a square base, a Buddhist 'chorten'.

They struggled towards it, holding on to each other to avoid being blown back down the steep, rocky incline, and urging the mules on when they were up to their girths in freezing snow. Near the shrine was a cleft that offered partial shelter from the wind and it was here they sank down to recover.

The journey behind them had been a nightmare, but what lay ahead promised to be worse. Ahead of them stretched the endless vista of the Pamir mountain chain, bleak, precipitous, and unwelcoming.

Matteo clambered over to join Niccolo and Marco. His face was set. 'The guides say they'll go no further!' he shouted, raising his voice above the wind.

'We paid them to lead us to the trade route across Pamir!' Niccolo protested, shocked.

'This is the start of it, they say. Now they're heading back.'

'Offer them more!'

'It's no use, Niccolo. They're afraid the mountain devils will catch them. They refuse to go further. They've never gone beyond this point.'

The two brothers looked at each other and Marco could see they were more than a little troubled by superstitious fear. 'God help us,' Niccolo muttered.

Without guides, their progress was more hazardous than ever. Jacopo, believing the superstitions about furred monsters, almost died when he spotted something coming down a slope towards him, but it was only a wild sheep. With a toss of its long, curling horns it loped off towards a ravine. Jacopo continued to be an extra burden for the others to bear. When they crossed a deep gorge on a rickety bridge, they had to blindfold him, as well as the mules, before they could get him over.

The blizzard caught them on a narrow track on a mountainside. It descended so suddenly and raged so violently that they lost all contact with each other. Marco, at the rear of the caravan, began to shout in desperation to the others, but the blizzard seemed to have swallowed them alive. Before he could even try to search for them, there was a low rumbling from above and a rising crescendo of noise, as an avalanche of thick, white, suffocating snow came rumbling down the mountainside. In the time it took him to call out his father's name once more, it poured over him, sweeping him from the track.

He awoke after what seemed like a sleep of years to find himself staring at the image of a Demon-God with burning eyes, its multiple arms brandishing weapons. Through the haze of incense fumes, he could make out the figures of tall, ascetic men in dark, red robes, like monks with shaven skulls. They came and went in eerie silence.

Where was he? And where were his father and Uncle Matteo? He tried to speak, but was too weak and light-headed. He looked down at himself and saw that he was lying on a bed of heaped carpets and wearing a loose, off-white robe.

As he watched from his bed, he saw one monk squat in front of a majestic golden Buddha, illuminated by the flicker of a thousand tiny candles. A nimbus of light seemed to form around the monk's head and then his whole body was haloed in light. Slowly, and with no visible effort, the monk rose into the air until he was level with the Buddha's head. Not sure if he was witnessing dream or reality, Marco fell back again, lapsing into sleep.

When he stirred once more, he discovered that he had been moved. He was in a small, bare room like a monk's cell, lying on a wooden bed. There was absolutely nothing in the room, except a copper bowl filled with water and a cloth on the floor beside him.

He tried to rise, yet even though he felt much stronger, it was some time before he could swing his legs off the bed. He sat breathless for a moment, then took up the cloth, dampened it and wiped his eyes and face.

The touch of the water revived him and he examined the cell again. It was lit only by a narrow, horizontal window, too high for him to see out. There was a door of old, bleached wood, studded with nailheads. He pushed himself up, breathing regularly to steady himself, and moved to the door. It was not locked.

He came out into a dimly-lit long stone corridor. There was no one in sight. The need to find out where he was became more urgent. The red-robed 'monks' had not appeared to mean him any harm, but he was cautious as he made his way unsteadily towards the brighter glow at the far end of the corridor.

He stepped out on to a balcony and stopped, gazing in wonder. The balcony on to which he had emerged was set high in the exterior wall of a small, austerely beautiful building, perched on a cliff face, its red stone walls at many different levels, topped by towers with golden pagoda roofs. Far below was a green and fertile valley sunk between towering, ice-capped mountains. The view was breathtaking. He stepped closer to the edge and looked down. The height and his lightheadedness made him pull back at once in alarm. Also, he had begun to sense that he was not alone.

He turned slowly. One of the red-robed men, tall and ascetic, his head shaven, was watching him from the doorway. At first sight he was forbidding, even frightening, and Marco recoiled, aware of the drop behind him.

'*U la lo ho*,' the man said. It was more of an invocation than a statement.

'*U la lo ho?*' Marco echoed. It was not a language he recognized. 'Where are we? Where is this place?' he asked in Afghan.

The man smiled slowly and shook his head. He stood aside and gestured to Marco to come with him. Marco was uncertain, but also weak and unsteady. The man came towards him, holding out his hand. Deciding to trust him, Marco let the man lead him back through the door.

The room he was taken to was the one he first remembered seeing. It was a long hall, lit patchily by hanging lamps and small windows near the roof. At the lower end, set between pillars with blue, red and gold-painted capitals, was the gilded, enigmatic Buddha. A row of pillars ran down on either side, splitting it into aisles like a Christian cathedral. The walls were covered with cycles of paintings of the lives and miracles of what could only be saints. In front of the main altar was a throne, with cushions on either side. The atmosphere was unearthly and mysterious.

Marco realized that his first impression had been correct. It was some kind of religious institution, like a monastery. The red-robed, shaven-skulled men who sat by the pillars were the monks. A larger group of younger men, in off-white robes like his, sat in a semicircle, chanting softly. Some spun what he later knew to be prayer wheels, others accompanied the chanting by a rhythmic beating of drums.

Directly ahead Marco saw a throne, where a very old man was seated. His head was shaven like the others, his slant eyes hooded, under tufted brows, his face a reddish brown and gnarled as a nut. He wore a high-collared blue and yellow brocade tunic, embroidered with gold, over his red robe. The old man's hands rose and spread wide, his head lifted, his lips moving in the incomprehensible words of an alien liturgy.

Who was he praying to? Those demons with glaring eyes and teeth like tusks, or the golden statue with the bland smile? In his weakened state, Marco felt confused and a little frightened. He clasped his hands together and tried to pray. '*Holy Mother of God, let me not be lost here among those heathen idolaters. Let me not be alone, abandoned here. Holy Mother, help me . . .*' His thoughts and his words were not coherent. He had a terror of having found his father only to lose him again; of being trapped in a land where there was no one to whom he could speak; of never being able to discover the way back to his own world. What would these people here do when they realized he was not of their faith? What might they force him to do? Where *was* he?

The chanting and drumming had stopped. He glanced up and saw that the Mass, or whatever it was, had ended. Some of the red-robed monks were leaving, others talking together quietly. The younger men around him were still seated, and were all looking at him. He froze, near panic.

A voice behind him said in Afghan, 'You are in the Lamasery of Muztagh-Ata, in the region of Pamir.' Marco swivelled round. One of the young men had spoken. He was slender and dark-skinned with brown, friendly eyes, calm and gentle. 'I could not answer you before.'

'Who are you?' Marco asked.

'I am a student, a novice. One day I shall be a Lama, a monk devoted to the doctrines of Buddha. Like you, I come from far away, from the kingdom of Kashmir.'

'How did I get here?' Marco asked.

'Our brothers found you half-buried in the snow. The flame of your life burned very low. Take my arm,' he said. 'The Father Abbot wishes to speak with you.'

The old man had left his throne and was coming towards them. The novices bowed and retreated. Copying the one with him, Marco also bowed and the old man nodded approvingly. Seen closer to, he was even older than he had seemed. He must once have been tall, but was now stooped by age. His expression was severe, inscrutable, and his hooded eyes transfixed Marco, seeming to see into his very depths. 'You have recovered, my son,' he said. '*U la lo ho.*' And he smiled. The smile transformed him, shifting the wrinkles set into a mask of severity by time. His expression became kindly and the eyes lit by his smile were wise and compassionate.

'You were carried here to die. But your Karma was not yet accomplished.'

'My . . . Karma?' Marco repeated, not understanding. He felt confused and unsettled by the strange surroundings and by the old man's penetrating gaze.

'Your destiny,' the abbot told him. 'Your life's journey to the One has just begun.'

A tinkling sound of bells came from outside, far in the distance, and was answered by the penetrating call of conches, shells blown by the Lamas. The sound triggered something in Marco's memory. 'I was on a path,' he said slowly. 'My father and uncle had been swallowed up in a snow storm . . . Then the whole mountain seemed to fall on me.' Memory rushed in on him and he shuddered. 'My father . . .'

'You spoke of him often in your sleep,' the abbot nodded.

'I have to find him,' Marco said agitatedly. 'I have to search for him!'

'He is safe,' the novice said. 'And your other companions.'

Marco looked from him to the abbot, not fully believing them. 'They nearly died hunting for you in the blizzard,' the abbot told him. 'Our brothers in Liu-ciu led them to safety.'

'Are you sure?' he asked. 'How do you know?'

The tinkling of the bells, near and far off, was heard again. 'These are barrel-bells,' the abbot explained. 'We use them to signal from Lamasery to Lamasery. We are never isolated. Just now, they are saying that you are whole again.'

The novice was smiling, and Marco saw that the others, who could not understand what they were saying, nevertheless were smiling also. And the Lamas who watched them. He felt ashamed that he had thought of them as heathens. 'I am grateful to you, Father Abbot, for all you have done,' he said.

The abbot's hand rose. 'It is to the Lord Buddha you should give thanks.'

Marco could see that the old man was expectant, even eager. 'How would I do that?'

The abbot indicated the paintings of the fearsome figures on the walls. 'When the Lord Buddha first came to our land he defeated the demons of superstition and made them his servants, the guardians of our frontiers. So now, whenever sin or disease have been defeated by his power, we say, the God is victorious. *U la lo ho*.'

'The God is victorious. *U la lo ho*,' Marco repeated, and the novices and Lamas echoed him.

The abbot raised a hand, 'Now, however, you must rest.'

'But what about my father?' Marco asked.

'Later we shall have news for you. Now you must eat a little, and sleep. Then we shall talk again.'

Marco bowed to the abbot and was led by the novices to their refectory, where he was given soup and milk and rice with curds, and tried to answer their questions. The name of his interpreter and new friend was Hafiz. He had been born in Kashmir of an Afghan mother and at an early age had been dedicated to the service of Buddha, the Enlightened One. Some of what he was told was disturbing to Marco, some he simply could not follow. 'Do not be surprised,' Hafiz told him, smiling. 'It takes us many years of study even to understand what is basic to all.'

As far as Marco could gather, there was not just one Buddha, but many, of which Sakyamuni, founder of the religion, was the most recent and the greatest. They preached self-denial and rejection of superstition, together with meditation and lack of prejudice and a determination to harm no living creature – and what Hafiz called a return to the physical world after death, a rebirth, reincarnation. Like Christians they believed that the soul does not die. On that Marco could agree. But further, they believed that the soul was born again in another body, according to how one had lived. Thus, a peasant who had lived a pure and useful life might be reborn as a landlord, then as a noble, and one day might be a king. Whereas a king who had been evil might descend by stages until his soul inhabited the form of a dog or a snake or a flea. The true aim was to purify the soul by degrees, in whatever station in life its present owner had his being, until it achieved an absolute purity and merged with the Divine, the Universal Cause. 'God?' Marco asked. Strictly speaking, Hafiz told him, there was no one God. Each man could become part of God through achieving his own personal salvation.

As they left the refectory, the youngest of the novices presented Marco shyly with a scarf made of a gauze-like material. Hafiz showed him how to wear it, tying it round his neck. 'This felicitous scarf is a sign of our heart's content to have you with us,' he explained. 'It is called "katak". By wearing it, you keep God's blessing on you.'

After he had rested, Marco felt stronger. He woke refreshed and clearheaded and Hafiz found him on the stone balcony, gazing again at the idyllic valley in its girdle of ice-capped mountains.

They were in that part of the Lamasery reserved for the reception of travellers and treatment of the sick. The Lamasery was larger than Marco had thought, and he marvelled as Hafiz showed him the workshops and stables and kitchens; the cells and towers, where adepts retired for long periods of contemplation; the shrines and statues, and the library, where scholar Lamas copied and studied sacred texts, parchment rolls preserved in leather cases, some of them reputed to be so ancient that they came from the time of Sakyamuni himself, the Gotama Buddha.

In the late afternoon, Hafiz led him to a long, wide terrace which still caught the sun, where the abbot sat on a wicker chair under a parasol. Near him two acolytes were kneeling, spinning prayer wheels.

'In turning the wheel,' Hafiz explained, 'we set the doctrine of the Buddha in motion.'

The abbot could see that Marco was still puzzled. 'All life is unending, a wheel, in which all live and die, to be born again. Each time, we hope to lose a little more of our imperfection, until at last we achieve Nirvana.'

'Nirvana?' Marco asked.

'The peace of Oneness with God.' Marco nodded. It was what he had discussed with Hafiz. 'By study and purification, man may bring closer the day when he reaches Oneness,' the abbot went on. 'But we must put aside the things of the world, for they do not last. All is a dream. Be not attached to anything, for too soon you will lose all that is dear to you. Take nothing as real – passion, envy, ambition. All is merely illusion.'

There was an almost hypnotic quality in the abbot's

voice and Marco gazed at him, feeling as though a shutter were being opened in his mind through which he could make out, half glimpsed, vistas of thought and experience which summoned him and, at the same moment, made him afraid. He had never before felt so aware of his ignorance, of the weakness of the foundations on which all his assumptions about life and the world, about the nature of man and religion, were based. He felt held by the abbot's eyes as though suspended in water and, if the eyes released him, he would drown.

Just then they were interrupted as one of the Lamas entered with a copper tray on which were several pots and bowls. With him was an acolyte carrying a silver tray with eight or nine small loaves.

'Will you join me?' the abbot asked. He was pouring a steaming, brown liquid from one of the pots into two bowls.

'If I may,' Marco said. 'What is it?'

'It is called tea,' the abbot told him. 'It is drunk with salt and butter.' He added a pinch of salt to each bowl, and a spoonful of butter. 'It gives strength.'

Marco took his bowl a little uncertainly, and sipped the hot liquid in which the yellow butter had dissolved. The taste was not immediately pleasant. The drink was probably medicinal, he decided. The acolyte was offering him the silver tray; he reached for one of the small loaves.

'Choose carefully,' the abbot said.

Marco saw that everyone was watching him tensely. It was odd; he realized that he must be taking part in some unknown ritual. Brother William and Brother Nicholas had often spoken of the need to guard against being trapped by heathen sorcery. He hesitated, taking his hand away quickly. 'No!' He shook his head. 'This is some witchcraft.'

He regretted it at once, seeing the dismay his refusal had caused. Only the abbot appeared undisturbed, his calm expression unchanged.

'Do not let appearances misguide you,' Hafiz said quietly. 'In inviting you to choose, we are asking your mind – freed from all outside influences – to lead you to choose your own destiny.'

'What you will find in the bread is a sign of your Karma,' the abbot said.

Marco set down his bowl of tea. 'I – I did not wish to offend you, Father Abbot. It is all so new for me, so different. I only want to try to understand.'

'You will,' the abbot promised. Again his eyes held Marco's. 'Inhale deeply. Then expel the air three times through your right nostril.' Marco imitated him. 'Thus you have let out "the white wind", anger. Breathe in again. Exhale through your left nostril and "the red air", lust, will leave you.' Again Marco obeyed. 'Now, from both nostrils breathe out, three times, and you will rid yourself of "the colourless wind", ignorance.' Marco imitated him carefully. 'Now concentrate on this thought: the three original sins, anger, lust and ignorance, are gone. Curl up your tongue—' The abbot demonstrated. 'Like this. Like the petal of a lotus flower.'

Marco opened his mouth and tried to curl his tongue, but was suddenly overcome by embarrassment and could not prevent himself from laughing. He stopped himself, worried that he had upset them, but the abbot smiled. 'You are on the way to freedom of the mind, my son. Laughter breaks the shell of the ego. Say the blessed formula, "*a-lia-ki*" – and choose.'

Again, the acolyte offered Marco the tray with the loaves. Marco put out his hand. '*A-lia-ki*,' he muttered, and took one.

'The choice has been made,' Hafiz intoned.

Marco was taut. He had not been sure what to expect. He breathed out and smiled. 'They're all the same.'

'No. They are all different,' the abbot told him. 'For example, one contains herbs. To pick that would mean you would have strength and victory over your enemies.'

Marco understood and nodded.

'The one with a sliver of wood,' Hafiz said, 'means that your fate is to be poor, a beggar who walks with a stick.'

Marco looked at the small loaf in his hand. The Lamas had rejected superstition, yet this was a ritual in which they believed. So it was not mere soothsaying. He broke the loaf open quickly. Inside was a tiny slip of paper with an unknown writing on it. He looked up and saw that the abbot was pleased. Hafiz seemed relieved. The other two were smiling.

'Your choice,' the abbot said gently, 'shows that you are born to be a seeker after truth and knowledge – and so worthy of our efforts to save you.' He laid his hand on Marco's. 'Stay here with us. You will study the mysteries and, being purified, acquire the powers to overcome your human weakness, to achieve Nirvana.'

Marco paused, torn, but finally shook his head. 'I – I cannot . . . I swore an oath,' Marco told him. 'To the Father of my Church.'

'An oath must not be broken,' the abbot agreed, after a pause. 'In truth, I already knew your answer.' He smiled and held out his hand for Hafiz to help him to his feet. He motioned to Marco, who matched his pace to the older man's as they walked slowly down the terrace. At its end, the abbot stretched out a hand, pointing to the valley below. 'See. Your companions are already on their way to join you.'

Marco looked and saw below, far away on the floor of the green valley the shapes of tiny horsemen riding towards them.

'I understand you, Marco,' the abbot said quietly. 'Your destiny is to travel. You will go from land to land, with your mind and body. As for us, we let only our minds travel for us, and perhaps we reach distances that are denied to many.'

Down below Niccolo, Matteo and Jacopo were riding sturdy hill ponies and their guides were tough Drog-pas in sheepskin coats and fur hats. The whole party reined in and stopped in the forecourt of the Lamasery. On either side of the long steps in front of the pillared main entrance were red-robed monks with red, pointed hats, the earflaps turned up. Some were playing flutes of hollow bones, others banging drums, while others blew copper and bronze horns ten to twelve feet long, whose bell-shaped mouths rested on the ground.

More monks filed out from either side of the entrance, spinning prayer wheels and chanting. They turned inward and broke off when the abbot came out with Marco at his right side. The abbot now wore a short, gold-embroidered cloak and a wide-brimmed, black hat with a pointed, red crown. Round his waist was a blue ceremonial belt and in his left hand a book of sacred texts.

The Drog-pa hillmen had dismounted. Seeing them kneel and touch their foreheads to the ground, the Venetians dismounted and bowed also. It was only as he straightened that Niccolo realized the young man in the off-white robe was Marco.

Seeing his father and uncle, Marco started forward, but stopped himself and turned to thank the Father Abbot, going down on one knee. The abbot smiled and touched Marco's forehead ritually with the end of his blue girdle, then with the sacred book. Marco hurried down the steps.

'We thought we'd lost you, boy,' Niccolo said gruffly. He looked at Marco awkwardly for a moment, then pulled him into his arms and hugged him. Matteo was hugging them both, laughing with relief, and even Jacopo was bobbing and grinning, thankful they were all together again. The hillmen sat on their haunches, applauding, delighted at the reunion of father and son.

'What was all that business with the book?' Matteo chuckled.

'He is the Father Abbot,' Marco said. 'He was giving me his blessing.'

'The blessing of a heathen?' Niccolo muttered uneasily.

'He is a wise and good man,' Marco said seriously. He smiled, as Hafiz and other novices came to them to present kataks, the gauze-like scarves, to Niccolo, Matteo and Jacopo. 'They took care not only of my body, but also nourished my soul,' Marco said. 'Here I have felt closer than ever to God.'

Rustichello laid down his pen and scratched the side of his nose. He had not been writing for some time. 'I think I'll leave that out,' he grunted.

'Why?' Marco asked in surprise.

The Prison Commander, Arnolfo, responded to a glance from Rustichello. 'It might be wise,' he agreed. 'If anyone of Holy Church were to read this tale . . . it might lead to questions. There is no point in giving unnecessary offence.'

'I'll leave in the bit about their weird beliefs, though,' Rustichello suggested. 'They are quaint, and quite amusing. Good stuff.'

Marco stifled a surge of irritation at Rustichello's ignorance. Argument, he had learnt, was useless.

'And what happened then, Messer Polo?' Arnolfo prompted.

Marco stirred. 'Our new guides led us by the shortest passes to the land of Turkestan, where there are mighty cities. Khotan, Lop and Karakorum. Why make a long story of it? We were further delayed by floods and tribal wars, which forced us to take detours. And my father and uncle could not resist trading, so to cross Turkestan took us another seven months. It was in the district of Chinchitalas that I saw the production of the cloth known as salamander.'

'Ah!' Rustichello looked up. 'Is it there that they hunt the fire lizards?'

'No, no,' Marco said. 'It is made from a fossil substance mined in the mountains there.'

'Oh, come now, Messer Polo,' Arnolfo objected. 'Everyone knows that the incombustible cloth is made from the skin of the salamander.'

'Then everyone is wrong,' Marco said simply. 'I have seen how it is made. This was some years later, when I visited the mountains with Zurficar, a close friend of mine, a Turk who was in charge of the mining operations in the province. I saw them take this fossil, which is not unlike wool, pound it and wash it to detach the fibres. It was then spun into thread and woven into cloth, which goes by the name of asbestos. When woven, it is placed in fire for an hour and comes out as white as snow.'

'No lizards?' Giovanni asked, disappointed.

'I never saw any,' Marco told him. 'But the cloth is considered so valuable for protecting precious relics that I brought a bolt of it home to Italy as a present to the Pope from one of the Mongol princes.'

Rustichello looked up from his writing. 'You had now been some two and a half years on your journey. Were you never to reach Cathay?'

'Before the end of that very year,' Marco said, and paused. 'But first we had to pass the terrible, burning desert of the Gobi.'

They left the city of Lop with its fountains and pleasant gardens before dawn, heading east–north–east. For ten days they had rested and prepared themselves for the crossing of what men called the Great Desert. Marco had heard many travellers' tales and had learnt to discount half or more as exaggeration; but nothing, none of the city-dwellers' fearsome descriptions of the wasteland that began beyond their doorstep, had even faintly pictured the sight that met his eyes when the sun rose.

There was no transition. The fertile land simply disappeared. All round him lay an endless desolation – hills, mountains, plains and valleys of rock and shale and sand. There were no beasts or birds, no growing things. Nothing lived in what the Mongols knew as the Gobi.

As seasoned travellers they had started early, so as to be some miles on their way before the break of day. Their mounts were well watered and they themselves were refreshed and fit. Yet in only a few minutes they were bowed down in their saddles by the merciless heat, parched by thirst, their eyes squinting at the reflected dazzle of the quartz in the sand and shale. As the sun rose higher, their torment increased a hundredfold, until, long before noon, Niccolo was forced to call a halt in the sparse shade of an overhanging cliff.

It was the worst time of year for a crossing, they had been told. Only small groups could attempt it. After the long summer, some of the few waterholes between which the track snaked were bound to have dried up and all provisions and water for themselves and their animals would have to be transported. The track they were following had been part of the jade and silk route for over a thousand years, traversing the Gobi at its narrowest extent. Even so, it would take a minimum of twenty-eight days.

At first, Marco was buoyed up by the thought that this was the final barrier before they came to the fabled land of China; but as the days wore on, each bringing more torture than the last, he began to fear that their long journey would end somewhere in this arid emptiness. A scorching wind sucked the moisture from their bodies and lashed them with fine particles of grit. In all creases of skin and where their clothes chafed, weeping sores developed, so that movement was agony. They could not march by night for dread of missing the trail signs, small pyramids of bones topped by human and animal skulls – grisly reminders that to lose the track was certain death. Much of the landscape was featureless and each time they rested or slept, they had to leave markers to remind them of the direction in which they were travelling.

They became used to seeing mirages of buildings and oases, lakes of shimmering water so real it took all their willpower to stop themselves racing desperately towards them. By night they were haunted by sounds that frightened and tantalized them. The wind and the soft slither of cooling sand on the slopes of the dunes became voices which whispered and sobbed and crooned their names. One night, Jacopo wandered away, stumbling off into the dark like a sleepwalker, not hearing when they shouted for him to come back. The voices had hypnotized him and he would have been lost had Marco not caught sight of his dark shape outlined for a second against the sky on top of a far rise. When he finally caught up with him, Jacopo was whimpering, 'Accursed . . . This place is accursed. It is the gate of Hell.'

At the start of the third week, their luck ran out. The main waterhole at which they were hoping to fill the skins for the last stage of the crossing had dried up. Marco and Matteo dug frantically, but any water lay too deep to reach. Even the dessicated thorntree which marked it was bent and dead, the water too deep for its roots. As darkness fell, Marco lay on his back, motionless, gazing up at the sky, an immense vault of indigo filled with countless thousands of stars. He had never felt so insignificant, his life or death of so little matter. He and his companions were merely insects crawling across the endless, wasted plain under the great void. Once he had laughed when his father told him that the nomad Mongols worshipped the desert heavens. Now, he began to understand something of the awe they felt before that vast Unknown.

The next day, as youngest and fittest, it was he who took the lead, fighting off his own weakness, supporting and driving the others on as they lurched and reeled beside their drooping horses, tongues swollen, throats raw and rasping. Yet even he could not beat the burning, pitiless sun as it rose to its zenith. Looking back, he saw that the others were near collapse. Matteo and Jacopo had sunk to their knees. Even his father could not go on and stood swaying, grasping his horse's saddle for support. 'We can't stop!' Marco urged. 'You've said it over and over again!' Niccolo only looked at him dully and shook his head. Somehow, Marco got Jacopo and Matteo to their feet and, holding their saddle girths, they staggered forward, shamming Niccolo into following them.

As Marco gathered together the halters of the pack ponies, he heard a pounding sound of horses in the distance. As he expected, he saw nothing, yet as he moved on, the drumming grew louder and, in spite of himself, he looked again. Off to the side in the heat haze, he began to make out impossibly tall, wavering shapes, black figures like riders on giant horses. He knew it was a hallucination, but the shapes were so menacing that he panted out hoarsely, 'Father! Father! Uncle Matteo!'

To his amazement, real riders were emerging from the haze, shrinking to life-size as they passed out of the refraction of the light; ten or twelve fierce warriors on shaggy ponies, their bearded, savage faces running with sweat and coated with grease. They wore thick felt coats, tanned leather doublets, sheepskins, lacquer breastplates, pointed leather helmets, and were carrying lances and round shields, with short, curved bows and arrowcases slung at their backs. They swept up to the Polos and round them, levelling their lances, some fitting arrows to their bows. Marauders, they were about to butcher the small group and rob them, when suddenly they reined in, as if on command, staring.

Ironically, Marco was half-prepared for death and could not understand when he saw them lower their weapons, leap from their mounts and kneel, bending their foreheads to the dust in reverence. Then he saw that his father had taken the golden passport from his pouch and was holding it up, unsteadily.

Marco had met his first true desert Mongols. The Devil's Horsemen.

They were the advance guard of a tribe which owed allegiance to Caidu Khan, nephew of the Great Khan, Kublai. As soon as they had tended to the Polos' immediate needs, they led them by the quickest way out of the desert to the scrub grassland to the north, where their tribe had found grazing for their cattle. After two days, Marco saw the smoke of cooking fires ahead and then a camp of black felt tents like a small city, with horses and cattle everywhere. The warriors were yelping in high-pitched excited cries, smiling and pointing ahead. Soon other riders came out to meet them and it was as the centre of a whooping, chattering cavalcade that the Polos came to the Chief's *yurt*, a domed tent of black felt standing on an enormous wagon at the heart of the encampment. The Chief's standard of yak-tails was planted in front of it. The flaps of the *yurt* opened and the chief himself, Bektor Khan, strode out to greet them, a vigorous, barbaric man in his late fifties.

After the ritual welcome and offer and acceptance of hospitality, they were ushered into the *yurt*. Marco had expected something backward and primitive; instead he found himself in a dwelling of some splendour. Its felt walls were painted white and hung with gilded, leather shields, ivory bowcases, curved daggers. Between the objects were coloured paintings of horses and riders, hunting scenes and delicate impressions of flowers and trees and bright-plumed birds, which he later realized had been crafted in China. There were carved and inlaid chests, and fine silk hangings screened off the far side of the *yurt* where the Khan's low bed was placed.

As Marco, Niccolo, Matteo and Jacopo took their places, sitting cross-legged with Bektor Khan and his eldest sons and advisers, the whole camp seemed to gather outside, chattering and laughing and peering in, until Bektor sent his personal guards to enforce a more respectful silence. They sat in a circle, with his wives and concubines and their children in a wider circle round them. Servants brought sweetmeats and poured cups of whitish liquid for the guests and elders. 'In the name of the Kha Khan, in the name of his nephew, Caidu, and in my name, you are welcome to my *yurt*,' Bektor intoned. Carefully emptying out a few drops of the white liquid on to the floor as a libation to the household god, Natigai, he drank to his guests.

About to drink in turn, Marco hesitated when Matteo whispered, 'Careful! That's *koumiss*. It's strong.'

'What's it made of?' Marco asked.

'Fermented mares' milk.'

Marco grimaced as he drank, but found it not unpleasant, like a sharp white wine. He was surprised to see his father take a necklace of rubies set in heavy gold from the bag beside him and present it to Bektor. 'We are honoured and grateful, Bektor Khan,' Niccolo said. 'And beg you to accept this trifling token of our thanks.'

There was a gasp of appreciation and the women craned forward as Bektor held the necklace up to the light, delighting in the rich, red sparkle of the jewels. 'You honour my poor hospitality with too great a gift, Polo Noyon,' he murmured. His eyes shifted to Niccolo. 'Where are you journeying to?'

'To Shangtu, the Summer Palace of the Great Khan, Kublai.'

'That is far.'

'But not as far as we have already travelled,' Niccolo said, and added pointedly, 'As his ambassadors.'

Bektor smiled and nodded. 'I am thricefold honoured. When you are rested, I shall give you an escort. I beg you to be my guests until then.'

Marco had heard that, unlike the Mohammedans, the Mongol women were free and equal with their men in daily life, not veiled and covered. Even so, he was surprised by their boldness. The younger ones near him kept smiling to him, giggling and whispering to each other. They wore loose robes of sheer silk, their hair long, partly braided and hung with golden trinkets and jewels. Some were very pretty, obviously from a variety of races, an unexpected number straight-nosed and fair-haired. Circassian mothers, Matteo explained.

'Who are they?' Marco whispered. 'The Khan's daughters?'

'His younger wives and concubines, more likely,' Matteo chuckled. 'They think you're very funny.'

'Why?' Marco asked indignantly.

'Because you have no beard. They think you look like a woman – or a Chinese.'

This was confirmed when Marco glanced at them and

they nudged one another, squealing with laughter. Bektor Khan was annoyed at being interrupted and scowled, but when he heard what they were whispering, he looked at Marco, stroked his own wild beard and chuckled. The other Mongols began to smile. One young woman, fair-skinned with wide blue eyes and a mischievous smile, reached round and stroked Marco's smooth cheek. He jerked his head away and the Mongols shouted with laughter, slapping their thighs.

When the ritual greetings were over, Bektor and some of his elders and guards showed the Polos round his camp. Jacopo stuck very close to them, frightened by the Mongols, who crowded round them, peering at the strangers and trying to touch them. 'Today we shall have an *ikhudur*,' Bektor told them, 'a great feast of rejoicing.'

Marco was hugely flattered, until Matteo told him that it was not entirely for them. The Mongols seized any excuse to give a party. There was only one thing they enjoyed more. Marco smiled, thinking he understood. 'You're wrong,' Matteo said drily. 'The one thing they enjoy more is killing. We're lucky,' Matteo went on. 'Bektor's overlord, Caidu, is always quarrelling with his uncle, Kublai. At the moment, they're at peace – otherwise, they might have sent our heads on to Shangtu, while the rest of us stayed here.'

Although shaken by his uncle's words, Marco was still fascinated by the camp, with its noisy enthusiasm for the *ikhudor*. Whole sheep, lambs and goats had been butchered and flayed for roasting over open fires, with children to turn the spits. Women were making dough, slapping the mixture down into flat, round loaves, while they laughed and sang. Children ran playing among them and dozens of dogs. Men were laughing, some playing flutes and drums, shouting greetings and questions, clamouring round them inquisitively. Their life seemed happy, noisy and carefree.

Suddenly there was a shout and the crowds parted. Marco saw a group of youths galloping towards them, yelling and brandishing their lances. For a moment or two, it was as if they were to be cut down, but at the last second the youths reined in and their mounts reared, pawing the air. They whirled round and dashed away into the space that had been cleared for them.

To the cheers of the whole camp, the youths raced back, crossing and recrossing in front of Bektor Khan and the Polos, standing on their horses' backs, swinging over their heads or from side to side, their feet tapping the ground and up again in a dazzling display of horsemanship. As two of them galloped towards each other, Bektor snatched the sheepskin hat from the guard nearest him and threw it up into the air. The lances of the two riders skewered it in mid-air.

The feast that night was like nothing Marco had ever experienced. He had no idea that human beings could drink and eat so much. From where he sat, outside the main *yurt* with his father and uncle among Bektor and his elders, the whole camp sounded like one huge revel. Enormous platters of roast lamb, beef, rice and fruit were continually refilled in front of them. The wives and concubines sat in a chattering group behind the men, and slavegirls brought an unending supply of *koumiss*. Girls with bright, swinging skirts and clinking beads danced before them, while behind the dancers, jugglers leapt and tumbled, spinning coloured dishes, balls, knives and clubs. All round them drunken Mongol warriors danced clumsily, stamping their feet, drinking and laughing, and the camp itself was an uproar of music, laughter, singing and occasional angry shouts.

Marco was wide-eyed, gazing at everything. He sat on the Khan's left, with Niccolo and Matteo in the more honoured position on his right. He could see Jacopo farther round the semicircle, frightened but stuffing himself with food and almost passing out drunk.

There were yells of approval and expectation as the girls and jugglers made way for the Shamans, the priest-conjurers in their multicoloured cloaks. Their feats of magic were as good as any Marco had ever seen, some simple, but others defying explanation, from live lizards and doves produced from empty wine cups, to swirling banners and streamers of bright silk that appeared out of thin air and danced to the play of the Shamans' fingers. At last, the Chief Shaman strode impressively out of the dark shadows by the *yurt* and bowed to the Khan. Over his robes he wore a cloak embroidered with magic symbols and a high, pointed hat with earflaps like wings. His long-fingered hands passed over the fire as he muttered the words of an incantation and the semicircle grew still and silent, watching.

The movements of his hands were almost too quick to follow, but as the crowd gasped at the leaping, changing colours his hands produced in the fire, Marco was sure he had seen them flash to the pouches at his belt. Just as he was laughing at the simplicity of it, he was startled like the others when the Shaman took a handful of powder from one of the pouches and threw it on the fire. There was a muffled explosion and a yellow smoke cloud sprang up. An exploding powder? Marco wondered. But then again, like the others, his attention became riveted on the smoke cloud. Within it a shape was appearing, a naked girl who danced slowly and sinuously, swaying her heavy haunches, her arms writhing before her full breasts. The Mongols were open-mouthed and Bektor's hand was half reaching out towards the dancer, when she began to whirl and her voluptuous body became more and more transparent and faded with the last tendrils of yellow smoke. Even as Bektor shouted for her to be summoned back, the Shaman threw again, this time producing a green cloud out of which came a snarl that brought instant silence. In the green mist a shape was forming, lithe-bodied, massive-headed, a savage lion that crouched, its hideous fangs bared in anger, and suddenly sprang straight for them. The women screamed. Some of the men grabbed their weapons and others fell backwards in fright. But the lion had disappeared, and as they all looked about in astonishment, Bektor's laugh was taken up and the whole group shouted with glee like children.

The Shaman's third throw produced a red cloud and in it Bektor Khan himself appeared, seated in full armour on his horse. At each apparition, Marco had cried aloud in wonder like the superstitious Mongols; now he too cheered at the tribute to his host. Bektor smiled to him, raising his silver cup, but Marco's was empty. The young concubine with the blue eyes and mischievous smile took the jug from one of the slavegirls and refilled it for him. As Marco looked up in thanks, she reached down again with a giggle and stroked his smooth cheek. The Mongols spluttered with laughter as she slipped back again to the other women, doubled over with amusement.

'How old are you?' Bektor asked Marco.

'Twenty-one, Signore,' Marco told him.

Bektor's eyebrows rose. 'How many wives and sons do you have?'

Marco was surprised. 'None , Signore. I'm not married.'

'Not?' Bektor echoed in astonishment. 'By the time I was twenty-one, I had five wives and seven sons.'

'Things are different in our country,' Niccolo said, seeing Marco's embarrassment.

'But surely not *that* different?' Bektor chuckled. The Mongols laughed.

The laughter was cut short by a shout and cheering. Two of the younger men had risen from the end of the semicircle and were throwing off their sheepskin coats. The Mongols applauded as they moved forward, pushing the dancing girls aside. One of the two, a tall, handsome young nobleman, turned and saluted the Khan, raising both arms high.

'My sixth son, Kasar,' Bektor explained, 'our champion wrestler. He is training to fight the Princess.'

'I'm sorry. Did you say, to fight the *Princess*?'

'Princess Aigiaruc, daughter of Caidu Khan,' Bektor nodded. 'They have seen each other and want to marry.'

He grunted with approval and applauded. Kasar had

just thrown the first challenger and was already making short work of a second.

'But why would he want to wrestle with her?' Marco asked.

Bektor was too intent on the contest to answer, but the man on Marco's right said, 'Some years ago, her father ordered her to take a husband against her will. To keep her independence, she swore an oath only to marry a man who could beat her in combat.'

'Surely that should be easy?' Marco smiled.

The man snorted. 'She has beaten the champions of six tribes already. She is as strong and as tall as a man, and as cunning as a fox. But she wishes a husband, and Kasar is the one. Every day, our young men help him to train.'

The young warrior wrestling with Kasar was desperate, clawing at his face. Kasar shook his head free, snarling, whirled his opponent round and smashed him to the ground. The warrior had angered him and when he tried to get up, Kasar kicked him in the ribs and face, knocking him down again. He stood raging and dangerous, glaring round the circle.

Marco looked to either side, but for the moment no one was rising to challenge the angry champion. The *koumiss* had gone to Marco's head and he had been stung by the jokes made about his apparent lack of manliness. Scarcely aware of what he was doing, he rose unsteadily and threw off his sheepskin coat. There were gasps, followed by some applause, as he moved forward.

'Marco!' Niccolo exclaimed warningly, and started up. But Matteo caught his arm, holding him down. The boy could not back down now.

Kasar turned like a young, maddened bull as Marco came towards him. About to rush forward, he stopped, puzzled. Marco had paused to bow to him. The Mongols laughed, but Kasar was no fool, and as his head cleared, he decided to treat the young stranger with caution. Once, twice, they circled each other, Kasar looking for the moment to attack, his powerful shoulder muscles knotting, his heavy hands crooked. Gazing back at the prince's killer's eyes, Marco began to feel that he had made a terrible mistake. Then all at once, Kasar leapt in, kicking viciously. Marco twisted to the side, but the Mongol's thick boot crashed into his hip, hurting him and sending him sprawling to his hands and knees. There was a gasp of alarm, and some cheering.

Almost immediately, Marco was on his feet again, just avoiding the lunging swoop of Kasar's arms. Again Kasar rushed in, aiming another kick, but this time Marco was ready and feinted to the side, grabbed Kasar's foot and twisted with all his strength. The twist and the Mongol's own momentum sent Kasar sprawling flat on his face. There was an even louder gasp of sheer astonishment, and Bektor shook his fist in fury.

The women screamed. Kasar had jumped to his feet again and sprang at Marco. They slammed into each other and began to struggle, their arms locked round each other's body, each trying to force his opponent round and back, off balance. Kasar released one hand and grabbed Marco's hair. In return, Marco jabbed his elbow up under Kasar's throat and, straining, managed to bend his head back. For all his youth and slimness, he was surprisingly strong and the Mongols grunted in amazement.

Kasar was coughing and choking, but his hold tightened until Marco felt that his back would break. It could not last; Marco knew he would have to find some way to break the bear hug, or he was finished. His feet fought with Kasar's in an attempt to trip him, but before he could even get a purchase, it was over. He had forgotten Kasar's favourite trick; as his feet shifted, he found himself swung round. With his right thigh locked round Marco's, Kasar heaved and Marco flew over, crashing to his back on the ground.

There was the briefest pause and the Mongols began to shout and cheer, crowding in. Marco was dazed and looked up to see Kasar coming towards him. He struggled for breath to defend himself, but Kasar was smiling and reached out both hands to help Marco to his knees. The last young warrior to be defeated was standing behind Marco and grabbed him by both ears, pulling outwards. As Marco's mouth opened in pain and surprise, Kasar took a jug from one of the slavegirls and upended the *koumiss* into Marco's open mouth, a great Mongol gesture of admiration and friendship.

Choking and spluttering, Marco was helped to his feet. Kasar hugged him, laughing and patting his back, and with his arm still round him, led him to Bektor Khan. Bektor had risen with Niccolo and Matteo and they smiled and applauded. 'Well done, son of Polo Noyon!' Bektor shouted. 'Well done!'

'Where did you learn to wrestle like that?' Niccolo asked, somewhat taken aback.

'At school, and the back alleys of Venice,' Marco panted. He was a little fuddled and chuckled. Niccolo and Matteo laughed with him and Bektor seized him in his arms, kissing him.

Bektor could see that Marco was not quite steady. 'The young man is tired after his journey,' he decided. 'It's time he slept.'

'High time,' Niccolo agreed.

Bektor clapped his hands. 'Nazura!' he called. Several of the younger wives and concubines rose with the Khan's oldest wife, smiled and left. Bektor raised his cup and poured some of its contents on to the ground. 'To the Spirits of the Eternal Blue Sky!' He drank from his cup, presented it to Marco who smiled and drank, then passed it to Kasar. There was a growl of approval and Kasar drained off what was left, hurling the cup away into the dark.

Beyond them, Jacopo lay sprawled forward, dead drunk and asleep, his cheek resting on a platter of rice and apricots.

The sounds of revelry in the camp went on without stop. For all his tiredness, Marco would willingly have kept on, but as Kasar and some of the young warriors led him to his guest *yurt*, he felt the weariness of the last days creep over him. Torches were burning outside the *yurt* and the flaps were closed.

In front of it, the group stopped. The Mongols were joking and friendly, patting Marco's back. Kasar ruffled his hair and stroked his smooth cheek. The others laughed, but Marco no longer resented it. He turned to his father and uncle who were with them, to say good night. They were surprisingly serious. 'Careful, Marco,' Matteo warned.

'Why?' Marco smiled. 'What do you mean?'

'The Khan has taken a liking to you. He has sent one of his women to share your *yurt*.'

As Marco stared at him, the flaps of the tent opened and they saw the oldest of Bektor's wives smiling and beckoning to him. She was not only the oldest, but the ugliest, bent-backed and half toothless. The Mongols were chuckling, tugging at Marco and urging him towards the *yurt*. Marco glanced at his father, who could not look at him. 'Get along, boy,' Niccolo said gruffly.

Marco was thrust towards the opening of the black tent. His sheepskin was thrown after him. Chuckling and joking among themselves, the Mongols were already leaving, taking Niccolo and Matteo with them. 'Good night! Sleep well! Good night!' they shouted. Marco took a deep breath to muster his courage and went inside.

Through the gauzy sheen of a gold silk awning, he could just make out someone sitting in the bed, waiting. He moved forward and drew back the curtain.

It was Nazura, the beautiful young blue-eyed concubine. Her hair had been combed out of its plaits and rippled in honey-coloured waves to her naked shoulders. As she sat up higher, the silken coverlet slipped from the swell of her round, high breasts, uncovering them. She was smiling, and bit her lip softly in her anxiety to please him. Her skin was as pure and white as milk.

Marco's tiredness had vanished. He let the sheepskin

drop to the floor beside him and smiled. Nazura smiled back and patted the bed beside her.

The next day, long single notes from the yak's horns of the guards on outlying picket notified the camp of the arrival of Caidu Khan. As the people of the tribe ran to form an avenue of honour, Bektor, with Kasar and his other sons, his wives and elders and the Chief Shaman, all dressed in their finest clothes, began to assemble outside the main *yurt*. Niccolo and Matteo were with Bektor, Marco standing next to Kasar.

A column of heavily armed horsemen was riding towards them. In front rode officials and handmaidens, serving the Lord Caidu and his daugher, who rode at their head, preceded by a warrior with Caidu's standard of seven black yak-tails. Caidu Khan was tall and hawk-faced, a brilliant Mongol leader and general, who had never accepted civilization. His cloak of marten skins was thrown back at the shoulders to show his gold-lacquered breastplate. One hand rested on the jewelled pommel of his long-bladed sword. By his side, no less proud and barbaric, rode the Princess Aigiaruc. She was strikingly beautiful, wearing a long white dress of fine felt. Her hair, from a South Russian mother, was red gold, long at the back, braided at the sides with pearls and gold coins, built out over the ears to support her headdress, a cone of birchbark covered with rare silk. She wore soft, white leather boots, a blue girdle around her waist and another over her breasts.

While all Bektor's tribe was shouting their welcome, Marco turned to his new-found friend Kasar. 'That's Princess Aigiaruc? The one you have to beat to marry?'

'If the Spirits of the Eternal Blue Sky will it,' Kasar muttered. He raised his eyes to the sky. 'May it be their wish . . .'

Caidu and Aigiaruc halted in the open space in front of the *yurt* and guards ran to hold their horses' heads as they dismounted. Marco could see that the princess was tall –

nearly as tall as Kasar and her father – and strongly made in spite of her beauty. For all her apparent aloofness, he caught the glance that she gave Kasar – only a fleeting look, but enough for him to tell that she was as much in love as his friend. As for her father, Caidu, after Kublai Khan the greatest of all Mongols, he seemed unyieldingly fierce and distant; yet just for a moment he revealed another side. At the corral a small boy led a little white foal towards him and bowed, presenting it. For a few heartbeats, Caidu's face softened as he accepted the gift, touching the heads of the boy and the foal in turn with a gesture of tenderness. Then he was his distant self again.

After another sumptuous meal in the main *yurt* Marco became aware of an expectant stillness in the crowd around him. A great drum was being beaten slowly and rhythmically and Caidu and Bektor were rising.

An oval sandy space had been cleared near the corral, marked out by lances and banners. At one narrower end was Bektor's standard, at the other was Caidu's. Kasar was already standing in front of his father's banner, with some of his warrior brothers massaging and greasing him. He wore only leather breeches and his broad chest was bare, marked by the scar of an old battle wound running diagonally across his ribs. He was a superb physical specimen, and as the Khans and their entourage took their places round the oval, Marco saw Caidu's eyes pass over him approvingly. Plainly this was the man he would welcome as his son-in-law.

The Khans sat at the middle of one of the longer sides with the Shamans and chief warriors opposite them. The men of the tribe and Caidu's escort squatted round the wrestling space with the women and children behind them The excitement was intense and grew to a crescendo as Aigiaruc and her handmaidens came to the far end and the princess took her place under her father's standard. Her hair had been braided and coiled round and behind her head. She was enveloped in a long cloak of sables and stood motionless and impassive, gazing at Kasar, as the

Chief Shaman offered up a prayer to the Spirits for a just and true verdict, according to the wishes of the gods and in keeping with her vow.

Marco was watching Kasar when he saw heads turning and looked round, joining in the gasp of admiration. Two of Aigiaruc's maidens had unclipped her cloak and drew it off. Beneath it she wore tight leather breeches like Kasar, moulding her lithe figure. Her waist was held tight by a silver belt. Above it, the surge of her breasts was restrained by a bodice of oiled leather, fastened at the back by thongs. Like Kasar she was barefoot. One of her handmaidens was offering her a pot of scented unguent. She dipped her fingers in it and greased her arms and neck. Not once did she or Kasar take their eyes from each other.

Caidu was carrying an ivory rod tipped with the golden miniature of a ram. He raised it and all chatter ceased. Only the slow beat of the drum was heard. Kasar's brothers and Aigiaruc's handmaidens moved out of the oval. The two of them still gazed at each other. Caidu's baton fell. The sound of the drum ceased. There was absolute silence.

Marco held his breath as Kasar and Aigiaruc advanced slowly towards each other. They were both very wary, both magnificently fit, assessing each other's stance and balance as they feinted and circled. Suddenly, Aigiaruc darted in towards Kasar's right side. He clutched for her, as she meant him to, for she stopped just short of him, caught him round the waist and hurled him down on his back.

There was a gasp of disappointment and some subdued applause.

'She's won!' Marco blurted, shocked.

'No, no, no,' Niccolo told him. 'In this contest it's the first to score three falls who wins.'

Kasar had risen quickly, flexing his shoulders to shake the sand off his back. He was clearly disappointed, but much more determined now and cautious. Aigiaruc had stepped out of range. She smiled to him, encouragingly, then became serious as they circled again.

Again the princess feinted, but Kasar made only the slightest reaction to it. He was not to be tricked again. Instead, he feinted twice himself, and the third time, when she reached out, seized her by the upper arms. They spun each other round, each hoping to knock the other off balance. Relying on his strength, Kasar stopped all at once and crushed Aigiaruc against him, locking his arms round the small of her waist. Fighting like a wildcat, she broke her arms out from between them and grabbed him in the same hold. Legs braced, they strained against each other, each trying to bend the other back or to the side. Marco was convinced that Kasar must prevail, but Aigiaruc was amazingly strong and did not yield an inch.

All the watchers were riveted as the silent struggle went on. Kasar and Aigiaruc were crushed together, gazing into each other's eyes, so close they could kiss. Sweat ran down their faces and their lips were snarling with effort. Suddenly, Aigiaruc clawed with one hand for Kasar's eyes. He ducked his head down and butted forward into her face. She gasped and their legs squirmed desperately, heels hooking as they tried to trip each other up, turning and panting. They both fell at last, rolling over and over, still clasped together.

Kasar broke the hold first and leaped up. Aigiaruc was after him, quick as a cobra, but he crouched, catching her round the thighs, and smashed her down on her back.

The crowd burst into a frenzy of cheering and applause. Bektor was elated and relieved to see Caidu also smiling.

'Kasar! Kasar!' Marco called, and others took up the cry.

Aigiaruc had propped herself up. She was astonished at being thrown, but smiled to Kasar, lovingly and gratefully. He was the one who would release her from her vow. He moved in, holding out a hand to help her to rise. Just as she reached for it, he thought better of it and jumped back.

Aigiaruc smiled approval. He was right to be cautious. The crowd laughed.

She rose by herself and paused, wincing with pain, holding her side and bending over slightly. Kasar stepped towards her, concerned. In a flash, her right leg shot between his. She was sideways to him and with a simple heave, she threw him down on his back.

This time, the crowd was so excited that they applauded her skill and cunning as wildly as if it had been Kasar who won the point.

'Two to her, one to Kasar,' Matteo murmured. 'He'll have to catch up this time.'

'He will,' Marco said confidently.

Caidu and Bektor were tense, leaning forward. Everything depended on the next throw.

Aigiaruc had stood back, allowing Kasar to rise. She was panting, her breasts heaving above the loosened neck of her leather bodice as she sucked in air. She watched Kasar carefully, tucking up some coils of her hair which had come loose. He rose more slowly, panting also, watching her with the greatest admiration and wariness as she began to circle again. He turned, keeping her in sight, beckoning to her to risk another trial of strength. To please him, she darted in. Their hands slipped and both lost their grips on each other's greased arms. They broke apart.

Again the princess darted in, but this time Kasar caught her by the neck and elbow. He forced her back, bending her like a bow; she stamped and swung her legs, finding a footing just in time to resist him. Her arms were clamped round his waist, her finely muscled legs braced, and he could not break her hold.

Marco was urging Kasar silently on when he saw the Mongol adjust his balance slightly. As Marco suspected, Kasar was about to try his favourite trick, knotting his thigh round Aigiaruc's. There was a sigh of expectation from the watchers. Kasar heaved to throw her over his hip, but her arms were tightly locked and she scarcely moved. As he strained to swing her, she gazed up at him, begging him with her eyes to throw her. He tried with his utmost power, but could not.

She was almost in despair, desperate to lose. But she had nearly waited too long, helped him too much. With an abrupt, raucously savage scream, she shifted her balance, applied the counter-throw and whirled Kasar over her hip. He crashed to the ground and lay half-stunned.

A cheer began, but died away instantly. Marco and the others were staring, unable to believe what had happened.

Kasar was trying to sit up. He gazed at Aigiaruc, lost. She was looking down at him, her eyes filling with tears. The man she loved had become just another beaten opponent; she could never see him again. She stared for a long moment at her father, Caidu, then moved slowly to the standard of the yak-tails. Her handmaidens hung the sable cloak round her shoulders. The crowd parted silently and she stepped out of the oval, walking disconsolately away.

Kasar lay like a broken man. His brothers hurried to help him up.

Marco was disturbed and incredulous. 'But why?' he muttered. 'She loved him. She could have let him win.'

Around them, the Mongols were all weeping. Matteo looked from Kasar, who stood with his head lowered, to Princess Aigiaruc, who was walking slowly away alone. 'She could not break her vow by cheating,' he sighed. 'And I presume, at the last moment, she could not betray her own skill.' He smiled wryly. 'And there's a strange object lesson for you, Marco – in the role and nature of women . . .'

Sometime later, Marco walked off by himself, still saddened by the despair of the two lovers. He needed a little time by himself to think over all that had taken place. Kasar had ridden off with only one companion, to be alone in the wilderness of the steppe until Aigiaruc had left his father's encampment. The princess, meanwhile, was enclosed and solitary in the main *yurt*.

In front of Marco in the corral was a string of pure white horses which had fascinated him earlier.

'You have an eye for horseflesh, Master Polo?' a voice said, and he turned to see Caidu Khan and Bektor coming towards him with his father and uncle.

Marco bowed, startled. '. . . I have learnt a little of them, my lord.'

Caidu nodded and indicated the white horses. 'You seem to admire these. Why is that? Because they are . . . more beautiful?'

From the worried glance between Niccolo and Matteo, Marco could tell that Caidu was somehow testing him. 'To compare them to other horses would be . . . like comparing the sun to a candle, my lord. They are not only beautiful. With their deep chests and strong legs, they must be as fast as the wind – and able to race from sunrise to sunset without faltering.'

There was a hum of appreciation from the listening Mongols. Caidu nodded, pleased. 'I told you he is more intelligent than he looks,' Bektor chuckled.

'He has learnt a little, as he says,' Caidu agreed. He stroked the muzzle of the horse Marco was fondling. 'These are very special – only sons of the royal house are permitted to ride them. They are descended from the battle steed of my grandfather, the great Genghis – the symbol of everything we are and have been. We Mongols are nothing without our horses. They gave us the Gobi and the power to conquer the world – and the power to keep it ours.' There was a murmur of agreement. He looked directly at Marco. 'So, on your journey to China, you have seen something of our ways. What will you tell of them?' Marco hesitated. 'You must not be afraid to say what you think.'

'That they are . . . hard, Caidu Khan,' Marco said. The Khan was drawing his sword from its sheath and testing its point and blade. Marco's eyes were on it as he added, prudently. 'But probably right for your people.'

Caidu smiled faintly. 'In other words, you see us as savages.' He released the point of his sword and this time it flew up, quivering a fraction of an inch from Marco's throat. Marco knew better than to flinch. Caidu smiled again more broadly and gave up the brandishing of the sword as childish, becoming serious. 'Yes, we are savages. Wanderers, nomads. We live in the desert, scrub and steppe lands, wherever there is grazing ground for our herds and horses. They dictate where and how we live. Our roots are in the wind, the mighty Genghis used to say.' His voice rose. 'Something my great uncle, Kublai Khan, seems to have forgotten. He wants us to learn nice manners, to live an easier life, in walled cities, to abandon the desert! No!'

At the growl of approval which greeted his words, Marco realized that Caidu was not speaking entirely for him. The Khan's eyes bored into his and Marco knew that he was being willed to act as an unofficial messenger. The words were meant to reach China. 'A true Mongol will never leave his horse and his *yurt*,' Caidu said deliberately. 'That is something else Kublai has forgotten. Do not be afraid to tell him I said so. He has heard it from me often enough. But he thinks that one needs a throne to rule – and a throne needs a solid, stable base. Well, I tell you, Master Polo, we conquered the world on horseback, and it is on horseback that we must rule it.' He smiled again at the rumble of agreement from Bektor and his elders and slid the sword back into its sheath. Marco bowed, tacitly accepting the embassy, although he wondered how he would ever have the chance to deliver it.

Caidu Khan sent a courier to Shangtu with news of the Polos' arrival and gave them an escort of his warriors to the fortress town of Suchow on the borders of North China. There, the escort set them on the post road to the summer capital and left them.

No further guides were needed. The post road was straight and well paved and was the first and most stupendous of the wonders which Marco now began to see. One to each province, the post roads stretched throughout the thousands of miles of the entire empire, with a posting station every twenty-five or thirty miles, each with four hundred horses in constant readiness. Imperial couriers were expected to cover a minimum of two hundred miles a day, and in an emergency, three hundred. Approaching each posting station they blew a horn in warning and a fresh horse was saddled and ready for their arrival, so that they only needed seconds to change mounts. In addition to the mounted couriers, there were the runners of the Khan's postal service. Between each posting station were others at every three miles. The unmounted couriers ran at full speed, never more than three miles, the jingling of the bells they wore at their waist alerting the couriers ahead so that messages and packages were carried on in relays. The service went on throughout the night by torchlight; in that way, a journey of ten or more days was reduced to under twenty-four hours. The Khan's law was absolute on those roads and it was said that a virgin could leave the shores of the Black Sea and, by keeping to the highway, arrive with both the gold and herself intact in China.

One thing puzzled Marco. Caidu's last words had been that the Great Khan would no doubt send them whatever escort he thought they deserved. When he asked his father what had been meant by that, Niccolo looked worried. 'Have you forgotten the reason the great Kublai sent your uncle and myself home to Europe?' he said.

'We have the Pope's letter and gifts, and the sacred oil,' Marco said. 'They're still in my pack.'

'And may seem little enough to bring back – after seven years' absence,' Niccolo grunted. 'If he thinks we have failed him, instead of officials to greet us, he may send soldiers to take us for punishment. Well . . . the summer capital is still forty days from here.'

'Niccolo!' Matteo hissed urgently. They saw he was pointing ahead at a troop of Mongol cavalry which had appeared round a bend in the road, cantering towards them. They were very warlike, but disciplined and in splendid uniforms, with spiked helmets, shining breast-plates and fluttering pennons.

The Polos stopped and gave the halters of the pack ponies to Jacopo, then rode forward slightly with Marco and stopped again, glancing at each other anxiously.

The cavalry troop approached swiftly and jingled to a halt.

The leading officer raised his hand. 'You are Niccolo and Matteo Polo?' he enquired.

Niccolo and Matteo had opened their pouches. For answer, they took out their golden tablet and held it up.

The officer gestured and the first pairs of troopers moved out and separated to line the road between the officer and the Polos. Behind them, and unseen until now, were three Chinese officials in summer travelling robes, with high caps of office. They rode forward and the chief official made a gesture of welcome. 'In the name of Kublai, the Kha Khan, the Mighty Ruler, Emperor of All Men,' he said, 'greetings to his Ambassadors, for whose lives and wellbeing he had almost despaired.'

The officer bowed in the saddle to Niccolo and Matteo and the pennons of the troop dipped in salute. 'We are sent to escort you to Shangtu, my lords.'

After all the stress and dangers of the long journey, the last few weeks passed like a dream for Marco. Travelling at ease with their escort, resting at the most sumptuous of the posting stations, with everyone showing them the utmost courtesy and deference, attending immediately to all their wants – life seemed to have taken on a fairytale quality.

At length, Marco saw before them a city like none he had ever seen. It was so vast, it seemed to overflow the plain in which it was set.

Shangtu.

It was surrounded by mighty defensive walls in which

were six huge gates, each one a fortress. Superbly armed Mongol soldiers on guard saluted as the ambassadors and their escort approached. Other Chinese officials in wide-sleeved silk robes were waiting to lead them to their quarters in the imperial palace.

The broad, bustling streets bewildered Marco and Jacopo with their teeming life and colour, all so exotically different from anything they had ever known. Horses, donkeys, camels, closed palanquins and carriages were part of the constantly moving stream. Butchers' shops, bakers' shops, merchants of cloth and spices and curiosities, vendors of sweetmeats and smoked fish, sellers of birds and ivories, restaurants and gaming rooms, temples and pagodas, and courtyards filled with sheep and goats: it was the profusion of everything which struck Marco, particularly the variety of the dress. A different shape and cut denoted each social class, from the loose tunics and calf-length cotton trousers of the poor, to the richly embroidered robes and elaborate headgear of the officials and nobles.

The palace to which they were taken spread over half the city, a huge edifice of marble and ornamental stone, its halls, chambers and roofs all gilded and its interior decoration a wonder of rich artistry and design. At one end the palace touched the city wall and from there another wall ran, enclosing sixteen miles of lush parkland, watered with streams and lakes and stocked with game. The huge park's only entrance was from the palace, and at its centre, by a grove of trees, the Khan had a second palace built entirely of bamboo canes, its gilded pillars with dragon capitals supporting a pavilion roof of split cane and waterproof silk. The whole, enormous collapsible pleasure pavilion – for that is what it was – was braced by hundreds of silken stayropes and could be taken to pieces and re-erected wherever the Great Khan wished. In Shangtu, Kublai stayed for the three hottest months, June, July and August, to escape the humid heat further south and to pursue his favourite recreation, hunting.

Marco was still marvelling when they were led to a marble bath house, where their travelling clothes were taken away to be washed and they sank up to their chests in steaming vats of hot water. Attendants wearing loin-cloths waited on them as they luxuriated, steaming out the aches and strains of the journey.

'I still can't believe it!' Marco exclaimed. 'This is all one palace?'

'It is,' Matteo told him. 'But it's only his Summer Palace.'

He and Niccolo laughed as Marco stared at them. 'I'd never really imagined it. Not even Bartolomeo could have imagined it!'

'Why did you think we were so eager to get back?' Matteo chuckled.

'I don't think he ever fully believed us,' Niccolo said quietly.

Marco was apologetic. 'Who could have believed? Everything, I mean. The priests all swore that if we went as far as this, we'd fall off the edge of the world.'

'Well . . . maybe if we went a little farther, we would,' Matteo said. 'Who knows?'

Marco was craning his head over the side of the bath, watching one of the attendants, who was shovelling something into the boiler. 'What's he doing?'

'Heating the water,' Niccolo said.

Marco held out his hand and the attendant put something hard and black into it. 'With this? But it's a stone . . .'

'It's a special stone known as coal.'

Marco turned the lump of polished coal over and over. 'Where does it come from?'

'They dig it out of the hills,' Matteo shrugged.

'Burning stone . . .' Marco marvelled. 'They'll *never* believe this!'

'Yes, they will,' Jacopo grinned. He opened his coat to show that he had hidden three shining pieces of the magic stone in his pocket.

From the bath house they were conducted to the quarters

allotted to them, and once again Marco marvelled at their cleanliness and tasteful elegance, at the inlaid floor, silk screens and carved jade ornaments, the fine porcelain and the sliding doors of waxed paper which opened on to a small, enclosed garden with a little fountain.

As he laid out on an ebony table the rolled and sealed scroll of Pope Gregory's letter with the box containing the precious ampoule of sacred oil and another box of ivory, carved with Christian scenes and topped by a golden dove, Chinese attendants entered, silent in their cloth-soled shoes. Marco found an attractive girl kneeling beside him, presenting him with a tiny bowl of tea on a lacquered tray, but when he smiled his thanks to her, she did not respond. He sipped the tea cautiously. 'Mmm,' he murmured. 'This is better than the tea in Pamir. I prefer it without salt.'

'No doubt,' Matteo chuckled.

Here, helped by the attendants, the travellers changed into their best remaining clothes. Marco was quite simply dressed in doublet and hose, but his father and uncle had all the appearance of Venetian grandees. The impression of grandeur was increased when the attendants brought Niccolo and Matteo Chinese cloaks of blue silk, exquisitely embroidered in silver with motifs of flowers. Others bowed and presented them with broad, silver-gilt linked belts, delicately chased, which were fastened round their waists, outside the cloaks.

'They're splendid,' admired Marco.

'They're badges of our rank at court,' Niccolo explained.

The attendants were dismissed, bowed, then left quickly in silence. 'Don't they ever say anything?' asked Marco.

'They're forbidden to,' Matteo said, 'unless they're asked a direct question. It would be a good rule for you to follow.'

'We are now going to the Great Khan, to report on our mission,' Niccolo said. 'You will come with us, Marco. Remember, he is the most powerful man on earth. Do exactly as we do. And stay well back. I'll present you when the moment is right.'

The outer court of the Imperial Palace was a sumptuous area, used both as a meeting place for courtiers and an anteroom for petitioners. Many nobles and high officials were waiting, some in Mongol dress, other in the costumes of Persia, India and Arabia. There were Buddhist monks with saffron robes and the distinctive shaven heads. Mongol Shamans, and black-robed Nestorian Christians, the strange sect from the Asiatic steppes, also waited. Marco observed that none of the religious groups stood anywhere near each other, but that all looked with interest when the Polos entered. Some were pleased to see them and bowed in greeting. Others, including the religious groups, were less pleased. The Shamans scowled and muttered.

On their way to the golden, emerald-studded door to the inner court, Niccolo and Matteo paused to bow and exchange words with old friends, and Marco had time to glance around. Two people caught his attention; a young Mongol prince perhaps ten years old, with a bright and lively face, standing with an emaciated older man, bald and gaunt, wearing the long red robe of a Tibetan Lama. Marco recognized the robe with pleasure. '*U la lo ho*,' he said, smiling.

'Where did you learn that?' snapped the man.

'God is victorious. The Lamas of Pamir taught it me,' Marco faltered, thrown by the Lama's cold gaze. Hastily he rejoined his father and uncle, who were angry with him for speaking out of turn. 'Who is that man?' he asked.

'Phags-pa is his name,' his father hissed sharply, 'the tutor of Prince Timur and Keeper of the Records – and, of everyone here, he's the one least likely to welcome us back. I warned you to be careful! He's a fanatic – one of the most powerful men in the empire.'

Marco committed another blunder at once. He made to step on the sacred threshold of the door that led to the Throne Room. Instantly the guards raised their heavy clubs. Niccolo stopped him just in time and showed him what to do. 'Stay behind us,' he ordered. He took off his shoes, then lifted the hem of his robe and stepped over the threshold. Matteo, then Marco, imitated him and followed.

The Throne Room was overwhelming in its splendour, but Marco hardly noticed the carved pillars, the gilded cornices and silken hangings. Nor did he pay much attention to the richly-dressed noblemen arranged down each side of the room according to rank. What captured his eyes at once was the figure of Kublai Khan himself, seated on a magnificent throne set on a high dais. He was a physically powerful man with a narrow downward-pointing moustache and a small tuft of beard. Though in his sixties, his fresh complexion made his age impossible to guess. He was supremely intelligent and ruthless, a brilliant military commander and a born leader of men, as befitted a grandson of Genghis Khan. He wore a robe of gold watered silk and a plain dark cap with a pleat falling at the back. Impassive and motionless, he watched the Polos advance.

Preceded by an official with a gold wand, they approached the throne and knelt behind the official. Marco, copying everything his father did for fear of making more blunders, was astonished to see him bow down until his forehead touched the floor.

'You may rise,' said Kublai. They rose to their knees. 'A welcome return after so many years. I feared that disease or some accident of war had prevented you.'

'We were delayed by both, Great Khan,' Niccolo explained.

'Is that why you have not brought the hundred wise priests I asked for?'

He was joking with them, but Niccolo and Matteo did not realize it. Matteo stuttered an apology about the enthronement of the new Pope, assuring Kublai that Rome had opened its arms and heart to him. Niccolo took the scroll from inside his coat and handed it to the Chinese official kneeling on the dais. 'His Holiness sends you this letter of brotherly greetings.'

'Brotherly?' Kublai did not like the word. 'He ranks himself as my equal?'

'As Supreme Pontiff of the Universal Church, Great Khan.'

'I doubt if his Church will be "Universal" until it has been accepted in my empire,' Kublai murmured, with a faint smile. A swell of laughter came from the nobles. Phags-pa had just entered with young Prince Timur and kneeled, smiling. But his smile became a scowl of resentment as Matteo produced the beautifully carved ivory box, the only one of the Pope's gifts which had survived the journey. He passed it to the official with the gold wand, who handed it to the Chinese chamberlain on the dais. At a nod from Kublai, the chamberlain opened the box. From it, Kublai lifted out a superb gold crucifix, studded with diamonds, and held it up admiringly.

'Strange. Yours is the only religion that has turned an instrument of death into an object of beauty – and a symbol of power,' he said quietly. He placed the crucifix back in the box carefully, almost reverently.

Niccolo hurried to follow up the favourable moment. 'We have also saved the rare gift for which you asked, Great Lord,' he said. He was signalling behind his back to Marco.

Marco had been kneeling, watching and listening, fascinated. He saw his father's signal and started to shuffle forward. It was awkward and he rose and walked to him, carrying his small box. Seeing Kublai's eyes turn coldly towards him, he knelt quickly again beside Niccolo and gave him the box.

'As a token of the Divine Blessing, His Holiness has sent you a measure of oil from the Holy Sepulchre in Jerusalem,' Niccolo said.

There was a loud murmur of interest. The Mongols, steeped in superstition, had heard that the sacred oil was mighty magic. Phags-pa tensed, his face dark with anger, as the box was passed up to Kublai and he laid it on his knees. Kublai saw Niccolo, Matteo and Marco cross themselves and hesitated before opening its lid and lifting out the small glass ampoule inside. The nobles craned their necks eagerly as he raised it.

'This is truly oil from the lamp that burns before your Christ's tomb?' Kublai asked.

Niccolo pressed his hand to his heart. 'Truly, Great Lord.'

Kublai's fingers moved to remove the waxed cork from the ampoule, but he stopped himself. He was not afraid, but cautious.

'Your golden passports were our safe conducts throughout your empire, Great Lord,' Matteo said. 'But if we survived the threats and dangers of your enemies and of nature, it was due to the power of the sacred oil.'

Very gingerly, Kublai replaced the ampoule in the box. He breathed out. 'A rare gift indeed . . . And one to be accepted with reverence.' He smiled. 'I see you have brought one of your race with you. Not one of your learned priests, surely?'

'No, Great Lord. This is my son, Marco, who has carried the sacred oil all the way here from Jerusalem. My son – and your servant.'

'If he serves me as well as his father and uncle, I shall be well pleased. How old is he?'

'Twenty-one,' answered Marco promptly.

There was a gasp of surprise from all sides that someone had spoken without first being addressed directly. Marco nearly bit his tongue, but Kublai made light of his error and continued as if unaware of it. 'I proclaim that your loyalty and faithfulness are worthy of all honour. Your possessions and treasures have been preserved for you. Whatever they are, from this day they are doubled.'

The nobles approved loudly and Niccolo and Matteo bowed in gratitude. Phags-pa, however, looked thoroughly annoyed and jealous at the warmth with which Kublai was treating the Venetians.

'You must translate the Pope's letter, and we have much to discuss,' Kublai went on. 'Meanwhile . . .' He touched the box. 'I shall send the sacred oil to the Empress Jaimu for safekeeping. You, Master Marco, since you have carried it so far, can carry it a little farther.' He gave the box to the chamberlain. 'Go with him.'

The chamberlain kowtowed and slithered backwards off the dais on his knees. Reaching Marco, he lowered his forehead to the floor again. At a nod from Niccolo, Marco took the box and rose to leave. He bowed to Kublai and turned round.

'Backwards!' his father hissed, out of the side of his hand.

Startled, Marco swung back, bobbed his head again to the Great Khan and retreated backwards up the Throne Room, his eyes cast down. Watching him, Kublai smiled faintly to himself at his new servant's lack of courtly polish. Yet when Marco glanced up from the door, the distant figure was as inscrutable as ever.

The chamberlain, a portly, meticulous man whose name was Chang Hsi, led Marco through a maze of corridors, painted passages crowded with treasures, stairways and marble halls adorned with swirling dragons. With the constant changes of level and direction, Marco soon became confused and gave up any hope of remembering the route. The palace, he realized, was one colossal labyrinth. His eyes were dazzled by the treasures they passed, sumptuous tapestries, giant glazed vases, statues of jade and ivory, jewelled aviaries, gold and silver fretted screens, murals of vivid mythological scenes covering entire walls, their landscapes so lifelike he felt he was looking at another world, and everywhere the theme of the swirling, golden, fire-eyed dragons. His senses reeled under the impact of so much beauty and richness.

At first he was amused by the self-importance of his guide, yet when he saw the deference with which he was treated by the many servants and guards who bowed or hurried to open doors for them, he began to understand that Chang Hsi was a person of some standing. He was also a useful source of information, explaining to Marco how he could differentiate between the many classes of servants by the colour and manner of their dress and between the eight grades of civil officials. The Mongols, conquerors and rulers of China, had their own grades of nobility and importance. To learn all the fine gradations, the degree of respect to be shown and form of address for each, would take many months. To administer his vast empire, Kublai Khan had taken over the whole apparatus of the Chinese civil service with its million or so employees. The numbers involved and the amount of control it exercised over every aspect of life and work in the Khan's dominions amazed Marco. He had once thought of Venice, the Jewel of the Adriatic, as the pinnacle of civilization. But what was she, compared to the culture and refinement, the sheer grandeur of Shangtu? And again, how different these people were from the wild nomads of the steppes, with their rough manners and roistering, violent ways.

Chang Hsi informed him that the Empress Jaimu was the First Lady of the Empire, the senior of Kublai's four wives, and mother of his heir, Prince Chinkin. Each of the wives had her own private palace and court, with a household, guards and servants numbering some ten thousand. Each was semi-divine, but the most exalted and honoured was the Empress Jaimu Khaitun.

When they finally arrived at the Empress's exquisite private palace and Marco was passed over to her own chamberlain and led past the eunuch guards to her boudoir, he was almost tongue-tied.

The room to which he was shown was like a silken pavilion, richly carpeted, with lacquered screens and delicately painted wall panels of peacocks, herons and ibises. Gentle tinkling music came from a corner where two girl musicians crouched, one playing a harp, the other a strange, two-stringed instrument. Two older ladies-in-waiting knelt by the door and two younger ones behind the empress's ivory chair. Yet he was surprised. Unlike the aloof and forbidding personage he had expected, she was charming and natural, wearing her regality lightly. In her sixties, she was still beautiful, although older in appearance than her ageless husband. Her hair was arranged in tiers of elaborate knots secured by gold pins. From her ears hung long jade earrings and she wore a simple, very tasteful gown of soft sage brocade, gathered at the waist with a peach-coloured sash.

Her welcome was designed to put Marco at ease and he detected something of eagerness, even anxiety, in it. When he knelt and presented her with the small box, she gazed at it for a long moment and, to his surprise, kissed it reverently. He saw a suggestion of tears in her eyes as she slowly opened the lid and uncovered the glass ampoule.

'I have waited and hoped for so long . . .' she whispered. 'It really has healing powers? It can work miracles?'

'The Holy Father himself said so,' Marco told her shyly. 'But only for those who believe in its powers. For those who have faith.'

Her fingertips hovered over the phial, but she could not bring herself to touch it. 'As I wish to have,' she said. Seeing his surprise, she took from a fold of her gown a silver crucifix which hung round her neck.

Marco was startled. 'I – I'm sorry, my lady. I had been told there are no Christians here.'

'I am descended from Wang Khan,' she told him, 'whom your people knew as Prester John.'

'I thought that was a legend,' Marco said wonderingly.

The Empress Jaimu smiled. 'No, my grandfather was leader of all the Khans, before the days of the great Genghis. He and his people were Nestorian Christians. Now the Nestorians' leader is my nephew, Nayan. I have heard from him of your Lord Christ – and also of your Holy Father, the Pope. Did he send his priests with you?'

'We arrived here alone, my father, my uncle and me,' Marco said carefully.

Jaimu nodded. 'That is a pity. Here we have only Nestorian priests, and Rome does not recognize them . . .

It was one of them who told me about this sacred oil, and it was at my request that the Khan asked for it. For . . . for a purpose. Come.'

She rose. Marco followed her to a folding screen which concealed one corner of the room. Behind it he was surprised to see an ornate silver and gold reliquary adorned with crosses in ebony and emerald. 'The Khan, my husband,' she explained, 'will not allow the body of your Christ to be shown on the Cross. He believes it is degrading to show a God so treated.' She opened the doors of the reliquary. 'I had this made to receive the oil – but I had begun to think it would always stand empty.'

She held the box out to Marco and he took the oil and placed it in the compartment in the reliquary. She closed the doors and placed her hands together, bowing her head in prayer.

Marco copied her, but was also watching her, still surprised and intrigued by her evident passion to believe. All that Pope Gregory had said to him, all the bright hopes of the start of his journey, came flooding back. Suddenly he felt uplifted, elated. Perhaps through him, the Pope's prayers for an alliance with Kublai Khan and his people might still be fulfilled.

Marco saw the Empress again that night at the great banquet given in honour of the return of his father and uncle.

The banqueting hall was the largest single room Marco had ever seen. About its edges were many musicians, playing continually. Rows of tables on descending platforms lined its sides, filled with hundreds of guests. At one end, Kublai Khan sat at a small table much higher than anyone else, with Jaimu alone on his left, both wearing imperial golden robes.

Lower, on their right, was a table for the Crown Prince Chinkin, a slim, handsome man in his twenties. The chamberlain, Chang Hsi, had told Marco that the prince was very intelligent and cultured, but reserved and solitary, unlike his son, a favourite with the Mongol lords, the little Prince Timur, who sat with other princes at a still lower table on a level with Kublai's feet. The princes' first wives sat in the same descending order on Kublai's left. The tables for the chief nobles, generals and officers of state were just below the level of the princes.

Niccolo, Matteo and Marco sat at the end of one of those lower tables to the side, where Kublai Khan could see them, as he could see everyone in the rest of the hall.

Food and drink were lavish, superbly prepared, the plates and drinking cups of solid gold. The lords-in-waiting who served Kublai and Jaimu wore silken scarves across their mouths and noses, so as not to contaminate their food. The chatter and gaiety was punctuated by a strange ritual. Each time one of the lords advanced to refill the Khan's goblet from the two-handled ewer of wine, he retreated and knelt, then all the musicians struck a crashing chord. Everyone at once fell silent as Kublai raised his goblet and the silence continued while he drank. When he set down the goblet, everyone cheered and the musicians began playing again.

Kublai was in an expansive mood, toasting the Polos often. The Buddhist Keeper of the Records, Phags-pa, watched him carefully, reading his expression as he smiled and nodded, listening to Jaimu. Phags-pa could guess something of what she was telling him from the way he kept glancing down at Marco. Although he was bland, revealing little in public, the Lama's mind was revolving over the problem of the same young man. Brilliantly subtle, infinitely cunning, he realized that the two older Polos were no threat. Their minds were exclusively on commerce, and their value to the Great Khan lay in their knowledge of international values and prices, and their organizing ability. The boy, Marco, however, was an unknown quantity. He had heard from the women in the Empress Jaimu's household who spied for him that Marco had made a very favourable impression on the empress, feeding her hunger for understanding of the Christian God. If she, in turn, infected the Great Khan . . . Yes, the son of Niccolo Polo would have to be watched very carefully. He could be the most insidious danger yet to Phags-pa's dream of making Buddhism the state religion of the empire.

Unaware that both Kublai and the red-robed lama were observing him, Marco was flushed and excited, fascinated by everything. He had eaten so much, of so many strange dishes, deliciously spiced and dissolving on the tongue, that for the time being he could eat no more, and sipped at his cup of rice wine as he watched the erotic dancing of the contortionists, lithe Tamil girls wearing only loincloths, with narrow bands of silk binding their breasts. They had formed themselves into living hoops, their bodies bent until their heads protruded from the forks of their thighs.

Marco was irresistibly reminded of the first night in Bektor's camp, the *ikhudur*. This whole evening was another *ikhudur*, only on a far grander and more lavish scale. The impression was confirmed when an Indian conjurer stepped forward through the departing dancing girls, to a shout of anticipation from the guests. He wore a full turban with an egret's plume, baggy trousers and a coat of many colours. He salaamed deeply to Kublai. When he straightened, his arms were filled with bunches of flowers, which he threw to the crowd. As he threw, the flowers became lengths of cloth, the same colour as the flowers, filling the air with bright streamers, apparently unending. He finished and, as everyone applauded, he threw up his hands again and sweets and sugared nuts, mixed with gold rings, showered down among the guests.

One of the rings fell on the table near Marco. He picked it up and tested it with his teeth. 'It's gold!' he exclaimed.

'Of course,' Niccolo told him. 'It's the way the Khan gives presents to his guests.'

The Indian conjurer was now salaaming and retreating. There was a flash of red smoke and a Mongol Shaman, gaunt and fearsome, stepped out of it in the middle of the hall, to gasps of astonishment all round.

Attendants were rolling forward the magnificent drinking cabinet which accompanied Kublai on all his journeys. It was made of rare woods, carved with gilded animals. On each side were gold taps, attached to hidden barrels inside, from which the attendants could draw wine, *koumiss*, camel's milk or flavoured mineral water. The Shaman was carrying a thin metal pipe. From the shelf at the top of the cabinet he took one of the gold drinking bowls and balanced it on the end of the pipe.

'Watch this,' Niccolo said.

The Shaman flicked his fingers and a long, thin taper appeared in them. As he pointed it at Kublai, the end burst into flame, to loud applause. The Shaman glanced up at the Khan, who smiled, motioning him to continue. The Shaman made a series of magic passes with the lighted taper, then touched the flame to the base of the pipe. There was a loud bang and flash which made the guests jump. Women screamed. Marco was startled, then amazed to see Kublai seemingly pluck the drinking bowl out of the air, where it had flown to him. Kublai was laughing and pleased, and once more everyone applauded. The lord-in-waiting filled the bowl; the musicians crashed out a chord and Kublai drank, to more applause, turning into cheers when he handed the bowl down to Prince Chinkin, who drank off the rest of the wine. They smiled to each other, obviously closely attached.

Marco applauded with the others, but he had already made a point of asking about the exploding powder, so was more impressed by the Shaman's skill than his 'magic'. He became aware of Kublai's eyes on him and smiled back, frankly and openly. Then something made him look round and he saw Phags-pa gazing at him from the other end of the long table. The Lama's eyes were shuttered and speculative. As Marco glanced at him, he looked away and raised his hand. All the musician's instruments sounded at once and the guests obediently fell silent. It was time for Phags-pa to claim the Khan's attention.

He waved his hand gently and a harp began to play. The music came from near the wine cabinet – but the harpist was not touching his instrument. As the musician scrambled back from it in fear, there was a murmur of superstitious dread from the guests. Marco saw Kublai frowning. As Phags-pa's hand moved again, more unearthly music sounded, although again no musicians were playing. As though despising the demonstration of his own powers, Phags-pa signalled to one of his red-robed, shaven-headed assistants, who stepped out, taking the Shaman's place. Somehow, the impassive Lama was a more awesome figure than the other magicians. As he flicked his finger, a hooded king cobra took shape in front of him, rearing up, swaying, its forked tongue flickering. The guests were silent in terror, cowering back.

The Lama flicked his hand and the cobra disappeared. In that second, Marco saw a look pass between him and Phags-pa. Then the Lama's fingers flicked towards Marco.

Marco heard the hiss of a cobra beside him and jumped, looking round in fear. There was nothing to be seen. The others at the table laughed quietly, uneasily. Matteo gripped the knife with which he had carved his meat. The hiss came again, nearer this time, and Marco laid both his hands on the table, sitting erect as the terrifying hiss came closer and closer. He was tense, perspiration sprinkling his forehead as he fought to hide his fear. The shadow of the cobra fell on the table in front of him, rearing over him. The hissing reached a strident peak. Then, abruptly, it stopped.

All this time, Kublai Khan had been watching Marco, his attention divided between him and Phags-pa, who he realized had been testing Marco's control. Kublai was the only one who saw Phags-pa's faint shrug as a signal to the Lama.

The Lama now raised his arms and twisted both hands at the wrists. A golden rain began to fall from nowhere, disappearing before it touched the guests, who nonetheless continued to clutch at it.

Unlike the others, Marco did not move. He looked at Phags-pa, who had clearly revealed himself as an enemy, he saw how the man sat, detached and icily contemptuous, despising the guests as they reached out for the illusory golden rain. Glancing up, Marco saw two others looking at him, the Khan and the Crown Prince, and was confused to find the prince smiling to him slightly, as if in greeting. Aloof and distant was how the chamberlain had described him, yet there was warmth and a shy friendliness in Chinkin's smile.

Marco applauded with everyone else as the Lama left the space between the tables and a group of dwarf acrobats came tumbling in. He drank and laughed like the others, giving no sign of the thought which kept growing in his mind. How shall I ever fit in here? What is to become of me?

Chapter Five

'Well? What happened then?' Giovanni grinned hopefully at Marco. 'Did you meet any more women?'

'Shut up, you idiot!' said Rustichello irritably. 'Let him have a rest.'

'But I want him to go on. His stories help to pass the time. They keep out the cold.'

'He's not just *telling* us what happened,' Rustichello pointed out. 'He's reliving it. And that takes it out of him.'

Giovanni looked more closely at Marco. He saw the strain and tension in his face, but he was impatient to hear the next instalment. 'You were telling us about meeting the Great Khan Kublai, at his Summer Palace. Did you stay there?'

'For a time,' whispered Marco.

'What was it really like?' Rustichello asked, taking up his pen once more.

'It was the most incredible—'

The description died on his lips as a key suddenly turned in the lock and the heavy cell door was flung open. Two Genoese guards came in – hard, efficient men, made all the more brusque by carrying out orders for which they did not care.

'On your feet! Against the wall!' shouted the older of the two.

Giovanni and Rustichello rose in surprise. They knew both guards well and had always found them friendly in the past. The older man was anything but friendly now as he jabbed a finger at Marco, who was still on his bed.

'You – hand over the writing! All of it!'

'What's wrong? What is it?' Marco asked.

'We have our orders.'

Without waiting for Marco, the guards seized the pages

of the manuscript from the table, then searched the whole cell with speed and thoroughness, rifling through clothes, overturning mattresses, confiscating every scrap of writing that they could find. They spread a blanket on the floor and began to throw everything into it.

Rustichello was horrified to see all his precious scrolls handled so roughly.

'Careful!' he begged. 'There's years of work there . . . Why are you doing this?'

'We have our orders,' the older guard repeated flatly.

The corners of the blanket had been tied together. Heaving it over his shoulder, the guard went out, followed by his colleague. Marco started forward after them, but he was halted by a look from the second guard. The younger man spoke quietly, warning. 'I'll tell you one thing – be careful. You tell some good stories. But somebody thinks they're dangerous.'

'Why?' Marco asked.

'Who knows? But when they *think* there's danger, there is. It's serious. For you.'

The guard went out and slammed the door shut behind him, and the rush of wind blew out the solitary candle. In the darkness Giovanni could be heard sobbing quietly. One of the items removed had been a prayer book that had once belonged to his father.

'Why have they done this?' Marco asked, troubled. 'Why?'

Rustichello, too, was mourning. Years of patient writing had been torn from him in a matter of seconds. He was distressed to have lost his version of Marco's stories. But if the written account had gone, there was still Marco's remarkable memory. 'It is better, perhaps, not to ask,' he said. 'Prisoners can only guess. But let us go on. You were at the banquet. What happened next?'

After a long pause, Marco spoke again. 'The next day, to my surprise, I was summoned to present myself to the Great Khan in his summer pavilion . . .'

*

Even in repose, the Great Khan managed to convey immense power and authority. Wearing a loose, dark robe and reclining on a silken couch, he took his ease in his enormous and luxurious *yurt*, situated in a quiet part of the wood. Light filtered in through fretted screens and made delicate patterns on the floor. All was silent and warm and soothing.

Marco knelt in front of Kublai, polite this time and minding his tongue. Out of the corner of his eye, he could see a low table on which a number of maps were scattered beneath a model of a warship, a large sailing junk. Marco was bursting with questions that he dared not ask. He wanted to know more about the maps and the model. He wanted the dripping sound explained. He wondered why Prince Chinkin, who sat on the floor with an arm over a stool, looked so tired and listless.

'You enjoyed our banquet?' Kublai asked.

'I was very honoured to be present,' Marco said.

'And the magic? I watched you as the Shamans performed their little miracles. You did not seem as impressed as some were.'

'I was impressed but not surprised. I know that holy men have strange gifts. I saw a monk at the Lamasery rise into the air.'

'Were you not afraid when the cobra started hissing at you?'

'Part of me was,' admitted Marco. 'And part of me was wondering how the Shaman had mastered the art of making us see and hear what was not there.' His eyes shifted to his side, caught by a strange-looking mechanism that seemed to be floating in a pool of water.

'You are here, but I see your mind is still travelling . . .' Kublai said drily.

Marco blushed guiltily. 'I beg your pardon, my lord. I will not let my attention wander again.'

'Why not take a proper look at it and satisfy your curiosity? It is one of our clepsydrae.' Seeing Marco's puzzlement, he smiled. 'A water-clock.'

'It is an instrument to mark the hours,' explained Chinkin, who was sitting on the floor nearby. 'The water seeps through an aperture at a regular rate. Those golden balls drop one by one into the little cups as each hour passes.'

'Amazing . . .' Marco marvelled. 'You tell the time by water! So you don't have to rely on the sun any more.'

'Are you always so easily distracted, Master Marco?' Kublai asked.

'Oh no, my lord! But it was something new. Any day in which you don't learn something new is wasted.'

The Great Khan laughed and he seemed younger than ever. 'You hear that, Chinkin? A fellow scholar. You two will get on well.'

Chinkin smiled.

'All I have studied is the world – and how to serve God,' Marco said shyly.

'You do not believe in magic?'

'In some magic, my lord,' Marco replied carefully. 'Miracles are magic. I must believe in miracles. But one can enjoy magic tricks without believing in them.'

Kublai was pleased with the answer. What the young Venetian lacked in formal education, he made up for in plain common sense and there was an honesty and directness about him that was very appealing. Kublai reached for a map that lay on the table. He unrolled it on the floor so that the whole of Tibet and Cathay lay at his feet. 'Where was this Lamasery?'

Marco shuffled forward on his knees. 'There, my lord,' he said, pointing to a spot in the mountains of north Tibet. His brow furrowed. 'There's a mistake here. That road is wrongly marked.'

'Are you sure?'

'Yes, we tried it. The cliffs have fallen and blocked the pass. We had to use this valley, further north.'

'Neither your father nor your uncle remembered that,' noted Kublai, relaxing on his couch again and appraising his young guest. 'The Empress Jaimu seems to be right.

She says you have a clearer recollection of the territories you have passed through than any traveller she has ever met.'

Shyness troubled Marco again. 'I remember what interests me, that is all.' He shifted his knees slightly to ease the discomfort, then saw that he was being watched. 'I'm sorry, my lord—'

'You are not used to kneeling. I understand. You may sit or stand, as you please . . .' Chinkin was surprised at this concession, but his father quickly added a condition. '. . . Though only when we are alone together.' Marco nodded in gratitude and sat back, stretching his legs out in front of him. 'Now tell me; what interested you?'

'Most things. People's customs and beliefs and ways of life. And many other things.'

'Such as?'

'What kind of crops they grow. How they care for the aged, for the sick. How they teach their children. Their trade – cotton in Kashgar, pearls in Baghdad, and so on. Whether they mine for metal or for precious stones – or for something unusual like asbestos.'

'Go on,' Kublai urged.

'Things like the wild sheep in Pamir with horns six palms long; the profit on the export of jade from Charchan; also, the reasons behind the legends, the truths behind the stories . . . What makes a people strong or weak, determined or uncertain.'

'You can hold all this in your mind?' asked Kublai.

'I made some notes to help me, such as the principal products of a district, and how many days it took to cross it, or the distances between towns.'

Kublai was fascinated. 'You hear this, Chinkin? What I have always said! This is exactly the information a ruler needs – he needs to know where to quarter his army, what revenue to expect, where there may be food to spare when other areas suffer famine. That's why we need accurate records, and why we must study them. We need to know our lands and our people better.'

Encouraged by this approval, Marco remembered something else. 'Caidu Khan says that the best thing for a ruler is to be there, to see for himself.'

'Did my nephew say anything else?' Kublai's voice was dangerously quiet.

'I hope I'm not speaking out of turn, my lord . . .'

'Continue.'

'Well, Caidu said that a true Mongol should never be far from his horse. That was what makes him invincible.'

Marco became aware of the anxious signals that Chinkin was sending him and realized that he had gone too far. He also saw, to his horror, that he had stood up while he was speaking. Throwing himself to his knees, he stammered an apology and bowed. Chinkin immediately came to his defence.

'He spoke in good faith, father.'

'I know.' Kublai was thoughtful. 'Do not be afraid, Master Marco. Too many people – all – only agree with me. It is refreshing to find someone who speaks so frankly.' Marco was relieved. A smile passed between him and Chinkin, the beginning of friendship. Kublai noticed and was not displeased. 'I admire Caidu,' he told them. 'He is a true Mongol. But he does not understand. I am going to say something for you both to remember – you, Chinkin, because one day you will succeed me, and you, Marco, because one day you may serve him. It is this: the world may be conquered on horseback. It cannot be ruled from it.' Both his listeners nodded seriously. 'Now, Master Marco, while your memory is still clear, I wish you to report to the Lord Phags-pa at the palace of records. He will want all the information you can give.'

'Yes, my lord.'

'Our Chinese mapmakers are excellent, but some of their maps are very old. Suggest any changes you judge are needed. You will find me grateful.'

'To help to repay your kindness to my father is reward enough, my lord,' Marco said sincerely.

He rose, bowed low, then turned to leave. Chinkin

tensed, fearing that this lack of respect would not be forgiven, but Marco recovered just in time and spun round to face the Great Khan, before backing slowly towards the exit.

When he was once more alone with his son, Kublai chuckled. 'His memory is not so remarkable for some things,' he murmured.

Drums rolled, gongs resounded, trumpets blared and a general clamour filled the air as the Imperial Summer Palace prepared for the hunt. To provide himself with sport and his hawks with food, Kublai had stocked the sixteen miles of enclosed parkland with deer, wild pig, hares and all manner of game. Watching the Mongol huntsmen prepare, Marco was spellbound. He was particularly impressed by Kublai's mew of gerfalcons, who numbered well over two hundred. He was also struck by the cheetahs, who were being restrained by their handlers on strong leashes, and whose occasional snarls showed teeth capable of ripping anything to pieces.

Marco walked on to where a group of young boys were riding frisky colts, making them perform all kinds of intricate movements. The coordination of animal and rider, of gesture and movement, of action and reflex, was so perfect that Marco began to clap in appreciation.

'They are the sons of the Great Khan's nobles,' Chen Pao, Marco's new Chinese servant, explained. 'They must learn to ride until the horse becomes part of them.'

'They don't have any saddles,' Marco noticed.

'Saddles are used only in war.'

Marco turned quickly, pointing, his eye caught by a new wonder, something which he had never seen before in his life. High above them, a huge green and red dragon was twisting and rearing against the clouds, its long tail snaking wildly. It seemed to be controlled by a small boy who held a length of twine and was surrounded by excited children.

'It's like a sail in the sky – kept afloat by the wind,' he breathed.

'A Dragon Kite,' Chen Pao smiled. 'Shall we go this way now, Master?'

Chen Pao was an educated, intelligent and deferential young man, who was sensitive to the needs of his new master. He set off at a leisurely pace so that Marco was able to absorb all that he saw around him. They walked past a group of Shamans, who muttered prayers and incantations, then scattered powder into braziers to send up spirals of multi-coloured smoke.

'They believe it is going to rain,' observed Chen Pao, 'and they are preparing to chase away the clouds.'

'They actually believe they can control the weather?' Marco laughed.

'It has been known,' Chen Pao said, seriously.

Together, they wandered on in the direction of the archery butts, where they arrived in time to see a feathered arrow smack into the centre of a target of rolled straw swinging from a wooden crossbeam. There was a vicious whistling sound as dozens of other arrows sped through the air to knock out the coloured centres of their respective targets.

'I've never seen such shooting!' gasped Marco.

'With their horses and their bows, the Mongols have conquered the world,' Chen Pao said. There was a slight edge to his voice, but when Marco glanced at him, he smiled.

'I want to try one of those bows,' Marco told him.

'If it is permitted to remind you, Master . . . you must change for the Great Khan's hunt.'

'With all those hawks and a thousand huntsmen, it's more like a war than a hunt, Chen Pao!' He looked upwards. 'I still think the rain will prevent it.'

As if in reply, the Shamans intensified their efforts to bring fine weather. Wearing pointed hats trimmed with hawk and eagle feathers, and with mirrors and amulets dangling around their necks, they moved rhythmically in a circle, beating their metallic drums. Every now and then, some of them would leap wildly into the air as if trying to strike the clouds with their fists and drive them away.

Marco returned to his quarters and immediately sent his servant to find one of the bows for him. He stripped down to his tights and took the short, deeply curved Mongol bow that Chen Pao brought him. Grunting hard, he tried to draw it, but could only move the bowstring a few inches. Chen Pao, standing by with a clean robe for him, watched with amusement as Marco tried a second time to draw the bow.

'I can't stretch it!' Marco complained.

'Only a Mongol's arrow is swifter than his horse. It takes time to learn how to manage both.'

'Which you can, Chen Pao. Well, show me!'

Chen Pao stepped back nervously. 'It is not permitted, master. I am Chinese.'

'I permit it,' Marco said.

'I am Chinese,' his servant repeated, with a shrug.

'And I am Venetian. Now take the bow.'

'No,' said Chen Pao, seriously. 'We are not allowed to handle these weapons.'

Marco considered him for a moment, then indicated the bow. 'What is this called in your language?'

'Gung, Master.'

'Gung . . .' Marco said after him.

Chen Pao was puzzled. 'Is it permitted to know why you ask?'

'If I am to speak to your people, I must learn their language.'

'But why should you wish to speak to *us*?'

Marco smiled. 'So that we can learn from each other.'

'Yes, Master. How can I help you?'

'To begin with, you can stop calling me master all the time.'

'But the Court Chamberlain sent me to serve you,' Chen Pao protested.

'Serve me, then. But when we're alone like now, why don't you call me by my name – Marco?'

'If that is in order, Mast – eh, Marco,' Chen Pao smiled.

'It is. Now teach me how to draw this blasted bow.'

Chen Pao laughed and put down the robe. 'Hold the bow to your right ear, and take the string in your right hand. Then you straighten your left arm as far as it will go.'

'For you obviously know a lot about them.'

Chen Pao whispered confidentially, 'I used to hunt on my father's estate near Ho-Kien-Fu before . . . before the Mongols occupied northern China.'

Marco made a second attempt to draw the bow and this time he was successful. He shouted out in delight, but his servant warned him not to release the bowstring with his wrist unprotected, or its force might cut his hand off. Together, and with great care, they slowly eased bowstring and bow back into position. Marco was panting when it was over. Something had occurred to him. 'Did you say the Mongols had occupied northern China? Don't they have *all* of it?'

'China is now divided into two,' explained Chen Pao. 'Cathay in the north and Mantzu in the south, beyond the Yangtse River. The Mongols have the north. But with bows such as these, the Great Khan will soon conquer the south.'

Still politically naive, an idealist, Marco was immensely impressed by his personal vision of Kublai Khan. 'But why should the grand design of having one country united under a single ruler be opposed?' He did not see the troubled look in his servant's eyes. 'Look what the Great Khan Kublai has done for this country. I have never imagined such a ruler. Look at how peaceful and contented all his people are. That surely proves the effectiveness of his laws.'

'It proves how strictly they are enforced,' came the quiet reply.

Chen Pao suddenly dropped to his knees, bowed his

head and kowtowed in the ritual greeting reserved for dignitaries. Marco turned to see that his father and uncle had come in, both dressed in the splendid hunting clothes that had been presented to them by Kublai. They chided Marco with being late for the hunt which was due to start as soon as the emperor finished his Council Meeting, but Marco had seen no need to hurry. The hunt would be delayed by the rain that was due to fall any minute. Matteo took him to the sliding door and opened it, in silence. The heavy clouds were being blown away by a lively breeze and the sun was now lighting up the Summer Palace. Marco was amazed. Had the Shamans really fought off the rain with their magic?

'Don't start asking how they do it – because we don't know!' Niccolo said gruffly. 'Just get dressed.'

Before they could continue the discussion further a Mongol officer entered, bowing deeply. 'The Great Khan to Master Marco. You are to attend him.'

'Is the hunt starting?' asked Niccolo.

'Not at the hunt, my lord.' The officer faced Marco. 'At the court of the Inner Council.'

Chen Pao was the first to recover from the shock and he helped his master quickly into his robe. Accompanied by the soldier, who was a member of the Khan's personal guard, Marco hurried to the Council Room in the sumptuous pavilion.

As befitted his majesty, Kublai Khan sat high above the others on a raised throne, wearing his richly embroidered hunting apparel. Prince Chinkin sat below him and to his right. Seeing Marco enter, he gave him a welcoming smile.

Highly nervous, but doing his best to conceal it, Marco went through all the proper rituals and was left by his escort kneeling in the centre of the room, with the members of the ruling Council of Twelve facing him in a semicircle.

Kublai, at the middle of the semicircle, began to question him closely about the territories that he and the others had travelled through. The ascetic Phags-pa, Keeper of the Records, listened intently to every answer. With the eyes of the Council fixed on him, Marco felt even more uncomfortable and under scrutiny, but concentrated on answering accurately and succinctly.

'. . . And the cities of Afghanistan?' asked Kublai.

'Strongly fortified, Great Lord. Many are built at the entrance to narrow passes. They are natural fortresses, easy to defend.'

Phags-pa addressed the Great Khan. 'Yet your grandfather, Genghis, the immortal Kha Khan, conquered all of them, Mighty Lord.'

'At a heavy cost,' Kublai reminded him.

'You say you lived for a year in Badakhshan?' The speaker was Argan, one of the leading Mongol generals, a dark, glowering, thickset man with an arrogant manner. 'Is that so?'

'Yes, General.'

'Describe it.'

Marco replied without hesitation. 'The people worship Mohammed. It is twelve days' journey across. Wheat is grown, and barley. There are mines of rubies, large quantities of silver and copper. The mountains take a full two days to climb. At the top are wide plateaux with good grazing. They breed fine horses and many sheep.'

'My General Argan also knows Badakhshan,' Kublai said.

Impressed by the accuracy of the details, Argan nodded to the Great Khan. Marco realized that he had been tested in public and was relieved that he had come through the test with honour. He could sense Chinkin's pleasure, too. Another general was signalling that he had questions. Kublai waved a hand to him. 'Proceed, Nasreddin. Ask what you wish.'

Nasreddin, a slender, watchful, Saracenic Arab, fixed his gaze on Marco. 'And from there you travelled to Turkestan. How far from Chinghintalas to Su-chou?'

'Ten days' journey, east-north-east.'

'And from Kan-chau to Etzina?'

'Twelve days, General. Its people live by agriculture and

rear cattle and camels. They also breed the best falcons. Forty days ride to the north is Karakorum.'

'It is just so, Great Lord,' Nasreddin conceded.

'Did I not tell you?' laughed Kublai. 'He is a living atlas of my empire – or such of it as he has seen. And what has impressed you so far of China, Master Marco?'

'So much, Great Lord,' said Marco with enthusiasm. 'First of all, its sheer size and wealth. Then the paper money, the burning stones which heat houses, the water-clocks, and the kites which fly in the air and carry messages.'

Argan grunted. 'Haven't you noticed anything a little less . . . obvious?'

'Oh yes, General. The way all people obey the laws. And more than anything else, the roads.'

'Roads?' repeated Nasreddin.

'For the Imperial couriers, with relay posts and fresh horses. Nothing shows more clearly the stability of the empire.'

'True again,' Nasreddin approved.

'Perhaps it is worth noting,' said Phags-pa drily, 'that his father and uncle wish to use those roads for trade purposes.'

'That is another matter, for another time,' Kublai decided. 'Your quarters are comfortable, Master Marco? You have all you require?'

'All and more than I deserve, Great Lord.'

Kublai smiled. 'As to that, we shall see. I shall summon you again.'

Marco bowed where he was kneeling, rose and bowed again. As he backed carefully out of the Council Chamber, he responded to a friendly smile from Chinkin. Argan and Phags-pa saw the smile and exchanged a quick, disapproving look, but Kublai was almost chuckling, delighted that Marco had lived up to the praise he had given him.

Sunshine reigned in an empire of blue sky from which all

rebellious clouds had been chased. Everyone was looking forward to the hunt and the impatience of the hounds and the horses was almost palpable. Marco, Niccolo and Matteo were part of the waiting crowd outside the pavilion, and they were as anxious as anyone to enjoy the thrills of the chase. Prince Chinkin rode up on a fine white stallion, escorted by Mongol nobles, soldiers and his own team of beaters. As he dismounted, he saw Marco and beckoned him over.

'It is an honour,' Niccolo told his son. 'Hurry!'

'And mind your manners!' warned Matteo.

Marco moved forward, with everyone watching. Self-consciously, Chen Pao followed, leading his horse. Chinkin indicated the space beside him where Marco was to stand, and he bowed in acknowledgement. More nervous than ever, Chen Pao took his place behind. A flourish from trumpeters announced the arrival of Kublai Khan himself. As he came out of the pavilion with Phags-pa, the waiting rows of nobles surged forward and dropped to their knees in homage. Argan knelt beside the young Prince Timur, the proud, pleasant boy who was next to his father, Chinkin, in line to the throne. Kneeling beside Chinkin, Marco saw that he was troubled by the closeness between his son and the ambitious general, then his attention was caught by Phags-pa, who had moved to confer with the Shamans. The priests had been studying the cracks in the horses' shoulderblades that they had been heating over a brazier and now delivered their report. Phags-pa turned back to the Great Khan. 'The signs are in favour, Great Lord. The Spirits bless your hunting.'

Kublai raised his arms in the air and the happy pandemonium of drums, gongs and trumpets started up once more. Grooms brought a superb white stallion to the bottom of the steps and Kublai climbed easily into the saddle. As he led the procession off towards the parkland, he held a gerfalcon on his gloved wrist and a small cheetah lay curled up on the crupper of his horse. To Marco's eager gaze, he appeared as a kind of patron saint of the chase.

The cavalcade followed Kublai, gathering speed slightly when they reached open country and causing the grooms – Chen Pao among them – to break into a trot to keep up. Marco was bolt upright on his horse, conscious of the honour of riding beside Chinkin.

'Do you enjoy hunting, Marco?' the prince asked.

'More than anything, Prince Chinkin. But as I told Chen Pao, this is more like going into battle.'

'It keeps us in practice for war,' Chinkin smiled.

The beaters with their gongs and bamboo canes had put up the first small flock of birds from a covert. Kublai unhooded his gerfalcon and sent it soaring into the sky in pursuit. It was the signal for the other hawks to be released and for the hunting to begin in earnest.

A herd of deer was flushed out of a copse by the baying of the dogs, and the cheetah who had looked so tame and docile on Kublai's horse sprang into life at his order and bounded off after the game. Other cheetahs were now unloosed from cages on the back of carts and Marco was stunned by their muscled grace and incredible swiftness. Horsemen spurred their mounts forward and the remainder of the hawks took to the air. The whole hunt was on the move now, a thousand horses and a huge pack of dogs thundering over the ground across a front that extended for hundreds of yards, and creating a noise that brought hares, stags, rabbits and more birds darting out of cover. Mongol arrows flew, rarely missing their targets.

Some hours later, after a long and tiring gallop, Marco and Chinkin turned into a clearing and reined in their horses. It was quiet, cool and shaded under the overhanging boughs of a large tree, and they were glad to rest. In the distance, the hunt could be heard continuing on its noisy and destructive way. Chinkin's beaters and Chen Pao, almost breathless from sprinting through undergrowth, found their way to the clearing. Chen Pao untied the leather bottle from his waist and offered the water on his knees. Chinkin shook his head, but Marco drank gratefully. More of the prince's beaters ran up, some carrying hares and pheasants, two with a stag slung between them on a pole.

'Marco – look!' Chinkin was pointing at a wild boar that came scuttling across the clearing. 'Spread out!' he ordered his men.

'Drive him this way!' yelled Marco.

The beaters dashed into the bushes in pursuit of the animal, which was grunting and squealing in fury. Marco and Chinkin selected their arrows quickly and drew their bows in readiness, but when the wild boar came crashing through the undergrowth and back into the clearing, neither of them let fly. Instead, Chinkin dropped his bow and grabbed at his throat as if choking. His eyes rolled, he gave a strangled cry and fell heavily to the ground from his horse.

'Chinkin!' Marco called, shocked.

Marco leapt from his horse and stared down at the rigid figure of his friend, who was shaking convulsively and emitting a strange moaning noise. Chen Pao and the others had plunged off after their quarry and did not hear Marco's cries for help. Kneeling beside the twisting, writhing body, he took off his leather belt and managed to force it between the teeth of the young Mongol prince. Even more violent spasms tormented Chinkin's body and his mouth was spluttering with foam. When the others came back into the clearing, Marco called for them to make a litter, but to his surprise, they simply turned and fled. Only Chen Pao remained and he stayed at a safe distance.

'Chen Pao! Quick – I need help here!' Marco shouted.

'No! No . . .' Chen Pao muttered, backing away.

Frightened by what he saw, the servant ran off as well, although Marco called to him. Marco held Chinkin, supporting him. The first fury of the attack had subsided and his body was no longer arching so violently, though it continued to tremble. Marco wrenched open Chinkin's collar and stroked his wet forehead. 'It's all right . . . I won't leave you,' he soothed. 'Try to relax. It's over now . . .'

As he tried to calm Chinkin, a patrol of Imperial Guards came racing into the clearing. As soon as they saw what had happened, two of them jumped on Marco and dragged him brutally away, while the others formed a defensive circle around the prince, their swords drawn. The officer in charge of the escort gave an order and Chinkin's horse was taken over to the circle.

'No! Don't try to move him!' warned Marco. 'He may have another attack!'

The soldiers who held Marco reacted with savage efficiency. They pushed Marco roughly to his knees and, while one man pulled his head forward by the hair, his colleague raised his sword, ready to decapitate him.

'Stop! His life belongs to the Khan!' someone shouted.

Marco recognized the voice of Nasreddin and almost passed out with relief.

The Great Khan Kublai paced up and down like a caged tiger, his anger barely contained. Marco knelt before him on one knee. They were alone in the pavilion.

'And then?' snapped Kublai.

'I forced my belt between his teeth, so that he would not bite off his tongue.'

Kublai winced. 'Had anyone told you before today that my son had . . . this sickness?'

'No, Great Lord.'

'But you understood what it was?'

'At the monastery school in Venice, a boy had the same sickness. I often saw him when he was seized by those fits.'

Kublai stood over him and fought down his anger. It was replaced with a heavy sadness, tinged with fear. He looked at Marco for a long time before deciding to confide in him. For once, his face betrayed something of his true age.

'The last . . . the last time, he could feel the attack growing and came to me. We were alone. No-one else knew of it, except his mother. Not even Chinkin's own son.' His voice became a hoarse whisper. 'Others who knew he had once suffered from the sickness thought he had recovered – until today! Do you understand? It is the most closely guarded secret.'

'So it must be,' replied Marco artlessly. 'Not even my father had heard of it.'

Kublai stiffened. 'You *told* him? And your uncle?'

'They wondered what was wrong,' said Marco, not realizing that he might be sentencing both Niccolo and Matteo to death.

'You were warned not to speak of it to anyone!'

'I wouldn't tell anyone but them, Great Lord. I wondered why it was kept so secret. Surely the people would understand?'

'They might,' sighed Kublai. 'They might even pity my son. But from the moment it was known, his life would be in greater danger from his own brothers than from his illness.'

'I do not follow . . .'

Kublai swung away from him. 'Why do you think I have kept Chinkin with me, and given my other sons their own provinces, their own countries to govern? To keep them from plotting together! If they suspected any . . . any weakness in him, then after my death the empire founded by my grandfather, Genghis Khan, would be torn to pieces. Ripped apart like an ox by starving wolves!' Kublai paused, lowering his voice. 'My guards have the strictest orders that anyone who witnesses one of his attacks – or comes to hear of them for any reason – is instantly to be put to death.'

Marco realized his danger at last and rose involuntarily. 'My father and uncle . . .'

Kublai's face was set. 'I have honoured them in the past – but there can be no exceptions.' He paused. 'And there is your servant.'

'Chen Pao?' It was another stab for Marco.

'When he is found, he will be executed. With the others.' Marco was stunned, unable to react. 'And then there is you. At least you do not beg for mercy. That makes it easier – because you tried to help. But I know now that in your heart you despise my son.'

'But I don't,' Marco protested.

'I preferred your silence!' Kublai said coldly.

'Chinkin is my friend!' retorted Marco with vehemence. 'I don't despise him. Why should I? If you want the truth, I was terrified of losing him. My only other real friend, Giulio, died on the journey. Since then, I've had no-one until now . . . You're *wrong!*'

Kublai stiffened. 'Wrong?' he growled. It was a word that nobody had dared to apply to him before.

'Yes!' continued Marco, unabashed. 'You talk about the falling sickness as if it was leprosy or something! Many people have suffered from it, famous men. Alexander the Great was one. And Julius Caesar, the noblest of the Romans.'

Kublai was astounded. 'Iskander? Kaisar?'

'It's an affliction, but it didn't destroy them. And it didn't affect anything else in their lives,' Marco said bluntly.

'But they were two of the Perfect Warriors. The whole world honours them.' Kublai was gazing at him.

'Well, they both had the falling sickness,' Marco said. 'Father Anselmo at school told us. He said it was nothing to be ashamed of. In ancient times it was considered a sign of greatness.'

'My son has the sign of greatness?' whispered Kublai.

Marco suddenly realized that he was standing and he fell to his knees. His heart was pounding audibly. He did not know how he had dared to speak so frankly. The silence stretched on for what seemed an age.

'Get up, Master Marco . . .' he heard the Khan say quietly. As Marco looked up, Kublai beckoned to him, headed towards the exit and swept out. Guards on duty outside knelt at once and Phags-pa came forward, bowing. Kublai halted the Keeper of the Records with a gesture and paused by the captain of the Imperial Bodyguard.

'From today, Master Marco will hold an honoured place at my court. He is to be admitted to me at all times – and his orders are to be obeyed.'

'Yes, Great Lord,' said the officer, with unhidden surprise.

What Kublai did next was clearly for the benefit of Phags-pa. He turned with a faint smile. 'You appear to have lost your belt, Master Marco.'

'Yes, Great Lord.'

'Then take this in exchange . . .'

Kublai unclipped a silver belt from his own waist and handed it over. The belt was studded with rubies and had a small dagger hanging from it. Marco accepted it in amazement, and bowed.

For a second, Phags-pa stared in disbelief, but recovered like a skilled courtier. He advanced and bowed, glancing up at the storm clouds that were gathering overhead. 'The Spirits of the air are restless, Great Lord,' he said. 'The weather is changing. That may have caused the recent . . . disorders. Shall I call the Shamans to disperse the clouds?'

'No!' announced Kublai. 'The hunting season is over. We shall return to Khanbalic.'

Phags-pa left to order the preparations for leaving. Marco thanked Kublai for the gift and asked permission to see Prince Chinkin. Soon afterwards, he was conducted into the pavilion of the Empress Jaimu, where his friend lay on a couch, covered with furs. The empress herself, drawn and anxious, held the phial of sacred oil that Marco and the others had brought from Jerusalem. Her cheeks glistened with tears as she gazed down at Chinkin.

'This is why I wanted the oil from the Holy Sepulchre,' she confessed. 'Because my son, my dear son, has the falling sickness. Our medicines, and the magic of the Shamans, have failed to cure him. If this fails also . . .'

She looked at Marco for reassurance and he gave her the only answer that he knew. 'The Holy Father said that it is faith that cures, Great Lady – not the oil itself.'

The Empress Jaimu nodded and crossed over to her son,

who lay weak and restless. With the utmost care, she poured a drop of the oil on to his fevered brow, then worked it gently into a sign of the cross with her fingertips. She repeated the process on his lips and on his chest. Chinkin continued to tremble and mutter. She bit her lip, glanced round and saw that Marco's hands were closed together in prayer and that his eyes were shut. Lowering her head, her hands clasped round the phial, she too tried to pray.

When she turned back to her son, she trembled. Was it possible? Chinkin seemed calmer and was falling into a deep and peaceful sleep.

The day was fine and clear and from the cleft in the hill could be seen a long view of a distant, fertile plain. The entire cleft, running back into the treeclad hills, had been turned into a corral for the Great Khan's herd of pure white horses. From them Shamans came, carrying the milk of the mares in silver bowls.

They climbed up to an altar standing before a shrine set on a low pyramid of white marble. On the altar stood a gigantic golden bowl into which the Shamans poured the milk. They were flanked by other priests of the court, saffron-robed Buddhists on one side, black-robed Nestorians on the other, but the ceremony was Shamanist.

To the side, Kublai Khan sat on a raised ivory throne. Chinkin, pale but recovered, was on his right, leaning on Marco's arm. The little Prince Timur stood beside them, troubled, glancing at his father who some said had been poisoned by the foreign-devil, his pretended friend. Beyond them were other male members of Kublai's family. On his left, on a lower throne, sat the Empress Jaimu with the Imperial Ladies. Kublai and all the Imperial Family were dressed in white robes and he wore a diadem of white gold bordered with pearls.

Facing them on the other lower sides of the human square were Phags-pa, Argan, Nasreddin and other members of the Council of Twelve, with rows of Mongol nobles, officers and court officials. They watched as more milk was poured into the golden bowl, while Shamans at each end of the altar beat their ritual oval drums, revolving slowly, muttering incantations to the Spirit of the White Horses.

Marco saw the looks directed at him by many in the assembly, Phags-pa's speculative, Argan's more hostile like some of the nobles, and knew that somewhere in the outer ranks his father was watching him anxiously, disturbed by his sudden prominence. 'Don't push yourself forward,' Niccolo had cautioned. 'It doesn't do to be too conspicuous. We're only tolerated here.' Yet sheer fascination swept away any disquiet he felt. Performed annually, just before the Khan returned to his capital, the ceremony was sympathetic magic, reaffirming the Imperial Family's link with the Mongol gods. He remembered how Caidu had told him that the white horses were the symbol of the power and majesty of Genghis Khan and that only his descendants were permitted to ride them. And Chinkin had told him that only they could drink the milk of the mares.

The Imperial Chief Shaman was standing at the altar, his arms upraised to the sides. All the time he had been chanting along with the others, but as the milk poured into the great bowl reached nearly to its brim, his voice rose in volume, so that it could be heard ringing out over the drums and incantations. '. . . Great Steed of Genghis, the Kha Khan, Lord of Lords, Emperor of All Men – the Rider of Heaven! To him, the Spirits of the Eternal Blue Sky gave the east and west, the north and south – to his invincible sword was given the riches of the world and the lives of the Sons and Daughters of Men . . .'

Other Shamans approached the altar and bowed as he spoke, pouring more milk into the bowl until it lapped the brim. The voice of the Chief Shaman carried on without stop.

'On his steed, the White Stallion of the Spirits, he bestrode the earth.

At his command, its dread hooves broke down mountains.

Its neighing shattered the strongholds of the Mighty.

Its nostrils breathed terror into the hearts of his enemies.

The passing of its white Tail was the hot wind of the Gobi.

Its white mane brushed the stars!
And high on its arching back sat
He who was hero, He who was wisest,
He who was conqueror of all –
He who was Mongol!'

His last word was almost a scream. It was taken up by everyone watching and even Marco found himself yelling, 'Mongol! Mongol!'

The golden bowl was full and the Chief Shaman turned dramatically, lifting his arms to Kublai.

Kublai rose and all present knelt, except for his immediate family and the Empresses. Kublai descended from his raised throne and advanced to the altar and the Chief Shaman with Chinkin, Timur and five other young princes. Marco went part of the way with Chinkin, supporting him, then knelt.

The Chief Shaman had scooped some milk from the bowl in a silver goblet and presented it to Kublai. Other Shamans presented goblets to Chinkin and the princes, then retreated and knelt. Kublai raised his goblet and poured some of the milk on to the ground in front of him. Following him, Chinkin and the others also poured some as an offering.

Kublai's voice rang out, magnified like the Shamans' by the configuration of the ground. 'May the Spirits of the Eternal Blue Sky grant to all living things – to all mankind, all beasts and plants and fruit – increase and safekeeping in the twelve months to come!' The white horses could be heard whickering and neighing in the silence as he and the princes drank off the milk in their goblets.

While they drank, the Chief Shaman and his assistants removed stoppers from the lower sides of the huge golden bowl and milk began to pour out over the altar. Marco, gazing at it, almost hypnotized, saw all the kneeling officials and nobles lower their foreheads to the ground. He also leant forward, feeling no awkwardness in the obeisance.

The milk, cascading over the altar, spread out, frothing and bubbling, sinking into the parched ground.

The Summer Palace of Shangtu had looked vast, glorious and permanent, but it fell with the ease of a house of cards. The soaring pavilions toppled down, tents were dismantled, carpets rolled up, furniture and furnishings were packed, and a whole army of servants made everything ready for transport to Khanbalic. Throughout, the drums kept up their insistent beat. The Great Khan Kublai was moving south-east to his capital.

Watching the departure from a hilltop, Phags-pa drew the attention of his companion to the sight of Crown Prince Chinkin riding at the head of his men, with Marco at his side.

'The sign of greatness,' murmured Argan scornfully.

'The prince appears to have recovered,' said Phags-pa. 'It is a blessing.'

'Is it?' snorted the general. 'His son, Timur, is worth ten of him, even though he is only a boy. Every day Chinkin becomes less like a Mongol, more poisoned by the foreigner's ideas and religion.'

'It is also his mother's chosen religion,' Phags-pa reminded him, 'and the Great Khan himself favours it.'

Argan snorted once more. 'He plays with Christianity! But not his son. Chinkin is weak and that philosophy, exalting weakness, appeals to him. Something must be done!'

'What *can* be done?' Phags-pa asked mildly. But his eyes were intent on Argan, as he waited for his response.

'Bad influences must be removed. They must be eliminated without mercy.'

As Argan spoke, his eyes were fixed on Marco.

The Imperial cavalcade wound slowly through a countryside that was surrendering its summer glow to the deeper colours of autumn. Niccolo and Matteo found the pace luxurious after the hazards of the journey to Kublai. Fertile valleys gave way to grassy plains. Wooded slopes and craggy mountains added to the impression of a constantly changing landscape. Marco was thrilled by it all. At one point, he and Chinkin came to the top of a rise that looked down on another lush, green valley. On impulse, they spurred their horses and raced each other at breakneck speed for the best part of a mile, taking their armed escort by surprise and leaving them far behind.

Niccolo and Matteo laughed indulgently at this exuberance, and Jacopo, plump again thanks to the rich diet, chuckled throatily. All three were pleased to see the developing friendship between Marco and Prince Chinkin, and not only because it raised their own status among the Mongols. Niccolo marvelled at Marco's good fortune and now had no regrets at all about having brought his son with him.

When the two riders reached the bottom of the valley, they reined in their horses near a sparkling stream to let them drink. Marco gazed around happily. 'Is all China so beautiful?'

'I don't know,' replied Chinkin. 'I suppose it is. I'm learning to see it with new eyes. Your eyes.'

'Those eyes see you in good health now.'

'Thanks to you, Marco,' Chinkin said seriously. 'My mother believes you were sent by your God.'

Marco grinned. 'I'm here because I pestered my poor father to take me! And also, because the Pope took pity on me.' He became serious, too. 'I did not believe my father when he told me how long and hard the journey would be. But if only to have helped you, it was worth it.'

'There are many who would not agree,' the prince confided. 'Even in my own household, there are some who watch. To report any sign of illness.'

'Then you must disappoint them,' Marco smiled.

Chinkin smiled back. The rest of the cavalcade was starting to catch them up, and as Niccolo, Matteo and Jacopo came towards them with their escort, the two friends kicked hard again and galloped off.

On leaving the valley, they found themselves in a totally different terrain. Low-lying bushes and shrubs abounded and there were cultivated fields where peasants tilled the earth or watched over small flocks of livestock. Smoke rose from the rooftops of scattered huts and the voices of children and dogs greeted them as they rode past. A thick forest made them slow their horses and pick their way carefully, but when they emerged from the trees, they were met by a sight that took Marco completely by surprise.

Ahead of them, like something left over from the age of giants, stretched the Great Wall.

'It starts up in the north,' said Chinkin, enjoying the other's gasp of disbelief. 'You must have seen it at Giungiam.'

'I had no idea! I thought it was a fortified valley defending the exit from the Gobi desert.' Marco stared open-mouthed at the massive, crenellated structure that snaked its way over the crests of the hills, reinforced at intervals by square towers. 'How long is it?'

'About one thousand five hundred miles, and wide enough for a cart and oxen to ride on. It was built a thousand years ago to protect the north-west of China against the barbarians.'

'Barbarians?' Marco asked, then understood and glanced at Chinkin in apology.

'Yes. The desert barbarians. The Mongols,' replied Chinkin, smiling.

The escort had now caught them up and gazed with

who lay weak and restless. With the utmost care, she poured a drop of the oil on to his fevered brow, then worked it gently into a sign of the cross with her fingertips. She repeated the process on his lips and on his chest. Chinkin continued to tremble and mutter. She bit her lip, glanced round and saw that Marco's hands were closed together in prayer and that his eyes were shut. Lowering her head, her hands clasped round the phial, she too tried to pray.

When she turned back to her son, she trembled. Was it possible? Chinkin seemed calmer and was falling into a deep and peaceful sleep.

The day was fine and clear and from the cleft in the hill could be seen a long view of a distant, fertile plain. The entire cleft, running back into the treeclad hills, had been turned into a corral for the Great Khan's herd of pure white horses. From them Shamans came, carrying the milk of the mares in silver bowls.

They climbed up to an altar standing before a shrine set on a low pyramid of white marble. On the altar stood a gigantic golden bowl into which the Shamans poured the milk. They were flanked by other priests of the court, saffron-robed Buddhists on one side, black-robed Nestorians on the other, but the ceremony was Shamanist.

To the side, Kublai Khan sat on a raised ivory throne. Chinkin, pale but recovered, was on his right, leaning on Marco's arm. The little Prince Timur stood beside them, troubled, glancing at his father who some said had been poisoned by the foreign-devil, his pretended friend. Beyond them were other male members of Kublai's family. On his left, on a lower throne, sat the Empress Jaimu with the Imperial Ladies. Kublai and all the Imperial Family were dressed in white robes and he wore a diadem of white gold bordered with pearls.

Facing them on the other lower sides of the human square were Phags-pa, Argan, Nasreddin and other members of the Council of Twelve, with rows of Mongol nobles, officers and court officials. They watched as more milk was poured into the golden bowl, while Shamans at each end of the altar beat their ritual oval drums, revolving slowly, muttering incantations to the Spirit of the White Horses.

Marco saw the looks directed at him by many in the assembly, Phags-pa's speculative, Argan's more hostile like some of the nobles, and knew that somewhere in the outer ranks his father was watching him anxiously, disturbed by his sudden prominence. 'Don't push yourself forward,' Niccolo had cautioned. 'It doesn't do to be too conspicuous. We're only tolerated here.' Yet sheer fascination swept away any disquiet he felt. Performed annually, just before the Khan returned to his capital, the ceremony was sympathetic magic, reaffirming the Imperial Family's link with the Mongol gods. He remembered how Caidu had told him that the white horses were the symbol of the power and majesty of Genghis Khan and that only his descendants were permitted to ride them. And Chinkin had told him that only they could drink the milk of the mares.

The Imperial Chief Shaman was standing at the altar, his arms upraised to the sides. All the time he had been chanting along with the others, but as the milk poured into the great bowl reached nearly to its brim, his voice rose in volume, so that it could be heard ringing out over the drums and incantations. '. . . Great Steed of Genghis, the Kha Khan, Lord of Lords, Emperor of All Men – the Rider of Heaven! To him, the Spirits of the Eternal Blue Sky gave the east and west, the north and south – to his invincible sword was given the riches of the world and the lives of the Sons and Daughters of Men . . .'

Other Shamans approached the altar and bowed as he spoke, pouring more milk into the bowl until it lapped the brim. The voice of the Chief Shaman carried on without stop.

'Bad influences must be removed. They must be eliminated without mercy.'

As Argan spoke, his eyes were fixed on Marco.

The Imperial cavalcade wound slowly through a countryside that was surrendering its summer glow to the deeper colours of autumn. Niccolo and Matteo found the pace luxurious after the hazards of the journey to Kublai. Fertile valleys gave way to grassy plains. Wooded slopes and craggy mountains added to the impression of a constantly changing landscape. Marco was thrilled by it all. At one point, he and Chinkin came to the top of a rise that looked down on another lush, green valley. On impulse, they spurred their horses and raced each other at breakneck speed for the best part of a mile, taking their armed escort by surprise and leaving them far behind.

Niccolo and Matteo laughed indulgently at this exuberance, and Jacopo, plump again thanks to the rich diet, chuckled throatily. All three were pleased to see the developing friendship between Marco and Prince Chinkin, and not only because it raised their own status among the Mongols. Niccolo marvelled at Marco's good fortune and now had no regrets at all about having brought his son with him.

When the two riders reached the bottom of the valley, they reined in their horses near a sparkling stream to let them drink. Marco gazed around happily. 'Is all China so beautiful?'

'I don't know,' replied Chinkin. 'I suppose it is. I'm learning to see it with new eyes. Your eyes.'

'Those eyes see you in good health now.'

'Thanks to you, Marco,' Chinkin said seriously. 'My mother believes you were sent by your God.'

Marco grinned. 'I'm here because I pestered my poor father to take me! And also, because the Pope took pity on me.' He became serious, too. 'I did not believe my father when he told me how long and hard the journey would be. But if only to have helped you, it was worth it.'

'There are many who would not agree,' the prince confided. 'Even in my own household, there are some who watch. To report any sign of illness.'

'Then you must disappoint them,' Marco smiled.

Chinkin smiled back. The rest of the cavalcade was starting to catch them up, and as Niccolo, Matteo and Jacopo came towards them with their escort, the two friends kicked hard again and galloped off.

On leaving the valley, they found themselves in a totally different terrain. Low-lying bushes and shrubs abounded and there were cultivated fields where peasants tilled the earth or watched over small flocks of livestock. Smoke rose from the rooftops of scattered huts and the voices of children and dogs greeted them as they rode past. A thick forest made them slow their horses and pick their way carefully, but when they emerged from the trees, they were met by a sight that took Marco completely by surprise.

Ahead of them, like something left over from the age of giants, stretched the Great Wall.

'It starts up in the north,' said Chinkin, enjoying the other's gasp of disbelief. 'You must have seen it at Giungiam.'

'I had no idea! I thought it was a fortified valley defending the exit from the Gobi desert.' Marco stared open-mouthed at the massive, crenellated structure that snaked its way over the crests of the hills, reinforced at intervals by square towers. 'How long is it?'

'About one thousand five hundred miles, and wide enough for a cart and oxen to ride on. It was built a thousand years ago to protect the north-west of China against the barbarians.'

'Barbarians?' Marco asked, then understood and glanced at Chinkin in apology.

'Yes. The desert barbarians. The Mongols,' replied Chinkin, smiling.

The escort had now caught them up and gazed with

that conquerors should be feared, not liked. The Council of Barons believes that the Chinese must be controlled with an iron hand, to prevent them rising against us.'

'But surely it can't go on forever,' he argued, thinking of Chen Pao.

'You are right.' Chinkin lowered his voice. 'I have no wish to succeed my father before his time has been completed. But one thing, above all, I shall try to do when my turn comes – to teach us all that we are the same nation. The only hope for the future is that one day the Mongols will no longer be thought of, nor think of themselves, as nomads and invaders, but as sons of the same mother: China.'

'Surely the Great Khan could do that now?' insisted Marco, stirred by his friend's determination.

'It is too soon.'

'Is that why I have seen no Chinese in positions of power?'

'Tens of thousands of them serve the Great Khan, but all positions of importance are given to Mongols or to foreigners who will be faithful out of self-interest. If the Great Khan is overthrown, so would they be.'

'Foreigners like Nasreddin?'

'Yes, he is from Bokhara, in Persia. Zurficar is from Turkey.'

'And my father, my uncle and myself,' added Marco, 'we are from Venice.'

Chinkin paused. His voice was sombre. 'There is one more powerful than them all – Achmet. He is the Regent. He governs the empire, when my father is not in residence in Khanbalic.'

'I have heard about him,' said Marco, inquisitive as ever. 'What is he really like?'

Chinkin reflected for a moment, then spoke in carefully neutral tones. 'Achmet is a Turk. He is very capable, attentive to my father's every wish. You will meet him in the morning when the city of Khanbalic welcomes our return.'

That night Marco had little sleep. His mind was restless, filled with thoughts of Chen Pao, of Phags-pa, of Achmet, and of the extraordinary turn of events that had made him, the son of a Venetian merchant, into the confidant of a prince.

Nothing that his father and uncle had told him, nothing he had already seen in Shangtu, prepared Marco for the sheer enormity of the city of Khanbalic. Built in the form of a square, its perimeter walls ran for all of twenty-four miles, and its twelve colossal gates were each guarded by a thousand men and surmounted by a splendid palace.

The Great Khan Kublai was greeted rapturously by the throngs of well-wishers, and he revelled in the joy and the celebration. Marco, too, found the combination of music, colour, excitement, pageant and continuous applause exhilarating, but it did not stop him from noticing that among the hordes of Mongol and Chinese faces were many from India, Arabia, Tibet, and other races he had yet to identify.

At the heart of the Khanbalic was the Forbidden City itself, residence of the Great Khan and a citadel of daunting magnitude. It was surrounded by four high solid walls, each a mile in length, and at each corner stood a fine palace that was used as an arsenal. As the procession approached the southern front of the city, Marco saw five massive gates ahead. The central one, only ever opened to admit the Great Khan himself, was now swinging back on giant hinges to give him his first glimpse within.

The cavalcade swept in through the central gate and Marco felt that he was entering a different world altogether, so complete was the contrast with what lay outside the walls. They were in the courtyard of the Great Khan's palace, a vast but delicate structure of golden and majolica domes, pink lacquered columns, marble walls and floors and intricate miniature gardens. Because only the Khan had the right to bright colours, being above all mortal men, all the houses in the outer city had been painted grey. In contrast, the multicoloured brightness of the palace was dazzling.

The courtyard was crowded with nobles, court officials and their wives and children, all dressed in ornate clothes, and all unnaturally quiet after the happy uproar outside. Buddhist, Nestorian and Lamaist priests stood in groups, while soldiers, standard bearers and musicians waited in their appointed places. At the very centre of the courtyard was Achmet, Regent and First Minister of the Khan.

Drums and trumpets sounded as the Great Khan entered the courtyard and every head bowed low in homage. Kublai dismounted, handed the reins of the white stallion to a servant, and strode towards Achmet, who was holding a sceptre of ivory and gold with a yak-tail at its tip, which symbolized his authority as Regent. Achmet, tall, dignified, shrewd, and with the distinctive features of a Turk, knelt before his master and solemnly returned the sceptre, yielding up as he did so the power that he had exercised in Kublai's absence. The Regent then lowered his face to the marble floor and offered his neck to the foot of the Great Khan in a ritual of total subjection. Music accompanied the ceremony and heightened its impact.

When the official reception was over, Achmet conducted the Polos to a spacious private chamber in the Regent's Palace. There he was able to extend an enthusiastic personal welcome to Niccolo and Matteo. He clasped their hands, smiling, 'My friends! A welcome return to Khanbalic – after so many years! As much as the Great Khan, I rejoice to see you.'

'No happiness could equal our own, my lord,' replied Matteo.

Achmet turned dark, smiling eyes on Marco. 'And this is the young man of whom I have heard such promising things.'

'My son,' introduced Niccolo, proudly. Marco bowed. 'As I have told you, Marco, Lord Achmet is our protector and benefactor in China.'

'And friend, I hope,' chuckled the Turk. 'It is not often that one finds such able counsellors in all matters of trade and commerce as your father and uncle, young sir. You have a high reputation to live up to.'

'Any talents I have, I have learned from them, my lord.'

'Well said!' Achmet turned back to the beaming merchants. 'Your positions in my department are, of course, yours again. Your staff has been expanded and you will find interesting developments, especially in the silk and spice trades.'

'We have made many valuable contacts with merchants in many countries in the course of our journey,' Niccolo said. 'My son has kept note of them.'

'Excellent! And naturally when the Great Khan has completed the conquest of the south, the opportunities for new markets and sources will be enormous.' He looked at Marco and spread his hands apologetically. 'I would offer you a post also, as assistant to your father, perhaps. But I understand that you have been attached to the household of Prince Chinkin?'

'Yes, my lord.'

'However,' Achmet went on. 'Remember I am your father's friend. If you need any help or advice, do not hesitate to come to me.'

The beauties of the Forbidden City were so great and extensive that Marco was reminded of his dream of paradise. Apart from the sumptuous palaces, each decorated with gold and silver and filled with rich hangings and superb furnishings, there were magnificent parks and gardens that displayed Kublai's rare talent for landscape design. Taking a keen personal interest from the start, the Khan had made good use of the soil excavated from the huge stew-ponds in his palace grounds, heaping it up to form a massive hill and planting it with evergreens selected by himself. His master-stroke was to cover the whole mound with lapis lazuli and then set a green palace on top of it, thus creating the most striking view.

But this delight began to pall on Marco after a while. It was not that he had tired of the glories of the Forbidden City, but rather that he had begun to think about their implications. How many shovels had worked to shift the thousands of tons of earth for the mound? What physical torment lay behind the moving of the stones and the marble? Who could remember the numberless deaths that went into the making of those mighty walls?

There was also another reason for his restlessness, which he confessed one day. 'I want to see outside, Chinkin.'

'Outside?'

For months, Marco had led a totally inactive life, penned up in the palace. 'Beyond the gates of the Forbidden City. I want to visit the real Khanbalic, where the ordinary people live and work.'

Instead of mocking him, as Marco had feared, Chinkin agreed to the idea eagerly. It would be an adventure for them both. Wrapping themselves in dark cloaks, they slipped out through one of the gates and suddenly entered a world that was bustling with life and noisy with argument. It was early evening, but the shops and the stalls were still trading, and Marco's first impression was of a rather more squalid version of the market he had seen at Yazd. Closer inspection of the people and sights of Khanbalic, however, taught him that it was very different. The poor seemed to live most of their lives in the streets. A man with two trained monkeys entertained a group of laughing children, letting the animals perform somersaults on his head and shoulders. A healer applied a mess of snake entrails and raw fish to the bald head of a patient. A doctor was sticking needles into his patient, apparently without causing him any pain. A juggler kept several clubs in the air while running through the streets and Marco and Chinkin were nearly trampled by the crowd hurrying to keep up with him.

Clean-shaven, obviously European, Marco attracted a

considerable amount of curiosity. On the other hand, Chinkin passed almost unnoticed, his appearance and clothes so normal that no one even remotely suspected his importance or that all their lives belonged to him, as heir to the throne of Yüan. To be treated as an ordinary human being was a strange experience for him. Once or twice, in spite of himself, he nearly became angry at the lack of deference, but laughed instead with Marco, and was refreshed by it.

Admiring a procession of young girls, dressed in festive costumes, gentle and reserved, moving with the shy grace of fawns, they saw them join a procession coming from a group of poor hovels, men, women and children dressed in white. They were carrying banners painted with pictures of toys and sweetmeats, led by a man holding a pole on which hung a lifesized paper cut-out of a little boy. Intrigued, they fell in behind the procession.

It led them to the internal courtyard of a Buddhist temple, where they met another procession, almost identical, led by a man carrying a paper cut-out of a girl child. As Chinkin understood, he stopped smiling and Marco was surprised to see tears in his eyes. 'They are two families,' Chinkin explained. 'One has lost a boy, the other a daughter. And the parents have met to join the spirits of their dead children in marriage.'

Watching the simple ritual, they saw a Buddhist monk uncover a large brazier and the two fathers throw the paper images of their children on to the flames. As they caught fire, twin spirals of smoke rose from them, joining and becoming one as they floated away on the evening air. Temple gongs rang out and everyone clapped their hands. The other children ran to the brazier, placing on them the banner painted with sweets and toys.

'Nothing must be denied to them,' Chinkin said. 'These are presents for the children's spirits, for them to have for ever. That way, you see, these people defeat death's attempt to cheat their children of the joys of life.'

Marco was moved and the two friends left the courtyard

quietly, not wishing to intrude any longer. At a stall, they bought some *satay*, pieces of river fish grilled on a bamboo skewer, and a napkin filled with steamed, fluffily white dumplings. They were delicious, washed down with tiny cups of cinnamon-flavoured tea.

Eventually they reached a broad street already ablaze with hanging paper lanterns and bright with many-coloured chrysanthemums.

'What's down there?' Marco asked, pointing.

'You don't want to see that part of the city,' Chinkin assured him with a smile.

'I want to see everything.'

'But that is the street of the Flower Houses, leading to the prostitutes' quarter.'

Marco stopped. 'You mean . . .?'

'Every city has its prostitutes. Even Venice, I dare say.'

'Oh yes . . .' Marco admitted, remembering Monna Fiammetta.

'In Khanbalic, they have almost twenty thousand.' Chinkin smiled at his friend's amazement. 'They are very well organized. There is a captain-general, with chiefs-of-thousand and chiefs-of-hundred responsible to her.'

'*Her!*'

'Women know best how to order women. If you really do wish to see everything, Marco . . .'

'No, no,' Marco said, stopping him from heading off towards the flower-filled street. He tried to affect a worldly indifference. 'When you have seen one such area . . .'

'My father would not agree with you.'

'The Great Khan comes *here!*' Marco was incredulous.

'No, of course not. He would never consort with common prostitutes. He has high standards where his concubines are concerned. He favours the girls of Kungurat province, because they have such fair complexions.'

'The Great Khan?'

'Forty new concubines are selected for him every two years.'

Marco was stunned for a moment. He knew that Kublai

had four wives and well over twenty children, but this was the first time he had thought of his harem. He was not sure whether to be shocked by his lack of moral sense or impressed by his stamina.

'Does your father have no concubines, Marco?' Chinkin smiled.

'Of course not!'

Chinkin laughed. 'How well do you know him?'

'Not as well as you know *your* father, obviously,' Marco said and they laughed, strolling back.

Marco's private quarters were near Chinkin's palace and, although not magnificent by Chinese standards, were quite the most comfortable and elegant in which he had ever lived. The floors were of inlaid satinwood and the rooms entirely lined with silk panels. Chinkin sent him paintings to decorate the walls and new furniture of gilded rosewood, while the Empress's gift, the one which Marco prized most highly, was a translucent pale-blue vase of exquisite lines, a precious example of the art of the mysterious island of Cipango. Marco's European clothes were now nearly worn out, so he had them copied by Chinkin's tailors. But over the months, he wore them less and less, preferring the mode of dress of the young nobles; loose trousers tucked into soft calf-length boots, a shirt and divided robe gathered at the waist, with a padded jacket or cloak in colder weather. Unlike the nobles, he did not go armed and wore only the silver belt with the short dagger given to him by the Khan.

His life was pleasant and ordered, in many respects ideal. His friendship with Chinkin deepened until they became almost inseparable, and the two of them spent much time with the old Empress, who liked Marco to tell her stories from the Bible and of the lives of the saints. In return she had bards to recite for them the epics and legends of the Mongols who he found to his astonishment had no written language, and whose literature and history were all oral. She herself told them of her own early days and marriage to Kublai, fourth son of the fourth son of Genghis Khan, the Rider of Heaven. Genghis, son of a petty chieftain, by his ruthless brilliance in war and ability to inspire absolute loyalty had made himself Kha Khan, Emperor of Mongolia, then with his armies and his irresistible Mongol cavalry had spread his empire over Cathay, Turkestan, Russia, northern India and Persia. He had been succeeded by his warrior son, Ogodei, who left the throne in turn to his nephew Möngke, Kublai's elder brother. When Möngke died, another of his brothers claimed the succession, but was defeated in battle by Kublai, who had himself proclaimed Kha Khan, founder of the dynasty of the Great Origin, Ta Yüan. Unlike his predecessors, Kublai never lived in the Gobi or at the old capital, Karakorum, but had established himself firmly in Khanbalic, known to the Mongols as Ta-tu, the Great City. The Spirits had told him it was his destiny to reunite China, divided since the far-off days of the T'ang Emperors.

With Chinkin, Marco also saw much of the Great Khan, becoming more and more impressed with his wisdom and magnanimity. Kublai liked Marco to ride with him in the early morning and questioned him closely on the history of the European kingdoms, their alliances and geography. He never talked down to the younger men and laughed and joked with them when they were alone, often sending for them when he needed relaxation from the cares of state. Marco felt no disloyalty in telling him all he knew, for Europe was in no danger from the Khan. His concentration was all on China and the East.

With the Imperial cartographers, Marco had worked over the maps of the areas covered by his journey, correcting and bringing them up to date. It was a work he enjoyed and wished to do more of, but he had no opportunity. As a member of Chinkin's household, he joined in the prince's life of cultured idleness. He told himself he should be grateful, that he was fulfilling as best as he could the Pope's wishes, by strengthening the

Empress's longing to believe and the Khan's knowledge of the Holy Father's power and influence. He could not debate theology with Phags-pa or the Confucians, the Chinese priests. The Nestorians he distrusted as heretics, although he found them sympathetic and sometimes attended their services, fascinated to compare them with the Latin Mass he knew and loved. He saw less and less of his father and uncle, who were immersed in the service of state commerce and their own trading ventures. He continued his study of Mongol and Chinese, but there were days when he felt restless and irritable. He was not used to a life of idleness.

Chinkin told him he needed a woman.

In Marco's household, there were several younger women, who were virtually his slaves, to do with as he chose. Yet although two at least were undeniably attractive, an innate belief in human dignity prevented him from taking advantage of them. He had been brought up to treat servants with respect, not as chattels. Besides, as Chinkin warned him, among them were bound to be some planted by Phags-pa, Achmet or any one of a number of other powerful figures, eager to have a spy close to the Khan's new favourite. The answer, Chinkin assured him, was simple. Among the beautiful girls brought to the palace for the Khan, those not selected as concubines were given to favoured noblemen, as were those of whom the Khan had tired. Marco had only to mention his need and any number would be provided. He could not understand Marco's reluctance, even horror, at the idea. Instead, once a month, Marco took to going to the Hall of Fragrant Lilies – on his own. He forced himself not to go more often, for the sensual pleasures provided by the skilful, bewitching singing-girls, trained in the arts of love since childhood, were intoxicating – and addictive. Many men had been known to ruin themselves financially and physically through over-indulgence.

One day, Chinkin led him to the Hill of the Hundred Brushes, a ziggurat of rising terraces where the Chinese came to consult the astrologers. Like the Mongols, the Han Chinese were extremely superstitious and no business, no journey, no active step of any kind would they take without consulting the stars.

The hill was crowded with clients, noisy with the cries of vendors of almanacs and amulets, sweets, cakes and magic philtres. Children ran laughing, trailing kites, and groups of friends, excited by good fortune or to drive off bad omens, exploded firecrackers, leaping and jumping as they crackled round their feet.

Marco was amused and intrigued by the lively scene. Fortune-telling seemed to him to be heathenish nonsense, yet in China it was an honoured science, based on an exhaustive study of the stars over thousands of years. It could not be lightly dismissed and, in spite of himself, it made him slightly uneasy.

They were on the highest terrace, and while they waited to consult an astrologer they looked down over the balustrade, over the slope of many-coloured roofs, over the golden spires, down to the lake of the park, reflecting the cloud-studded sky.

'This is the roof of Khanbalic, Marco,' Chinkin said. 'Here the wise ones come to be closer to the sun, moon and stars.'

They walked on, inspecting the rare and valuable instruments; jade astral disks with a sighting hole in the centre, astrolabes, small and large armillary spheres and a curious, long bronze tube resting on a tripod. Seeing their interest, an astronomer turned the tube on its pivot, aiming it in the direction of a wooded area beyond the lake. Chinkin smiled. 'Can you see anything over there?' he asked Marco. Marco looked, but it was too far to make anything out clearly. 'Take a look through here,' Chinkin said.

Marco looked through the lower end of the tube. At first he saw nothing. But as the astronomer adjusted the hinged lenses, he gasped. In the eye of the telescope he suddenly saw a section of the distant wood with startling clarity. A rider was galloping on a path through the trees, the banner attached to his saddle-bow of white and green, the colours of the Khan, whipping through the air.

'At night,' the astronomer said, 'it shows you the moon's face.'

Marco touched the tube with awe. Only a few months ago, he would have thought such a thing to be magic. Now he knew it was science, part of the incredible science developed by the people of China over untold centuries, before even the Roman Empire rose and fell, when Greece was still in her infancy.

'Come, Marco,' Chinkin said. 'I think the astrologer is free now. It is our turn.'

With some reluctance, Marco followed Chinkin to an old man who waited patiently, his thin hands folded in the sleeves of his black silk robe. He looked up as they approached, assessing them shrewdly, and bowed to Chinkin where he sat. 'Is it you who wishes to consult the stars, my lord?'

Chinkin was holding himself very erect, but could not disguise a shudder of disgust, almost fear. 'No, I have no wish to know the future,' he said. 'My friend wants to ask when the war with the South will end.'

'And whether peace will follow victory,' Marco added.

The astrologer stared at him fixedly for a moment, then reached for his astrolabe. With a barely perceptible creak, the instrument began to turn very slowly. After raising his eyes to the sky, the astrologer took a square ruler and followed the imaginary lines that converged at the centre of his jade disk. His gestures were practised and graceful and Marco was fascinated.

'These are the signs of the heavens,' the astrologer announced. 'The small faces the big. Amid the tears and mourning stands one great banner. Not gold, but iron will come to the throne.'

'Tears and mourning?' Marco's smile faded.

Chinkin was disturbed. 'Let's get away from here,' he said, taking Marco's arm and pulling him away.

The astrologer, who had been writing out his prediction, looked up in surprise. 'Wait, wait!'

But the two friends were already hurrying down the stairs.

'You gave in to fear, Marco,' Kublai Khan said sternly. 'You and my son opened the door to the heavens and then turned away from their answer.'

They were in the Audience Room at the Great Khan's palace and each was wondering how he knew exactly where they had been. They had taken such trouble to conceal themselves that they had thought their expeditions had gone unnoticed. Kublai disillusioned them.

'Listen to me carefully, both of you. There is no place under the sun where the Khan's watchful eye does not reach.'

'You've been having us followed, father?' asked Chinkin, tensing at the thought.

'You did not imagine that I would let you wander around without protection?' Kublai waited for an answer. 'Well?'

'I simply wanted to see the city as the people see it, father.'

'It was my fault, Great Lord,' Marco said. 'I asked Prince Chinkin to show me the real Khanbalic.'

'Wherever *I* go – *that* is the real Khanbalic,' the Khan said. Then he smiled, and they realized he was not angry. 'I know that both of you must find the Forbidden City narrow and confining. It is only natural that you long for fresh sights. But from now on, have no illusions. You are of the Royal Household. There is *always* someone watching you.'

'Yes, father,' replied Chinkin, subdued.

'The same applies to you, Master Marco.' Kublai paused. 'Even when you visit the Flower Houses.'

'Yes, Great Lord,' he muttered, embarrassed.

Kublai chuckled. 'Well, since you are both so anxious

about the war with the Sung, perhaps you would care to hear what my council has to say on the matter? General Bayan has arrived from our headquarters in the South. I suspect that he is far better informed than a Chinese astrologer . . .'

With Marco, Chinkin and a wedge of Imperial Guards at his heels, Kublai led the way to the Council Chamber, a vast hall with lacquered, dark red walls that looked the colour of blood in the flickering torchlight. While the Great Khan ascended the steps to his throne, Marco stole a quick look around the Council. Phags-pa was there, the proud Argan and the slender Nasreddin. Achmet occupied a central position, as befitted the First Minister of the Empire. Beside him was a squat, powerful, middle-aged man in the garb of a Mongol general.

Chinkin took his place below his father's throne and Marco knelt respectfully at the side. The Great Khan addressed the man beside Achmet. 'For many years, General Bayan, I have had a dream – to complete the conquest and, for the first time, to unite all China under one rule. To make her the heart of the empire.'

There was a pause, then Argan spoke. 'I ask your pardon, Great Khan,' he said with a bow, and turned to the general. 'For ten years, Bayan, your armies have been fighting the Sung without breaking their resistance. Far too many Mongol warriors have been taken to the Eternal Blue Sky.'

'There is no great victory without great sacrifices,' replied General Bayan firmly. 'The Sung army is like a serpent; when it is hit, it grows new limbs and new strength. For every fortification that we destroy, ten – a hundred – take its place.'

'Whatever the sacrifice,' Achmet said smoothly, 'it is worth it. The empire needs the riches of the South. Their fields are the most fertile in all China.'

'The South is a refuge for rebels and agitators!' insisted Phags-pa. 'It must be brought under control.'

Bayan faced the throne. 'Great Khan, you have forbidden unnecessary bloodshed or destruction of crops, villages and cities. I know that the spirit that guides you is as great and wise as your dream, but . . . but we keep hoping that the Sung will surrender. To have a real knowledge of their state of morale, we have to penetrate their lines and observe them at close quarters. The problem is that their frontiers are so well guarded and the Emperor Tsu-Tong refuses to admit even ambassadors.'

It was a tough speech and it produced a long, brooding silence. The Great Khan Kublai drummed his fingers on the carved arm of his throne while he considered. Eventually, he nodded to Bayan. 'Very well.' He turned to Marco. 'You have begged me to employ you. There is a mission for which we think your talents may be ideally suited.' Marco tensed, aware that every eye was on him. 'You will go as my envoy to the Sung Emperor. You will take a message to be delivered to his hands only. In it I will suggest a meeting between us which he, surely, is bound to refuse. Your real mission, therefore, is to keep your eyes and ears open and to report fully all you see and hear.'

Marco hesitated. 'I don't know the southern regions, Great Lord.'

'A Chinese from the South will travel with you. He is a man of science and letters.'

'You will also have an armed escort,' Nasreddin assured him. 'As a foreigner, you may ask questions without being accused of spying.'

Kublai's gaze tested Marco. 'You realize it may be dangerous. Do you accept?'

'I am grateful to be given the chance to repay your kindness, Great Lord,' Marco said. 'My only fear is that I might fail you.'

'Your fear is a guarantee of your success,' Achmet approved.

Marco answered with a bow. Although he was grateful for a chance to repay the Khan's generosity, he was apprehensive about the task which he had been given. His curiosity to see southern China was tempered by the fact that it was a deadly country for anyone travelling in the service of the Mongol emperor. There was a strong possibility that he would not return alive.

Escorted by four heavily armed soldiers and riding in the company of the austere, impassive Wu Sheng, a Chinese official of the third grade, Marco left Khanbalic with his orders and journeyed south.

His progress was unimpeded until after three days his party reached a series of canyons set in rocky countryside. They were moving in single file between high walls of red clay when they heard an ominous rumble above. Boulders came crashing down in profusion at both ends of the canyon, sealing them in completely. It was the perfect place for an ambush. Before the Mongol escort had even unsheathed their weapons, Sung warriors jumped out from the rocks and held poisoned lances at the throats of the travellers. At the same time, archers appeared along the top of both sides of the canyon, their bows drawn and arrows at the ready.

Shaken by the suddenness of it, Marco held up a red, lacquered cylinder bound with ribbon and seals. 'A message from the Khan to the Emperor!' he called.

'We bring a message for the Emperor Tsu-Tong!' shouted Wu Sheng. 'Take us to him!'

Bound and blindfolded, Marco and Wu Sheng were led away.

After a long and taxing journey, they reached a fort, as night was falling. They were ushered into the courtyard and pulled roughly from their horses. Though their blindfolds were removed, their hands remained tied and the Mongol escort were pushed to their knees. A tall, smart, dignified Chinese official approached and spoke to Wu Sheng in the local dialect. Wu Sheng listened intently and then turned to Marco. 'This is the commander of the garrison, Yang Ku. He says you are to give him the letter, Master Marco.'

'The Great Khan's order is that I am to deliver it personally to the Emperor,' Marco insisted. He turned to face Yang Ku.

'The Emperor has sworn to see no more ambassadors from the Mongol Khan,' Yang Ku told him. 'I will deliver it myself. You will wait here until an answer is received.'

'How long will it take?'

But the garrison commander was no longer listening. An officer had hurried up to him and was whispering to him. Yang Ku gestured brusquely to a guard. Marco was searched, roughly, and the Great Khan's private letter snatched from a hidden pocket. Before he could protest, a blindfold covered his eyes once more.

Marco was hurried across the courtyard, up a flight of stone steps, in through a low archway, along a narrow corridor paved with flagstones, and into a room that smelled of damp. A final shove forced him to his knees and he stayed there, trying to make out what the whispered voices were saying. After some minutes, the blindfold was removed. When his eyes had grown accustomed to the light, he saw that he was in a sparsely furnished stone-walled chamber. Standing in front of him was a proud, impressive Chinese woman of about thirty, her finely moulded features suggesting beauty and strong will at the same time, her pale skin set off by her shining black clothes. She was clearly of high rank. 'So this, then, is the spy?' she asked, the Khan's message in her hand.

'Yes, my lady,' said Yang Ku respectfully.

'Leave us!' she ordered the guards, and the men left at once. 'You may stay, Yang Ku.' The woman studied Marco carefully. 'Is it our courage or our fear you have come to spy on? When I heard about your capture, I wanted to come here personally to take a look at the Khan's stupid cunning. Kublai could have sent someone a little less . . . obvious. You are from the West, are you not?'

'Yes, my lady, from the most serene Republic of Venice.'

'And you have come under the pretext of bringing me a message?'

'The Khan's message is for the eyes of the Sung Emperor,' he argued. 'I don't know who you are, my lady.'

'Don't lie to me!' she warned, erect and disdainful. Her eyes bored into Marco's, trying to gauge his honesty.

'I would not dream of it, my Lady,' he said earnestly. 'I am nothing but the Khan's envoy to the Emperor Tsu-Tong.'

'My son has taken Tsu-Tong's place on the throne,' she announced. 'I am the Empress Sie Chi, Regent of the Empire in my son's name.'

Marco bowed low, then smiled. 'So the letter has been delivered into the proper hands. My mission will be over when I can take your answer to the Great Khan.'

'What answer!' she snapped, waving the letter. 'He suggests a meeting on the Yellow River! As if I could accept such a proposal!' She hurled the cylinder across the room and stood up, looking much taller somehow in the majesty of her anger. 'It's a trick! A cheap trick to enable you to pass through our lines and spy on out defences!' Her hand swung back to strike Marco. He gazed up at her in silence, without flinching, and after a moment she turned away. 'You see? You cannot even deny it.'

'I will not deny that I shall tell the Khan all I have seen and heard,' he admitted. 'But the Khan is sincere. He knows that sooner or later the South will fall to his armies and he wishes to prevent more bloodshed and destruction of crops and villages.'

Her anger smouldered again. 'Does he expect us to surrender?'

'The Great Khan wishes to reach an honourable agreement with you and your noble family.'

'There is no honour for one who betrays his country,' Sie Chi said icily.

'For the first time ever, China would be united in peace,' Marco urged. 'This is the wish of the Great Kublai Khan.'

'Who can believe the word of a man who has left nothing but destruction behind him?' she sneered. 'He has created deserts where once wheat and rice grew!'

'The Great Khan fears a famine. His orders are that the fruits of your fields are to be respected, and the lives of your people.'

Suspicion narrowed her eyes. 'I know what happens to the cities that open their gates to your Khan – cities that trust him and surrender without a fight. Blackened stones and ruined walls are all that remain of them. We will not be deceived by his cunning – you may return and tell him so.'

Marco did not feel brave, but it was worth any sacrifice to help to put a stop to the endless slaughter and to repay Kublai's trust in him. 'If you wish, my lady, I will stay here as a hostage until your answer has reached Khanbalic,' he said quietly.

There was a silence. A door creaked behind him and Marco turned to see a small boy standing on the threshold, his ornate robe far too grand and stately for him, his bright, curious eyes those of a child caught up in a world he does not understand. After staring at Marco for a moment, the boy slipped quietly out again and shut the door behind him. The Empress had recovered her composure and reached a decision. She was visibly impressed by the barbarian envoy's courageous frankness and by his belief in Kublai Khan's goodwill. 'Yang Ku – take this man away and treat him well. Tomorrow, he will have my answer to his master.'

Yang Ku and Marco bowed and left. In the corridor outside, the rope was untied again and Marco's hands freed. While the garrison commander was giving orders to some guards, the young envoy had a chance to reflect on the strange events in which he had been involved. If the Emperor Tsu-Tong was no longer on the throne, where *was* he? How long had his wife ruled, and what authority did she have among the people of southern China at large? Who was the boy, and why was he dressed so formally?

Marco thought he heard something from within the room where he had just been interviewed, and a new question preoccupied him. Why was the ice-cold and haughty Empress Sie Chi weeping?

As soon as the first lookout at Khanbalic saw the returning embassy on the horizon, word was hurried to the Great Khan and a Council Meeting summoned at once. Immediately Marco arrived, weary and travel-stained, he was rushed to the Council Chamber, where he delivered his report to the assembled lords and caused many murmurs of astonishment. Kublai's eyebrows arched in surprise.

'Southern China is ruled by a child and by a woman?'

'The Sung Emperor has fled with his harem to an island in the ocean,' Marco explained. 'The garrison commander gave me the details.'

'Tsu-Tong has abandoned his empire?' Kublai was shocked.

'The throne has passed to his son – with the Empress as Regent. A very brave woman.' Marco had been struck by Sie Chi's dignity and had come to feel deeply sorry for her. In a world where men ruled almost exclusively, only an exceptional woman would even dare to take on the role of a Regent.

'Let us hear what the Empress says in reply,' suggested Kublai.

Phags-pa rose with the letter that Marco had brought back with him. ' "To Kublai, Great Khan of the Mongols. Your words promise peace, but your soldiers' lances bring war. Our honour wills us to resist to the last. Our hearts are heavy with apprehension for our people and for the fate of Hangchow, our capital city, the most beautiful jewel in the Sung crown. Who could allow it to be destroyed . . ." '

Kublai raised his arm abruptly to indicate that he would speak. Phags-pa stopped at once.

'She has told us everything,' the Great Khan declared.

'Everything?' Nasreddin was dubious.

'In what way, Great Lord?' So was Argan.

'However much she intends to resist, in her heart Sie Chi has already accepted defeat. She is begging me to spare her city – and I shall. Where is the Empress now, Master Marco?'

'At Siang-yang-fu, I believe, Great Lord.'

'Half of Bayan's army is encamped there,' Argan said with vehemence. 'They are only a few miles from Siang-yang-fu, which is a small city.'

'In other words, she is trapped,' Achmet smiled.

'Are you certain of this?' Kublai asked Marco.

He was hesitant. 'I . . . I think so, lord. On our return journey we saw Sung warriors, part of the Imperial Guard, heading there.'

Marco looked around to gauge the reactions to his news. Nasreddin clearly accepted it as the truth and was smiling at the opportunity it gave the Mongol forces. Achmet was less certain and toyed meditatively with his beard. Phags-pa was inscrutable as ever, but Chinkin was plainly troubled. Argan, breathing heavily through his nose, was still unpersuaded.

Kublai addressed his Regent. 'Send Bayan this order: his entire army is to move in and attack.'

'Will you base your decision on the report of this boy?' demanded Argan, pointing a stubby finger at Marco.

'For the chance to end this war in one move,' said Kublai, evenly, 'I command Bayan to lead the attack.'

Silence fell as they all considered the implications of the decision. It was Phags-pa who finally broke the silence. 'If Master Marco's information is incorrect,' he warned quietly, 'our armies could march into a trap, Great Lord.'

Marco felt more uncomfortable than ever. One way or the other, his report would lead to death and destruction. Either the Chinese would be routed and their Empress captured, or the Mongol forces would be led to their slaughter by a cunning deception. Bloodshed hung on his word, an enormous responsibility for him to bear. His eyes were troubled as he thought about it. He had come to the East as the companion of his father and hated his role as a spy. Too much was expected of him, too much depended on him, too many would die as a result of him. He began to pray quietly to himself.

Captain Arnolfo, the Prison Commander, was standing when Marco was escorted into his office by the prison guards. Beside him was a short, barrel-chested Dominican friar with a tonsured head and a stern expression. In front of the two men was a table, and Marco was quick to note that all the items confiscated from his cell were still intact – Rustichello's manuscripts, Giovanni's missal, and all the other books and objects.

Arnolfo pointed to them. 'As an act of benevolence on the part of those who defend our faith,' he began, 'it has been decided to let you keep all you have dictated to Rustichello of Pisa. Your stories have won many admirers. But your imagination runs too wild – you touch on subjects that—'

The friar interrupted sharply. 'You touch on subjects that are dangerous snares to those not protected by faith. Idols, false prophets, Buddha, Mohammed! The Devil has many faces and speaks with many tongues. Woe betide those who yield to his enticements!'

'This is just a warning,' added Arnolfo, in more reasonable tones, 'but I advise you to remember it when you begin to invent—'

'I have *invented* nothing!' Marco protested, unable to contain himself any longer. 'It is all true – and I could prove it if I had my notes.' Hope brightened his face. 'Perhaps the Church of Venice would help! If I asked my father and my uncle to collect the notes I made during our stay in China.' He appealed to the friar. 'In God's name, father, ask the patriarch of the parish of San Felice to help me!'

The friar seemed quite unmoved, but the Prison Commander at least considered the request and promised to see what could be done. Marco thanked him, emphasizing the importance of the notes now that his memory was no longer as reliable in every particular as it had been. Imprisonment had not only made the Venetian thin and pale, it had started to affect the faculty on which he had always prided himself most.

'So many things to remember! People, places, dates . . .'

'I will look into it, Messer Polo. Meanwhile, you are permitted to continue describing your travels. But be careful.'

Marco Polo reached out and picked up the manuscript.

Chapter Six

Victory lit the Forbidden City and turned a dark night into a blaze of glory. The green-and-white standards of the Mongol Khan headed a brilliant procession of banners and flags into the immense courtyard, which was flanked on one side by the Hall of Supreme Harmony, and on the other by the Hall of Perfect Harmony. Torch-bearers walked alongside the standard-bearers, forming a ribbon of fire that picked out the variegated hues. A low drumming accompanied the procession, until it forked and sent its twin prongs down the two long sides of the courtyard towards the throne area at the northern end. Then, with astonishing precision hundreds of torches and lamps flared into life in the four bamboo towers that rose in the corners of the central square of the courtyard. Almost simultaneously, the drumbeats quickened and built to a crescendo.

Presiding over it all was the Great Khan Kublai. Dressed in the flowing robes of a Chinese potentate, he sat on a gold and ivory throne set on a raised and carpeted platform. To his right was Chinkin, with his own son, Timur; to his left was the Empress Jaimu and her court ladies. Immediately below the imperial family was the Council of Barons with Achmet, Phags-Pa, Nasreddin, Argan, Caidu, Bektor and Nayan prominent.

Marco watched with a mixture of excitement and detachment, at once part of the whole experience and an objective observer. He was interested to see how the magnificently barbaric Caidu and the handsome, dignified Nayan, Kublai's nephews and lords of their own vast territories, held themselves aloof from the others, although they shared their pride in the victory of Mongol arms and diplomacy.

Strident fanfares announced the entry of General Bayan, returning in triumph to Khanbalic with his army. The Mongol warriors who preceded him carried the banners of the defeated Sung Dynasty, and these were laid symbolically at the feet of the Great Khan. Bayan and his commanders approached the throne and knelt in obeisance. Kublai then rose and opened his arms wide in a gesture of welcome, and Bayan mounted the steps and knelt in front of his sovereign. His voice echoed around the whole courtyard.

'The last Sung fortress has fallen, Great Lord. All the South lies under your heel.'

'Rise, Bayan, sword of the empire!' ordered Kublai, offering him his hand to kiss. 'From today, you shall have the custody of all you have conquered. I proclaim you Regent of Mantzu in the name of my grandson, Timur.'

Chinkin inclined his head slightly at this and Timur swelled with pride. General Bayan moved across to stand behind them and take up his new position. To Marco it was like a mythical tapestry unrolling before him. He was riveted by what he saw, the colour and ritual. Then suddenly there was heard the tramp of booted feet and Marco's earlier detachment disappeared altogether.

Escorted by Mongol soldiers, the Empress Sie Chi entered, accompanied by her small son, the former child emperor, both dressed in white robes – white being the colour of mourning in the Sung culture. As soon as she was seen, all Chinese dignitaries in the Imperial court knelt down and Marco was interested to note that Wu Sheng was among them. Mother and son walked alone with firm steps to the foot of Kublai's throne and waited calmly, without showing any sign of fear. Beautiful in her tragic dignity, Sie Chi glanced around and her eye caught Marco's long enough to make him lower his head. It was his information which had sent General Bayan into Siang-yang-fu, and he felt directly responsible for the humiliation of this beautiful woman and the conquest of her people. His sympathies were with the Empress and her son at that moment, and he found it hard to accept that his loyalty to one person had meant betraying another.

He recalled the way that he had defended Kublai to Sie Chi and spoken of his magnanimity. She clearly expected nothing from Kublai and was now looking at him levelly, her pride protecting her like a coat of armour. The Khan's grim face slowly softened and he rose to bow his head in the ritual courtesy reserved for honoured guests. The watching Chinese dignitaries and officials gasped audibly, touched by this display of quite unexpected generosity, and Marco felt tears threatening. With simple but eloquent gestures, Kublai invited the Empress and her son to take their places to his left with the princesses and other ladies of the Imperial Family. As the couple slowly mounted the steps, a hesitant applause broke out, building to a cheer. On reaching the place assigned to her, the Empress Sie Chi herself smiled faintly, graciously, in acknowledgement, glancing again at Marco.

Marco had been observing Wu Sheng throughout the applause, noting how the austere man had blossomed in joy. Clearly it was a very special moment for the Chinese, many of whom were weeping. It was Matteo who drew his attention back to the throne.

'Go on, boy!'

'Do as he says!' urged Niccolo, pulling his son's sleeve.

When Marco turned towards Kublai again, he saw to his utter amazement that the Great Khan was beckoning him to take a place on the elevated area reserved for nobles and dignitaries. It was a public acknowledgement of the part that he had played in the overthrow of the Sung Dynasty. Hands trembling and cheeks burning with embarrassment, Marco walked self-consciously to kneel before the Khan and take the place indicated, with the eyes of the Forbidden City upon him.

Chinkin and General Bayan gave him welcoming smiles, the friendly Nasreddin beamed, and Achmet nodded his approval of the high honour that had been bestowed. When he saw the glowing pride of his father and his uncle,

Marco felt strong enough to ignore the disapproval on the face of Phags-pa and the open irritation of General Argan.

Drums pounded and a dazzling and lavish entertainment began.

Braziers were lit in each of the four bamboo towers and huge copper mirrors were suspended over them so that a vast, shimmering circle of intensified light was created below. Into this circle came a great swarm of acrobats and jugglers who exhibited their skills in a breathtaking exhibition of tumbling, vaulting and balancing tricks.

They ran off into the darkness and their place was taken by a wave of dancers. The lithe, young bodies moved with such sinuous grace and liquid ease that the whole courtyard was filled with undulations of brilliant colour. Each gesture and movement blended perfectly with the languid sounds of the stringed instruments so that dance and music seemed one. The effect of hundreds of performers forming endless elegant patterns delighted the senses.

They vanished like the acrobats and their gentle music gave way to the warlike beat of the Mongol drums. Hundreds of young athletes, champions of the martial arts, surged into the light. Each man, barefoot and stripped to the waist, tested his blade by slicing thick bamboo canes. Then the warriors paired off and a series of ferocious duels took place, blade striking blade with such force that sparks flew. Tension among the spectators was at its height because they knew that a misjudged swing or a late parry could be lethal. Marco, like the others, cheered in a mixture of fear and excitement.

As suddenly as they were lit, the fires in the bamboo towers went out and covers fell over the braziers to snuff out the flames. The warriors fled into the darkness and a new wonder took their place, a huge fire dragon that snaked its way around the courtyard, then shot up a high wooden ramp and soared into the air. There it began to explode over the heads of the spectators, sending up cascades of multi-coloured sparks and clusters of brilliant lights into the night sky.

As the glittering display of dancing and magic unfolded, Marco soon found himself clapping spontaneously with an almost childlike delight, joining in the frenzy of applause and excitement which reverberated round the courtyard. It was a fitting end to the celebration of such a notable victory, both for Marco personally and for the Mongol empire and its mighty ruler.

In the days that followed, Marco's standing in the court changed dramatically. Where before he had been largely ignored, or at best tolerated by most of the Mongol nobles as a friend of the Crown Prince, he was now sought out by them and showered with invitations to dine and to hunt. The foxy Chinese officials, who usually payed little attention to temporary favourites, expecting them to topple from grace sooner rather than later, now realized that he had become someone to reckon with and treated him with cautious respect. He won good opinions for his lack of vanity and unaltered politeness to all, not showing the usual arrogance of those suddenly advanced in rank.

One change pleased him. He was no longer addressed in slightly condescending style as 'Master Marco'. He had become 'Messer Marco' and received salutes from the guards and the bows of those of lesser status. Jacopo chuckled and took to bobbing and touching his forelock, whenever they met. Having been such a liability on the journey, he was proving himself a treasure now that they had settled. He still grumbled at being so far from home, but the thought of the rigours of the return was so terrifying that he tried to make the best of it. He had become the lord of Niccolo and Matteo's kitchen, a benign dictator over their other servants, and was now plumper than ever, teaching Venetian cooking to the women and to one in particular whom he had moved into his own quarters. 'Not as pretty as one of our girls, maybe, Ser Marco,' he chuckled, 'but then her manners are a lot better than most Italian women's. And she's more biddable.'

Another change was important. Marco's life was much safer. Chinkin had told him that, according to rumour, Argan had publicly sworn to have him strangled, and Marco had experienced the uneasiness of those who depend on great men's affection. Now, with the protection of Achmet and Bayan as well, and the friendship of Nasreddin, he felt much more secure. Phags-pa tended to avoid him as much as possible, their only open argument coming when Kublai decided to celebrate the Christian festival of Easter with an official feast. It was only settled when the Khan announced that the court would also observe Passover with the small Jewish community, Ramadan with the Mohammedans in honour of Achmet, and whichever day Phags-pa cared to nominate as the birthday of Buddha. Argan was muzzled, and was carefully polite to Marco when they met, biding his time.

Marco's status was further increased, when he travelled with Chinkin representing his father to the great *Kuriltai*, the council of all the Mongol Khans, at the former capital, Karakorum. Present, apart from all the chieftains of the steppes, such as Bektor, were all the ruling sons of Kublai, with Caidu, Nayan, and representatives of the Golden Horde of Russia and the Il-Khans of Persia. The purpose of the *Kuriltai* was for each to report on the development, security and needs of his area, a colossal stocktaking of the empire, to hear the confirmation of the conquest of southern China and to reaffirm their loyalty to the Kha Khan. Of them all, the one most likely to cause trouble was Caidu, lord of the Central Steppes, but he had been chastened by his uncle's victory over the Sung and held his peace. Through him, Marco met his cousin, Nayan, lord of North Mongolia. The leader of the Nestorians, an unaffected, extremely likable man, the very model of a chivalrous hero, Nayan wore the Cross on his tunic. Marco was impressed by him and, in turn, told him of the Empress Jaimu's influence over her husband and how close Kublai had come at times to accepting the Cross himself. It made Nayan think. The assembly strengthened Kublai's position as supreme ruler and was another diplomatic triumph for his young ambassador.

It was then that Marco met and became friendly with Zurficar, the Turkish mining expert, and explored with him the mines and deposits of the southern ranges of the Altai Mountains. The report he brought back was of immense value in assessing the mineral resources of the empire.

After his embassy to the Empress Sie Chi, Marco continued to take a deep interest in South China and commissioned the learned Wu Sheng to find books for him on its history, politics and literature.

The South was a constant topic of discussion, for although it had officially been overcome, it covered so many thousands of square miles that it was a further three years before the conquest was complete. In that time, debate raged over how best to administer the territory and treat its conquered inhabitants. Kublai, supported strongly by Chinkin, favoured a policy of reconciliation and absorption. Achmet saw it as a source of much-needed revenue and taxes, with which view many agreed. The Sung, it was held, should pay for their defiance. Phags-pa saw it as a land of idolaters, Taoists and Confucians, who should be converted or eradicated. Kublai tended to agree with him, the native religions were a possible rallying ground for rebellion, always simmering in such a vast area and one that was so difficult to police. In spite of doubts expressed by some, including Chinkin and Marco, the basic Chinese religions were forbidden.

To Marco's shock, he discovered that a large percentage of the Mongol nobility considered the best alternative would be to slaughter the entire southern population systematically and turn the thousands of square miles into one gigantic grazing ground for their horses. It was hard for Marco to believe that they were serious, yet they were. Only the urgent need of the North for the grain and rootcrops of the more fertile South, which required armies of peasants to tend them, prevented more from agreeing.

At the prompting of Achmet, whose chief responsibility was for the Imperial treasury and granaries, Kublai gave Marco a mission which to him was heaven-sent. He was ordered to make a six- to twelve-month survey of the produce, industries and agricultural capabilities of Mantzu. Only pausing to take leave of his father and uncle, of the Empress Jaimu and of Chinkin, who longed to go with him, he set off with a strong escort, a train of servants and the reserved, scholarly Wu Sheng, who had become his personal assistant.

The decision had been taken to stay mainly in the eastern regions, since to cover the entire area would take many years. They travelled south-east from Khanbalic to the great River Kara-moran, which the Chinese knew as the Hwang-ho, the Yellow River, and crossed at last into Mantzu at the large city of Hwai-ngan-chou, a flourishing seaport and trading centre. From there they rode along the stone causeway stretching for many miles across the marshes of the Hwang-ho delta to the silk-manufacturing city of Pao-ying, heading on by smaller cities to the rich and magnificent city of Chinju. Here they were three days' journey from the ocean and coming to the heart of the salt-producing region of Yangchou, with its miles of docks and its numberless temples and mansions. Here, in the main mines, thousands of slave workers toiled under the whips of the overseers to pile up huge mounds through which water was filtered and the resulting brine conveyed by pipes to be boiled in immense, shallow vats. The end product was pure high-quality salt and the value to the Khan's treasury of the tax on it alone, in this one region, was nearly six million gold ducats.

Heading for the Yangtse, they turned west on Marco's orders before they reached the river in order to see again the fortress to which Marco and Wu Sheng had been taken as captives of the Sung. Here the Mongol commander insisted on lodging the whole party for the night. Ironically, Marco and Wu Sheng were entertained to dinner in the very room in which he had been made to kneel to the

Empress Sie Chi. The memory of the two days he had spent here as a captive was very keen and the officers listened attentively when he told them of it.

He saw the commander whisper to one of his men, who left the room. The commander turned to Marco. 'I imagine you wondered if you would ever see Khanbalic again. Well, I have a gift for you, Polo Noyon – something to help you remember that time even more clearly.' His officers laughed and Marco was puzzled, but the commander would only say, 'It's a modest gift. Wait and see.'

Marco was laughing with them when the door opened and a prisoner was dragged in, his hands bound tightly in front of him.

'Over there,' the commander pointed, and the prisoner was led to the centre of the room and pushed to his knees. The commander and officers were chuckling at Marco's puzzlement, but he saw that Wu Sheng was troubled and looked again at the prisoner. The man raised his head. He had been brutally treated. He wore only a simple, torn tunic; his face was bruised and emaciated, yet his eyes had not lost their pride and defiance. It was Yang Ku, the former garrison commander.

'Do you recognize him?' the Mongols asked.

'Yes,' Marco said. 'He was captain here, under the Sung.'

'That's right,' the Mongol commander laughed. 'Well, now he's your slave – to do with as you please.'

Marco got up from the table and walked round it towards Yang Ku, who watched him impassively. Marco stopped, and the Mongols smiled with anticipation when they saw him take the dagger from its sheath at his belt. Wu Sheng was nibbling fastidiously at some spiced cashew nuts and laid them down, folding his hands to conceal their involuntary tremor.

Yang Ku's eyes went from the dagger up to Marco's face.

'Do you remember me?' Marco asked, thickly. 'Yesterday I was your prisoner – today you are my slave.' Yang Ku was silent. 'Do you deny it?'

'How can I?' Yang Ku said. 'It was written.'

He closed his eyes as Marco reached down with the dagger until its point touched his chest. The dagger slid lower and slipped under the cords binding Yang Ku's wrists.

'I pronounce you free,' Marco said, 'in the name of the Great Khan.' As Yang Ku opened his eyes, staring up at him, Marco cut the cords. 'Stand up.'

There was a murmur of consternation from the Mongols and a muttered objection, which was broken off as soon as Marco invoked the name of Kublai. Wu Sheng's eyebrows rose and he looked down at the table, quite expressionless.

Yang Ku climbed stiffly to his feet, rubbing the skin round the sores at his wrists where they had been chafed nearly raw. He was unable to speak and still gazed at Marco, dumbfounded.

'The Great Khan has forbidden reprisals,' Marco told him. 'You may go; no one will harm you. Or you may stay with me, if you prefer.'

Yang Ku glanced round at the commander and the Mongol officers, fearful that they would only take him prisoner again. His look when it returned to Marco was humbler, a mixture of gratitude and injured pride. 'If . . . I may leave here with you, sir,' he said quietly. 'Then with your gracious permission, I will go back to my village, where my brothers still live.'

'Why?' Marco asked.

'It will be easier to hide my shame there.'

The following morning, as they moved on, Wu Sheng drew up level with Marco. 'That was a fine thing you did,' he said. 'I was proud of you.'

Marco looked at the Chinese in surprise. It was the first word of praise he had ever had from him. But the old official was as expressionless and as aloof as ever.

That day, Marco had his first glimpse of the Yangtse.

He had seen many rivers, from the Tigris to the Hwang-ho, but never one that was eight miles wide.

It was like a sea. Marco and the others with him gazed wordlessly at the mighty expanse of water, its opposite shore so distant it could barely be made out through the light haze. Its surface was filled with water traffic, in a seemingly unending procession of large and small sailing junks, barges, rafts and sampans. Some of the junks were the biggest ships they had ever seen, with distinctively high sterns and forecastles, two to four masts and sails made of ribbed matting.

They rode on to the east, coming to the busy riverport of Sinju, where in one ordinary day Marco counted five thousand ships at anchor, loading or discharging cargoes. From the Mongol collector of customs he learned that upwards of two hundred thousand vessels travelled upstream every year.

The Yangtse, known to the Chinese as Ta Jiang, the Great River, was China's main commercial route, and the statistics he began to gather about it from navigators and trading captains seemed scarcely credible. Later he verified them for himself. The river was over three and a half thousand miles long, rising in the snows of the mysterious land of Tibet. It was fed by over seven hundred tributaries, ran through sixteen provinces and had on its banks more than two hundred cities, many of them far larger even than Sinju. It flowed from west to east, and the most precious gift given to China by the gods was a prevailing wind that blew in exactly the opposite direction. When the wind died, horses and trackers dragged the ships upstream using three-hundred-foot ropes made of lengths of split bamboo bound together, stronger and more durable than hemp.

Marco spent the next three months exploring the lower and middle reaches of the industrial centres of Nanking and Siang-yang-fu to Chungking, built at the meeting-place of the Yangtse and its mighty tributary, the Chia-ling, focus point for all the trade of the vast hinterland from Kweichow, Yunnan and Tibet. Above Chungking, the Yangtse was known as the River of Golden Sand, from the silt rich in gold dust brought down from the mountains by its waters. Marco sailed downstream by junk through towering, prehistoric gorges, where the river ran like a millrace over perilous rapids, with ancient shrines and monasteries perched on its crags, leaving on his mind an unforgettable impression of lovely and savage grandeur.

After a sail of thirty days he came again to the broad, lower reaches, disembarked his party and rode south for the trade centre of Chin-kiang-fu, and from there by way of the splendid city of Soochow, famous for its silks and the production of ginger, to the southern capital of Kinsai, called by the Chinese Hangchow. While Soochow meant 'city of Earth', Hangchow meant 'city of Heaven'. The name was not lightly given, for as Wu Sheng told him, travellers from all over the empire who visited the city said on reaching home that they had been in paradise. Throughout his long stay and his many return visits in later years, Marco never found cause to disagree.

Capital of the South for centuries, Hangchow was situated between a broad river and an extensive freshwater lake. It was a city of canals and fine houses, mostly of carved wood; but there any comparison with Venice ended. It had grown and grown over the years until it was fully a hundred miles in circumference. The current in its innumerable watercourses carried all its filth and rubbish to the sea, fifteen miles distant, leaving the city healthy and clean, with pure air. Its streets were spacious, allowing easy passage for large carriages, while the canals were equally wide, spanned by some twelve thousand bridges, those over the main channels built of stone, with high arches under which the biggest ships could sail. Apart from countless small markets and shopping areas, there were ten main squares, each side half a mile long, spaced out on either flank of the main thoroughfare, which crossed the city from end to end. The squares were surrounded by tall houses, the lower storeys given over to shops selling everything conceivable, from jewellery and wine and fashionable clothes to Persian rugs and exotic spices. All the riches of the East were on display, for Hangchow was one of the leading centres for trade with India and Arabia. Bearded and turbaned merchant captains were to be seen everywhere, and three days a week, each market was filled with forty to fifty thousand country people selling meat and fowls, game, fruit, fish and vegetables. Their carts were so loaded it seemed impossible to sell so much, yet each day they were cleared.

In trying to estimate the number of inhabitants, Marco was told by the customs officials that the amount of pepper consumed here every day in cooking was forty-three cartloads. At two hundred and twenty-three pounds to the load, it appeared far-fetched, until he saw from the census figures that the city had over one million six hundred thousand houses. At an average of five to a family, not counting servants, itinerant workers and untold thousands of visitors, the number suggested boggled the mind. There was no other city of this size on the face of the earth.

Created by the cultured, pleasure-loving Sung, Hangchow had many superb mansions and palaces, academies, temples and public buildings. Marco delighted in the good manners, friendliness and hospitality of its people, who had been so secure and prosperous for so long that they willingly accepted the change of government, merely in order to be left in peace. One feature which surprised him were the hundreds of bath houses, used every day by the populace, both men and women, who had a passion for cleanliness. With Wu Sheng he toured the places of interest in each quarter, from the lighthouse-like Drum Tower from which a watch was kept for fires, to the lake, where twin palaces on its two central islands had been turned into luxurious restaurants and where many exquisitely painted houseboats served as floating cafés and social clubs.

More to Wu Sheng's liking was the Great Library, where the archives and records of the Sung were stored, hall after hall stuffed with scrolls and bound manuscripts, the works of poets and historians and novelists, and the most revered religious writings, so ancient that the parchment could not be touched for fear it might crumble away. There, Marco saw another wonder which was worth the whole trip; a printing press with movable type, turning out book after book. The idea that hundreds of copies of any work could be produced in a matter of days, instead of just one copy being made laboriously by hand over several months, was staggering. He marvelled at the implications for the West if books became cheap and general, available to everyone and not just to the Church, the noble and the wealthy.

Of almost equal fascination was the Customs House, for another reason. While the municipal board of trade could give him no accurate account of the amount of merchandise produced by the city's twelve thousand workshops, the customs officials had a much clearer idea of the yearly revenue collected. Every commodity paid a duty, from three per cent on spices to ten per cent on imported goods. Marco inspected the annual account of the city's revenue as it was drawn up. It came to twenty two million four hundred thousand gold pieces.

As an important visitor, Marco was lodged by the municipal governor in one of the city's most sumptuous Flower Houses, maintained for visiting dignitaries. Its chefs came from the former royal palace and the 'food of Kinsai' which had seemed so delicious to him in Khanbalic was as nothing compared to the real delicacies which now became his daily fare. When he had completed his business and remained a further two weeks purely for enjoyment, it required the most determined effort of will to make himself leave.

He travelled slowly south-east again into the coastal province of Zaitun, to inspect the main seaports, Fuchau and the even larger Amoy, where the volume of imports exceeded even that of Hangchow. It was there that he saw ocean-going junks for the first time, huge wooden vessels with four or more masts and a single giant rudder worked by six men. They were matched only by the massive dhows which he was told came from Madagascar and Zanzibar, two island kingdoms off the east coast of Africa, trading in elephant tusks, pearls and ambergris. Even with all imported goods paying a duty of ten per cent and freight charges of thirty to forty per cent, traders made enormous profits. The revenue to the Khan was incalculable.

Marco sailed back to Hangchow with the friendly captain of an Arab dhow, who showed him the mysteries of the compass, a Chinese invention which had made the crossing of the oceans much safer. He returned in leisurely style to Khanbalic with Wu Sheng on an official barge which took them all the way on the Grand Canal.

To his surprise, he was met on arrival by Prince Chinkin with a guard of honour. He had left Khanbalic known to a small number of people in the Imperial Palace, and had returned famous.

As they rode to the Forbidden City, Chinkin explained. The mass of reports which Marco had sent back during his trip contained not only accounts of places, resources and products, but descriptions of the local inhabitants, their customs and religions, of unusual events and striking buildings, of everything that had intrigued, amused or impressed him, from the mile-long pontoon bridge at Fuchau and the lion traps of Zaitun to the method of testing for virginity in Tandinfu and the stupendous golden palace of the former Emperor Tu-tsong at Kinsai, with his harem of one thousand concubines. Gradually, as the details mounted, the interest of the Khan and the Council had been awakened, then spread from the Palace of Records to the court and nobility, and to the city, until everyone was agog for each new despatch. No such description of south-eastern Cathay and the four principal provinces of Mantzu had ever been compiled before. 'You have revealed a world of wonders, Marco,' Chinkin told him. 'How I wish I could have been with you! Yet through your reports, I have seen it with your eyes.'

Niccolo, however, was less effusive in his welcome. 'Little did I think the day would come,' he growled, 'when my chief claim to fame would be that I am Marco Polo's father.' He was not entirely joking.

Kublai, however, greeted Marco affectionately. 'Like a lost son', as was whispered to Phags-pa. Achmet was in attendance and the First Minister's welcome was as warm as the Great Khan's. At one stroke, Marco had silenced the doubters throughout the empire who had questioned the expense in time and lives of invading Mantzu. At the same time, he had proved how much more lucrative it was to administer and draw continual profit from the South, rather than plunder it and lay it waste in one orgiastic bloodbath. It was a triumph for Kublai's policy of reconciliation and integration.

The day after he returned, when Marco came to present a summary of his reports in person to the Council of Twelve, the Great Khan personally invested him with the title of Nöyök, and stamped the warrant and gold tablet with the sign of a lion's head confirming his rank as a baron – the equivalent of a Mongol army commander of ten thousand men. His ennoblement was loudly approved by the Council. Even Phags-pa bowed and congratulated him.

'The trouble is,' Argan grumbled, 'now more than half the court wants to know when we are all going to move to Hangchow.'

'Never,' Kublai said flatly. 'It is too seductive. It turns a man's thoughts only to comfort and pleasure. And here at Khanbalic we are closer to the heartland of our people. We must never forget where we came from, and we must not let the reins of the empire become any longer.'

Marco spoke and was questioned for three hours, and by the end any lingering doubt had vanished. Properly exploited, South China could treble the annual revenue to the Treasury and fill the Imperial granaries five times over.

'Yet the amount actually received is nothing like the figures suggested,' Phags-pa observed. 'Less than half.'

'It will take time to set up a really efficient administration,' one of the Mongol councillors said.

'Precisely,' Achmet agreed. 'In dealing with such an immeasurably vast area, it will be many years before our assessors can work out exactly what taxes and tithes are due.' He smiled. 'Even Messer Marco covered only four out of nine provinces.'

As the discussion continued, Kublai saw Marco frowning and held up his hand. 'What is it?' he asked. 'Does something trouble you?'

'I was just thinking, Great Lord,' Marco said. 'Why not use the Sung archives.'

'The Sung . . . archives?' Phags-pa queried.

'They have governed the South for over three hundred years, and their people paid taxes.'

Chinkin had already understood and was smiling.

'So?' Kublai prompted.

'They were highly organized and kept written records,' Marco replied. 'Among them, tax records for every district, town and city. I have seen them with my own eyes. They are stored with the rest of the archives in the Great Library at Hangchow.' Kublai's mouth had opened. He closed it with a grunt and slapped his hand on his knee. 'There may be changes since their last census,' Marco went on, 'but their records could at least form a basis from which your tax assessors could work.'

For several moments, the Council sat silent, admiring the brilliant simplicity of the suggestion.

'The answer was so obvious, no one ever thought of it,' Achmet laughed. 'You are a wonder, Messer Marco!'

'Those archives must be secured and examined,' Kublai said.

'At once, Great Lord.' Achmet bowed, and turned to Marco. 'You have saved us perhaps years of needless work.'

Marco went with Chinkin to pay his respects to the Empress Jaimu, who received them in her private chamber, where everything was chosen with her usual perfect taste and bore the Khan's personal colours; delicate shades of green in the carpets and wallhangings, contrasting with the pure white of vases and ivory chairs. Behind a sliding screen of sage green silk showing the loves of Genghis and Borchei stood the reliquary with the holy oil, next to a small altar with a silver and jade Cross hanging above it. In front of it, Marco noticed a prayer stool.

Her grandson, Chinkin's son, Timur, was with her and watched in annoyance the ease and friendliness with which she greeted Marco. Timur was now eleven, sturdy and handsome, reaching the early manhood of Mongol boys, with nothing of the sensitivity and languor of his father. He wore buckskin breeches and a short yellow cloak trimmed with red sable, open to show the falcon amulet on his bare chest. It was deliberately non-Chinese.

In a niche by the entrance hall of the chamber, a girl plucked gentle melodies from a lute and handmaidens served them tea flavoured with mint in the Arab fashion and tiny almond cakes shaped like waterlilies.

'I am always anxious when you are gone from Khanbalic,' Jaimu told Marco.

'I was never in any danger, your Imperial Majesty,' Marco assured her.

'In the South there is always danger,' Chinkin said.

Timur snorted. 'Our troops are firmly in control. *My* troops.'

'Nevertheless, your Imperial Highness,' Marco said mildly, 'since several cities there have over a million inhabitants, not to mention the metropolis of Hangchow, it is fortunate that the Sung are a peaceful people or no garrison could contain them.'

'The answer to that is simple,' Timur smiled. 'One of Bayan's advisers recommended that any revolt could be forestalled by the simple expedient of executing everyone with the surname Li, Wu, Chang and Chao.'

'But those are the most common names in China!' Marco objected. 'It would mean executing eighty per cent of the population.'

'Exactly!' Timur laughed. 'Isn't it an amusing thought?'

Chinkin flushed and made to speak angrily, but Jaimu looked at him, stopping him. 'Such gallows humour is hardly suitable here,' he said coldly.

Timur shrugged and bowed to Jaimu. 'If you will excuse me, grandmother, I am expected at the archery butts. Father—' He bowed again to Chinkin, nodded curtly to Marco and swaggered out. Marco smiled. Timur had spoiled his exit, boylike, by pausing to take a handful of the little almond cakes.

'I should have kept a closer eye on his education,' Chinkin said.

'It would have made no difference,' Jaimu told him. 'He is pure Mongol.'

They made plans for Chinkin and Marco to spend some time with the Empress Jaimu when the court moved with Kublai to the Summer Palace, but as things turned out, they were not all to meet again for another year. For after only a month in Khanbalic, the Great Khan sent Marco on another mission. And on this trip, much to his sorrow, he was told he would not need Wu Sheng to accompany him.

Kublai Khan, aware of the unsettled nature of much of the South, was anxious to avoid any trouble with the most powerful of his neighbours before the pacification was complete. He had already formed an alliance with the King of Korea, who had agreed to accept his overlordship and to pay a yearly tribute. A similar submission by the King of Burma, whose country shared a border with China just beyond the Mekong River, would remove the only remaining danger. No threat was to be expected from the smaller kingdoms of Siam and Champa. Marco's latest task was to assess the readiness of the king to fight or submit, and to gauge the wealth of Burma and Bengal.

'It is an admirable policy of the Great Khan,' Marco said seriously. 'To prevent war by a system of alliances.'

He was sitting in the courtyard garden of Wu Sheng's house, a grey-roofed, grey-walled building in the prosperous quarter where many of the higher-grade Chinese officials lived.

'To *conquer* by alliance,' Wu Sheng corrected quietly. He did not wish to offend Marco by appearing to doubt the universal benevolence of the Khan.

'Don't you see?' Marco went on earnestly. 'To be under the Great Khan's rule will be of inestimable value to those people. There is no suggestion of destroying their sovereignty or way of life. The Khan only wishes them to share in the benefits of his empire.'

Wu Sheng took some nuts from the dish in front of him. 'These have always been my weakness,' he said. Extraordinary, he was thinking, how after all he has seen, he still keeps his political naivety . . . 'May I remind you of the words of the blessed Meng-tzu, disciple of the all-wise Confucius, as you name him? "Do not allow yourself to speak of mere personal or political advantages. Justice and humanity are all in all. Let them suffice as objects to be sought after rather than material prosperity." '

Marco would not argue with him. As a Chinese, he was bound to see things differently. In any case, the sage, Mencius, was only underlining, centuries before, the wisdom of the great Kublai, as the Chinese would surely realize one day themselves.

They talked for a while in generalities. When Marco rose to leave, Wu Sheng said, 'I am sorry my wife and daughters were not here to meet you. They are visiting their maternal aunt at Cho-chau.'

Marco hid his surprise. He had never heard mention of a family, even of a wife, before. Throughout their long travels together, Wu Sheng had never once spoken of them. It was as if some restraint had been removed from between them and the old official felt he could now trust him. But why conceal the existence of a wife and daughters?

Two days later, Chinkin rode with Marco as far as the unique marble bridge with twenty-four pillared arches spanning the Hun-ho river, ten miles south of Khanbalic; and there the two friends parted company. Marco travelled on south with his interpreters and armed escort, through the extensive silk- and wine-producing region of T'ai-yuan-fu, crossing the Yellow River again into the province of Si-ngan-fu, and journeying on through the mountainous provinces of Hanchung and Szechwan, skirting Tibet. From there he crossed the Yangtse into the rich province of Yunnan, its seven regions split between the Great Khan's fourth son Hukaji and his grandson Essen Timur.

Again, the reports Marco sent back were a blend of factual statistics and observations on the life and customs of the regions, from Akbalic, the main centre for the production of ginger and spices, to the turquoises and knobbed pearls of Ning-yuan, and the noble city of Ch'eng-tu-fu, formed of three separate, walled cities united inside one massive wall. He told how on the borders of Tibet merchant caravans, to protect their horses against tigers and lynxes, would build fires round clumps of thick bamboos near their campsites, and how the heat made the bamboo expand and burst in a series of tremendous explosions, frightening away all wild animals for miles; he described how in the same area men refused to marry virgins, but only girls who had considerable experience of the opposite sex; he told how Essen Timur's Master of the Hunt had showed him how to spear giant crocodiles, whose tender flesh was much prized as a delicacy, and whose gall was used as an ingredient in many medicines.

For the first three months of his journey he enjoyed lavish hospitality, being received with all the honour due to a personal ambassador of the Great Khan. But as he left Yunnan, he passed out of Kublai's realm and his route became harder and more dangerous. Now he journeyed on through the difficult passes of the mountains which ran directly across his route and into the trackless, uninhabited jungles of northern Burma, where Marco saw snakes of enormous length and the escort had constantly to be on guard against bears and lions, and herds of elephants and rhinoceroses. They came at last to the Irrawaddy and rode along its bank through its ever-widening valley plain, sleeping at night on rafts anchored in midstream as protection against the tigers which infested the region, until they arrived at the magnificent city of Pagan, capital of Burma.

Pagan had been a political and religious centre for hundreds of years, and over the centuries, craftsmen had flocked to it in the wake of priests and scholars. Their art had made the city resplendent, with many fine houses and palaces. What struck Marco most were the number of golden-roofed temples, shrines and monasteries. Attached to each was a school or academy where boys and girls were taught by saffron-clad Buddhist monks, just as men and women mingled freely in daily life. Most notable of all buildings was the tomb of Anawrahta, founder of the kingdom. At the head and foot of the marble sepulchre stood twin towers shaped like pyramids, high and broad-based, topped by symbolic globes. One pyramid was entirely sheathed in gold, the other in silver, and round the globes were hung little silver and gold bells which tinkled with the motion of the wind. The base of the tomb itself was covered in silver plate and its top in solid gold.

The King of Mien, as they called their country, received Marco and his messages of friendship from the Khan Kublai with reserve. His spies had informed him of smouldering revolt in Mantzu, and he knew that the Khan's eyes would shortly be turning to the west. He had no intention of letting Burma become a satellite kingdom of the empire, accepting the laws and policies of the Mongols, whom he and his people thought of as barbarians. He was more interested in Marco himself and entertained him for several days, questioning him on his travels and the nature of the western world.

For his part, Marco swiftly realized that there was small hope of returning with a favourable answer. The king would not deliberately offend the Great Khan, but took care to show his ambassador sections of his formidable army at exercise, pointing out that it was reinforced by Shan mercenaries, the most redoubtable infantry in the East. The king could barely conceal his displeasure when Marco declared his intention to visit Bengal, in spite of assurances that it was purely for personal interest. Accordingly he left Pagan early the next morning before the king could take steps to prevent him.

With a Bangala guide, he rode along the sandy coastal plain beneath the Chittagong hill region, with its bamboo forests teeming with elephants, many-hued birds and rhesus monkeys, until he reached the flats of the delta basin where Bengal's main rivers, the Ganges and Brahmaputra, join together and flow with many others through a vast marshy plain to the sea. Here the people were mostly Hindu, with many Mohammedans. Its ruler, descended from the Mohammedans who had replaced the former Buddhist kings a hundred years before, welcomed Marco effusively. He was eager to receive the Khan's offer of protection, guaranteed by his co-religionist Achmet as a shield against the King of Burma, whose aim was to annex Bengal. The King's displeasure was explained; and now Marco knew of the Khan's interest in Bengal.

A few days later, Marco joined the prince and his courtiers on a hunt for a group of man-eating tigers. They set off, riding on elephants, with beaters and a pack of mastiffs, the prince's hunting pavilion drawn behind by huge oxen on four carts lashed together. The mastiffs were the tigers' natural enemies, the only thing feared by the great striped cats, he was told, and he saw how they flushed out the group from a covert of cane, dashing in fearlessly to bark and snap at the tigers' haunches. The tigers of Bengal were the largest and most ferocious in the world, but they ran from the dogs. Marco and the prince followed the biggest of them, a superb specimen ten feet long, which had ravaged the villages of the area for months. When the mastiffs finally cornered it in a clump of trees and it turned, crushing their skulls with its huge paws and snapping their necks with its fangs, the courtiers and beaters hung back, terrified by its rage and awesome roaring. Marco and the prince went forward into the trees and slew it with one arrow each from their bows. They returned in triumph to feast in the mobile pavilion, but found news waiting for them which cut short his stay. The King of Burma was amassing an army to invade Yunnan in South China and had given orders that Marco was to be arrested and beheaded on his journey home.

Riding back quickly to the harbour of Chittagong, Marco hired a fast galley to take him and his escort past the heavily guarded ports of Burma and land them on the coast of Siam farther to the south. From there they travelled overland with a series of Mon and tattooed Khmer guides to Kweichau province in Mantzu, then back west to Yangch'ung in Yunnan. In Yangch'ung, Marco was relieved to find General Nasreddin at the head of twelve thousand Mongol cavalry. His presence was no mystery. Marco's despatches had alerted Kublai to the possibility of a preventative attack coming from Burma and he had hurried Nasreddin south to protect his sparsely defended border.

Prince Essen Timur, Viceroy of the province, was also at Yangch'ung, and Marco was able to tell him and Nasreddin what he had learnt; that the King of Burma intended to march on Yunnan and destroy the Mongol force there, so that the Great Khan would be deterred from ever again stationing a permanent garrison on his frontier. Marco was disturbed to think that it was possibly his report that had prompted the Burmese to act, but Nasreddin reassured him. The conflict was bound to come sooner or later.

Already the Burmese army was in Yunnan, approaching Yangch'ung, and scouts came in by the hour with reports from the parties of skirmishers Nasreddin had sent out. Their news was alarming. The army advancing against them was much larger than had been supposed. Reliable information put the enemy forces at forty thousand cavalry and foot soldiers, together with two thousand fighting elephants, each carrying a wooden castle on its back with fourteen to sixteen archers. Most probably, the King intended not merely to crush the Mongol defenders, but to occupy the whole province. Marco could see that Nasreddin was disturbed – understandably, since he had only twelve thousand men to face some sixty thousand and the elephants, which were reputedly terrifying in battle. Mongols had never fought against them before.

Next morning, word came that the Burmese were encamped only three days' march away. Marco and Essen Timur expected Nasreddin to withdraw and wait for reinforcements, as the odds were so much against them. The Saracen did just the opposite. 'If we are to fight, then the sooner, the better,' he said. 'And at a place which *I* can choose.'

Marco rode with Nasreddin, Essen Timur and the vanguard. The scouts had reported the Burmese to be advancing across the Yunnan plateau, making for the broad valley which led to Kunming, established by Kublai as the provincial capital. Nasreddin took up a position blocking the valley, with his right flank against a thickly wooded forest. Calling in hundreds of the local inhabitants, he had defensive ditches and pits dug along the front line to hinder a headlong charge by the enemy, leaving slanting paths through them for his own cavalry. That done, he settled down to wait.

The King of Burma, having pillaged the surrounding country, had stopped to feast and rest his men. Clashes between his outlying pickets and the Mongol skirmishers roused him and, learning that Nasreddin's smaller force was within reach, he broke camp and advanced to within three miles of their position before nightfall.

Marco had dined in the general's campaign tent with Essen Timur, Nasreddin and his senior commanders. Afterwards, he walked with Nasreddin round the lookouts, watching against a night attack. In the darkness, the glitter of the enemy fires could be seen and their occasional, exultant yells, mingled with the disquieting trumpeting of the elephants, carried through the still air. In spite of himself, Marco shivered and drew his cloak about him. He had fought before, but never in a pitched battle, never endured the hours of waiting for the killing to start.

'You're not a soldier,' Nasreddin said quietly. 'You don't have to stay here.'

Marco shook his head. 'I couldn't leave now. Many will die here tomorrow – possibly because of me.'

'I told you to forget that,' Nasreddin said. 'One day the Great Khan would have had to confront Burma anyway. It's better to get it over with.'

Marco could see his lean profile etched against the night sky, intent, listening to the distant murmur from the Burmese lines. 'Will that be the last enemy, then? Will the wars be over after this? That's worth staying and fighting for.'

Nasreddin's sceptical smile was a white glimmer in the dark.

Before dawn, Marco joined the commanders of thousands as they gathered in the general's tent. 'Is it true the odds are four to one?' one of them, Toktai, a battle-scarred veteran of many campaigns, asked.

'Perhaps more,' Nasreddin said. He saw the commanders shift, troubled. 'But what's important is that some of them are raw troops, others are mercenaries. They haven't fought together as a unit like we have. Certainly not so often.' Some of the commanders grinned. 'Remember, the numbers may be against us, but at this moment they are afraid – because they have never crossed steel with the Mongols, whose very name strikes terror to the whole world.' There was a growl of agreement. 'So fight well,' Nasreddin went on. 'The Burmese think they have us trapped. We'll teach them what it means to put their heads into the lion's den.'

Before dawn the next morning, Essen Timur's bodyservant approached Marco with a suit of the Mongol cavalry armour, made of thin, overlapping metal plates which covered the wearer from the neck to the elbow and to the lower leg when riding. Marco refused it, but Essen Timur said, 'Either you wear it or you go back and wait for us at the Viceroy's palace. I'm not going to be the one to tell my grandfather that a Burmese lance went through you, because we didn't make sure you were protected.'

The armour was easier to wear than Marco had expected, and left his arms and legs unrestricted, but he would not accept the cumbersome helmet. In its place, Nasreddin gave him a pointed, Saracen cap of steel with a projecting piece in front and a fringe of chainmail at the back to guard the nose and neck. After all that, Marco was disappointed to be ordered to take a place beside Toktai, a battle-scarred veteran who was in command of the two thousand held in reserve behind the main lines.

'Don't worry,' Toktai told him. 'If it's fighting you want, we'll all see enough of it before the day is out.'

As the sun rose, they became aware that the enemy was already on the move, a tremendous mass of animals and men rolling forward. As well as the fighting troops, there were campfollowers, cooks and baggage trains drawn by oxen, armourers, arrowmakers, musicians and herders to manage a thousand spare horses. The moving mass crowding into the valley seemed irresistible and Marco was tense, gripping the long-bladed cavalry sword he had been given. 'Relax,' Toktai said. 'Nothing'll happen for an hour yet.'

He was right. At less than a mile from them, the Burmese ground to a halt and they watched as the king, with almost insulting slowness, marshalled his forces, stationing the elephants in front in a wide block, with two extended wings of cavalry and infantry a slight distance behind them and strong reserves to the rear. Marco could make him out as he rode with his generals and standard-bearers and saw him, quite distinctly, pause to laugh at the comparative insignificance of his Mongol opponents. When the King had finished riding along his lines and speaking to his men, he raised his ivory baton and the kettledrums of his corps of musicians boomed out, followed by the rattle of smaller drums and the sound of pipes, flutes and brazen horns. With the Burmese shouting and clattering their weapons against their shields, the din was indescribable, echoing and redoubling from the sides of the valley. It was all part of maddening the trained elephants for the charge. Marco's throat went dry. The great beasts, half armoured, their tusks sheathed in steel, the wooden turrets attached to their backs and filled with bowmen, were a sight to chill the blood, as was the sheer multitude of the enemy, their arms brandishing spears and maces. Marco heard Toktai clear his throat and spit, and copied him. The barrel-chested Mongol chuckled.

The Burmese King hoped to provoke the Mongols into one of their famous headlong charges, but none came. Each man of Nasreddin's superbly disciplined army, divided into tens, hundreds and thousands, knew the orders and watched their immediate officers. When the enemy drums began, they swung as one man into their saddles, but continued to sit stone-still, looking ahead. Nasreddin's plan was to wait until the elephants were committed to charge, then to outflank them. Once his cavalry had hit the Burmese wings, the elephants would be of restricted use, for fear of trampling their own men.

It began perfectly. The enemy started to advance, preceded by the two thousand battle elephants, trunks tossing, sail-like ears flapping. As they lumbered forward, their speed gradually built up and their trumpeted calls rang out. The gap between them and the bulk of the Burmese army increased, growing wider every second.

When the moment finally came, Nasreddin gave the signal and the three front ranks of Mongol cavalry dashed forward, threading through the lanes in the defensive lines and forming up at once to sweep to the charge. The plan was for them to split, allowing the elephants to pass through their centre. The sight of the charging behemoths, their shrill trumpeting and the thunder of their heavy feet did not affect the Mongols, but their horses were terrified and began to wheel round, trying to flee. Their riders could not restrain them and Marco, horrified, saw Nasreddin's cavalry reduced to an ungovernable rabble, milling about in mindless confusion.

The elephants were racing towards them and already the archers on their backs were firing, beginning the inevitable slaughter. The mahouts, the elephants' handlers perched on their necks, goaded them to drive them on, but the Mongol commanders, remembering Nasreddin's contingency orders, began leading their men off to the side and the horses responded, ready to do anything to escape the approaching monsters. Within seconds they had reached the first trees of the forest on their right and were soon swallowed up. The elephants, unable to halt their headlong career, went crashing in after them, uprooting trees and bushes, raging to get at them.

To his dismay, Marco saw Nasreddin give the signal for the two remaining lines of Mongol cavalry to fall back and they began to retreat the four hundred yards to where he waited with Toktai's reserve squadrons.

It was easy to understand why the order had been given. The main Burmese army, scenting victory and seeing over half of the Mongol force chased into the woods, was streaming towards them, their cavalry, their long pennons fluttering and lances levelled, racing ahead of the infantry, straight towards the depleted Mongol lines. Off to his left, Marco saw Nasreddin sitting coolly on his black horse, as though merely observing. Prince Essen Timur was arguing and gesticulating, but the general paid no attention. How could he be so cool? Marco wondered. What was he waiting for?

All of a sudden, he heard Toktai grunt and saw for himself. The leading ranks of Burmese cavalry had reached the concealed defensive pits and ditches. As the flimsy covers gave way, horses and riders pitched forward, many of them falling, with the riders behind them unable to draw up in time and ploughing on into and over them.

'Soon be our turn,' Toktai muttered and hitched at his belt with his free right hand. On his left forearm was his small, round Tartar shield. Marco slid his left arm through the straps of his own shield and gripped the handhold. Then his head turned quickly.

The elephants were coming out of the forest in disarray, their handlers urging them back. Some had lost their mahouts and were mixing with the others in panic, preventing any orderly formation. Marco saw that the Mongol cavalry who had appeared to be in flight had dismounted, tethered their horses to trees and were now attacking the elephants on foot, streams of long-shafted arrows from their powerful bows driving the huge beasts back. Ignoring the archers in their turrets, the Mongols shot at the elephants themselves, aiming for the eyes, the trunk, every chink in their armour. While they trumpeted shrilly, trampling bloody swathes through them, the Mongols still darted round them, firing volley after volley, until the behemoths, stung with arrows and screaming with pain, turned tail and fled. Eight or nine, pierced through the eyesockets to the brain, toppled over dead, their huge limbs still twitching.

The stampede of the rest took them through the left flank of the Burmese cavalry and straight for the massed ranks of foot soldiers, who broke aside in terror as the crazed elephants smashed into them, out of all control, screeching and trampling and pounding in all directions and throwing the infantry into confusion.

Suddenly Nasreddin's sword arm swept down. '*Hai yai yai yai – Nasreddin!*' Toktai bellowed, and Marco found himself yelling with him as the so far uncommitted Mongol ranks raced forward, cleared the hideous barrier of threshing bodies in the ditches and charged full tilt at the demoralized lines of Burmese cavalry. It was now that Marco discovered the value of the short Mongol stirrups, which permitted the Mongols to drop the reins and stand erect, guiding their battle-trained mounts with their calves, while they let fly their arrows as fast as they could. The Burmese sent back answering volleys, but since they wore no armour, the damage inflicted on them was much greater.

Then the two forces clashed together and there was no more time for shooting. It was cut and hack and parry. Marco saw Toktai splitting skulls with a spiked iron mace. His own sword was in his hand and he slashed about him, unaware of anything except the need to turn the enemy's flank. Forgetting the men of his escort riding round him, still trying to protect him, he fought his way forward, hacking and thrusting at the bodies and faces of the enemies in his path. He was at the apex of one of many wedges the Mongol cavalry had driven deep into the enemy ranks. Even so, the outcome was by no means certain.

Suddenly the Mongols who had driven off the elephants emerged from the woods, having remounted, and charged into the enemy's wavering left flank, rolling it round. The whole line began to inch back towards the foot soldiers.

The king tried to summon up his reserves and threw detachments of infantry forward to cover the retreat of his cavalry, but the confusion was too widespread. This was the fighting the Mongol veterans knew best and now they began to cut paths for themselves through the retreating cavalry and into the foot soldiers, killing with a dreadful and joyous ferocity.

The Burmese campfollowers were already straggling away, and panic was spreading to the rear ranks of foot soldiers, who could only see the swaying, struggling mass in front of them and hear the clash of arms and the shouting, the neighing of horses and the shrieks of the wounded. They began to give way, many turning to hurry after the campfollowers, despite the king's efforts to rally them. Without the weight of the reserves behind them, the front ranks also started to yield ground and all at once, like a dam collapsing, they were in full retreat. As the decimated remains of the cavalry also took to flight and the King of Burma abandoned the field, the retreat became a rout. Isolated pockets fought on hopelessly, but the

Mongols left them surrounded and chased after the fleeing enemy, cutting down all they overtook, butchering them as they ran, until the valley was one long charnel ground of the dead and dying.

Marco took no part in the pursuit. He reined in, amazed to find himself still alive and so far from where he had been stationed. The sun was high in the sky, a little after noonday; they had been fighting for over six hours. His right hand felt numb. As he looked at it, he realized that he was spattered with blood, his right arm red to the elbow. He let the sword fall from his hand and gazed round at the carnage. Of the last two hours he had little memory, only of hacking and thrusting, of snarling, screaming faces. He was panting in short, shallow breaths. He was not even sure that he had killed anyone, but the blood was a sign that made him tremble and its smell, as he became aware of it, made him want to retch.

The prince's yak-tail banner and the green-and-white Imperial banner of Nasreddin had been set up on a low mound to the side. He rode towards them and discovered Nasreddin there with Prince Essen Timur and some of his senior commanders. They smiled in relief when he approached and Nasreddin sent his lieutenant to hold Marco's bridle as he dismounted.

Toktai was with them, the broken shaft of an arrow protruding from a gap in his armour above the right elbow. 'I told them I'd lost sight of you, Lord Marco,' he chuckled. 'It could've cost me my head.' He gave no sign nor sound, only a slight narrowing of the eyes, as a Chinese surgeon cut the arrowhead out of his thick arm.

Essen Timur was drinking from a gold-rimmed bowl. He gestured with it and his bodyservant brought it to Marco. 'Not wounded?' Essen Timur asked. Marco shook his head. 'Praise the Spirits of the Eternal Blue Sky,' the prince said. 'Their arms protected you.'

Marco drank deeply, the cold dry wine in the bowl burning his parched throat. He looked at Nasreddin. 'You knew!' Marco said to him, almost accusingly. 'You knew what would happen.'

Nasreddin looked at him and passed his hand over his close-trimmed beard. 'I did not really know,' he admitted. 'But I hoped.'

Essen Timur laughed. 'Never expect a general to confess that luck played any part in a victory. It is always his brilliant tactics.' The commanders were smiling. His eyes on Marco, Nasreddin gave one of his quick, slightly twisted smiles.

Of Marco's escort of eighteen, seven had been killed. He said a prayer for them, and for all the dead of both sides. For many nights, and often in years to come, he woke sweating and shaking at the memory of those blood-filled hours; but the King of Burma had been defeated and never again would he menace the empire. Some two hundred of the elephants had been trapped in the forest. They were brought under control and local handlers fetched to replace the slain mahouts. Ever afterwards, elephants formed part of the Mongol army. It was a notable victory.

The sequel to the battle was the stuff of legend. Shortly after Marco's return to Khanbalic, where he was heaped with honours, despite his protests that he had done little, Kublai Khan decided to make a decisive end to the threat from Burma. He ordered the leaders of the two thousand acrobats and jugglers retained by the court to take their men and conquer the southern kingdom. It was a gesture intended to display his scorn of enemies. In reality, the jugglers were backed by an experienced commander and a considerable army. But the 'army of jugglers' became a tale told from the Flower Houses of Khanbalic to the bazaars of Cairo. When they had successfully invaded the country and taken the city of Pagan, they sent word to the Great Khan, offering to demolish the wonderful towers of gold and silver at the tomb of Anawrahta, whose value was inestimable. But Kublai had heard from Marco that they had been erected to perpetuate the memory of the dead king and for the welfare of his soul. He gave orders that they were not to be harmed, as the Khan of the Mongols did not plunder the dead.

The wars to unify China and to secure its frontiers were over.

'I know how much you have prayed for this day,' Marco said. 'How you have prayed for peace.'

The Empress Jaimu offered her jewelled hand to Chinkin and her son helped her up from the cushioned ebony bench where she had been sitting. She shook her head sadly. 'Peace is an unknown word to us Mongols, my son. It is merely an illusion – like a dream that lasts a night and leaves only regret.'

'But the Khan's last enemy is defeated, my lady,' Marco pointed out. 'There will be no more wars. Now the Khan wants life in the South to be improved, for everyone.'

'He always knew how it would end,' said Chinkin. 'Even the astrologer's prediction only confirmed his victory.'

'It sounded so alarming to us at the time,' Marco smiled, 'and yet it seemed to please your father.'

'What did the prediction say?' Jaimu asked, intrigued.

Chinkin tried to remember the exact words. ' "The small faces the big. Amid the tears and mourning stands one great banner." ' He shrugged. 'Well, we saw the little son of the Sung Emperor bow before my great father.'

'And certainly there were tears,' she murmured.

'And my father's banner standing alone over his defeated enemies.'

'Yes, but how would he explain the last line?' Marco wondered. ' "Not gold, but iron will come to the throne." '

'As you know,' explained Chinkin, 'he has made my son, Timur, Regent of the South. In our ancient language, Timur means iron.'

'So the astrologer was right!' Marco laughed. 'The Great Khan's dreams have been fulfilled.'

The Empress was solemn. 'There is always a new frontier to be crossed, always a new land to conquer.'

They were disturbed by the light rustle of silk robes and three young ladies-in-waiting to the empress came in and bowed. Belonging to the Pai minority, they wore the traditional red-bordered robes and each carried a stringed instrument. The Empress gave them the slightest nod and they sat cross-legged on the floor in the far corner, playing soft, sweet music that seemed to bathe the senses.

The empress moved to a small table and picked up a beautiful porcelain vase decorated with characters and scenes in relief. She caressed it lightly as she studied it. Her voice was still tinged with sadness. 'There is a distant country, a kingdom of islands that is said to be rich in gold and jewels. Once already the Khan has attempted to force them to submit to him.'

'Attempted?' Marco was puzzled.

'The invasion was badly planned,' said Chinkin. 'Lack of organization meant that our ships were scattered and destroyed.'

'What country was it?'

'It is known as Chipango,' the prince replied. 'Some call it the Kingdom of the Islands.'

'Your father has never forgotten that defeat,' Jaimu sighed. 'I've even heard him saying that name in his sleep . . . Chipango . . . Chipango . . .'

'But how powerful is this Kingdom of the Islands? How big is its army?' asked Marco.

'We know very little. Only what we learned from those who survived the expedition.'

'The Mongols were defeated? I can't believe it!'

'Don't you think this vase is lovely?' Jaimu asked, and touched a second, faintly tinged with green, veined like a leaf. 'And this other one? They were made by a man from those islands. He was wounded in battle and brought back here as a prisoner. He began modelling things while he was in captivity – small animals, vases, bowls. I was impressed by his art and arranged for his release. For a roof and workshop to be given to him. That man is everything I know of Chipango.' The gentle music was still wafting through the room as she paused and glanced over at the crucifix. 'When the wind blows from the steppes, the Khan's horses scent battle and blood – then no-one hears my voice . . .'

Marco, gazing at her, was moved by her hopelessness. Yet she could not be serious. Kublai Khan had no reason to go to war.

While his wife extolled the art of Japan, Kublai thought only of its conquest.

Accompanied by Argan, Bayan, the enormously obese King of Korea and Admiral Won, Commander of the Korean fleet, the Great Khan strode into the Main Hall, where Chinkin waited by the raised, golden throne. Round the walls hung the banners of the principal Khans of the empire.

As Kublai entered, the loud buzz of argument ceased at once and everyone present knelt in ritual greeting. He proceeded to the throne and seated himself above the Council of Twelve and all the Khans who had been summoned to his capital. Marco stood behind the Council, watching as Kublai motioned the King of Korea to a throne on a lower dais, then indicated the king's companion, 'Admiral Won, Commander of the Korean fleet.' He remembered something and smiled. 'Of three thousand ships.'

Most people were impressed, Marco saw. Achmet was smiling, Phags-pa inscrutable.

Kublai turned to the king and introduced the most important dignitaries to him. As each was named, he came forward to the throne, bowed, then knelt. Marco was placed at an angle to the throne and was able to see the faces of those who were being presented. Caidu Khan came first, nephew of Kublai and governor of the regions of the Central Steppes. Dressed in a large, ram-hide cloak, Caidu limited his greeting to a short nod, then locked eyes for a moment with Kublai. Marco noted the hard look that passed between them. Bektor came next, head of the nomad families of Ganzu, a little uneasy in the grandeur of the palace. Then Marco saw Kasar, his son, being introduced, and recalled the wrestling match. He smiled, wondering how he had ever had the nerve to challenge such a powerful opponent.

Kublai pointed to a strongly built Mongol warrior of noble bearing, who wore a tunic decorated with a small, bronze cross. Marco was pleased to see him. 'Nayan, descended from the line of the Great Genghis, my ancestor. He has chosen a new God whose sign is the Cross.' Kublai smiled benevolently at Nayan. 'A God from far away, but who is yet another powerful ally of the Mongol people.'

Marco was amusing himself by trying to guess the weight of the King of Korea, whose neck seemed to consist of successive rolls of fat, when the Great Khan's next words jolted him. 'Marco Polo, a young man from the city of Venice, our envoy and faithful servant . . .'

Rising quickly, Marco moved round and knelt in front of the throne, collecting an interested nod from the King of Korea. Because the King knew most of the others in the room, further introductions were unnecessary.

Kublai began the *Kuriltai* by telling his Council and his visiting Khans that ambassadors had been sent to Japan to demand the surrender of the emperor.

The news caused ripples of alarm, and Caidu's reaction was one of real anxiety.

'I know what is in your minds and hearts,' Kublai said. 'I, too, have not forgotten our defeat. But that defeat served to make me wiser. The errors will not be repeated. And when the united fleet attacks the islands, our dead at the bottom of the sea will be the first to celebrate our revenge. Our ships which will attack Japan will be as invincible as the horses of Genghis Khan!'

'Great Khan,' said Caidu, stepping forward, 'this is our weakness – a Mongol is not a warrior without a horse. We fight for you, but only as far as our horses can reach. The sea cripples us, Great Khan. Think on this.'

Marco noticed the nods of agreement from Nayan and some of the other Khans, but he also saw the irritation of the King of Korea.

Achmet sought permission to speak. His voice was conciliatory. 'The noble Caidu urges prudence, and prudence is the greatest virtue. And yet there is nobody present who does not know of the difficulties faced by many regions in our empire. Flooding, epidemics in the North, the threat of a famine in the war-ravaged South . . .'

'War is never a solution,' Nayan interrupted.

'It is, if the reward of victory is gold, more gold than any other kingdom has ever seen,' Achmet argued, smiling.

'Who has been to this kingdom to count its wealth?' asked Nayan. 'It is Japan's *iron* we have seen so far, not its gold.'

Kublai signalled to the Keeper of the Records. 'Phags-pa, you have told me that you have brothers of your faith living in those islands, those who turn the prayer wheels as you do. Let us hear wisdom from you.'

The silence was tense and the Head Lama hesitated. 'I say Caidu warns with reason.' Phags-pa's words always commanded prestige and there was a murmur of approval. 'Yet Achmet's eyes see far,' he continued. 'What he sees is such to fill the heart with hope. Perhaps the last word should be left with the stars, Great Khan . . .'

Kublai realized the danger of waiting for a delayed reply from the astrologers. 'No,' he announced, rising. 'The last word will come from my ambassadors. And the final decision will be mine – and mine alone!' His voice echoed down the vast hall.

Marco bowed along with everyone else. As he raised his eyes again, however, he saw that Caidu Khan still stood, staring fixedly at Kublai, as if in defiance.

'*Kuai! Kuai! Mufan! Daozi!*' Quick, quick! Rice! Fetch another knife! Jacopo bustled about, giving orders to the Chinese servants.

He had important guests to impress, for the Polos had invited Caidu, Nayan, Bektor and Kasar to their residence in the Forbidden City, and they were all relaxing around a table in the small, internal courtyard. Jacopo, who was behaving more like the landlord of an inn than a servant himself, hustled the others into bringing in traditional Chinese dishes and jugs of rice wine. The warm sun, the fresh air and the delight of being reunited with Niccolo, Matteo and Marco had improved the nomads' mood and many toasts were drunk.

Caidu glanced up at the patch of sky above them and asked the Venetians how they could bear to live behind so many walls. 'There's no horizon in this City. You are like prisoners in a great golden prison. I can understand how the Great Khan has forgotten the Mongol way of life.'

'He dresses like a Chinese,' Bektor grunted through a mouthful of rice. 'His nails are painted and his hair perfumed!'

'He's surrounded by too many people and tries to keep them all happy,' Nayan said. 'He behaves with God in the same way. He accepts all faiths. If only he had one himself.'

'Keep your faith to yourself,' Caidu growled. 'What I'm saying is – sea battles are not for Mongols. We have nothing to gain by attacking Chipango, and everything to lose.'

'That is what the Empress Jaimu believes, too,' Marco told them. 'She says that the people of the islands possess great virtues and that it would be wrong to declare war on them.'

'What are you talking about?' Niccolo asked, sharply. 'Everyone knows that in Chipango all the houses, churches and palaces have roofs of gold.'

'Indeed,' Matteo agreed, 'and the country has vast reserves of silver and jewels – although no merchant has been there.'

'Riches to make your head spin!' Niccolo assured them.

'But how do you know, father? Uncle Matteo has just said that no merchant has ever been there!'

'You heard Phags-pa – Achmet sees further than the rest of us, Marco. He knows about Chipango. He has his informers. The King of Korea—'

'My opinion,' Kasar belched, 'is that the king is too fat. He can hardly move his belly. He talks bravely of war, but he'll never lift his huge backside off the throne to take up a sword.'

'Probably not,' Marco laughed.

Matteo tried to school his nephew. 'The king does not need to fight with his sword. Achmet has made sure that he will serve the Great Khan like the rest of us. We must *all* serve the Khan. Don't forget that, Marco.'

The speech had made Caidu impatient and he drank from the wine jug nearest him, emptying it. His disaffection with the Great Khan was as strong as ever. The tension was eased by the arrival of Jacopo and a small cortege of cooks and servants. Each of them set a bowl in front of someone at the table.

'Eat and enjoy,' invited Jacopo, grandly, bowing.

Marco looked doubtfully at his bowl and saw something that looked like long strings of wet dough. Puzzled frowns all round the table showed that the dish was a novelty to everyone and this made Jacopo smirk. The Mongols were the first to try the new delicacy. Dipping their fingers into the bowls and wincing at the heat, they drew out large helpings. Before their hands reached their lips, however, the long, slithery strings were slipping from their grasp and clinging to their beards or stuck to the front of their tunics. Niccolo and Matteo fared no better, and Marco managed to drop a whole handful on to his lap. He yelped. Failure spurred them on to fresh attempts, but these were equally disastrous. Annoyed at first, then desperate, they eventually gave way to laughter.

'How the devil are you supposed to eat it?' Matteo demanded.

Jacopo stepped forward to instruct them. Thrusting a finger into a bowl, he wound a coil of the strings around it, then put the finger straight into his mouth. When it reappeared, the strings were gone and Jacopo munched contentedly.

'What is it?' Marco asked.

'Threads of wheat dough with butter and spices,' Jacopo told him. 'A Chinese delight.'

The others were soon feeding themselves in the prescribed way and good humour reigned at the table. Jacopo felt that his status had been raised considerably with the other servants.

When the guests had gone, Marco rested and dozed for a while.

But soon he awoke thinking about the Council Meeting and was very troubled by the notion of an invasion of Japan. This unprovoked aggression was not what he had expected of Kublai. The words of the Empress Jaimu kept coming back to him and he found her counsel very persuasive. Kublai, with the instincts of a Mongol, could only think about another country in terms of conquest, but Marco was a traveller with a traveller's insatiable curiosity.

It was his curiosity which made him rise. An hour later, escorted by a Mongol guard, he left the Forbidden City and went into the busy streets of Khanbalic. It was evening and the light was failing swiftly as they began their search. After zigzagging through a maze of alleyways in the poorer districts, they at last found the house that they sought. The guard took down a hanging lantern and they entered a small courtyard containing only a tiny vegetable patch and a pile of rubbish. A low door in a wall allowed them through into a second courtyard and it was there, on a bench near a tree, that Marco saw him, indistinct in the violet shadows.

He was sitting in front of a potter's wheel, turning it by pressing a pedal and working clay skilfully with both hands. The wheel stopped when they approached him and he left his hands protectively round the bowl he had been making.

'You can work in the dark?' Marco asked, surprised.

'For me there is no dark,' the man said. 'No night or day.'

It was only when he moved closer that Marco saw the potter was blind.

'Who are you?' the potter asked.

'My name is Marco Polo. I am in the service of the Great Khan. I have seen your work – and heard your story from the Empress Jaimu.'

'You know the Lady Jaimu?'

'It was she who showed me your work. I have come to ask you for information – about the Kingdom of the Islands.'

'Why?' the man asked cautiously. 'There is fear in your voice. A threat . . .'

'No, you hear a desire to learn – that is all. I wish to tell the true from the false.'

The potter smiled wryly. 'It seems, my friend, that you are as blind as I am at this moment. I must rely on memory – you, on imagination.' The wheel had started up again and his hands continued to mould the wet clay. 'My country, the Chinese call Je-pen-quo. It means land of the rising sun. It is well-named, because the sun loves it and makes it beautiful. In the early morning, the roofs of the houses and the pagodas shine like gold. And in the evening, the girls sing and the air is full of music and friendly voices. Even the wind is friendly in my land.'

'Is it a country of peace, then?'

'Peace? No, my friend,' the potter sighed. 'My people are divided by many things – religious quarrels, disputes over land, rich lords jealous of what they have and always ready to fight each other for more. Then there is the pride of the great families, of the men of war we call samurais. They are both generous and cruel – born to fight, they never lay down their swords.'

'But how could a country so divided drive off the Mongols?' Marco wondered.

The potter held out a hand towards him and stretched the fingers wide. 'These fingers are different from each other, aren't they, my friend? But watch!' He closed his hand into a tight ball. 'Now they have become a fist, united and strong. When my country comes under attack, all disputes and quarrels end at once. Everyone obeys the emperor's voice and that of the shikken, his regent, and the shogun, his great general. It is as though Chipango beats with only one heart.' Clouds drifted over the face of the moon and the potter was veiled in shadow. As darkness thickened, the wheel continued to turn rhythmically and the hands to mould the vase. Marco listened to the sounds and felt he had begun to understand something about the spirit of the people of Japan.

'Doubts, uncertainties, discussions are all behind us now! The Emperor of Chipango has given us his answer.' Kublai's anger was fearsome. 'My ambassadors have been beheaded! We are left with only one choice. War! War until our enemy has been destroyed!'

The Council was in a turmoil at the news, and the other dignitaries were equally alarmed and bewildered. Chinkin looked anxious and the declaration of war was like a physical blow to Marco, who was shocked to see Kublai driven by the sheer lust of conquest.

Nayan raised a hand to speak and was ignored by Kublai, but he refused to be silenced. 'Do not listen only to the voice of anger, Great Lord! The grief we feel today could be a thousand times greater tomorrow!'

'As always, we are ready to fight for you against all enemies,' Caidu swore fervently, 'but we will not fight against reason! We must consider and discuss it further.'

Choking with emotion, Chinkin tried to put in his plea for a delay. 'Listen to them, father. If we rush into a—'

'Enough! Enough from all of you!' Kublai exploded. 'I have lost patience with your quibbling, your caution! They are other words for fear and cowardice! You say: we are ready to fight – but not on the sea. Yet the world that the gods gave to the Mongols is made of earth *and* water.' He announced his decision yet again. 'Our answer to Chipango is war! War! War!'

Kublai stormed out of the Council Meeting with the King of Korea waddling after him. Consternation made the hall echo with noise for a long time as the others discussed what had happened. But all that Marco could hear was the turn of a potter's wheel and the gentle swish as hands moulded wet clay.

Niccolo and Matteo had been honoured by a visit from Achmet, and they had given him the warmest welcome. When the real reason for the visit became clear, however, the Venetians felt an anxiety natural to a father and an uncle. Marco was sent for. His enemies had waited long for this moment and now, it seemed, he was in serious trouble.

'I will be open with you, Marco,' Achmet said. 'Phags-pa has warned the Khan that you are a bad influence on Prince Chinkin, that you distract him from his duties and poison him with ideas that are foreign to the Mongol spirit.'

'It is not true!' Marco protested. It was incredible. All he had done was to agree with Chinkin and a few others that there was little justification for the war against Japan. Now a great gulf had opened before him.

'I know,' Achmet assured him. 'Your friendship is a good one. Those who criticize you are envious. But sometimes when one protests against envy, one only makes it stronger.' He glanced at the others, then announced his decision. 'No, it is better to avoid the evil altogether. I will appoint you to a post in the South, far from here. Your father, I am sure, will agree.'

'We are at your command, Lord Achmet,' Niccolo bowed.

'But why must I—'

'You, Marco, have not hidden your impatience to travel again,' Achmet interrupted courteously. 'This will satisfy your impatience and give you an opportunity to use those talents that the Khan values so highly.'

'How, my lord?'

'You will co-ordinate the production and shipment of salt, and head a group of my tax collectors, collaborating with them in drawing up a tax census of the city and district of Yangchou.'

'But I have no experience in tax matters,' Marco argued. 'And I only know that district from one short visit, my lord.'

'Your Uncle Matteo will go with you. He will be a useful companion and adviser.'

'I know the governor of Yangchou well,' Matteo said, trying to encourage his nephew. 'He will help you, if you need it.'

'Strange though it may seem,' Achmet smiled, 'inexperience is often a useful ally. It prevents one from digging too deeply and becoming lost in the shadows.'

'I do not understand,' Marco said, baffled.

'Nor I,' Matteo admitted.

'When the moment is right, Marco, you will understand these matters better,' the regent promised. 'For the time being, understand two things: first, the empire's treasury is low and in need of new payments from any source possible; second, you must avoid giving your trust even to those who seem to be your friends.'

'When are we to leave?' Marco asked.

'At dawn tomorrow.'

'So soon?'

'The Khan has been informed of everything and relieves you of formal audience. He has much on his mind at the moment, as you well know.' Achmet paused. 'Take care. You must get away. He has affection for you, but you have seen how unpredictable his anger can be.'

Niccolo bowed. 'I am grateful to you, Lord Achmet. I hope that my son will prove worthy of your trust.'

'Dawn tomorrow?' Marco repeated.

'You will want to take leave of Prince Chinkin,' the regent said. 'I suggest you do that now.'

'Thank you, my Lord.' As Marco bowed and left, he felt considerably dejected. In spite of what Achmet had said, he had the unmistakable feeling that he would be leaving Khanbalic in semi-disgrace.

When he finally tracked down Prince Chinkin, his friend was relaxing in his litter in a wooded area in the hills near Khanbalic. It was a favourite spot for both of them, peaceful and enchanting, the buds of the cherry blossom just beginning to open. The eight litter-bearers were resting. The air was clear and fragrant, and Chinkin lay with the curtains open. Marco obviously had much to say, but he seemed hesitant. It was some time before he broached the painful subject of his estrangement from Kublai. 'The Great Khan has kept me at a distance since I tried to ask him to think again about his plan to invade Japan.' Marco paused. 'He told me he would consider what I said. But I have never seen him so cold and remote.'

'The humiliation of that old defeat embittered my father.' Chinkin frowned. 'Try not to judge him. He is driven by old passions. His wisdom, as well as his prestige, has suffered. Today, more than ever, he leaves the business of governing the empire to Achmet and Phags-pa.'

'Both able men.'

'Power corrupts even the best, Marco. Too much power is like too much strong wine – it makes a man forget his finer feelings.'

'Yes.' Marco nodded.

Chinkin waited. 'You have something to tell me.'

'I have come to say goodbye – for a time,' Marco said quietly. 'I am being sent on a journey.'

'A journey?' Chinkin was surprised that he had not heard of it.

'To the South. Yangchou.'

'Again? For what purpose?'

'To oversee the collection of taxes,' Marco said. 'Achmet proposed the appointment, your father agreed to it, Phags-pa endorsed it.'

'Yes,' Chinkin said bitterly. 'They all want rid of you.'

'But why?' Marco asked. 'All I have done is agree with you.'

'And because of that, my father wants to separate us. As his heir, I am allowed no opinions but his. As for Achmet's motive – who knows? He is eager for the gold of Japan. Perhaps he fears you might still make my father think again about invading.'

'And Phags-pa?'

'The simplest of all. He is afraid that your influence, added to my mother's, will lead us to choose your religion instead of his.'

'I wish I understood him better,' Marco said.

Chinkin shrugged. 'He's a fanatic. He will not rest until Buddhism is our state religion. To him, that justifies everything.'

'So that is why he distrusts the Chinese?'

'Except the Buddhists. He believes that we Mongols must build a culture of our own. You know that we do not possess a written language and therefore cannot record our history and legends. Well, Phags-pa has begun to invent a language for us – a system of signs and letters. Just another way of stopping that which was destined to move, "Our roots are in the wind" – that is what Genghis Khan said. Our language lives in the words passed on from mouth to mouth, not in signs made on parchment or stone.'

'You talk like Caidu,' Marco smiled.

'And Caidu talks like me.' Chinkin sat up and tried to climb out of the litter. 'Help me, Marco.'

'You shouldn't move,' Marco reminded him. 'Rest is the best medicine.'

Chinkin had recently come close to having another attack of his sickness and it had weakened him. The physicians had advised rest and fresh air, but Chinkin was never the most obedient patient. In spite of his obvious breathlessness, he tried to explain things to Marco.

'The power game is much stronger than we are. Achmet sends you to the South and Phags-pa backs him. In this, the two rivals are in agreement. But their motives are very different. Who knows which one of them will gain most from this movement of a pawn on the chessboard? But remember, Marco; the pawn is the last to find out.' Leaning against a tree, he closed his eyes for a moment. His next words were a whisper. 'How I wish I could go with you, my friend.'

'It won't be long before we're together again,' Marco promised. 'And you will be healthy again then. This weakness will have passed. You will be fit and healthy and happy.'

Chinkin shook his head and grasped the tree tight. 'When the days of a Mongol chief, or his son's, are drawing to a close, he is taken to a tree and stood up against it, so that his measurements can be taken. Then the tree is hollowed out. When the chief dies, the trunk will hold his body, deep under the earth, and a new tree, young and strong, will be planted on his unmarked grave.' His voice was weaker now and had a dreamy quality that alarmed Marco. 'My great father has decided that I should live in Shangtu, until I have recovered my health fully.'

'The country air will help you,' encouraged Marco.

'No, my friend. It is too late.' He embraced the trunk against which he was leaning. 'I think I have already found my tree . . .'

Japan had changed everything.

It had brought out a streak of vengefulness in Kublai that warped all his better qualities. It had meant disagreement and division in the Council of Twelve, and thrown old rivalries into sharper focus. It had made the Empress Jaimu sadder and lonelier, and sent her to kneel more often before her crucifix. It had caused uncertainty and unrest throughout Khanbalic, and its wider effects were starting to be felt in the Mongol empire at large. By the anxiety and stress that it brought him, it had laid another heavy burden upon the failing health of Prince Chinkin.

The changes from Marco's point of view had been deeply disturbing. He had lost the ear of the Great Khan; he had been the victim of political intrigues at Court, and was to be parted from the friend he loved most in the world.

'The Treasury needs money to finance the war against Japan, Marco,' his father had reminded him. 'Don't forget – this appointment is a great honour.'

Marco was doubtful. 'If it had been given to me solely on merit, I might have welcomed it,' Marco admitted. 'But now . . .'

The night before he left to take up his new appointment, Marco lay awake for a long time, plagued by questions to which he had no answers. What had Achmet meant when he had talked about inexperience being a useful ally? When would he see Chinkin again? How would the war with Japan end? Who had really made the decision to send him away from Khanbalic?

His father, too, occupied his thoughts. Now that he was about to leave him for some length of time, he realized how much he cared for him. Niccolo Polo had always been wary about his son's involvement in court affairs, partly because he had regarded that involvement as potentially dangerous for Marco, but also because it had kept father and son apart. On the long journey to the East, they had really begun to know each other, to understand each other. Since they had been in Khanbalic, however, Marco's assignments and his preoccupation with Chinkin had drawn him further and further away from both his father and his uncle. He had lost something in the process and he regretted that.

Marco was still thinking of his father as he finally drifted off to sleep, but he did not dream of Niccolo. Instead the image which surfaced time and again was of the hand of a blind Japanese potter, clenched into a fist.

*

Next morning, before the sun had appeared above the grey rooftops of the outer city, Marco, Matteo and their four Mongol guards rode through the southern gate of Khanbalic. Contemplation had made Marco determine to take a more positive attitude to the mission. He knew that some of the answers that he was seeking lay ahead of him. In addition, he had felt the promptings that all born travellers feel at the prospect of exploring new territories.

After several days of maintaining a steady pace, they came to the summit of a wooded hill and looked down on a vast, curling stream that flowed between reeded banks. 'The Yellow River,' Matteo identified.

'We'll make camp here and start for the river at first light,' Marco decided. 'The governor of Yangchou will have a junk and a new escort waiting for us.' He turned to the guards. 'Then you can ride back to Khanbalic.'

They dismounted and the guards began to remove the saddles and packs from the horses. Marco and Matteo went off to collect wood for a fire. As they sat around the flames in the twilight, Matteo's mind was nudged by fantasy. 'I'm – I'm really grateful for the chance to come with you,' he confided. 'I have often heard of a wise man, as old as time, who lives in the hills near Yangchou. They say he knows the secret of eternal youth. He's the one who has the secret of transforming metal into gold.'

Marco was amused by his uncle's new obsession with alchemy. 'Yes, and there's also a giant, and a dragon with seven heads, and an eagle as big as a—'

'You can mock, Marco, but I intend to search for that man. And if I find him, we'll return to Venice rich enough to dictate the law to the Doge and all the Senate.' Matteo held his palms out to warm them over the flames.

'Be careful, Uncle Matteo,' Marco warned, mocking him with a Chinese proverb: 'Remember that the perfect man may be able to walk under water – but fire burns.'

Matteo snorted, yet joined in Marco's laughter.

As he lay snug in his blanket and breathed in the crisp air, Marco realized again how right Caidu Khan had been.

Life in the Forbidden City, albeit luxurious, was strictly confined. In his new post he would have much more freedom. In rank, he would come directly after the military governor. It was a responsibility, and a challenge. He might even be able to do some good.

For Matteo, visiting the city for the first time, Yangchou was a revelation.

'Look, Marco – streets of water!'

'Just like Venice,' Marco nodded. 'I told you.'

'And bridges . . . And houses – just like ours!'

They were in a narrow, flat-bottomed barge, and a boatman was taking the two of them, accompanied by a pair of armed guards, along a still canal of blue-green water past the white stone or tarred wood façades which Marco remembered so vividly from his last visit. He was entranced. The glories of Hangchow had made him forget how beautiful Yangchou was.

Activity surrounded them. Other boats plied up and down the canal, and the steps along both banks were covered with Chinese women performing household chores, drawing water, beating wet clothes on stone slabs, preparing food, mending, emptying, gossiping or shouting at groups of playing children. The place had a warm vitality that reminded the visitors even more of Venice.

As their barge swung round into an adjoining canal, they saw that Yangchou was in fact very different from their own city. Carpenters were working on a strange boat, whose unusual shape was further distorted by an enormous prow that rose out of the water majestically in the shape of a fierce, carved dragon. On a bank, two bamboo carts with big, rickety wheels were rolling along, powered by sails that billowed in the stiff breeze. In the sky above, a man hung suspended from a huge kite, whose flapping wings gave it the appearance of a giant butterfly. Bells rang out from the many Buddhist temples.

It was evening when they reached the landing stage of the palatial governor's residence, and torches had been lit. Still dazzled by all that they had seen, Marco and Matteo took one last look across the panorama of rooftops and pagodas and spiked towers, and turned to see their host, Matteo's old acquaintance. The governor was a corpulent, thick-necked, balding Mongol in his sixties, who chuckled and bowed to Matteo as they disembarked and walked up the steps to meet him. Matteo took his place behind Marco, who presented his credentials and was then greeted formally, in accordance with his status as representative of the Great Khan.

'I welcome you to my house, Lord Marco, and to the province which the Great Khan has entrusted to my care. I am Chin Mei, governor of Yangchou.' He bowed, then indicated a shorter, bearded man with watchful eyes and a fixed, deferential smile. He wore Turkish dress with a white turban. 'And this is Talib, head of the Imperial Tax Collectors – a relative of the noble Achmet.' Talib inclined his head very slightly. He would be Marco's chief assistant. 'All that we have is at your disposal. Please enter.'

The dignitaries bowed and formed a procession, and the governor led his guests inside. Marco and Matteo were both careful to follow his example and step over the threshold without touching it.

Music floated through the building as they were conducted to a large room furnished with rich silken hangings and Persian carpets. Food and drink had been set out on a low table and the guests took their places on soft, perfumed cushions. While they went through the ritual offer and acceptance of hospitality with their host and his entourage, dancers moved gently to the music.

Once oblations of wine had been poured to Natigai and food smeared on the mouth of the god's image, the governor beamed amiably. 'This is a peaceful region now. There was trouble for a while, but it is over now.'

'What are the feelings of the people towards the Great Khan?' Marco asked.

'They fear and therefore respect him,' came the chuckled reply. 'They respect us, too. While they obey, no harm comes to them. A few heads had to roll to teach them their manners, though.'

The dancers came to the end of their performance, and were dismissed. At a nod from the governor, the lesser dignitaries bowed and retreated to the door. Only Marco and Matteo remained with Chin Mei and the Turk, Talib.

'I am honoured by your hospitality,' Marco said to his host. 'And I am very impressed by Yangchou. It is extremely beautiful.'

'Of course, you have been before,' Chin Mei said.

Marco nodded. 'On my second mission for the Great Khan.'

The governor fingered the cylinder which contained Marco's credentials. 'I remember your return to Khanbalic with the letter from the Sung Empress,' he said. 'I was then on General Bayan's staff. I am happy to welcome you back in more peaceable times.'

Marco, however, found it hard to believe that the region was quite as law-abiding as the governor claimed, and was keen to question him more closely. 'We have been told of growing unrest in this region, of revolts . . .'

'There have been a few incidents,' the governor admitted, 'but nothing serious. Isolated outbreaks, that is all.'

'On the way here, for instance, I saw something painted on a wall,' Marco remembered. 'What was it . . . ? "The Khan spared walls and houses, but turned hearts to ash and rubble." '

'Such ingratitude!' the governor snorted. 'A madman, obviously.'

'Obviously,' Talib echoed.

Matteo coughed. He had something else on his mind. 'I have heard, governor, of a wise man in these parts, who—'

'I don't think this is quite the right moment, Uncle Matteo,' Marco cut in quickly, and turned to the governor. 'We have a lot of hard work ahead of us. Naturally I wish to study the tax registers.'

'You will find everything you need. Talib has been preparing for some time. He is eager to help you.'

Talib smiled. 'I suggest that you rest for a few days, get to know the city a little. That will give me and my assistants time to complete our documentation.'

'I already know the city. We need the lists prepared by your assistants so that we can check them,' Marco insisted.

'When the time comes,' Talib promised smoothly, 'you shall have whatever is necessary without having to ask for it.'

The governor rose and the others followed. 'Unfortunately, since word has only just reached us of your appointment, we have not yet arranged quarters for you. In the meantime, you will be my guests, until we can select a suitable residence – one worthy of your new rank.'

Marco and Matteo bowed and followed their host to the door. Guards with blazing torches were waiting outside to conduct the guests to their apartments. On impulse, Marco looked back into the room. Talib was hovering where they had left him, and there was something furtive in his manner. For the briefest second, Marco saw what appeared to be a flash of contempt in his eyes; then he bowed deferentially to the honoured guest.

Marco left and the door clicked shut behind him.

Closer acquaintance with the city showed them that it was not at all like Venice. Yangchou was the conquered capital of a region that was now occupied territory and evidence of Mongol overlordship was everywhere, most notably in the blank expressions of the populace.

Marco watched how some of the revenue was raised for the Imperial Treasury. The branch-streams of the city were all crossed by stone bridges of great size and beauty, some with a span as wide as half a mile. Trade took place on these bridges, and every morning the booths and stalls were set up, just as in St Mark's Square. What made it different from Venice was that an army of the Great

Khan's toll-gatherers kept close watch on the trading and exacted the customs payable for every item that was sold. The daily income from this source was large, but Marco could not help wondering how the dealers and merchants of his own city would react to such a punitive tax on their profits. Uncle Zane would have been horrified.

A systematic tour of the province was even more sobering. Accompanied by an armed escort and a large retinue of tax assessors, Marco and Matteo left to inspect the smaller cities, townships, villages and farming and fishing communities. The trip had taken nearly two months to arrange. First the records of the Sung tax department had to be produced, but somehow these were never available, or were just being sorted out, or brought up to date. Meanwhile the time was filled with a ceaseless round of official functions, receptions and banquets given by the governor. Marco was an important personage and it was flattering, but he became increasingly irritated by the delay and by Chin Mei's constant hints that things were best left to run themselves. Marco had no intention of being a figurehead, and finally he exploded, threatening to dismiss the entire tax department for inefficiency. The records were delivered the next day, wagonloads of them. There were thousands of scrolls, in such a jumble that he was not surprised Talib's staff had found difficulty in making abstracts of them.

He could not find any specific fault with Talib. The man was willing to help, anxious to please; but in spite of it, the things he promised were never done – or not adequately. He blamed his restricted staff. His department was strictly according to the rules, but was overwhelmed by the size of the task it faced. To be really efficient, he would need a whole regiment of assessors and collectors. Marco sympathized with him, yet it was difficult. He simply did not like the man.

He did what he should have done at the beginning, and sent for Wu Sheng. The old mandarin was delighted to have a chance of working with Marco again. Recruiting a handful of Chinese former civil servants, he began the work of straightening out, tabulating and indexing the records. Meanwhile, Marco went on his tour with Matteo.

They gave themselves six weeks and by working virtually without stop, covered nearly everything they wanted to see. They went everywhere, armed with the interim tax summaries provided by Talib, inspecting, assessing, making detailed notes of their own, comparing their findings, from the giant workshops where armour and leather accoutrements were made for the Khan's soldiers, to groups of peasants toiling in the paddyfields, to the spinners and weavers of fine silks and cloth of gold.

The wealth the province produced was astounding, yet it was of little benefit to many of its people. The riches went straight to the Khan's Treasury and to the Mongol barons who now owned the factories and great estates. China had been unified, but the South was not administered, merely exploited, as a source of slave labour.

One memory always remained with Marco. Matteo and he had paused to watch a cargo of rice being loaded at a quay. Peasants climbed a bamboo ramp to empty the contents of their sacks into the hold of a high-prowed junk, an unbroken line of them, like patient, hard-working ants. The Khan's guards looked on. There was no violence, only repetitive, unremitting toil. One peasant had emptied his sack and come back down the ramp. When he reached the shore, one of the guards stopped him, took the limp sack and tipped it up. A few grains of rice fell to the ground. Without speaking, the guard signalled and another joined him. Together, they prodded the peasant into a bamboo thicket and began to beat him unmercifully, on the grounds that he might have been planning to keep the grains of rice. He made no sound. Matteo had to stop Marco forcibly from interfering.

Ever after, when Marco thought of that man, he remembered the part he himself had played in bringing the South under the control of the Mongols. He was less and less proud of what he had done. Yet to the governor,

Talib and others, everything was excused by the needs of the Imperial Treasury and the increased demands placed on it by the forthcoming invasion of Japan. 'Slavery paying for conquest,' Marco said. Matteo told him to remember where his loyalties lay.

One thing pleased Marco. He had at last chosen somewhere to live. He had insisted that it be outside the city and a villa was suggested halfway between Yangchou and the river. It was well-built, attractive, not too ostentatious, with three acres of pretty, enclosed garden. The governor had been worried about security, but its walls were stout enough to be defended in case of trouble. Matteo and Wu Sheng moved in to live with him. Matteo had converted a small outbuilding into an alchemist's laboratory where he spent most of his free time; but Marco liked nothing better than to ride out into the country, preferably without an escort, or to sail on the river.

One day, he hired a skiff for himself, Wu Sheng and two guards. The wind carried them lazily upstream against the current and for a time they simply relaxed, watching the herons and water buffaloes and the local fishermen. Marco was fascinated by some men fishing with cormorants. The birds with their slender, hooked beaks skimmed over the surface and swooped below it, coming up each time with their throats bulging above the ring placed round their necks to prevent them swallowing their catch. They returned to the boats and the men stroked their necks gently, easing the trapped fish up from their gullets.

On a rise of the shore beyond the fishermen stood a small village. On impulse, Marco steered towards it and was intrigued to see that it appeared to be deserted. He tied up, disembarked with the others and climbed the stone steps from the landing-stage to the carved lions at the top.

There was no one in sight. Wu Sheng and he looked round and set off down the single main street, followed by their two guards who had drawn their swords uneasily. They turned a corner into the central clearing and realized why the street and houses had seemed deserted. In front of a granary, which once might have been an old temple, a stage had been erected. A cloth stretched between two poles served as a backcloth and everyone in the village was gathered for the performance of a mime show.

When Marco and the others appeared, the actors froze in their positions and the heads of the audience swung round. They had been laughing, but the sound cut off. The sudden silence, the staring audience and the actors in their crudely painted masks made it an eerie scene.

Marco signed to the escort to put away their swords and to stand behind the bulk of the spectators on the threshing floor. Followed by Wu Sheng, he sat cross-legged at the side and waited.

One of the actors, standing at a corner of the stage without a mask, seemed to be the leader. Making up his mind that there was no danger for the moment, he clapped his hands for the performance to continue.

One actor wore a makeshift costume representing a government official, and heavy padding had endowed him with vast rounded buttocks. A mask expressed the sour and corrupt nature of his character. Two other actors, also masked, were dressed as peasants and stood beside a large sack of rice.

First imperiously, then threateningly, the official ordered the peasants to open the sack. He picked up a handful of rice and let it fall through his fingers. Satisfied, he gestured to them to tie the sack, but they had no rope. Taking his dagger out, the official cut through the belt that one of the peasants was wearing.

Marco was disturbed by what he saw, particularly by the actor playing the role of the official. It was almost as if the young performer was acting *at* him, identifying Marco as a symbol of officialdom. Wu Sheng, amused at first by the graphic mime, was also beginning to feel uncomfortable.

The satire continued, with the official ordering the peasants to lift the sack on his back. He then began to plod across the stage with it. One of the peasants imitated his pompous waddle, but the other slid out a knife and crept silently after the official. When he raised it, some of the audience glanced nervously at Marco, but the actor plunged his knife into the bottom of the sack. As rice came streaming out, a small boy grabbed a pot and rushed over to catch it. The two peasants performed mocking pirouettes behind the back of the official, who gradually straightened as the load got lighter. As the official left the stage with an already half-empty sack, the small boy followed to catch the rice, grinning at the audience.

Laughter and applause broke out. Marco and Wu Sheng joined in.

Then the leader of the actors came to the centre of the stage, bowed ironically to Marco and started to recite. The poem was old, the actor's tone varying from serious to mocking, but the overall effect was bleak.

'Friends, I'm a government official. I take paradise and leave hell for you. Those who suffer are better off, after all. These thoughts came to me in the city today. Looking at the people, I asked myself how I could steal more rice, when they only had a handful. Those who don't pay their taxes go to the pillory; those who don't pay taxes, pay with their blood; in front of the old man and child who are weak with hunger, I know not how to hide my shame.' He covered his face with his hands. An astonished silence fell over the audience as he bowed and went behind the backcloth.

'Will you have him flogged?' Wu Sheng asked quietly.

Marco shook his head. He rose, and followed by Wu Sheng, made straight for the door of the granary. He pushed it open and went in. The actor who had played the official and one of the peasants had removed their masks. The other peasant stepped back, seeing Marco.

'I knew you would come to this village one day,' the leader of the actors said. He was young and good-looking, intense.

'Why did you challenge me on that stage?' Marco demanded. 'Your words were like a whip on my back.'

'I'm sorry,' shrugged the young man. 'Perhaps I should have thanked you.'

'Why should you thank me?'

'For the mercy you showed Yang Ku.'

Marco and Wu Sheng were surprised. 'Yang Ku?' Marco said. 'Do you know him? Where is he?'

The actor hesitated. 'At his father's house, not far from here.'

'Take me to him.'

'But I have thanked you for him.'

'It's not gratitude I want,' Marco said. 'It's help.'

'The help of a beaten man?'

'I mean him no harm. Take me to him,' Marco repeated. 'Please.'

The young Chinese actor studied him as if trying to gauge his sincerity. At length he nodded. 'Follow me – but without your escort.'

'This is my assistant, Wu Sheng. He also knew Yang Ku, when he was an officer of the Sung.'

Finally the young man nodded and led them through the straggling alleys of poor, mean huts rising behind the central compound. On the higher edge of the village was a small, stone dwelling with a courtyard at the front. As the visitors approached, they saw an old man sifting grain through a sieve, a younger man plaiting rushes, and a peasant woman trying to coax her child into a tub of water.

Yang Ku came out of a doorway on the other side of the courtyard. He was dressed in rough clothes, but still had the dignified bearing that Marco remembered from their first meeting at the fort. Though watching them guardedly, Yang Ku bowed.

'I ask you to receive us in your house as your friends,' Marco said. 'For you are my friend.'

'You command. I obey.' Yang Ku's voice was neutral.

'I command you to stop obeying. I need your advice.'

There was a pause.

'What we need is tea, perhaps,' the young actor said.

Yang Ku signalled to the woman who was washing the bawling child and she hurried off. The visitors were taken to a roofed area where planks of wood had been laid across stones to serve as benches. Yang Ku bowed to them to be seated.

'Our house is your house. By receiving you here, we are also trusting you with our lives.'

There was a moment of awkwardness as Marco wondered what he meant, but it was dispelled by the arrival of a beautiful young Chinese girl, bringing a tray of tea which she proceeded to serve with ritual courtesy. When she came to fill Marco's cup, she took his hand and kissed it. The actor rose to object, but Yang Ku restrained him gently. He introduced the young woman. 'My daughter, Mai Li. I'm afraid that she forgets that the modesty of a shadow is more becoming to a young girl than light.'

Mai Li blushed, but said shyly, 'You saved my father's life. I am grateful.'

'You see, my noble friend,' the actor explained, 'the Khan's tax collectors are not only interested in our rice and grain. We have to keep our women hidden from their sight, too, especially if they are pretty.'

At a thought, Marco glanced at Wu Sheng. Surely that was not why he, too, had concealed his daughters?

'You came to ask my advice, you said,' Yang Ku reminded him.

'It occurred to me you might be able to help,' Marco told him earnestly. 'I am trying to establish what would be a fair taxation for the people of the South.'

'A fair taxation!' the actor exclaimed. 'Taxes have never been fair. Those who have little pay heavily, and those who have much hang on to it.'

'Things can be changed,' Wu Sheng observed quietly.

'What is your name, friend?' Marco asked.

'Chien Hu, sir,' the actor replied.

'Justice will come, Chien Hu. But first we need help to

draw up lists, to calculate rates and quantities, to see that they are correct.'

Chien Hu was roused. 'The names, the numbers of inhabitants, the amounts produced – all may be correct! But what if a father is ill and cannot work, or if crops have been destroyed by hail, or a granary hit by lightning?'

'What do you mean?'

'There is a law. The Great Khan decreed that if a village or a district suffers from hail or lightning and the crops are ruined, as ours were, taxes should be suspended for three years.'

Marco was about to reply, when he noticed that he was being watched. A pair of eyes gazed at him through a grating in the wall behind Yang Ku; dark, lustrous eyes that he felt he recognized. Yang Ku noticed his guest's interest.

'My house cannot keep its secrets . . . Come here, my child!' he called.

There was a stifled laugh from behind the wall and a figure came through the rush screens towards them, head bowed. Marco saw the peasant costume and realized that the eyes had belonged to one of the actors in the play. The mask had hidden the face, but accentuated the large, expressive eyes which he had remembered.

The figure raised its head and Marco was astounded. '*Che bella! Bella . . . !*' he murmured, involuntarily.

The girl's eyes widened.

He was looking up into the face of a beautiful and demure young woman. Her hair was a deep, shining red-gold. She was European.

Chapter Seven

The miracle happened late one afternoon. When the door of the tower cell opened, five people came in. Captain Arnolfo led the way, followed by a dignified, ascetic man in his fifties, and an intellectual young monk with a reserved manner. But it was the two Genoese guards who claimed the attention of Marco. They were carrying a heavy wooden chest which he recognized at once. They set it down near the table and went out. Marco took a step towards the chest, but stopped at a gesture from Arnolfo.

In the presence of the visitors, Arnolfo, normally pleasant, sounded curt and officious. He called Marco forward and introduced the two men. 'This is Brother Damian – and Messer Pietro de Abano, doctor of medicine and astronomy at the University of Padua.' Marco bowed, but received only the faintest of nods from the monk and de Abano in return. The Prison Commander indicated the chest. 'The Holy Church has agreed to your request for the notes you left behind in Venice. They have taken into consideration your desire to prove the truth of your stories and to avoid dangerous errors.'

'As there is still no peace between Genoa and Venice,' de Abano explained, 'I was asked by the Patriarch and Doge of your city to act as intermediary.'

'Everything possible has been done to help you, Messer Polo,' Arnolfo said.

Giovanni grinned. 'There'll be no more excuses for not finishing the story now!'

Marco was finding it difficult to restrain himself from reaching for the chest and throwing open the lid. Rustichello watched him with understanding, knowing what an immense difference the notes would make. Gaps had started to appear more frequently in the narrative and contradictions had become more obvious. Failures of memory had led inevitably to repetition. The contents of the wooden chest would cure these deficiencies, and the writer also rejoiced.

'I gathered all I could find,' said de Abano, taking some sheets of parchment from inside his dark robe. 'I read everything, as the authorities ordered me to do before handing the documents over to you.'

'It is the sacred duty of the Church to defend the truth,' Arnolfo commented, with a slight bow towards Brother Damian to warn Marco.

The young monk responded. 'A duty towards God and the souls He has entrusted to us, in order that they may reach salvation against every danger, open or hidden.'

'You will have your notes,' de Abano promised, sensing Marco's impatience, 'but I must confess there are several things I do not understand.' He spread the sheets carefully on the table. 'As you know, my science is medicine and also astronomy. I have spent a lifetime searching the heavens, and yet I have never seen stars such as those you describe here.' His finger pointed. 'I have been unable to identify this one here, for example.'

'It's a great star in the shape of a sack,' explained Marco, 'and with a sort of double tail. It can be seen beyond the equator.'

De Abano studied another sketch. 'You write here that the Great Bear and the North Star become visible the moment one has crossed the southern tip of India, sailing from the East . . .' He glanced up questioningly. 'Are you sure? Might it not be that you mistook one constellation for another?'

'There was no mistake.'

'Just by following that star,' Rustichello said, repeating what Marco had taught him, 'one could navigate from the Indian sea all the way to Europe. What Marco has described to us will open new paths – even for those who go by sea.'

'Let the learned judge these things, Master Rustichello,'

Arnolfo warned. 'This is not an occasion for your flights of fancy.' He bowed respectfully to the academic. 'If you allow me, Messer de Abano, I would recommend to my Venetian "guest" more prudence, and less presumption in asserting things which cannot be proved, and about which his memory is confused.'

'Messer de Abano,' Marco said, earnestly. 'In China, there are hundreds of men, thousands, who study the stars. They have built instruments to measure their courses and their evolutions. They print almanacs and calendars, where they note, day by day, the phases of the moon and the conjunctions of the planets and stars. Nothing is done there without consulting the stars.'

'Superstitions!' exclaimed the monk. 'Magic enchantments!'

Rustichello tried to answer. 'The Bible is full of—'

'Our science, our knowledge comes from God,' Brother Damian said positively.

'Also my eyes,' Marco insisted. 'And what my eyes have seen, I have set down faithfully. And yet I have not had time to tell half of what I have seen.' He paused and looked around the others. 'There is a stone which, when suspended in a box, always points to the north. In China, travellers who use it, whether on land or sea, by day or night, can always find their direction.'

'Is it possible?' Arnolfo wondered.

'No,' de Abano doubted.

'He has seen paradise!' Giovanni said, trying to be helpful. 'He has been to Mount Ararat and seen Noah's Ark.'

'The Ark?' In spite of himself, the monk was excited.

'No, Giovanni,' admitted Marco, 'I did not see it. Though I passed by the mountain and was told it was there.' He shrugged. 'I only describe what I have truly seen.'

'You have been given repeated warnings,' de Abano told him. 'Do not let your imagination deceive your memory and lead you to cross forbidden boundaries. If you venture beyond what the Holy Church teaches as certain or possible, you will find only heresy or blasphemy.'

Marco was suddenly alarmed at what he might have said without thinking. He had no wish to offend the Church and thereby lose access to his precious notes, perhaps even cause that part of the story already set down to be confiscated and burned. It was on the *written* chronicle that Brother Damian concentrated . . .

'You are a sensible man,' the monk told Rustichello, 'even though you deal in fairytales more than reality. Point out the dangers to him. You, too, have a very definite responsibility.'

Rustichello was tense. He had been given a direct warning that, in writing down Marco Polo's account, he would be held accountable to the all-powerful and suspicious Church. The warning imposed enormous restraints upon him. It was almost as if he was being ordered to eliminate from the narrative those parts that made it so unique and extraordinary. The notion of censoring Marco's story was a betrayal of all his instincts as a writer.

'There is nothing more to be said,' de Abano concluded, solemnly.

He nodded to Marco and left the cell with the others. As soon as the door slammed shut behind them, Marco and Rustichello seized the chest and lifted it up on to the table.

Giovanni tried to dispel the gloom left behind by the visitors. 'Lesson for today, Messer Polo. Leave the stars alone.'

Marco opened the lid of the chest and looked inside at the rolls of parchment. A sheet of rice paper lay on the surface and he picked it up.

Giovanni bounced up and down with anticipation. 'Tell us about the girl! At the riverside village.'

'You think of only one thing!' Rustichello complained.

'I knew there had to be another girl sooner or later,' Giovanni confided. 'He may have been to all those different countries, but he's a Venetian at heart. Now we come to the part of the story that will make the Holy Church blush!' He laughed aloud and tugged at Marco's sleeve. 'We're listening. Who was this girl from Europe? How did she land up in the middle of China? What *happened*?'

Marco was not listening. He had been looking at a drawing of a Buddhist shrine and it had drawn his mind back into a past more real than the present.

It was some time before Marco saw the girl again – although he thought of her constantly.

He was aware that he had not fully won Yang Ku's trust. He was too firmly identified with the occupying power. The strongest resentment had come from the younger man, Chien Hu, whom he had been told was a poet and only occasionally came to the village. The theme and direction of the amateur mime plays were his work. Marco suspected his interest in the village was largely because of Yang Ku's daughter, Mai Li. He questioned Wu Sheng about the need to conceal young women, and his assistant, with some embarrassment, confirmed it. 'Not only from the Mongols,' he said. 'It has always been difficult in China, if a powerful man happens to feel desire for the wife or daughter of someone weaker. That is why our maidens are taught to behave with modesty and why they are rarely seen in public.'

In a way it was an oblique warning to Marco. He called on Yang Ku several times, but did not meet either of the girls. To his polite enquiries, Yang Ku replied that Mai Li was his only daughter. Monica was a guest, about whom he could say nothing without her permission. Without demanding that she was brought to him, Marco could go no further. He could only hope that by earning the confidence of the local people, the barriers would gradually come down.

Although he could not forget her, he was too busy to brood and was soon too occupied to have time to visit the village.

He had more duties than he would have thought

possible. Wu Sheng reported that the existing Sung records for this province were not as useful as they had hoped, since there were considerable gaps. New lists had to be compiled containing innumerable time-consuming and laborious details.

In addition, since the abolition of the Chinese civil service by the Mongols, who distrusted it as a potential focus for organized resistance, many functions which its officials would have carried out passed to Marco; there were appeals to be heard, arbitrations to be made, awards and relief and punishment to be decided. And all the time the pressure kept growing for more money to finance the invasion of Japan. Huge fleets and unprecedented numbers of soldiers were being built up at Amoy, Fuchau and other ports further north. They needed equipment, food, pay and clothing. There was unrest as the Military Council brought in conscription and young men were drafted from the farms and cities into the reserves of the Khan's army. No exceptions were permitted. The law insisted that the conscripts were to be stationed a minimum of a hundred miles from their homes to prevent them from refusing to suppress their own people, in case of revolt.

The single largest provider of revenue in the province was the salt trade, as Marco knew. Fortunately, he had already studied it out of interest, and now was able to put his knowledge to practical use to improve production. He also did what he could to improve conditions for the workers, especially in the mines, where he had never forgotten the prematurely aged men and women, with weeping sores, their lungs tortured from permanently breathing salt, staggering under the lashes of the overseers.

Talib and the governor assured him that attempts had been made before to make the administration of the province, both in production and tax collection, more efficient and less of a burden on individuals, but they had never succeeded. That was no excuse not to try, Marco told them. They were silenced when the revenue from

Yangchou rose by an appreciable twelve per cent, and that from salt production by an amazing twenty per cent.

It had been months since Marco's last visit to Yang Ku. On a day when some of his appointments were unexpectedly cancelled, he rode out from his villa without calling for an escort. He only meant to ride a little, but almost subconsciously found himself making for the river and the now familiar rise above the ruins of an ancient Taoist sanctuary from the days of the Ch'in dynasty. Marco was not careless riding alone. Even his Mongol guards and Talib's assessors had noticed a change in the attitude of the people to him. As he passed, townspeople and peasants no longer turned away with lowered heads as before. More frequently, they bowed respectfully in token of his efforts to treat them fairly and with justice. Sometimes children waved to him or brought him shy offerings of wild flowers.

Coming to the village that day, Marco tethered his horse and walked at his leisure through the alleys to Yang Ku's house. The gates of the courtyard were closed and no one answered when he knocked. He was afraid there was no one at home, but pushing at the gate as he turned to leave, he saw it swing open and went inside.

A fieldworker in baggy trousers and smock, wearing sandals and a wide bowl-shaped straw hat, stood with his back to him. Yet from the narrowness of the shoulders and the slightness of the body, he knew the masculinity was assumed. His heart leapt. Then the peasant looked round, startled, and he recognized Mai Li. Clearly, she had been hurrying away from the gate just as he opened it.

Following her involuntary glance to the side, he saw a second figure by the stonebuilt well, identically dressed. It was Monica. She smiled nervously, seeing him.

Their obvious fear of him upset Marco and he had to force himself to be casual. He took off his cap and bowed, smiling. 'Excuse my intrusion,' he said. 'It's a great pleasure to see you again.'

Mai Li stood motionless, with her hands clasped under the slight swell of her breast, but Monica came towards him hesitantly. Some strands of hair had escaped from under her coolie hat and she took it off, copying him. Her thick hair fell free in lustrous, Titian waves. She was even more beautiful than he had remembered. And he had not been mistaken: without doubt, she was pure European. All the questions he had ever wanted to ask her surged through his mind.

'Forgive us for not opening the gate to you, Lord Marco,' she said. Her voice was low, her accent of the Chinese higher class. 'But as you can see, there was no one with us.'

Marco smiled. 'You can chaperone each other.' Monica glanced at Mai Li and he wondered if perhaps he had mistaken her.

Mai Li was coming forward. 'Your pardon, my lord,' she said, bowing, 'for not greeting you properly.'

Marco was still trying to put them at ease. 'Oh, I prefer my friends not to bow to me,' he said. 'And we are friends, aren't we? After all, I've been here several times. Although—' he glanced at Monica, 'although unfortunately, neither of you were at home.'

Mai Li had noticed his glance at Monica and smiled prettily. She bit her lower lip. 'We were sorry to miss you, my lord,' she told him. 'We have talked about you often.'

Again Marco saw a swift look pass between the two girls, a hint of mischief from Mai Li, of embarrassed reproof from Monica. Before he could follow it up, he heard a noise from the wooden steps to the raised door of the house. Yang Ku had come to the door and paused, watching. About him, too, there was a suggestion of anxiety.

Marco bowed. 'I have taken the liberty to call again, Yang Ku.'

Yang Ku came down the steps, not losing his watchfulness. 'We are honoured,' he said quietly. 'But we have just returned from the fields. Perhaps Monica and Mai Li should—'

He broke off as the gate behind Marco burst open and

a Mongol officer came in quickly, followed by three soldiers. The officer's sword was in his hand and his men carried lances. 'Stand where you are!' he shouted, and gestured to his men to search the house.

Marco saw Yang Ku's head jerk towards him accusingly. He turned to the officer. 'What do you think you're doing?' he asked sharply.

The Mongol officer whirled round angrily, and stopped in some confusion as he recognized Marco. He bowed jerkily. '. . . My lord!'

'What is this?' Marco demanded. 'What are you doing here?'

'Searching this village for deserters, my lord.'

The soldiers had hesitated just as they were about to go into the house, waiting for further orders. Marco looked at them and back to the officer. 'Well, you won't find any here,' he said coldly.

The Mongol came to attention and signed brusquely to his men to leave. He moved to the gate, turned and bowed to Marco. 'A thousand pardons, my lord.' He went out and the gate closed.

Yang Ku, Monica and Mai Li were still tense, watching Marco. The incident had made him angry and embarrassed. 'Has this happened before?' he asked.

'Once or twice,' Yang Ku answered carefully. 'Our young men are ordered to serve in the Khan's army. Some are the only means of support their parents have, and they try to escape. Soldiers are sent to hunt for them.'

Marco could hardly look at Monica and Mai Li. 'It is still no reason why you should be treated like criminals,' he muttered. His head rose as he heard a woman's voice cry out from the village, a long, wavering scream. 'I'll put a stop to this,' he promised. 'I'll clear them out.' He left quickly.

None of the other three moved for a moment after he had gone. Yang Ku swung back to the house. Chien Hu was at the top of the steps. In the doorway behind him were two young and very frightened men. 'Get back inside,' Yang Ku said. 'You can leave when it is dark.'

Marco went directly to the military governor and protested at the brutality of the random search in the village. Much damage had been done and two totally innocent people wounded. He knew these villagers well, Marco said. They were simple and law-abiding. The governor assured him that orders would be given for the community above the sanctuary to be treated with consideration. When he came home, Marco told Wu Sheng what he had done and Wu Sheng was disturbed. 'It might have been wiser not to draw too much attention to your connection there,' he said.

Two days later, returning from a meeting at Sinju, Marco ordered his small, official junk to land him and his uncle on the north bank and to pick them up again in an hour. He walked with Matteo along the track to the main fields, where they could see a long line of peasants stretching right to the water's edge. Buckets were being dipped into the river and passed from hand to hand along the human chain, until finally they were poured into the irrigation channels in the field. It was necessary in high summer, but back-breaking work under the hot sun.

Marco found Yang Ku sitting in the shade of a large tree with the poet, Chien Hu, and introduced his uncle. As they talked, Marco's eyes were restless, watching the coolies. At last he made out two slighter figures among the men and waited until one looked up. It was Monica. There was a water jug under the tree and he picked it up and walked over to her, offering it to her. She smiled and tugged at the sleeve of the peasant next to her, Mai Li.

Matteo took hardly any notice of the three of them, until he became conscious that Yang Ku and Chien Hu had fallen silent. Marco was handing the water jug to the taller of two young coolies. Monica drank and passed the jug to Mai Li. As she smiled again to Marco, her head rose and the shadow of her wide-brimmed hat cleared from her face. Matteo saw the smooth skin, only lightly tanned, the clear, dark hazel eyes, the straight nose, finely moulded, the soft, full lips. Even though her hair was caught up in a twist of rag under the hat, she was breathtakingly lovely. Matteo's mouth opened.

Matteo half rose to his feet as Marco returned. 'But – But—' he spluttered.

'Yes, that is one of the reasons I brought you,' Marco told him.

'You knew about her?' Matteo asked, still thrown.

'Of her existence only. Scarcely more than you.' Marco turned to the two Chinese, who were expressionless. 'It is natural that we should be interested in someone who is clearly from our own world,' he said.

'It is natural,' Yang Ku conceded, but said nothing more.

'Has there been any more trouble?' Marco asked, after a moment.

Yang Ku had the grace to look ashamed. 'Not for us – thanks to you. But there have been raids on two villages along the river. By orders of the governor.'

'Things will improve,' Matteo promised. 'But you cannot expect that your people can break the Great Khan's laws without ever being punished.'

'When the laws are just, our people obey them,' Chien Hu said.

'Governments make laws for which it is not always easy to see the reason,' Marco countered. 'Trust in the Great Khan's wisdom.'

'How can we?' Chien Hu asked. 'To the governor and Talib and others like them, we are only beasts of burden.'

'When I report to the Great Khan and to the Lord Achmet, I shall tell them what is good here and what needs to be changed,' Marco assured him. 'I will ask him to improve conditions here.'

Yang Ku smiled. 'You have brought a season of hope with you, Lord Marco, after a long winter.'

'But his goodwill cannot cure the ills from which we suffer,' Chien Hu commented drily. He looked at Marco. 'You are not one of us; you come from another land. Your admiration for the Khan blinds you.'

'That is enough, Chien Hu!' Yang Ku said firmly. 'Whatever else, you owe Lord Marco respect for what he has already done for us.'

It created an awkwardness and shortly after Marco and Matteo left to return to their waiting junk.

As he watched them walk away, Chien Hu apologized. 'I am sorry for what I said. But it is hard for me to forget that he is a servant of the enemy.'

Marco had made Yang Ku think. 'Perhaps it is time to stop talking of "the enemy" and to try to work, like him, for peaceful change. Today I felt ashamed. From the moment he gave me my freedom, from the moment he entered my house, he was no longer a stranger. He is a brother and friend of the Chinese people.'

Marco had satisfied what he could of his uncle's curiosity about Monica by the time they reached home. The little he knew, however, only raised more questions to which Marco himself longed to have answers. He had begun to despair of ever breaking through Yang Ku's reserve.

It was with surprise, therefore, that he found Wu Sheng waiting for him one day soon after, betraying an unaccustomed excitement.

'The headman at the village, Yang Ku,' Wu Sheng smiled. 'He has invited you to dine with him. Also to bring Messer Matteo – and my unworthy self.'

In the week before they were to dine with Yang Ku, many people noticed Marco's abstraction. He thought of little else but Monica – that he would have the opportunity at last to talk to her. He was determined. If the girls were segregated again and did not appear, he would insist that they were fetched. Jacopo, who had recently joined him at Yangchou, chuckled at his master's preoccupation and made jokes about it, before becoming sulky, offended that he had not been invited, too.

'You'll meet her soon,' Marco promised him.

Jacopo was so happy at the prospect that it led to a row with the dumpy Chinese woman with whom he shared the kitchen, whom he had brought from Khanbalic. 'She was really jealous,' he said proudly, the next morning. He had a livid welt across the side of his face and a scratch on his chin. 'Never seen her like it.'

Marco bathed and chose his clothes with care on the day. It would not do to go dressed as a Mongol noble and the fashionable court robes he wore on formal occasions were too gaudy. He decided on what he most often wore for riding, softsoled boots, leggings which served him as trunk hose and a short tan tunic, with the belt given to him by Kublai Khan.

Instead of Mongol guards, the party took some of their Chinese servants to light them on the road home. Marco, Matteo and Wu Sheng all looked forward to the occasion for their own reasons, but that evening there was also a special excitement which Marco and Matteo could share with no one else. The battle fleets had sailed for the islands of Je-pen-quo, land of the rising sun. Whatever they thought about the rights and wrongs of the invasion, after so much preparation and involvement, they waited eagerly to hear the outcome.

The lanterns hanging in the courtyard of Yang Ku's house were the first surprise. The next was to be greeted by their host, wearing the costly robes of a Sung aristocrat, a black, wide-sleeved overmantle, embroidered with golden hawks, over a cream robe with a belt of carved jade. Chien Hu was with him, dressed more soberly in a dark scholar's gown.

When they had seated themselves on cushions in the living room of the house, plain but scrupulously clean with whitewashed walls and red lacquered rafters, Mai Li and Monica were summoned. Marco could not prevent himself from staring as they came in and knelt, honouring the guests. It was the first time he had seen either of them dressed as women. Even their walk had changed. He had been glad that neither of them had adopted the recent Sung habit of binding the feet, but even so they moved with tiny, shuffling steps. Their clothes matched Yang Ku's in elegance. Mai Li's dress was of powder blue silk, her hair swept up in glossy folded wings, fixed by gold hairpins ending in the form of lotus flowers. Her face was delicately made up, kohl blackened her eyelashes and rouge blushed her high cheekbones and the centre of her budded lips. Monica had only her natural colouring, but a faint flush warmed her beauty. Catching the light of the lamps, her upswept hair shone now copper, now chestnut, now pure gold. The silk tunic over her emerald underdress was of soft moss green, with a collar of peach folded across her breasts, leaving the line of her neck and the notch of her throat bare. Her body was fuller than Mai Li's, though still slim, the curve of her breasts high and rounded. The filmy silk of the underskirt revealed the sweep of her long, finely-shaped legs. Her eyes lowered at the unhidden admiration of the three guests.

Marco replied gracefully to the greeting from Mai Li, as daughter of the house, then turned to Yang Ku, complimenting him on the loveliness of the two flowers which grew unseen in his garden. Matteo and Wu Sheng added their compliments; then the older female servant brought tea which Mai Li and Monica served, and the conversation switched to weather, crops and the time-honoured methods of fishing in the Great River.

Marco was grateful to Yang Ku. This evening was his method of apologizing for the suspicion of the past, his gesture of acceptance. Certain areas were still closed to discussion, but these were fewer and fewer. Even Chien Hu seemed more subdued, not twisting every remark to politics, and only becoming animated in a friendly argument with Wu Sheng over the literary merits of popular songs, 'the new lyric poetry', as he called them. Wu Sheng was delighted when a dish of roasted walnuts appeared specially for him. Marco smiled with the others, yet it occurred to him that it argued a very precise knowledge of all of them. Probably every detail about them was related by their servants. The Chinese had a love of gossip.

The meal was delicious, simply presented, rice, mushrooms, bean curds, flaky river fish in strips, and cubes of lamb served on lettuce, with unsweetened jasmine tea instead of rice wine, which Marco found cloying. Afterwards, Chien Hu was persuaded to recite some of his short lyric poems, which were unexpectedly moving, and Mai Li sang, accompanying herself on a five-stringed harp. Later still, they walked out on the flat roof to enjoy the night air, and Marco found himself alone at last with Monica.

The rooftiles reflected the moonlight, the stars filling the sky above the river valley. From the sleeping village below them came the occasional, muted murmur of voices. Far off, a dog was barking. Rising from beyond the wall beneath them was a faint perfume of night-scented stock. And over everything lay the whispered murmur of the Great River, rustling over pebbles, sighing through reeds, lapping gently against its banks.

Marco looked from its shimmering, silvered expanse below them to Monica, who stood with her hands on the parapet, gazing out. Her profile was perfect, classical. 'I can't remember when I've enjoyed an evening so much,' he said.

Her head turned to him. 'It is not me you should compliment.'

'But you are part of it,' he said, and paused. 'My Uncle Matteo is right. You are very beautiful.'

She looked away modestly and hesitated. 'I suppose I was a surprise to you.'

Marco laughed. 'Surprise is not putting it strongly enough. To meet someone like you here . . . Where do you come from?'

'Here,' she said simply. 'I was born here.'

'In this village?' Marco asked, puzzled.

'No. Further south, in Amoy. Now I live here with my father and Mai Li.'

Marco did not understand. 'Your father – Yang Ku?'

'He is not my real father, of course,' she smiled. 'My real father died when I was very small.'

'What was his name?'

It was hard for her to pronounce. 'De Vig-lio-nis . . .'

'De Viglionis?' Marco repeated. 'Monica de Viglionis . . . But that's Italian! You are Italian, like me.'

'No,' she corrected. 'I am Chinese.'

'But how did you—?' Marco stopped himself. Every answer she gave made him understand less. He smiled, shaking his head. 'I'm lost. Who *was* your father?'

'A merchant,' she said, 'so my mother told me. They both came from far away, and the ship they were on was blown to India by a storm. They lived there for a few years, then sailed on to Amoy, where I was born. My father was often away on voyages, then one time he came back with a sickness and died. My mother and I moved to a house in Hangchow, but she died not long afterwards.'

Marco was serious. 'I know how it must have felt. My own mother died when I was a child. But how did you manage? Who brought you up?'

Monica hesitated again, but she could see now that Marco was to be trusted. 'The Empress of the Sung appointed a guardian for me. I was raised by a lady of her palace.'

Marco at last understood. 'And that's where you met Yang Ku.'

'Where I met Mai Li,' she corrected. 'The daughters of the nobles each served for a year, as ladies-in-waiting. We became friends. Father – Yang Ku – told us that if anything bad ever happened, we were to come here.'

'But why here?' Marco queried. It was a question he had asked himself often. 'He was a commander in the Sung army. Why is he living in this little house, in this little village?'

Again Monica hesitated. 'His family owned all the land

round here, for many miles, until it was taken by your Khan. Yang Ku feels responsible for the people. He lives here to be near them, to do what he can for them.'

'Of course . . .' Marco breathed. Everything fell into place, and his admiration for Yang Ku increased.

'I am sorry we have been so distant,' she said. 'But you cannot blame us. We can only feel bitter about your Khan.'

'Then that could be a greater tragedy than your defeat,' Marco told her, his voice deliberately even. She looked at him, tensing, her eyes bright in the moonlight. 'I think Yang Ku is beginning to realize that. In Mongol, the Great Kublai is known as Setsen Khan – the Wise Khan. His most cherished wish is to reunite China, not just by conquest, but to make her one nation again, with everyone sharing in her bounty. For the sake of your people, you should help me to help him.'

His conviction seemed to impress her. Her body lost its tautness. She was evidently thinking over what he had said, but before he could go on, Mai Li turned to them and their group reformed. The time had come for the guests to leave.

After his first real meeting with Monica, two matters took Marco away to Khanbalic for a period of six weeks. First, he was required to submit his annual report; and secondly, it would soon be the Great Khan's birthday, the twenty-eighth of September, and all his senior officials were required to attend the celebrations.

Marco knew he would miss Monica. Although he could not pretend their relationship was anything more than friendly, he felt a beginning had been made. He would have preferred to stay, but he had no choice. It was an essential part of his duties to present the annual report in person, and no excuse would be accepted for failure to attend the birthday festivities. No one would miss them willingly, in any case, since they were a most splendid and lavish series of receptions and entertainments and an excellent opportunity for the Khan to shower generosity on his followers.

Khanbalic was already celebrating, when Marco, Chin Mei and Matteo arrived at the end of August. But it was not in anticipation of the birthday. Niccolo was among the officials of the Treasury Department waiting to welcome them at the eighty-feet-high Chienmen Gate. As they walked in procession through the outer city under ceremonial umbrellas, preceded by a guard of honour and followed by a twenty-piece band of horns and flutes, drums and cymbals, Niccolo told them excitedly above the din that word had just been received that part of the Mongol forces had landed successfully on the first of the Japanese islands, and was advancing with little resistance. The jubilation extended to the Council Chamber, and the Great Khan greeted Marco with much of his old affection, leading the applause when the totals of the contributions of his province to the cost of the invasion were read out.

Marco saw that Phags-pa did not join in the congratulations. The Head Lama, more gaunt and wizened than ever, his red robe more ostentatiously frayed and dirty to show his contempt for worldly comfort, had thought him safely disposed of, under partial disgrace. Watching Marco return to reap the rewards of success yet again was obviously a bitter experience for him. Together with the noticeable rise in numbers of Nestorian Christians throughout the empire, it would only serve to make Marco more dangerous.

Afterwards, Marco was able to spend a few hours with Chinkin, who seemed to have fully recovered. As they walked on the series of arched bridges connecting the islets of the long lake, Marco told him of Monica.

The prince was happy for him. 'Have you ever thought how everything in your life, Marco, seems to be destined?' he remarked. 'And now the proof. You are sent to the one place in all the millions of square miles of the empire where, unknown to you, is a woman of your own race.'

Chinkin was keen to meet her, to see her for himself, and Marco invited him to pay a visit, of state or incognito, to Yangchou.

Chinkin's smile was tinged with sadness. 'There is nothing I would enjoy more, my friend,' he said. 'But the days when we rode and hunted, or explored our little corners of the world together, are over. After this walk, I shall have to rest for at least two days. No, I did not tell you that to alarm you. Only to let you know that my father will not permit me to travel more than three miles from him – and from the Imperial physicians.'

Shortly after seeing Chinkin, Marco, his father and uncle were summoned to attend the Lord Achmet. Niccolo was almost overwhelmed by the praise heaped by the regent on his son.

'No appointment has been more triumphantly successful,' Achmet declared. I am to inform you that the Khan has granted you one of the robes of cloth of gold to wear at the festivities. Need I say more?'

Marco heard his father and uncle gasp. The superb robes presented by the Great Khan to his senior barons were beyond price, and to be granted the right to wear one was a signal honour. He could only bow in gratitude.

Achmet's private office was decorated more in Arab than Chinese style, with fretted screens, lush carpets from Bokhara and a miniature fountain trickling in the raised *diwan* area at the far end. On one wall hung the green banner of the Prophet, and a copy of the Khoran bound in silver lay open on a folding stand. Achmet sat cross-legged on the *diwan*, a dish of sweetmeats beside him, which he nibbled constantly. He was no longer lean, as he had been when Marco first came to China. His body had been swollen with excess. His head was swathed in a white turban trimmed with gold lace, and he wore a robe brocaded with pearls and precious stones. He smiled benignly as Marco asked permission to speak in confidence.

Marco told him of the difficulties he had faced and of the obstruction put in his way by Talib and his staff. While he did not have proof of individual corruption, it was an undeniable fact that of a considerable number of payments made to the state revenue through Talib, many had deductions made, some of more than half. At least half of the tax collected never reached the Treasury.

Achmet had taken a sugared almond from the dish and sat motionless with it raised to his lips. '*Half?* Are you prepared to make an accusation?'

Marco followed the advice his father and uncle had given him. 'I have evidence of the crime, Lord Achmet,' he said, 'not yet of who commits it.'

Achmet let the sweet drop and flicked the powdered sugar from his fingers. 'This is extremely serious,' he muttered. 'There are, of course, authorized deductions at source for departmental expenses – but fifty per cent?'

'What do you wish me to do, my lord?' Marco asked.

'For the time being, nothing,' Achmet declared. 'Continue to gather evidence, but keep it to yourself. When we are ready, we will produce it and make a fearful example of the guilty. Such wickedness must be punished with the full rigour of the law.' Marco bowed. 'But tell me – many local officials make personal fortunes out of graft and bribery, by doing favours for people. It is the rule rather than the exception. You must have been approached yourself?'

'There have been suggestions,' Marco admitted. 'I ignore them – unless they are repeated. Then, I point out to whoever is concerned that he risks grave penalties.'

'So you sacrifice the fortune?' Achmet studied him and after a moment inclined his head in a gesture of unfeigned respect. 'You are an example of incorruptibility to us all.'

As he finished speaking, a sound from outside startled them; the brazen clanging of a great bell. It was the tocsin, the alarm bell, and Achmet pushed himself quickly to his feet. Niccolo and Matteo were rising also, and paused, listening intently. Behind the solemn peal of the bell they could make out the sound of slow drumbeats.

'The drums of mourning . . .' Achmet muttered. 'What has happened?'

The door was thrust open and his chief eunuch hurried in, bowing jerkily to excuse the intrusion. He dropped his ceremonial whip of knotted silk and fell to his knees, agitated, his plump hands clasped. 'F-forgive me, my lord,' he stammered. 'The Great Khan sends for you most urgently. News has come from Japan . . .'

The main hall of the Imperial palace was lit by tall silver candelabra. Imperial Guards in blue felt armour with spears wound with gold thread lined the walls, shoulder to shoulder under the dragon tapestries. Gathered in a wide semicircle round the throne dais were the members of the Civil and Military Councils, while the nobles of the court were crowded in the body of the hall, watching and listening in shocked silence. It was a state trial, held with all the abruptness and severity of the ancient Mongol laws.

The accused were General Argan and the Korean High Admiral Won. Both knelt within the semicircle facing the dais, their hands tied behind their backs. They were flanked by officers with drawn scimitars. Between them and the dais were two lines of officers wearing jade, silver or gold belts of rank, the lines facing each other.

From his place among the barons, Marco could see Chinkin, pale and drawn, seated on his lower throne. At the level of his head stood the Imperial seven-jewelled throne where Kublai Khan sat, between two ten-foot statues of lions. Over his head hung a huge bronze eagle. The accused were sweating with fear, gazing up at Kublai's set, implacable face. There was no trace now of Argan's arrogance and Admiral Won was shaking uncontrollably.

The Mongol invasion of Japan, thrust forward by Kublai's dreams of conquest, had ended in disaster. They had sailed with a mighty fleet carrying a hundred and forty thousand warriors. Part of the force had breached the defences at Hakata Bay and begun their assault on the southern island of Kyushu, but arguments between the commanders over who was to lead and whose tactics were to be followed had delayed the landing of supplies and reinforcements. While the two commanders argued, a violent hurricane had blown up, even fiercer than the typhoon which had stopped the first Mongol attempt at invasion. The Korean and Mongol fleets were smashed and scattered, the force already landed was abandoned, to be slaughtered by the Japanese. Of the hundred and forty thousand, less than one in five survived.

Marco remembered the blind potter Akira and his certainty that his homeland was divinely protected. It might be so, Marco conceded. But by which god? Or was there really only One, prayed to by different names and different forms of worship? With his orthodox upbringing, the thought was disturbing to him.

'. . . There was no way we could have known what was going to happen!' Argan was explaining. 'Without warning, the sky went dark and the storm swept over us. The sea became a hell spitting up demons! Our ships sank under waves as high as mountains. A wild wind filled with lightning sent prow crashing against prow. The Japanese prisoners cried out "*Kamikaze! Kamikaze!*" The wind of God . . . It was the end of us.'

Kublai's hard eyes shifted to Admiral Won.

'I was against the attack!' Won blustered, trying to shift the blame. 'Against it, Great Lord! I didn't want to risk the fleet. I suggested that we wait for the calm, but your general was too impatient. I had to stop him from rushing to destruction.'

'You were as eager for battle as I was!' Argan snarled. 'You boasted that no one could sink your ships!'

'If I had been in command,' Won snapped, 'no one could have sunk them.'

Argan appealed to Kublai. 'It was not we who lost, Great Khan. It was hell who won the victory.'

He fell silent. Kublai was rising. He was ghostly pale and his figure was stooped. To Marco, he seemed somehow to have aged.

'It was not hell's victory, Argan,' Kublai said. 'You were defeated by the faith of our enemies against your stupid pride. The united faith of the people of Chipango against your divided leadership, your incompetence!' He glanced round at the silent members of the Councils. 'Have we heard enough? Does anyone dispute my right to pass judgement?' No one dared to speak or to move. Kublai looked back at the two accused. His voice was pitiless. 'I sentence you to death, in the manner prescribed for cowardice and treachery. Your heads will lie in the dust – with our humiliation.'

Argan had begun to shake convulsively. Won uttered a babble of protest, but the two guards behind them placed a foot on each of their backs and forced them forward to lie face down on the floor. Kublai descended the steps of the dais and all heads bent forward, in fear as much as homage. His head lowered, Marco felt a fear of the Khan such as he had never known before. His heart was pounding as the soft slap of Kublai's felt-soled boots and the swish of his robe approached him and passed. He risked a look and one of the guards pushed him brutally to the floor with the butt of his lance. Marco lay still. Sensing the mood of the Khan, the fanatical guards were ready to kill.

Won was executed directly after the trial and his body thrown to the wild dogs.

Argan, as a Mongol noble, was taken to a barren, rocky island, where his hands were wrapped in newly flayed buffalo hide, sewn with gut. When the hide dried, it became so tight it could not be removed. He was last seen rooting for insects with his mouth like an animal, and died of hunger.

Kublai had gone into seclusion. He sat for days in the secret courtyard, where he had once made a garden of bare earth and sparse grass brought from the Gobi. He saw no one but Achmet and Phags-pa. When Marco tried to use his right of access, he was told it was rescinded.

'It is much,' Achmet told him, 'that you have been left in your position. Return to Yangchou, and remember, discretion is everything. Gather your evidence, and when the time is ripe, we shall denounce those criminals and you will regain the trust of the Khan.'

It was sound advice. He travelled back to his province with Matteo, who was impatient to resume his occult studies.

Marco's return to Khanbalic had been chastening. In the South he had seen what Mongol overlordship meant in practical terms to a conquered people, and he had hoped that Kublai, in whom he passionately believed, would redress their wrongs. But the Great Khan had revealed himself as a despot. His vindictiveness and inability to admit any fault in himself, his irrational anger against anyone whom he even thought was critical of him or who had counselled him against the disastrous attack on Japan had altered Marco's view of him as an all-wise, tolerant and humane ruler. Once the empire had seemed to be a golden land ruled by a demigod. Now he was losing his naive hero worship of the Khan, and it was painful.

One thing he had to look forward to; seeing Monica again. His spirits lifted on the road from Yangchou when his villa came in sight, and there was Jacopo waving and his servants bowing and smiling, and Wu Sheng bowing gravely from the doorway.

'Welcome home, Messer Marco! Welcome home, Messer Matteo!' Jacopo called, hurrying forward to greet them. He was so excited that, when Marco dismounted, he almost hugged him. He recollected himself in time and bowed.

'You fat rascal,' Marco chuckled, 'you haven't changed a bit.' He took Jacopo in his arms, slapping him on the back.

As they walked to the door, Jacopo said, 'I know someone who'll be glad to see you.' He whistled. 'You're right about her, Messer Marco. She's . . .' He clicked his teeth.

'Monica?' Marco stopped. 'You've seen her?'

'Been here a couple of times, she has,' Jacopo smirked. 'To find out when you were coming back.'

The news that Monica was as keen to see him again as he had been to return lifted his spirits still more. He had to restrain himself from riding straight to the village. That, however, would cause embarrassment both to Monica and to Yang Ku.

'Patience, my boy,' Matteo told him. 'Try to achieve serenity.'

While tea was served for them in the salon, Wu Sheng said, 'I have some information for you, which may be of interest.' From his manner, Marco knew it must be something important. 'I have made the acquaintance of a farmer, a simple man who lives by growing and selling vegetables.'

'Yes?'

'The last time I passed through his district, he complained to me that the tax on his vegetable fields had been raised from ten cartloads to fifteen. I promised to look into it. As the assessment had been made personally by Talib, I checked the records without anyone knowing.' He paused. 'Only five cartloads were declared.'

'And Talib disposed of the rest . . .' Marco smacked the arm of his chair. It was a petty matter, but the first direct proof linking Talib with the misappropriation of public funds.

'There is more,' Wu Sheng said. 'And more important. A cross-reference in one of the Sung records to another scroll. But the scroll deals with a section of Yangchou for which, according to Talib's office, no records exist. It is not that they never existed, but that they have been deliberately removed. And we have proof.'

In his absence, Wu Sheng had found just what was needed to bring criminal charges against Talib and his assessors and collectors. Marco thanked him and told him of Achmet's warning to keep their findings secret until the Treasury Department could deal properly with the matter of corruption. Because of the loss of confidence in the administration due to the failure of the invasion, now was not the time. Marco promised Wu Sheng, however, that he would take some action of his own in the near future.

He was afraid that he had delayed too long and that work in the fields had already stopped for the day. But when he rode through the fringe of trees, the lines of peasants were just beginning to straggle away towards the village.

As always it was difficult to spot her. Then he saw one of the shapeless figures in their conical hats step aside and walk towards him. It was Monica, smiling, carrying her mattock over her shoulder. The slighter figure of Mai Li followed her at a distance.

He reined in and dismounted.

'You've come back,' she said.

'An hour or two ago,' he told her. 'I was afraid you'd forgotten me.'

Monica smiled. 'I was sure you'd forgotten *me*.'

They laughed, then neither could think of anything to say. Monica shifted the heavy wooden mattock on her shoulder.

'Let me,' Marco offered. He put out his hand and, as she let him take it, their fingers touched. It was for less than a second, yet both were conscious of it. All the things Marco had meant to say flew out of his head. All he was conscious of was that they were together and that she was happy to see him.

Monica glanced round at Mai Li, who was hanging back. It embarrassed her, because she knew Marco would realize that they had talked about him and arranged for Mai Li not to intrude. She made to walk on and Marco fell in beside her.

'Uh – don't you find it hard, working in the fields?' he began.

'At first,' she said. 'Now I'm used to it.'

He hefted the mattock. 'This is heavy. Doesn't it spoil your hands?'

'Not really.' She showed him her right hand, palm up, and only realized what she had done when he clasped it gently from underneath. Her hand was firm and strong, yet not calloused.

They smiled to each other. If they were truly alone, he might have kissed her. But Mai Li was catching them up and Monica drew her hand away.

'Mai Li,' he said. 'You are prettier than ever.'

Mai Li blushed and glanced teasingly at Monica. 'We wondered when you would return, Lord Marco.'

He walked with them both as far as the steps up to the village. An old woman bobbed to Marco and gave them some apricots from her basket. They stood eating them and talking for some time, without any of the restraint that inhibited them when Mai Li's father was present.

Over the next few weeks, Marco managed to meet Monica again several times, either at the fields or at Yang Ku's house. They were never completely alone, but it came to be accepted that she was the main reason for his visits. Yang Ku saw what was happening and it disturbed him. Yet provided the proprieties were observed, he did not interfere.

Marco also spent much of those weeks travelling in the province, speaking to merchants, farmers, shopkeepers and factory owners. One day, Talib and his first chief assistant assessor were called to a meeting at the military governor's residence. To their surprise they found Marco there, with Matteo and Wu Sheng. The governor was uncomfortable as he explained that the meeting was at the request of the civil administrator, Lord Marco.

'We have been informed that guards from your department have forcibly driven off cattle and commandeered grain from two communities in the district of Kuanhu,' Marco said.

Talib had always considered Marco courteous, reasonable and easy to handle. 'They were behindhand with their tithes,' he shrugged.

'No tithes were due from them,' Marco said. 'Or do you not know the law?'

Talib was thrown by Marco's unaccustomed bluntness. He glanced at the governor, who did not help him. 'I do not understand,' he smiled.

'In one,' Marco went on, 'half the crops had been eaten by locusts. In the other, cattle had been lost through an outbreak of plague. In those cases, the Great Khan's law states that such communities will be exempt from taxes for one year. Furthermore, their losses will be made good to them by the state.'

Talib looked again at the governor, who said, 'That is the law.'

'Obviously those people did not explain their difficulties,' Talib said smoothly. 'I shall see that what was taken from them is restored.'

'Your department will also make good the losses,' Marco insisted.

Talib bowed. 'Certainly, Lord Marco.' He relaxed, thinking the meeting was over.

'It has also come to my attention,' Marco continued, 'that in some cases you have changed the scale of duties. Goods imported by sea pay ten per cent, not twenty. Sugar and spices, three and a half per cent, not fifteen.'

Talib and the assessor were shaken by his determination. 'But I – I thought the Lord Achmet had explained to you?' Talib protested. 'All the expenses of our department and of the army of occupation are paid out of those revenues. With rising costs—'

Wu Sheng had handed Marco some papers, and now he interrupted. 'The governor has informed me of the amount needed for his army. At my request, Lord Achmet has sent me an estimate of departmental expenses in this province.' Talib blinked. 'They are covered twice over by our revenue from salt alone.'

'Not counting the revenue from silk, wine and coal,' Matteo put in. 'And the ten per cent on farming and livestock. That's worth another fifteen million gold pieces.'

'Any increase in revenue will come from greater prosperity in the province,' Marco said firmly. 'These rates have been officially approved. You will not seek to change them without my permission.'

Talib was floundering without the support of the governor. 'I – as always, there will be full consultation.'

'More than that,' Marco assured him. 'Wu Sheng will scrutinize all tax demands and records. Messer Matteo will be responsible for trade estimates. I myself shall continue in charge of the salt revenue.'

Talib was staring at him. 'But . . . I understood from Lord Achmet that the organization of the department was not to be altered.'

'Since I am responsible for the civil administration of this province,' Marco said, determinedly, 'it shall be run as *I* decide. All financial reports are to be submitted first to me and *no* penalties are to be enforced without my approval.' He waited for Talib's acknowledgement.

Talib's eyes were venomous. For a moment, it looked as if he would be defiant, but he had no grounds. 'Yes, Lord Marco.'

'That is all,' Marco said.

After the meeting, Matteo excused himself and hurried away. A significant development in his occult researches, he told them. Marco went with Wu Sheng to the record office, where a team of clerks were already taking charge of the records to prevent any more from being destroyed.

When their business was completed, Marco left Wu Sheng at the villa and rode to the river. He was in time to walk home with Monica and Mai Li, who invited him in to share their evening meal.

At the house he was surprised to hear a voice he recognized and to find Matteo there with Yang Ku and

Chien Hu. Over the past months, he had seen little of the poet, who explained that he had been given a licence to bring out a volume of his lyrics and had been busy supervising the printing, exacting work which left him hardly any spare time.

Mai Li went to take command of preparations in the kitchen and Monica fetched a pitcher of wine. While she poured for them, Marco asked his uncle why he had not waited so that they could come here together. 'It was just something that occurred to me,' Matteo said evasively. 'I thought Yang Ku might be able to help.'

'If it is in my power,' Yang Ku said courteously.

'I have heard that a number of wise men have come to live in the hills here. Men who have withdrawn from the world to live closer to nature and to learn her secrets.' His voice shook with eagerness. 'Are there such men?'

'You are talking of the "Immortals", the followers of Tao, the path of true wisdom. You wish to contact them?' Yang Ku asked.

'Is it possible?'

'If your desire is genuine, you may try. But be careful. To climb up where they are is to peer into an abyss. My father told me once of a woodcutter who came across two old men playing checkers on the mountainside. The woodcutter was fascinated and stayed to watch till the game was over. When he eventually got back to his village, he no longer recognized his house or the people in it. Centuries had passed while he watched.'

Matteo shivered pleasurably at the tale.

'If you wish,' offered Chien Hu, 'I will take you up into the hills. Perhaps it will help you to understand our land and our people better.'

'That would be wonderful!' Matteo breathed. 'When could we go, Chien Hu?'

'It would have to be tomorrow.'

'Tomorrow?'

'I'm going away for a while and won't be back until after the Festival of the Dragon Boats.'

'What is that?' asked Marco.

'A festival in memory of one of our ancient poets, who was drowned in the river. Our people take their boats out and sing songs and recite poetry; then they throw rice and sweets into the water for the fish to eat, so that they will leave the poet's body untouched.' Chien Hu made an expansive gesture.

'Tomorrow is a rest day in the fields,' Monica said. 'May I go with them?'

Yang Ku had been half-expecting the request. 'You have no fear of the "Immortals"?' She shook her head. 'Then I do not forbid it.'

Monica smiled to Marco.

'Tomorrow.'

Matteo echoed him. 'Tomorrow . . .'

The man was squat and ugly and wore green clothes that merged with the thick vegetation on the hillside. He watched the four figures as they made their way slowly up the steep gradient, then turned and began to climb, making his way towards one of the highest points in the range, keeping well out of sight of those below. He came to a rope bridge that had been slung across a deep crevasse. Taking out a knife, he crawled forward cautiously on his stomach and reached out to cut at some of the ropes securing the bridge to the poles. He dislodged a small rock in the process and it dropped into the void, taking many seconds to hit the bottom. When the ropes were cut, though not severed, the man scrambled back into the rocks.

Ten minutes later, the four climbers reached the bridge, panting heavily from their efforts. Matteo was breathing hardest and he slumped against a rock face. 'Let's rest again . . .'

Marco smiled. 'It was your idea to come, Uncle Matteo.'

'The worst is over,' Chien Hu told them.

'Thank goodness for that!' Matteo puffed. 'We must have been climbing for hours!'

They looked back down the hill and saw the river far below, coiling through fertile countryside and vanishing into the horizon. The village where Monica lived was now no bigger than a few bricks.

'Is that bridge safe?' Monica asked, watching it sway in the wind.

'I'll go first,' Chien Hu volunteered.

He led the way on to the bridge, holding the guide ropes on either side and moving nimbly. Though the bridge swayed violently, he reached the other side without difficulty. Monica followed him, then Marco, but at a slower pace, planting his feet carefully and not daring to look down. Matteo only ventured out across the crevasse when Marco was almost at the other side. But their combined weight was too much for the cut rope, and the remaining fibres began to part.

'Hurry!' yelled Chien Hu, spotting the danger.

Paralysed by fear, Matteo felt the bridge sink lower. He was right in the middle of the structure and gripping both sides with desperate hands. The ropes were parting on the side to which he was crossing and he could see the fibres twisting and springing free.

'Quick, Uncle Matteo!'

'Come on!' Chien Hu urged.

The two of them dived towards the support poles and grabbed hold of a rope each, just before the last threads snapped. They were now taking the full weight of bridge and passenger, and it cut deep into their hands. Matteo inched forward, shaking all over, certain that it was only a matter of seconds before he was hurled to his death. The strain on Marco and Chien Hu was almost unbearable and the ropes were now beginning to slip through their burning palms. If they did not let go soon, they too would be catapulted out into space.

As Matteo inched closer, his nerve started to fail.

'Don't look down!' Marco ordered.

'Reach!' Monica called. 'Reach out!'

With a last effort, Matteo lurched forward and groped

for her wrists, feeling the bridge fall as he did so. For a long, terrifying minute, he was dangling over the edge of the crevasse, his weight supported by the waning strength of the girl. Then Marco and Chien Hu grabbed him. The bridge had shot back across the gap and cracked like a whip against the other side. Matteo closed his eyes in prayer. Slowly, painfully and carefully, they pulled him to safety.

'I thought you told us the worst was over, Chien Hu,' he gasped, lying flat out.

'The ropes were deliberately cut,' their guide said. 'Someone knew we were coming.'

Monica looked from him to Matteo, worried.

'I'm not ready to join the "Immortals" yet!' Matteo smiled, recovering his sense of humour with his breath.

They rested and then pressed on. After a short but awkward journey over sharp rock, they reached a large cave, lit by a fissure that ran the length of the vaulted roof. At the mouth of the cave, a bubbling pot was resting on a resinous wood fire. Chien Hu produced a torch from his bag and lit it from the fire, then led the way into the shadowed interior. Monica took Marco's arm.

The cave was damp and cold, but its atmosphere was strangely reassuring, giving out an aura of holiness. The torch revealed a wall covered in ideograms, a heap of scrolls and books on the ground. As the light moved down the cave towards the far corner, it revealed what at first looked like a statue, so still and lifeless did it seem. Marco and Matteo started slightly with the shock, but Chien Hu and Monica had expected to find the old man and were not alarmed.

Though clearly venerable, the Immortal was yet ageless, and Marco was reminded fleetingly of Kublai. The man's face, bare arms and bare feet had the greenish tinge of old bronze, and there was an insubstantial quality about him, as if he had been evoked out of the air. His eyes had both the wisdom of age and the sparkle of youth, and his voice seemed to emanate from the rocks all round him.

'You who come from those regions where time finishes, do you desire to look into the infinite?'

'Two of us are from the village, old man,' explained Chien Hu. 'We bring with us travellers who have crossed mountains, seas and deserts to get here.'

'The desire to know, to learn new things, led us,' Matteo said reverently.

'Know not to know,' replied the Immortal. 'This is the only wisdom. The wise man forsakes pride; he does not seek power or success. He follows the laws of nature, from which all things are born and by which all things are governed, not by force but by the natural curve of space and time. Two opposite forces exist in nature, forces engaged in continual exchange, maintaining a constant equilibrium. A circle divided into two equal parts is the symbol of these two forces. On one side is the masculine force, Yang; on the other side is the feminine, Yin. Yang is heat, the sun, the earth, the desert. Yin is cold, shadow, the moon, water.'

Monica's hand tightened on Marco's arm.

Matteo was trembling with excitement, certain that they had found the mystic he sought, who possessed the magical powers of which he had talked so incessantly. He was about to put a question about gold, but again the old man seemed to anticipate it. In one fluid movement, he got up, crossed to the pot on the fire and stirred it so that the bubbles increased.

'I have seen nature's secret paths. They lead to a distant place where time and space have different values. There death can be defeated, or held at bay – and matter transformed.'

'Yes . . .' Matteo was tense.

The Immortal turned to him. 'But the wise man does not seek only that which seems to him profitable and positive. He sees also the virtue of negative qualities. It is the empty space of a container that makes it useful; without the hole in its centre, the wheel serves no purpose. Does nature not work continual marvels? Seas turn to desert, creeping worms turn into butterflies that hover like feathers on the wind. Nature makes cinnabar red, but fire turns it first white, then grey. Lead and mercury, heated over flames, become gold.'

Matteo had stepped towards the pot and was peering at its contents with an expression of wonderment. The liquid boiled and bubbled, then it began to change colour very slowly, until finally it shimmered with gold reflexes. Matteo stood over it, bathed in its light.

'But man must conquer himself before he can conquer nature,' the Immortal counselled. 'Man cannot change things by force, only by following their natural development.'

'You tell us you know the path that leads beyond time . . .' Matteo's words tailed off to a tense whisper. 'A path that leads to a place where death does not exist?'

By way of answer, the old man took the torch from Chien Hu and held it near his own face, illuminating the deep lines etched in his tightly-stretched skin. They were amazed that he could be so close to the flames without flinching.

'I live in this timeless zone and yet I am preparing for the journey into the next dimension, for the moment when my last evening falls.'

With a gesture of his hand, he signalled to them to leave the cave and followed behind them, pausing in the entrance. The daylight was dying. For a moment they had a bewildering impression that while they had been with the old man, a whole season had gone by, that time had played a weird trick on them.

The Immortal spoke. 'For seven years, I have not eaten cereals. I take my nourishment from cypress berries, pine resin mixed with honey and dates. Slowly but surely, my body is being purified. As you see, I am already mummified. But I am a living mummy, because my body will never die.'

He raised his hand, went back into the cave and out of sight. They looked in after him, but there was no sign of him. He seemed to have merged with the stone. Monica shivered. After a few moments, a thin wisp of smoke rose from the cave into the limpid evening air, the only witness that he had ever really existed.

The trip into the mountains seemed to bring Marco and Monica closer together.

Shortly after their visit to the Immortal, Monica looked up from her work in the fields one afternoon to see Marco standing watching her. With no hesitation, she laid down her hoe and went to meet him. They began to walk along the riverbank.

'I keep thinking about that old man,' Marco said. 'Wondering if he was real – if what he told us was true.'

'So do I,' Monica admitted. 'I felt that he was holy at the time.'

They had circled the low hill of the village and had reached the other side, which Marco did not know. The higher ground closed in towards the riverbank, giving the feel of a narrower valley. There was no one else to be seen. Everyone was in the fields or at the fishing nets. They were walking through scattered yellow flowers, like star clusters. He bent and picked one. When he gave it to her, she smiled and they walked on slowly. She took off her hat, shaking out her hair.

There was one question he had not asked. 'Are you a Taoist?'

'No.'

'What are you?'

She thought for a moment. 'I'm not sure. With my mother, I used to go to a Nestorian church.'

'A Christian . . .' He knew it was irrational, but he was relieved.

Monica trailed the flower across her lips. 'My mother told me about Christ and the Virgin, and how he died. I always liked him. He seemed more human than the other gods.'

'He was not God, but the Son of God,' Marco told her.

She smiled. 'That is how I think of Buddha.' She noticed his surprise and explained. 'When I was younger, I was also taught to love Buddha.'

'There is much of his teaching that seems very like our Lord's,' Marco accepted.

They were coming to a bend in the river, where it had scooped out a small bay. The bank sloped down to a lower level. Beyond the shallows of the bay lay a deeper pool. They went down and sat on the springy grass, watching the purl of the water in the shallows.

Monica was combing out her hair with her fingers, loosening its waves. Marco lay on one elbow, watching its glow against the sun. 'It's strange . . .' he said. 'You look like an Italian, but you think like a Chinese.'

'That is because I *am* a Chinese,' she told him.

'But you're not,' he smiled.

'You are a Venetian, because you know it in your heart,' she said softly. 'How do you know what is in my heart?'

He had no answer. He lay still, watching the slither of the thick coils of her hair as her fingers raked them. Her posture was unconsciously provocative, her raised arms lifting her breasts against her tunic, legs tucked under her, drawing the cotton of her trousers tight against her long thighs. In a moment he knew he would reach for her . . . He sat up, hugging his knees, to stop himself.

'Do you have rivers near Venice?'

He laughed. 'Many. Round the lagoon. I used to spend hours there.'

'Do you swim?'

'Of course.'

'Do the young ladies swim – in Venice?' she asked, teasing him with her smile.

Marco laughed. 'When there's no one looking.'

She glanced along the riverbank. There was no one to be seen. 'Well, then . . .' She smiled to him and rose and in the same moment, drew off her light tunic. Under it she wore only a silken shift. Marco gazed up at her. Her flame-coloured hair fell to the creamy slope of her shoulders. Her figure was slimmer than he had imagined, her breasts higher and fuller, pointed under the flimsy silk. With neither coquetry nor modesty, she stepped out of the loose trousers. The shift was still creased to her narrow waist and reached only halfway down her sleek thighs. She was very lovely.

She smiled to him and moved down to the edge of the water.

Marco rose quickly, taking off his tunic shirt, watching her as she began to wade towards the pool. She looked back and smiled. Stripped to his short drawers, Marco followed her into the water, but stopped, gasping at its unexpected coldness.

'Coward!' Monica laughed. She held out her hand and he joined her. Hand in hand, laughing, they ran towards the pool. As they came to it, Monica held slightly back, so that Marco was in front of her. She lunged with her shoulder, sending him yelling and splashing into the deeper water, then dived after him.

Marco surfaced. Shaking the water out of his eyes, he saw her swimming towards the other side. He struck out after her and had nearly reached her when she dived out of sight.

He looked round, smiling, expecting her to bob up again near him. There was no sign of her. Then he saw the glimmer of her body in the clear water as she came to the surface near the opposite side of the pool. He struck out after her again.

Monica came up out of the pool and stood on the edge of the shallows, in the sun. She tossed her long hair back from her face and smoothed it with her hands, then smoothed the water from her forehead and cheeks, bringing her hands to rest in front of her torso, joined as if in prayer. Marco climbed out of the pool and paused, looking at her. She smiled to him very faintly. The wet shift had become transparent, clinging to her, to the swell of her hips, to the slight pout of her belly with the dark notch under it.

He came towards her and she did not move. As he reached her, she separated her hands and placed them on his shoulders. His arms went round her tightly and they kissed.

Her lips were closed and inexperienced, but opened under his. Her body was trembling. Feeling her warmth and nakedness, her lithe strength against him, Marco was roused instantly. He had never wanted anyone so much, and his arms tightened round her, drawing her closer.

Monica's senses were reeling. She had yearned for him, yet nothing had prepared her for the passion that now overwhelmed her. She was yielding, cleaving to him . . . But gradually something that had been protesting in a corner of her mind broke through, the spectre of all the warnings, teachings, taboos of her upbringing. In her momentary detachment, her awareness of his hardness pressing against her, the rubbing of his legs against hers, made her cry out. She tried to push him away from her, but in his need for her the agitation of her body only stimulated him more. His clasp became fiercer on her and his hands moved, one rasping down her back to force her loins more insistently against his. She sobbed, and her limbs felt weak, yet she clung to him, yielding again.

They turned, stumbling together for the grass and the sunlight. And stopped, shocked by the sound of laughter. It was high-pitched, bubbling amusement.

They looked up the slope and saw a small boy watching them, his finger in his mouth, giggling. Another boy joined them, and a little girl, also laughing. The little girl waved.

Afterwards, Monica was distant for a few days, afraid of the feelings which had so nearly made her lose control of herself. Gradually, however, as they made more opportunities to meet, her need for Marco overcame her fears. When she at last gave herself to him, her passion matched his.

Marco was smiling to himself, thinking fondly of that first time by the river, as he dressed on the morning of the

Festival of the Dragon Boats. He had given the servants, except for the watchmen, a holiday for it. Matteo, Wu Sheng, Jacopo and he were all going to Yangchou together. Later he would join Monica on Yang Ku's boat.

He was looking forward to it all, when Jacopo came to tell him that Matteo was not in his room and that his bed had not been slept in. He was not in his laboratory and no one had seen him since the previous evening. He must have left during the night or early morning.

Marco knew at once where he had gone. His uncle had been slightly irrational ever since the visit to the Immortal. He had put himself on a rigorous diet of bran and seeds, although Wu Sheng had warned him of the dangers of dabbling in necromancy without proper guidance. His weight had fallen alarmingly and he had become listless, losing interest in his work, spending hours in silent brooding.

If he had gone off alone into the mountains, he was in some danger. There was little chance of his finding the right way to the cave among the countless other paths they had crossed. Marco would have to go after him – but he knew he could not find it alone either.

Meanwhile, the folk celebration in the canals of Yangchou was well under way. A noisy, high-spirited crowd lined the canalsides and leaned out of windows laughing and waving, while people in the boats waved back as the water procession wound slowly past.

On many of the dragon-boats musicians played string and percussion instruments and the crowd sang to the bright, lively music. The boats bumped and jostled one another in cheerful confusion and the passengers traded jokes and greetings, scattering rice and sweets on the water in honour of the dead poet.

In Yang Ku's boat, Monica and Mai Li were happy and excited, dodging handfuls of thrown rice and waving to the spectators, when Monica heard a voice hailing them from the bank. It was a worried-looking Marco, with

Jacopo waving with both arms beside him. She pointed them out, and Yang Ku shouted, 'Coming! Wait there!'

'It's my uncle!' Marco shouted to them over the hubbub. 'I think he's gone back up to the mountains!'

'Is he alone?' Yang Ku called out.

'I think so. I must try to find him. Where's Chien Hu?'

Mai Li looked up quickly at her father. For some time, Chien Hu had been part of an organization which helped deserters from the Khan's army to find refuge further south, secret and dangerous work of which no one knew, least of all Marco. He had used the festival to smuggle a group out of Yangchou. 'He's in Soochow,' Yang Ku shouted. 'Won't be back until tomorrow!'

Marco was more worried than ever. In the inhospitable terrain of the mountains, anything might happen to Matteo, alone and enfeebled. With Chien Hu's help, he had been sure of finding him. Now that hope was gone. He watched as Yang Ku steered the boat alongside and reached down to pull Monica up to the bank.

'I'll come with you,' she said. 'Between us we can remember the way.'

Marco smiled in relief and heard Yang Ku call, 'We'll keep a lookout for him here!' Marco told Jacopo to round up the servants and to help Yang Ku to form a search party if Monica and he were not back by morning.

Unnoticed by anyone, someone else was observing the scene. The squat man who earlier had cut the ropes of the swing bridge was steering the dragon-boat behind Yang Ku's. He had tried to force his craft through to the bank, but had found his path blocked. He hissed through his teeth as he saw Marco swallowed up by the crowd. In a mob like that it would have been easy to slip a knife through his ribs. After following Monica, he had succeeded in losing both the cheese and the mouse. He spat and his eyes shifted to the boat with Yang Ku and Mai Li.

Marco rode with Monica to the mountains and up the trail as far as they could urge their horses. Just as they dismounted, they had a piece of luck, coming across

Matteo's pony, which he had left at a shepherd's hut. The man showed them the path 'the barbarian Wise One' had taken, and they left their own horses with him, hurrying on on foot. At least, they knew now they were on the right track and that Matteo really was heading for the Immortal's cave.

The shepherd had warned them to take care, for the weather was breaking, but as yet there was no sign of it. The sun was burning hot, the air humid, and soon they were breathless as the rocky ground became steeper. The going was too hard for talk and after two hours, they were happy to sit and rest beside a mountain stream.

Monica still had some pellets of sweetened rice in her pouch and they ate some. While she replaced the rest carefully in case of need, Marco lifted off her straw hat, freeing her hair. She laughed and shook it back. Although he had learnt that compliments made her uncomfortable, he could not resist it and murmured, '*Bella* . . .'

She smiled. 'You called me that once before.'

'Do you mind?'

'No. But it's so strange. It's what my mother used to call me.'

Marco laughed. 'I always knew it! You see? You're Italian.'

'But what does it mean?' she asked.

He touched her cheek gently. 'It's an Italian word for what you are – beautiful.' Her smile faded. 'Surely I haven't said anything wrong?'

She was embarrassed. 'You know I'm not. Not beautiful.'

'You can't believe that?'

'I've always hated the way I look,' Monica told him. 'Ever since I was little.'

He suddenly understood. 'Because you weren't like the other girls?' He chuckled. 'You wanted almond eyes and a nose like a button?' He took her hand. 'Always remember that to me you are *bellissima* . . . Very beautiful.'

He drew her closer and they kissed. They had not seen

each other for over two weeks and the kiss became prolonged. When they broke apart, they looked at each other for a long moment. 'We have to find your uncle,' Monica whispered.

Reluctantly, Marco helped her up. She put on her hat, leaving her hair unbound. When they started off, they had to climb a jumble of boulders to get back to the path. He put his arm round her waist. 'I love you,' he said. She smiled to him and swung herself up.

Marco climbed after her to the path, but then hung back, watching her walking ahead of him. However close they had been, there had always been areas which he could not reach, silences which he accepted as modesty, beliefs which were too ingrained for him to challenge.

After a time she became aware that he was some distance behind her and waited for him to catch up. 'I love you,' he repeated. '. . . That's something you've never said.'

'But you know I do,' she smiled.

'Only you don't say it.'

She was troubled. 'It's not easy. A Chinese says, I honour you. He does not speak his love aloud. It is fragile and precious. He keeps it safe, locked in his heart.'

'You're not Chinese, though. You could shout it, if you wanted to. All you have to say is, I'm yours. I want to go on being yours.'

'You are everything I want,' she said quietly, sincerely.

There was something he had tried not to ask, but had to. 'And what happens when I leave Yangchou? Will you come with me?'

She had grown taut. 'To live among the Mongols?'

'To live with me. I want to look after you. I want to protect you.'

'It would be running away from my own people,' she tried to explain. 'There's so much—'

'For God's sake, you're not Chinese!' he burst out. 'You sound like Chien Hu!'

'I wish I was him!' she flashed back. 'I wish I was a man. So that I could fight!'

Marco gazed at her, shaken. Things were coming out between them, attitudes which he thought he had long ago overcome. 'He's not still thinking like that? It's madness! South China is the Khan's now. He will never let it go!'

Monica was already regretting what she had said. She had gone further than she had intended. She moved closer to him. 'I – I don't know what made me say that,' she apologized. 'Forgive me.' She put her arms round him. 'Hold me.'

He hugged her to him tightly, feeling her heartbeat, knowing she was torn by conflicting feelings. 'We have to think of ourselves,' he said. 'I want to marry you. I don't ever want to be without you.'

She tried to smile to him. She knew he was right, that years of conditioning, of seeing the struggle only from one side, had entrapped her. 'Kiss me, Marco,' she pleaded. 'Please . . .'

Their kiss was long and, in part, healing.

They climbed on, and at first the going was not so hard. Much of the heat seemed to have gone out of the sun and there was a light haze, unusual in the mountains. Constantly on the lookout for Matteo, they entered a narrow defile that wound exhaustingly upwards. Marco would never have believed that his uncle could get so far in his weakened state and was becoming increasingly anxious. The light appeared to be fading, too. It must be later than he had thought.

They emerged from the defile on to a long, stony slope, and stopped still, seeing the reason for the fading light. Thunder clouds were massing all along the tops of the mountains, black and dark purple, blanking out the sun. Even as they looked round for somewhere more sheltered, an ominous rumble of thunder sounded away to their left. He took Monica's arm, urging her upwards.

The rain began with a scatter of fat, heavy drops borne by a cold wind that made Monica shiver. 'There's an overhang there,' he told her, pointing up to their right.

'We must get to it.' She nodded and they began to scramble upwards as fast as the slope would allow.

All at once, a great clap of thunder jolted them, much nearer, seeming to shake the slope. As they looked up, partly deafened, they saw lightning crackling among the clouds obscuring the peaks. The skies opened. Rain drummed on the stones and sparse grass of the slope, drenching them in seconds. A vicious fork of lightning ripped across the escarpment above them and he heard Monica gasp. An icy wind swirled fiercely along the slope, threatening to hurl them back, and they had to crawl on their hands and knees, slipping and slithering on the wet stones, dazed by the reverberating thunder, which had become almost continuous.

Once under the lip of overhanging rock they were out of the worst of the rain, but the icy wind still buffeted them. Marco felt Monica against him. He looked round desperately and by the livid light of the storm saw a dark fissure in the rock wall beyond them. Half-carrying her, he inched towards it. It was the entrance to a cave. Something lay heaped beside it, a pile of old tree branches. Not knowing what lay within, he took one as a defence and holding Monica behind him, edged into the cave, which opened out beyond the narrow entrance into a small room. It was empty, but more wood was stacked against the wall and there was the blackened ring of a fire. In the flashes of lightning, he made out a sleeping area towards the rear protected by a low wall of stones and a drainage channel. It was filled with soft, dry sand.

Outside, the storm had begun to rage in earnest. His saddle cloak was hanging in a tight roll at his back. He shook it out, covered the sleeping area with it and laid Monica on it. She was still trembling, numb with cold. Thunderclaps boomed and rolled outside. The cave was illuminated brightly by a sudden burst of lightning at the entrance and she cowered back.

Marco had taken out his knife and a piece of flint he always carried. He prayed it was not too wet. As he scraped some shavings of wood, he kept talking to reassure her. 'The Mongols are afraid of lightning,' he said. 'Even my friend Chinkin is like a child in a storm. You'll like him. He can't wait to meet you. I'm as fond of him as you are of Mai Li. Like a brother – as she is like your sister.' Marco smiled to reassure Monica. 'You're not afraid, are you?'

Her teeth were chattering. 'Not – not when I'm with you.'

'What is this place?' he wondered.

'A shelter . . . for shepherds,' she told him.

Both of them had begun to shiver, and as Marco set to work lighting a fire with the help of flints and tinder, he was aware of his clothes clinging to him clammily. 'We'd better get these wet things off.'

He stripped off his sodden tunic and hung it on a ledge on the wall. He found an earthenware jug there, but it was empty. He looked round and was alarmed to see Monica's pallor. She was too weak to sit up and lay just where he had left her, her fingers plucking at her tunic. He hurried to kneel beside her, taking her hands and chafing them to bring back the circulation. Her hair was streaked across her face and he smoothed it back, then lifted her, catching her tunic at the waist and pulling it over her head. Her body felt deathly cold and he rubbed her sides and back, shifting round to let the meagre heat from the now-flickering fire reach her. He laid her on his cloak and took off her trousers, hanging them and her tunic over the wall of the sleeping area.

Her shift was sticking to her. 'Better take that off, too,' he decided. She managed to push herself up to sit and he drew the shift off. Now she was naked and he gathered up the edge of the cloak, draping it round her shoulders. Her colour was coming back and she managed to smile to him. She was sitting with her hands in her lap, the cloak round her shoulders, the firelight gleaming on the gourds of her full breasts. He touched them softly, feeling their coldness. His hands smoothed over them and under them, warming her skin. Their pale tips stirred and grew darker. Her eyes were fixed on his. Two spots of hectic colour burned in her cheeks. She reached out, wrenching open his shirt, and pressed forward, flattening herself against him. His arms swept round her and she toppled back on the soft sand.

Her mouth sought his and they kissed fiercely, her legs coiling and straining. Their love-making was sudden and desperate with the need to assert their living humanity against the terror of the storm.

All that night they lay entwined, while outside the rain streamed down and the thunder rumbled and crashed. Their love-making, now hungry, now tender and prolonged, was only broken when one or other moved reluctantly to put more wood on the fire. Sometime in the early hours, they fell asleep.

A little later, Marco came awake. The storm was over and the cave was warm and peaceful. He was too drowsy to waken fully. He saw Monica laying sticks across the fire. Her hair had dried and hung to below her smooth shoulders, its tangled waves matching the dark smoky red of the flames. He did not speak and she came back to him, settling again by his side, propped up on her elbow. His eyes had shut, but he could feel her gazing down at him. 'I love you,' she whispered. 'I love you. I love you . . .'

When Marco woke again, it was just after dawn. Monica had gone, but as he sat up, she came in from outside, dressed and carrying an armful of sticks.

'What are you doing?' he asked.

'Gathering wood,' she smiled. 'We must leave new wood for anyone else who comes.' She had filled the earthenware jug with rainwater from pools in the rocks and brought it to him.

He drank and drew her down beside him. As soon as he had dressed, they would have to resume their search for Matteo. 'Lie beside me just a minute longer,' he said. He turned her face towards him and kissed her gently. '*Bella, bellissima*,' he murmured. 'I love you, Monica. You see, I am whispering it like a Chinese, so that only you can hear.'

She held him tighter. 'I love you, too,' she said, 'more

than anything in life.' And his heart rose, knowing that the words he had heard during the night had not been a dream.

Outside, the ground steamed as the sun sucked up the last traces of the storm. Climbing was much easier and in less than an hour they came in sight of the Immortal's cave. Almost at once, they found Matteo.

He was lying flat on a low rock, quite motionless. Marco's first thought was that his uncle had either fallen from higher up, or been attacked. But when they got close, they learned that their fears were groundless. Matteo, very much alive, was lying with his eyes closed, going through his breathing exercises.

'Where have you been, Uncle Matteo!' Marco demanded.

Matteo sat up. 'I'm seeking the path, the Tao,' he said, mildly. 'Since I left home, I've eaten only berries and grass.'

'We've been searching for you since yesterday,' Marco told him. 'Why did you go off like that?'

'No cause for alarm. I will teach you, too . . .' He showed them the green paper that was in his hand. 'This was all I found in his cave. The Wise One has gone. Disappeared.' He held up a piece of paper with its red circle pointing upwards, then he filled his lungs once again. 'The sun responds to this sign. I feel its fluid entering every fibre of my being.'

He tried to stand up, but almost fell. He was evidently very weak and not at all sure where he was.

'Have you been out here all night, Uncle Matteo?'

'Probably.'

'In all that rain?'

'I didn't notice any rain,' Matteo said, surprised. 'I was meditating. I saw things I've never dreamt of before.'

'You were delirious, that's all,' said Marco.

'He needs food,' Monica said.

They sat him down and she took the balls of rice wrapped in a leaf from her pouch. They had to force him to eat but slowly he started to recover. He seemed to be coming out of a kind of trance. It was some time before he noticed that Marco was supporting him with one arm, while keeping another around Monica.

'Yin and Yang,' he smiled. 'Male and female.' With his finger, he drew a wavy line in the air. 'Life. Happiness.'

Marco and Monica burst out laughing. After all their anxiety, it was such an anticlimax.

The journey back down the mountainside was not too difficult. All the time, they expected to meet Yang Ku's search party, but there was no sign of it. They walked with arms linked, supporting him, and he was able to sit on his pony. The sun and the movement revived him further and they were relieved when he began to talk normally, even apologizing for all their trouble.

When they got within sight of the village, however, their mood changed abruptly. Thick, dark smoke could be seen curling into the air and faint cries could be heard.

As they galloped as fast as they could towards the settlement, the smoke became thicker, the cries louder. They dismounted and raced up the steps, gasping at the horror which confronted them.

A man sat weeping, his head in his hands. Marco grabbed him, asking what had happened.

'Mongols . . .' the man muttered. 'Soldiers. They attacked us without warning. My wife . . . my wife . . .'

The horror mounting in him, Marco set off in the direction of Yang Ku's house, the others following at his heels. They passed an old man, spreadeagled on the ground, blood oozing from a gash across his throat. They saw frightened animals stampeding everywhere, in and out of houses, over the bodies of dead villagers. Then they reached a blazing hut, outside which a woman was screaming hysterically, 'My baby! . . . *My baby!*' Her child was trapped inside and the flames were too powerful for her to get back inside. Marco tried to force his way through the door, but was beaten back by the wall of heat.

As the woman's cries rose even higher, a man came

struggling out of the blazing doorway with the child wrapped in a blanket in his arms. Thrusting the bundle at the woman, he staggered a few paces and collapsed, a blackened, gasping, half-dead figure whose clothes and face had been badly burned. Matteo knelt beside him, staring in disbelief at the ravaged face, then crouched, listening for his heartbeat. It was Jacopo.

'Is he still alive?' Marco asked his uncle. It did not seem possible that Jacopo could survive.

'I'll stay with him. You two find Yang Ku,' Matteo said.

Monica was already running on and Marco hurried after her through the stricken village, picking his way over slaughtered animals.

When they came to Yang Ku's house, they stopped in shock. All that remained were a few blackened stone walls standing amid a pile of burning débris. A figure sat hunched in misery by an overturned cartload of hay.

'Father!' Monica ran to embrace him.

'Yang Ku – what happened?' asked Marco.

He was still weeping as he looked up. 'Soldiers came for the girls. They've taken Mai Li. The soldiers have taken Mai Li. I heard her calling for help . . .' Monica held him tight and cried with him. 'Chien Hu came, but he was too late to save her. We – we couldn't save her . . .'

'Where is Chien Hu now?' said Marco.

'I don't know. He's gone, too . . .'

'Help me, Monica. We must get him away from here.' They lifted the sobbing Yang Ku to his feet. 'We'll take him to my villa.'

Supporting Yang Ku, they moved slowly away from the charred remains of his house and his source of happiness.

'No explanation was given, nor did they say where they were taking her, or why!' Marco's anger gave his words extra force. 'Her father is nearly out of his mind with grief!'

He was in the main room at the governor's residence. While the governor's brow was furrowed as he listened,

Talib looked bland and unmoved. 'Is she beautiful?' he asked.

'What does that have to do with it!' Marco demanded.

'A great deal,' the governor told him. 'It's only the prettiest girls who are taken by those sent to find concubines and younger wives.'

Marco was appalled. 'But that's hideous – barbaric!'

The governor shrugged. 'It's the custom. The great lords send down raiding parties to pick up ten or twelve likely young women for their harems.'

'Find them!' Marco insisted. 'Get them back!'

'They'll be well on their way to the North by now,' the governor said.

'In that case I shall go to Khanbalic at once and denounce these acts of violence!' Marco said thickly.

'Before you go too far,' the governor warned, 'we have information that that village was a nest of rebels.'

'That is totally untrue!' Marco snapped. 'I know that village. No people in the South were more peaceable, more ready to accept our rule.'

The governor glanced at Talib. 'The information *I* was given was different.'

Marco's head turned sharply to Talib, realizing the Turk's vindictiveness lay behind the atrocity. Talib flinched and hurried to explain himself. 'I've had long experience in these matters, Lord Marco. And I know this province even better than you do. However, it was pure coincidence that the raiding party chose that village.'

Marco knew he was lying and said coldly, 'Nothing can justify the burning of homes and the ravaging of women. I shall report to the Khan . . . to Lord Achmet.' He looked at both men in turn. 'I shall ask that Chinese be appointed to rule over Chinese. In that way, the Khan's laws will be administered fairly.'

'There is another law in government circles,' Talib reminded him, a hint of threat in his voice. 'The great have eyes only for great things. It is a law that excludes pity – but it is the only one that guarantees the empire's survival.'

Ignoring him, Marco addressed the governor. 'You have sworn an oath of obedience to the Great Khan. And it is to him that you will answer for your loyalty . . . and your honesty!'

Marco stalked out. The governor stared after him, beginning to wonder if Talib, with his promise of riches, was after all the wrong ally to have chosen.

Marco rode out to his villa at full gallop, blaming himself for having delayed so long in denouncing Talib and the corrupt governor. After speaking to Matteo, he told Monica and Yang Ku to prepare for a journey. He arranged for Wu Sheng to take charge of the office in Yangchou, then Marco and his uncle went to see Jacopo.

The servant was lying on a bed, so completely swathed in bandages that only one eye and his mouth were visible. Chinese tended him with patient concern and moved silently about their work.

'We're leaving, Jacopo,' Marco said. 'Monica and Yang Ku are coming with us.'

'As soon as our business is finished at Khanbalic,' Matteo added, 'we're going home. To Venice. We'll send for you.'

'Home, Jacopo!' Marco said. 'Think of that.'

There was a pause. Jacopo's blistered lips moved. 'No, Master Marco. This is my home.'

'But you've talked of nothing but Venice ever since you've been here!' Matteo reminded him. 'Just think of all the things you'll be able to do when you get back – with money to spend.'

'No,' Jacopo croaked. 'I've made up my mind. I'm staying here.' His eye turned to the Chinese woman, crouching patiently beside him. 'I want to stay with these people.'

'Stay?' Matteo could not hide his surprise.

'The flames took half my face away. If I returned to Venice, I would be seen as some sort of monster. Here the people treat me with kindness and affection, like an unfortunate brother. So – leave. I will stay.'

'You haven't thought enough about it,' Matteo argued.

'I'm sorry. I have served you as faithfully as I could, but now . . . I realize that this is my true home.' Jacopo's hoarse voice had grown fainter and the woman looked at him anxiously.

'Jacopo—' Matteo protested.

Marco touched his uncle's arm, stopping him. He looked down at the bed, at cowardly, funny, fat Jacopo, who had saved the life of a child. To part with him after all that they had been through together on their travels was a wrench, but Marco had been moved by what Jacopo had said. Bending down, he kissed him gently on the forehead.

They arrived at Khanbalic as night was falling. The first thing he discovered was that the Great Khan and Chinkin were both in Shangtu, so he could not appeal to them immediately, as he had intended. Marco told his uncle to take Yang Ku to their home. Fearing for Monica's safety in the Forbidden City, he had decided on other lodgings for her and led her off through the winding alleyways. A man hid, waiting for them in the shadows by the gate, and followed them silently, unseen.

When he came to Akira the potter's house, Marco asked his friend a favour and the blind man agreed at once. Monica was to remain with him in the anonymity of Khanbalic's suburbs. 'You'll be safer here,' Marco told her. 'It won't be for long.' She was troubled, but he kissed her, calming her fears. On the days of their journey to the capital, they had discussed the future, planning to marry as soon as possible and return to Venice. But there were other urgent matters to be dealt with first. Marco promised to return as soon as he could and watched Akira lead her into the house. As she looked back he made himself smile.

Next morning, Achmet had three visitors. His eyes

travelled from Niccolo to the hunched, kneeling Yang Ku, and ended at Marco. 'You have come back earlier than I expected,' he said, with a hint of disapproval.

'I lost faith in what I was doing,' Marco told him. 'I had seen the Khan's justice betrayed. People stripped of everything they owned. Villages burnt. Violence of every kind. Murder, rape . . .'

'He is still very young, Lord Achmet—' Niccolo apologized, alarmed at what his son was saying.

'I beg you to help Yang Ku!' Marco pleaded. 'They took away his daughter, Mai Li. She is his only child.'

Perplexed, Achmet glanced at Yang Ku, who still seemed dazed by all that had happened. 'Khanbalic is a huge city. His daughter could be anywhere. Be reasonable, Marco. I understand the grief you feel for your friend and his daughter, but there are rules and customs which I have to respect – even if I would prefer not to.'

'Is stealing a daughter from her father a rule to be respected?'

'Marco!' his father snapped.

When Marco saw Achmet's expression, he knew that he had offended him deeply and was shocked at his own lack of control. He bowed and apologized as humbly as he could for forgetting himself.

Achmet relaxed a little, and considered his request. 'I will see what I can do. There could, however, be serious difficulties with certain powerful people. I warned you before to guard against snares and traps. There are those who hate you and your Chinese friends. Religious fanatics.'

Marco understood. 'Phags-pa? But it's—'

'No names!' Achmet warned. 'I know what you mean. I have seen many monks yield to the temptations of the world . . .' He turned to a vase of flowers and admired them, lifting a hand to brush the petals of one bloom. 'For what concerns this man here, if an injustice has been done, then we will put it right. Our loyalty to the Khan—'

'That's the point!' Marco interrupted impetuously, making his father writhe with embarrassment. 'I want to tell him that the South will never be united with the North unless it has the same rights and the same protection. Chinkin speaks the truth when he says that all Chinese must be brothers!'

'Such passion, Marco!' Achmet smiled, raising a hand to silence him. 'You say that you want to speak to the Khan about the problems of the South, but the Khan has many problems and does not wish to be distracted with more. That is why he has men like me to take care of them, men who spare him the burden of day-to-day difficulties. You will only irritate him. I am the one you must come to,' he emphasized. '*Only* me. And I will listen to you, like a brother or a father.' He paused and walked over to Marco. 'I have told you before that there are those who consider your talents dangerous. But I will watch out for you. Your father and uncle value my protection. My advice has always brought honour and profit to the Polo family.'

'We are deeply grateful, my lord,' Niccolo bowed.

'But if that profit is ill-gotten?' returned Marco. 'If it has cost the blood of others? Then there is no honour. I have investigated the chief tax collector of Yangchou, a man called Talib . . .'

'Talib is already under suspicion. Go home and make a report, a written report which I can submit to the Council,' Achmet replied. 'And do not speak of it to anyone. Talib has powerful friends.' He smiled. 'And do not worry. I shall have a search made for this poor man's daughter. If it is humanly possible, she will be found.' He clapped Marco on the shoulder, dismissing them. Throughout, he had not once looked directly at Yang Ku, who had knelt with his head bowed, grieving. He now shuffled out backwards still on his knees, in the manner prescribed for suppliant Chinese.

Marco could tell that his father was anxious, but he himself felt relieved, and safer after the regent's offer of help. He decided to bring Monica to his own home. When he left Achmet's palace, he went straight to Akira the potter's house. But there another shock awaited him. Monica had gone.

'The man said that he had been sent by you to escort the girl to your home,' Akira explained.

'I sent nobody!' Marco protested. 'How could you let her go?'

'His voice sounded honest. And Monica seemed to know him.'

'How *could* she?' Marco's voice was full of pain and shock.

'Do not ask me, my friend. The girl welcomed him, that is what happened. She trusted him enough to go with him.'

'But who was he? What was he like? Can you describe him?' Marco saw the sightless eyes turned towards him, and cursed his thoughtlessness.

The potter smiled. 'All I can tell you is that judging from his voice, he was from southern China.'

'When did he come?' asked Marco, even more puzzled.

'Not long after you left.'

'I must find her! Even if I have to turn Khanbalic upside down!'

'You will not have to wait long,' Akira warned quietly. 'Terrible days are in store for this city . . . The gods are weaving them.'

Marco was scornful of such superstition. 'No-one knows what the gods intend.'

'Do not mock me, my friend. Was I not right in what I said about the invasion of my country? Tell your Great Khan Kublai the truth, as I told it to you a long time ago. There is no hope of victory for those who fight against a confederacy of love.'

The following night the quietness of the courtyard outside Achmet's residence was disturbed by an excited murmur of voices. A huddle of servants carried bundles of unlit torches, as if waiting for a signal to light them. That signal soon came.

'The Prince Chinkin has returned! Hurry and inform the Lord Achmet!'

The Chinese dignitary who had given the order was flanked by two guards, each with a lighted torch. One of the guards rushed to light the torches of the servants with his own brand. The courtyard brightened.

At the command of the dignitary, the fat major domo had run quickly to the pavilion. He was accosted by a member of the Regent's Bodyguard, who thrust a lance across his path.

'I have to speak to Lord Achmet on the prince's orders,' the major domo explained.

The guard stepped aside to let him pass. He went into the pavilion and along the marble corridor. When he reached a flight of steps, he took them in twos and hurried along another corridor at the top. He was panting when he knocked on the door of the bedroom and let himself in. There was a stifled grunt of annoyance. The room was dimly lit and Achmet was in bed on the far side. Without daring to look, the servant delivered his message.

'Prince Chinkin has returned, my lord.'

As Achmet levered himself up, the naked young woman under him whimpered. 'What?' asked the regent, surprised. 'Returned?'

'He's in the Hall of Supreme Harmony. He's waiting for you, my lord.'

The major domo backed out of the room, bowing.

Achmet got out of bed, dismissed the concubine with a wave and grabbed a robe. A summons from Chinkin at that hour of the night could only mean a matter of great urgency – and secrecy. Achmet could think of several reasons for both.

In a few minutes he was walking across the courtyard outside the Imperial Palace, escorted by a servant with a lighted torch. He hurried into the building and was conducted to the Audience Hall. It was virtually in darkness, the only illumination coming from a pair of candelabras at each end of the hall. Achmet saw the figure on the imperial throne, slumped back in the position that was usual to Chinkin since his last bout of illness.

'Welcome back, your Royal Highness!' Achmet bowed, walking towards the throne. 'In what way can I be of service to you?'

The figure rose up, stepped into the light, and suddenly lunged at him. Achmet had time to cry out only once before Chien Hu's dagger pierced his heart. Even as the body was falling, Yang Ku leapt out of the shadows to thrust his dagger into the regent's back.

The assassins exchanged a grim look of satisfaction, then the sound of running feet turned their thoughts to escape. Alerted by Achmet's scream, guards, sentinels, archers and servants came racing in. Chien Hu tried to run towards the far door, but two arrows hit him simultaneously and he was knocked flat, sliding for several yards on the marble floor.

Yang Ku, who had darted back into the shadows, moved cautiously along one wall towards a side door. But a sharp-eyed guard had seen him and he was caught and overpowered. As they dragged him out past the dead body of the regent, he saw the pool of blood spreading rapidly and allowed himself a bitter smile of triumph.

While uproar was breaking out in the Imperial Palace and guards were running towards it from all directions, Monica, dressed in the robes of a nun, took advantage of the confusion to enter the regent's pavilion by a rear door. She followed the directions she had been given by the other rebel conspirators, moving with urgency and speed, but taking care not to be seen by the eunuch guards. Eventually, she came to the night quarters where the concubines were housed. Taking a deep breath to give herself courage, Monica began her search.

On either side of a long corridor were a number of

small cubicles with curtained doorways. The first was empty and, peeping in, Monica saw that it was furnished simply with a bed, cupboard and stool. The odour of perfume was strong. When she looked in the next cubicle, it was occupied by a naked Chinese girl, who clutched a robe to herself, surprised by the intrusion. Monica went on down the corridor, faster now, tugging back each curtain, looking in and hurrying on. She was soon being followed by a group of chattering concubines and slave girls, who watched her with a mixture of curiosity and annoyance. Some of them were no more than thirteen or fourteen.

The further she went, the larger and more noisy became the group behind her. Thinking she was mad, they were afraid to stop her. Some called for the eunuchs. Others were laughing. She came to the last cubicle, hesitated, looked back at the sea of faces and pulled back the curtain.

She froze in horror. 'Mai Li . . .' she whispered.

A silk scarf had been tied to a beam. Mai Li dangled in space, her face distorted by the torment of her strangulation. Unable to bear the shame of being a concubine in Achmet's palace, she had taken her own life.

Monica let out a long, rising, anguished cry. Two harem guards seized her and she was hurried away.

Niccolo Polo lay in bed, wishing that his son would stop moving about the room so restlessly. He had something important to tell Marco, though he was not sure how he would react. Grief and exhaustion were making Marco edgy and unpredictable.

'I've looked everywhere for her, father! All over the city. I've asked everyone who could possibly know . . . But the only ones who might be able to help, the Chinese officials, are being dragged from their homes and butchered in revenge for Achmet's murder.'

'It is to be expected,' Niccolo said. 'Many of them were involved in an uprising in the palace.'

Marco was stunned. 'Against the Great Khan?'

'Against his administration. The death of Achmet was to be the signal.' Niccolo could see that his son's mind was racing with the implications. 'You think the girl was taken from the potter's house by this Chien Hu?'

'He's the only one it could be!' Marco saw it all very clearly, and was embittered. 'It was all Achmet's fault! He was a devil! Why didn't I realize it before? The corruption in the South – it was all his doing. The killings, the raids on the villages, the attempt on my life . . . He made me think it was Phags-pa. But *he* was the one who had Mai Li taken away. It was done to humiliate my friends, and me with them. Achmet and that creature, Talib!'

'Talib is one of Achmet's illegitimate sons.'

'His *son*?' Marco could barely take it in. Talib's relationship to Achmet had always been vague. 'Why didn't you tell me before?'

'I didn't know until recently. I made enquiries. Many leading positions are held by Achmet's "sons".' Niccolo paused. 'That report he asked you for – he was only playing for time. Your uncle and I think that he intended to have you disposed of. We were planning to have you smuggled out of Khanbalic.'

Marco sank to the couch. 'He used me – used us all.'

'Monica and your friends used you as well,' his father said quietly. 'To get to the Forbidden City.'

'I don't know. I don't know anything any more.' Marco sounded desolate. 'I feel as if everything's crumbled, my hopes, my plans . . . everything.' He refused to accept that Monica had been using him like the others. 'I know, whatever happened, that Monica loves me. If only I knew where she was. I'd trade my life for hers!'

'Pray God it doesn't come to that,' Niccolo said, moved to see how much his son cared for the girl. 'There is still something you can do.'

'Is there?'

'Remember who you are and what you have become in the years since you have been here. Appeal directly to the Great Khan, the Empress and Prince Chinkin.'

'But the Khan refuses to see me. The Empress has little influence with him. And Chinkin is still in Shangtu.'

'Then report first to Phags-pa. He will be regent, now that Achmet is dead. Any help must come from him.'

Marco was more troubled than ever. 'Appeal to Phags-pa?'

'It is your only hope . . . It isn't much, I know.' Niccolo paused. 'You love her very much, don't you?'

Marco hesitated, torn. 'I will go to Phags-pa tomorrow.'

That night he was far too tired to sleep. A night and day of searching for Monica had left him exhausted, yet when his body gave up the search, his mind continued. Why did she go with Chien Hu? How much did she know about the plan to assassinate Achmet? Where was she hiding and when would she try to contact him? What if she no longer loved him?

The audience with Phags-pa was embarrassing, but by no means fruitless. Though the Lama did not hide his dislike of Marco, he listened with interest to the detailed report of corruption in the South. A skilled interrogator, his questions probed and pierced, and Marco was made to feel particularly uncomfortable when talking about his friendship with Monica. He accepted, however, that Phags-pa needed to know every relevant piece of information and answered as helpfully as he could. At the end of the long interview, he was rewarded with a rare, if almost imperceptible, smile from the monk.

'The Great Khan should hear this at once.'

'May I speak with him?' begged Marco.

'No. But you may be present while I do. We must leave for Shangtu in an hour . . .'

They rode out with an armed escort on the post road

towards the Summer City, maintaining a hard pace all the way.

The City of Pavilions was as magical as ever on the horizon, but Marco had no thoughts of the past. His love for Monica dominated his mind completely. Just before he had set out from the Forbidden City, he had learned that she had been put under arrest for her supposed part in the murder of Achmet. It horrified him to think that he was actually riding away from the place where she was being held, but he knew that her fate lay at the disposal of one man, and that man was in Shangtu.

When they arrived, Phags-pa went into the imperial pavilion and Marco was left waiting outside like a stranger. He remained patient. Though eventually admitted to the presence of the Great Khan, he was warned that he must say nothing whatsoever.

Kublai himself did not even glance in his direction and only referred to him in the third person. In view of their earlier closeness, Marco found his treatment hurtful, but he was willing to endure any humiliation to help Monica.

'I have already given the order for the two assassins to be executed. The other person . . .'

Marco's heart constricted.

'What other?' Kublai asked.

'A third person was arrested after Achmet's murder – a young woman. She is from the South, too, the adopted daughter of Yang Ku, one of the assassins. It seems that she was involved in the plot to provoke a revolt of all Chinese officials and servants in the Forbidden City. She is also . . .' He cleared his throat. 'She is also very close to Marco Polo.'

Marco wanted to tell them *how* close, to plead for her, defend her; but to speak would have been to worsen her situation, if that was possible. And Marco was there very much on sufferance. All he could do was to wait until Kublai, perturbed by what he had been told, announced his decision.

'You may tell Lord Marco that it is time he learned to

distinguish between those who deserve his friendship and those who do not,' Kublai said, his voice cold and detached. 'All Achmet's helpers and accomplices will be executed. The spark of revolt must be extinguished.'

'All, Great Lord,' Phags-pa agreed.

There was a pause. Kublai's eyes flicked towards Marco, but he was adamant. 'All those who took part in his murder and the attempted revolt must also die – including the girl.' He turned and stalked out.

Marco's eyes closed. He felt Phags-pa's hand under his arm, helping him up.

Chapter Eight

Khanbalic was the capital city of death.

At every corner, bodies were hanging from stakes and gallows, and the stench of rotting flesh was overpowering. The streets were hushed, the houses shut, the marketplaces empty. Armed guards patrolled outside the Forbidden City, marching up and down past mound upon mound of human heads. The sky itself seemed to be mourning, its black clouds hanging low in great folds, its distant thunder like the solemn beat of a drum.

Marco was horrified by it. As he had feared, Kublai had taken revenge not only on the plotters, but on the Chinese population at large. His action had been swift, ruthless and comprehensive. Thousands had been slaughtered, thousands more mutilated, and hundreds still awaited their sentences. Khanbalic was a charnel house.

Phags-pa had been given the task of implementing the policy of savage repression, and he had done so with frightening efficiency. Since they had returned from Shangtu, Marco had not stopped pleading with him.

'I have no choice,' Phags-pa repeated. 'I must obey the Khan's orders. Consider yourself lucky that he is not punishing you as well.'

'She is innocent!' Marco swore. 'You can save her, if you wish. You *must* save her!'

'Yang Ku has been beheaded, but the revolt will not die with him,' Phags-pa told him. 'She considers herself his daughter; as such, she could become a dangerous symbol.'

'For the love of God, for the love of *your* God, because I pray to him as well – have mercy! You, a man of faith, must show mercy.'

They were standing on the steps of a Buddhist temple in the Forbidden City and the intensity of Marco's appeal made it echo around the courtyard. Though his face remained impassive, Phags-pa had been reached at last. 'The power of prayer is invincible,' he said, quietly. 'Perhaps a way to save her can be found . . .'

'Anything! I will do anything!'

'The cost will be high.'

'How much? I am willing to pay any . . .'

Phags-pa shook his head. 'You still haven't learned to read men's hearts, have you, Marco? The cost will be high, but you will not have to pay it in money.'

Marco could not understand him. 'What will happen to her?'

'I must make arrangements. Come to me in three days.'

'Three days?'

Marco wanted to ask more, but the Lama was already mounting the steps. He paused. 'Trust me. And if you love her, be prepared to make the greatest sacrifice for the sake of that love.'

Phags-pa disappeared into the temple as a bell rang out, and Marco was left to puzzle over what he had meant.

For the next three days Marco was in an agony of apprehension. Fresh lines of prisoners went to their deaths each morning and Marco was there to scan each face, fearing that Monica might be among them. The love which had begun the moment he had first seen her, and which had finally reached expression in the cave on the mountainside, now intensified to a great, aching obsession.

When the waiting period was over, he hastened to the first minister again. They set out on a journey.

As they travelled through the outskirts of the city, they came to cultivated fields, where peasants worked without daring to lift their heads, past mean hovels from which frightened woman and children peered out. On either side of the road were bodies impaled on stakes, rows of spikes topped with severed heads, grim reminders of the Khan's anger. Marco had to turn away from the sight.

They arrived at Chen De in time to see columns of Biskuni, Buddhist nuns, climbing the steps towards the

Temple of the Great Buddha. The nuns moved slowly and modestly, each carrying a stick of incense in one hand and a lighted torch in the other. Phags-pa conducted Marco to a shadowed area just inside the door so that they could witness the ceremony.

The nuns were shuffling silently towards a huge vase that had been filled with sand and placed before the altar. With measured gestures, they each plunged their sticks of incense into the sand-brazier and sent pale blue smoke rising aromatically to the roof. As the nuns filed past Marco, he looked at each one carefully, but their heads remained lowered and their eyes averted.

Then, only feet away from him, she appeared.

Monica was dressed in the same robes as all the others. Her hair had been shorn, her head shaven, yet it only seemed to enhance her beauty. She looked pale, lovely and tranquil as she moved forward towards the sand-brazier. Marco was so overcome that he opened his mouth to call to her, but Phags-pa touched his sleeve to remind him to remain silent. He could do nothing but watch and suffer and love.

'This is the last time you will be permitted to see her,' Phags-pa murmured. 'She is safe, as I promised. But for you, it will be as though she were dead.'

Marco had made the sacrifice. In order to save her life, he had sworn never to see her again. If he so much as tried to make the slightest contact with her, he knew that she would be killed.

'We must leave,' Phags-pa said.

Monica had reached the altar. As she approached the vase, she turned abruptly and looked back down the pillared aisle of the temple. Her eyes searched quickly, until at last they met Marco's. For a brief, poignant moment, their gazes locked. She was trying to tell him something, something which at that distance he could not read. Then the temple bell sounded and she turned back. Placing her stick of incense in the sand-brazier, she waited until its smoke had drifted high up past the impassive face of the great Buddha, then bowed her head and shuffled on with the others.

Marco had lost her forever.

He was not given time to mourn for her. The next day, a courier arrived from Shangtu with orders for Marco to lead an Imperial embassy to India and Ceylon. He had no choice but to obey.

With the other members of the embassy, Mongol lords and Chinese secretaries, he travelled south to Amoy, stopping on the way to greet the new military governor and civil administrator appointed by Phags-pa. Wu Sheng had been placed in full charge of tax collection, a post which he fulfilled admirably and fairly. Marco also saw Jacopo, who was recovering steadily, already able to sit up and order the other servants about with almost as much high-handedness as before. He was overcome with emotion when Marco told him he had made the villa over to him, to be his completely when Wu Sheng retired and returned to Khanbalic.

From Amoy, Marco and his embassy sailed in one of the huge ocean-going junks for the subject states of Annam and Malaya, and from there on to the Andaman Islands and India. To distract himself from thoughts of Monica, Marco had the captain teach him the mysteries of navigation and spent long nights alone on watch. His pain at losing Monica had become a rage at her betrayal, a fierce anger with her for joining those who had planned the assassination of Achmet and the abortive rising of the Chinese palace officials in Khanbalic. How long had Yang Ku known that Achmet was the real enemy? Why had he not told him? Yet he refused to believe that Monica had known. She was tied to the Sung by a lifetime's affection and loyalty. Her adopted sister had been kidnapped and ravaged. He could only imagine her torment when Chien Hu asked for her help. All her life would urge her to agree, while her love for him would fight against it. In the end, forces beyond her control had driven her. His heart softened and, sometimes, the Chinese helmsmen saw tears on the cheek of the strange, aloof lord as they sailed through the night.

At last, they landed in Maabar on the east coast of India and were received graciously by its king, or *devar*, Sundara Pandya. Lodged in a cool, marble palace, Marco was entertained by an unending series of receptions and visits. The country was rich and strong, controlling four other provinces, the federation known as Greater India. Its richness came mainly from pearls, of which it was the world's principal supplier, carrying out an enormous trade with the Orient and Arabia. Its people mostly went naked, except for a loin pouch. The King's loincloth was encrusted with jewels, while golden bangles set with gems covered his arms and legs, pearl rings decked his toes and round his neck was a priceless necklace of one hundred and forty matchless pearls and rubies, one for each idol worshipped by the state. Marco could not compute the fortune the King wore on his body alone.

Gradually he was distracted from his sombre memories by the fascination of the country and its customs, which from long habit he began to study. The Yogis reminded him of the Immortal in the cave in the mountains near Yangchou, while the Brahmins in appearance were more like Mongol priests, although their teachings echoed those he had heard years before in the Lamasery in the Pamirs.

He was also amazed by the erotic temple rituals, in which hundreds of naked girls leapt and danced to entice the god to have intercourse with the goddess to ensure harmony and fruitfulness. He had had no sexual thoughts since the harrowing days at Khanbalic and his reactions to the lithe, tumbling bodies disturbed him. Yet when carefully selected young women, scented and depilated, were provided for him, he could rouse no interest in their firm, brown flesh.

The King of Maabar refused to pay tribute to Kublai, but was anxious not to offend such a powerful monarch and swore a pact of eternal friendship with the empire, loading Marco with presents of pearls and rare cloths. Satisfied, Marco headed north for the kingdom of Hyderabad, ruled by the widowed queen, Rudrama Devi. Since the death of her adored husband, she had refused to remarry and had become famous for the freedom and justice of her reign. She also swore friendship with Kublai and presented him with a chest of magnificent diamonds from her mines at Golconda.

Marco sailed south again to pay homage at the tomb of the martyred St Thomas, revered equally by Christians, Mohammedans and Brahmins. He took away some of the red earth from the ground round the tomb, known to be an infallible remedy for many illnesses. He journeyed on south to Chola and to Comorin on the very tip of the vast continent and, at last, turned south-east for the fabled island of Ceylon.

Ceylon was not quite the land of necromancers, fairies and mythical beasts that he had been led to expect, but it delighted him nonetheless with its happy, graceful, naked people, its golden coral beaches and its perfect climate. Its king, Chandra Banu, a man of great charm and gentleness, welcomed Marco effusively as representative of the Great Khan. Among the wonders of Ceylon which he showed Marco was an almost inaccessible mountain which was said by the Saracens to be the grave of Adam, the first man, but which was also hallowed by the Buddhists as the site of a monument to Buddha. On the top, reached by an exhausting series of chain ladders, was a sanctuary in which precious treasures were kept, two of the teeth, a lock of hair and the begging bowl of Buddha himself, a shallow and austerely beautiful object, made of green porphyry.

In the weeks that Marco spent with him or toured the island, the King grew progressively more worried. His greatest treasure and the pride of the kingdom was a ruby, flawless and of wondrous colour. It was unquestionably the finest in the world, a span in length and of the thickness of a man's arm. The King, from occasional remarks made by Marco, was in no doubt that the Khan coveted it and was terrified to refuse, picturing to himself his peaceful, idyllic island overrun by Mongol hordes, pillaging, burning and raping. As the embassy drew near its end, he summoned Marco and as a token of loving esteem for the Great Khan, offered to send him the begging bowl of Buddha instead. Marco accepted in Kublai's name, with profound gratitude. The King was equally grateful and relieved, showering Marco with gifts and conveying him to his junk in the state galley.

Marco bowed low as the junk sailed, and the Chinese sailors astonished the watchers by letting off a stream of rockets and firecrackers. Things could not have turned out better. He had only had a passing interest in the ruby, as a rarity, and had always known it was completely unobtainable. His father's training had stood him in good stead. The main object of the whole embassy had been to secure, by any means, the porphyry begging bowl, the most reverenced and holy relic in the Orient.

They sailed home with favourable winds and travelled straight to Khanbalic. News had been sent ahead of their safe arrival and of the success of the embassy, but he was surprised by the procession which came out to meet him as he rode towards the main gate of the city. It was led by Kublai himself, on foot, followed by Phags-pa and the members of the Civil and Military Councils, the lords and dignitaries of the court, all walking, at the head of an uncountable multitude. Their feet were bare and they were dressed in simple robes with no ornaments.

As Marco dismounted and took the bowl from his saddle bag, Phags-pa and the lords and attendants, everyone in the crowd, knelt. Holding the bowl carefully, Marco walked forward to meet Kublai, to kneel and present it to him. Kublai took it reverently and passed it to Phags-pa, whose hands trembled as he touched it. Kublai raised Marco and embraced him, all the disagreements and differences of the past wiped out in the emotions of that moment. It was only when Marco saw to his surprise that

Phags-pa was bowing to him that a thought occurred to him; a strange, disturbing thought. He had come to China inspired with the idea of bringing the empire into the arms of the Pope. What if now, instead, he had helped to turn it inevitably to Buddhism?

After his two-year absence, his father and uncle noticed a change in him. It was not merely that he was older and now wore a light beard. He was leaner and more self-contained, his manner more serious, a man used to command. Yet when he told them of his travels, his eyes had their old vitality and curiosity.

Having last seen him in despair, Niccolo and Matteo were glad for him. He had come through pain to maturity. In answer to their unspoken question, he told them that he had not forgotten Monica, but had accepted that their story had ended. He did not tell them how dear it had cost him. On the years of the embassy, however, the ever-changing sights and experiences, the dangers and excitements, had slowly brought his bruised spirit back to health, as he suspected the Khan had known it would. Kublai was not a monster as he had once thought of him, just as he was not a god. Monica was not faithless. They were all pawns in the blind game of fate.

Niccolo was happy to tell his son of his own preoccupations. With Phags-pa's help, he and Matteo had opened the post roads at last for trade. The Lama was proving to be an enlightened and astute first minister. A stream of goods was being shipped to the West. 'Sometimes, I long to go with them,' Niccolo sighed.

Marco confessed to the same feeling.

'Why don't we go, Niccolo?' Matteo asked. He had now outgrown his obsession with mysticism; his brother had pointed out to him that excessive dieting made him look older and that he was spending more gold trying to create it by magic than he would ever recover.

Niccolo sighed. 'I put that question to the Great Khan himself. He only turned his back on me.'

'He can't keep us here forever,' Marco argued.

'Can't he?' Niccolo said.

Marco was disturbed by what his father had told him. So effectively, they were prisoners. But he was also worried by news of Chinkin's suspected failing health and made up his mind to visit the Empress Jaimu at his first opportunity.

When he was admitted to the private chamber in her palace, Marco found her surrounded by several elderly ladies-in-waiting. Prince Timur was there as well. Delighted to see Marco again, the Empress waved him to a cushion and he squatted in front of her. As always he was able to relax with her and talk with the openness of a son to a mother.

'You are kind to come and see me so soon after your return from Ceylon,' she said. Time had deepened the lines in her face, but her voice was as gentle and soothing as ever. 'I know how hard these years have been for you. Chinkin told me how you had to give up the girl you loved. I'm afraid there was nothing I could do to help you.'

'At least she is safe,' Marco said, with resignation. 'And I have learnt not to believe that love conquers all.'

'You will find happiness again, Marco. I pray for it.'

She held out her hands to him in a gesture of affection and comfort. Marco rose and kissed them, an action that surprised the watching Timur. Sensing his surprise, Marco turned to him and gave a slight bow. 'The Empress has treated me with kindness from the moment I first arrived in China, Prince Timur. You were only a young child then.'

'A child whom you often robbed of its father,' Timur remarked, evenly.

'We shared youth and the same desire to know the world,' Marco explained. 'But how is your father?'

'In the old days, I would have had to ask you.'

'Chinkin is quite well, Marco,' the Empress said, with a frown to her grandson. 'Still weak, but recovering in the healthy air of the Summer City. In fact his health has improved sufficiently for him to take a new wife – Princess Kokachin of the noble Baya'ut family.'

Marco was delighted with the news. But when he met his old friend beside the lake at Shangtu, he was disappointed to find him still looking pale and drawn.

'This is further than I've been for weeks, Marco. It's quite an adventure,' said Chinkin, pausing for breath as they reached the water's edge.

'Lean more heavily on me.'

'Here am I, hardly able to walk a few hundred yards, while you have travelled halfway across the world.'

'Not on foot,' Marco smiled.

They came to a bench and rested. Chinkin let out a sigh, then noted the other's questioning look. 'I'm getting better slowly. I'll be well again soon, they tell me. Very soon, I hope.'

'You'll *have* to be,' Marco said, teasing him. 'In time for the wedding.'

Chinkin hesitated. 'She's very beautiful, poor child.' The Prince's voice was tinged with sadness.

'Why do you say that?'

'She's from a royal family whose daughters can only marry Khans or princes. As proof of her father's loyalty, she's been given to me.'

'You will make her happy,' Marco assured him.

'Like my other wives? Whom I haven't seen for a year? My heart is not strong enough for love.' Chinkin gazed out over the lake, his eyes clouded. 'And if I recover and marry her, what sort of life will she have as my widow? Each day and month that passes is stolen time.'

'Don't talk like that!' Marco protested.

'I don't have to pretend with you, my friend. Whatever the doctors say, I know that the flame of my life is about to be snuffed out. It could happen at any moment.' He tried to smile, but could not.

'That is why you must rest,' Marco said, quietly.

'And to think of everything that might have been, and now will never be.' Chinkin shivered as if suddenly cold. 'I've been a failure, Marco. My brothers have all been given kingdoms to rule over. Even my son, Timur. Not me.

All my life I have lived in my father's shadow. I, who dreamed of uniting North and South.'

'It's beginning to happen!' Marco told him, sincerely. 'The signs are there.'

'Very faint signs. It's happening so slowly and with such difficulty.' He leaned heavily against Marco's shoulder and his strength seemed to be fading gently away. His pallor was now even worse and his breathing more irregular and snatched. Marco held him. 'It's turning cold, Marco. Take me back inside.'

As they headed slowly back towards the pavilion, Marco remembered the tree that his friend had once chosen and feared for him.

The rage of the Great Khan Kublai had continued for a long and dangerous time. Furious over the botched invasion of Japan, he had been given an excuse to vent that fury after the assassination of Achmet and the attempted insurrection. His entire empire had felt the force of his uncontrollable anger. Eventually, however, his rage had subsided and he accepted the need to re-adopt his policy of reconciliation. One sign of it was his summons to Marco to join the discussions of the Council of Twelve on the continuing pacification of the South. Kublai sat on his raised throne, Phags-pa presided over the barons themselves, Timur and some high-ranking dignitaries completed the assembly of Mongol power and wisdom.

For all that had happened, Marco's feeling for the people of the South remained strong and affectionate. He spoke up for them without reserve as he made his report. 'The people of the South are ready to accept the empire, Great Lord – if they can be shown that your government sees them as citizens of it and not merely as defeated enemies.'

'How can we do that?' asked one of the councillors.

'By giving them justice and by showing them that we trust them in turn.'

'Is that possible?' Timur was dubious.

Phags-pa gave him his answer. 'Lord Marco has already proved in one province that it can be done,' he said calmly, surprising Marco by this support from such an unexpected quarter.

'We give our thanks to Lord Marco,' Kublai announced, a hint of a smile displaying all his old affection. 'To thank him better, I shall order a solemn celebration for the Christian festival of . . . what do you call it?'

'Christmas, Great Lord.'

'But, Great Khan,' one of the councillors objected, 'to honour the Christians just now? When Nayan and his people are a growing danger!'

'Nayan is calling on his people to revolt,' another insisted. 'He is using his faith as an excuse to rise against you and split the empire.'

'It has little to do with his faith,' Kublai pointed out, bluntly. 'He has been crazed with ambition and the treacherous advice of Caidu.'

'Surely, Great Khan, by celebrating the birth of Christ, it is as though we are saying to the people that the sign of the Cross that Nayan wears is *worth* veneration?'

Marco stiffened at this insult to his faith, but he managed to hold back his reply. Kublai noted this, then spoke to the whole room with a forcefulness which left his listeners in no doubt about his position.

'I shall tell you, Phags-pa, and all of you. There are five prophets who are worshipped throughout the empire – Confucius, Buddha, Jesus Christ, Moses and Mohammed. It is wise to venerate them all, so as not to risk displeasing the one who is the greatest in the Eternal Blue Sky. And until the day we face him, we cannot know which He is.' His voice hardened. 'As far as Nayan and Caidu are concerned, they know that my patience will not bear much more of their arrogance. And if they have ears, here, among us . . .' he glared all round, '. . . let them listen well: their days are numbered! They will not be able to stand against my anger, whatever symbols they have on their banners and shields.'

The suppressed fury of the speech seemed to make the whole room throb. As before the attack on Japan, Marco felt a terrible premonition that another storm was approaching.

Not long after, the premonition seemed to have another cause. The condition of Prince Chinkin worsened, and he was brought to the Forbidden City. Even the sacred oil and the prayers of the Empress Jaimu could not save him this time, and he began to fade rapidly.

Refusing to accept Phags-pa's reluctant conclusion that they must submit to the Will of God, Kublai kept insisting there must be a way to cure him. Mongol pride stirred inside him. Yet despite all the efforts of the Shamans, nothing could be done to avert the course of destiny. Within a few days, Chinkin's soul was speeding to his homeland.

The ceremony was held that night in the courtyard in the presence of all the nobles and dignitaries. Marco, Matteo and Niccolo took up their positions to watch. The Shamans began with a ritual dance to the beating of the drums, the same ominous sound that had warned of the defeat by the Japanese. In the fiery torchlight, they danced themselves into a state of exaltation, a few so overcome that they lost consciousness and fell to the ground. The mixed sounds of the drums and their voices, imitated animals and birdcalls, were frightening and eerie. As they moved, they seemed to undergo a kind of metamorphosis into animal forms. Several waved their arms to mime the flight of birds, others reared like horses or jumped like deer.

'Why are they doing that?' Marco asked.

'To suggest the various forms – human or animal – that Chinkin's soul may have taken,' Niccolo explained.

The Chief Shaman had been dancing near three tree trunks that had been erected, two crowned with a horse's skull and the third with hawk's feathers. As if in a trance, the man suddenly stood rigid while his body was racked by great spasms. His cries were shrill and demonic.

Several other Shamans tied a sort of leather harness around his waist and hung on to the straps as he continued to jerk and twitch and sway. To Marco he seemed possessed by demons.

The Chief Shaman began jerking even more, kicking out his legs, then trying to leap into the air, but the others held him back with the straps as if restraining a wild horse. His screams and his struggles intensified until, all at once, he fell silent and his body stiffened. The Shamans immediately dropped the straps and crouched around him. Drums all round slowed their beat as the Chief Shaman raised his arms and chanted.

> 'The horse of the Steppe has neighed!
> The strong bull of the earth has bellowed!
> I am above you all, I am a man!
> I am Man!
> Created by the Lord of Infinity!
> Come, O Horse of the Steppe, and help me!
> O Lord of Power, command!
> O Spirits of the Eternal Blue Sky,
> take this soul by the hand and lead it,
> show it the way, the road to its home,
> back from the distant mountains.'

He finished by flinging his arms high, imploring the stars of the night.

The drumming quickened its beat again and attention turned to a Ladder of Knives, which had been constructed from thirty-six gleaming blades. It flashed in the firelight, its edges razor-sharp and menacing. As the drumming reached a frenzy, one of the Shamans burst out of the group and approached the ladder, the first to reach the needed state of trance. Marco gasped as he placed a bare foot on the first lethal blade. Kublai was intent, watching.

'The Ladder of Knives stands for the Tree of Life,' said

Matteo, nervously. 'If he reaches the top and comes safely down the other side – Prince Chinkin will live.'

The Shaman ascended slowly but without fear. Marco winced each time a foot was placed on a new blade and made to take the full weight of the man. He could not understand why the Shaman's soles were not cut to ribbons. Did the priests really have the power to defeat death itself in this way?

When the Shaman reached the top of the ladder, there was a gasp from the watching crowd and Kublai, fraught with anxiety, took a step forward. The descent was slower and more hesitant. The Shaman felt for each knife with his foot and tested it before lowering himself. All drums had ceased now, all voices were still. The tension was almost unendurable as the man came closer and closer towards the ground and towards the working of a miracle. Like everyone else in the courtyard, Marco was willing him to succeed. The man had only two more knives left to go.

As he felt for the second to last blade and let his full weight ease down, the knife sliced right through his foot and sent blood spurting out.

With a cry of pain that rang round the courtyard and terrified all who heard it, the man fell to the ground in agony. Kublai's body sagged and Marco joined involuntarily in the cry of despair from the whole watching court that silenced the drums.

The Empress Jaimu was in her garden when Marco was taken out to her. She sat among delicate flowers and blossoming trees, but the colourful abundance of nature only served to heighten her attitude of sorrow. Marco waited patiently until she was ready to look up and speak to him.

'I have taken the Princess Kokachin into my household,' the Empress said, almost whispering. 'She will be honoured as if she and Chinkin had been married.'

There was a long pause. 'Will he be buried here in Khanbalic?' Marco asked.

'No. In the homeland of our people on the Altai Mountains. The burial place is secret. Nobody knows of it.'

'I wish I could help to escort the body.'

'It would not be permitted,' she told him. 'And . . . there are other things. All his horses must be killed, as well as all those people who cross the path of the funeral procession on its way to the mountains.'

'All of them?' Marco was shaken.

'When the Great Genghis died, twenty thousand people were sacrificed for him.' Seeing Marco's revulsion, she tried to explain. 'The Great Genghis respected the law – and it was obeyed by many generations of Khans before him.'

Marco could not accept the notion of a single death that led to so much needless bloodshed. It was yet another painful reminder of the fact that he was an outsider in an alien culture. Chinkin was a Mongol Khan and would be buried in the manner befitting his status, but all the same it was hard to believe that gentle, tolerant Chinkin would have wanted the slaughter of his herds of horses, or have approved the murder of innocent people.

'You are going away, I hear,' Jaimu said.

'Yes, I came to say farewell. The Great Khan is sending me North to take his embassy to Nayan. I hope to prevent war.'

'My heart goes with you, Marco. You are the only one who can speak to Nayan. I pray God that he listens.'

The alternative was unthinkable. Marco took his leave.

The vast tented camp stood near the edge of the Mongolian desert. Thousands of warriors had gathered under Nayan's banner, which bore the Nestorian Cross: they were hard, fierce, barbaric fighting men, toughened by the nomadic life. As he rode through the camp with his escort, Marco was struck by the number of warriors who had gathered to support Nayan; it was a much bigger force than he had expected, and one that seemed ready for battle. Hostile stares came from every side and he saw more than one sneer of contempt, but he kept going until he reached Nayan's *yurt*. Guards wearing small bronze Crosses on their tunics stood outside the door and challenged him as he approached.

Hearing the noise, Nayan himself came out of the *yurt* and welcomed Marco. The Mongol leader had his beautiful Circassian wife with him, but he kissed her forehead and she went back inside so that he could parley. He knew of Marco's sympathy and greeted him warmly.

Marco dismounted and sat in the shade of the *yurt* with Nayan, who looked older and more hardened. They talked at length about the terms which the Great Khan was prepared to offer. But even as Marco was urging the importance of a peaceful solution, the sounds of war were all around him – warriors testing or sharpening their weapons, blacksmiths busying themselves at anvils. Nayan's expression gave no hint of his true feelings.

'You would do better to stay here with us, Marco Polo,' he smiled. 'One day, perhaps soon, my uncle will make Buddhism the official religion of the empire. Especially if Phags-pa has his way.'

'It has too many Muslims and Christians for that,' Marco said.

'The empire is not united and Kublai cannot keep it together by force. He will try to unite it with religion – and fail.'

'The Empress Jaimu could dissuade him,' Marco began. 'She—'

'She is his wife,' interrupted Nayan, 'and a Mongol woman. With death in her heart, she would choose to follow him.' He shook his head and sighed. 'If Chinkin had lived, maybe things would have been different . . . I hear that the Khan has taken his death very badly.'

Marco was about to reply when a group of Mongols

came riding past. He recognized one of them; the beautiful, barbaric warrior daughter of Caidu Khan. But by the time he had started forward to greet her, the Mongols had ridden on.

'Someone you know?' asked Nayan.

'Caidu Khan's daughter, I'm sure. Aigiaruc.'

'It is possible,' Nayan said casually.

'I saw her wrestle once, years ago. It is not something you forget.'

'I suppose not,' Nayan smiled.

'She's a long way from home,' Marco observed.

'She must have come for the hunting,' replied Nayan. 'Some of her tribe usually ride north at this time of year.'

Marco hesitated. 'I'm still not sure what message to take back to Kublai, Lord Nayan.'

'You may tell the Great Khan this: that Nayan respects him because he shares his blood; he admires the Khan's skill as a warrior and has not forgotten his many victories. But he will not sacrifice his independence and that of his people in order to satisfy the Khan's ambition as emperor.'

The interview was over. Marco bowed and mounted his horse. His escort at once reined in alongside him. As Marco raised his hand in farewell, Nayan stepped forward to him, his voice low. 'Have you forgotten, Messer Polo, that you came to the East as an envoy of the Pope, to spread the word of Christ? Now I can see in your eyes that you consider me a fanatic. Be careful. There is One greater than all of us, who sees everything and whose judgement is final.'

Without replying, Marco spurred his horse and galloped away. Nayan had touched a deeper chord than he knew.

When Kublai heard that his peace terms had been rejected, he made no comment at all. The death of his son had afflicted him so deeply that he hardly heard what was being said to him. Age had suddenly stamped itself on his face, turning him into a shrunken old man with wrinkled flesh. Marco repeated his news and offered to return to Nayan with a fresh offer, but still Kublai would say nothing. Phags-pa terminated the audience and Marco had to leave.

He went straight to the Empress.

'That is how he has been since Chinkin died,' she explained. 'Nothing interests him any more.'

'He leaves everything to Phags-pa?'

'And Timur, who is his heir now.'

'When I told him what Nayan said, he was hardly listening.'

'Nothing makes him break his silence,' the empress sighed. 'Except when the ambassadors came from Arghun, Khan of Persia, to ask for a royal princess to be sent as a wife. When I told him that Kokachin would be chosen, he wept like a child.'

'What was decided?' asked Marco, anxious to know about the future of the princess who had once been Chinkin's intended bride.

'Kokachin will be Arghun's wife,' the empress said practically. 'It's a useful alliance. Arghun is loyal, but the marriage will make the bonds tighter. Yet it is a long and arduous journey to Persia for her.' She looked towards the crucifix for a moment, then turned and spoke with intensity. 'You must speak to Kublai again, Marco. *Make* him listen! Tell him that Nayan's only concern is for his people! He must allow Nayan and Caidu to keep the freedom of our ancestors. He cannot imprison them inside walls and cities.'

'I will do my best,' he promised.

Marco returned at once to Kublai and requested another audience. Phags-pa and Timur were with the Khan in his private chamber, and they showed alarm when Marco told them of seeing Caidu's daughter with Nayan, and of the extent and nature of the enemy forces. Kublai ignored all that was said, and did not even look up when there was a soft knock on the door, and the guards admitted a courier.

'An urgent dispatch from the North, Great Lord!'

When there was no response from the Khan, Phags-Pa took the scroll and dismissed the courier. It was the first time that Marco had seen the Lama lose his iron self-control. When he read the dispatch, Phags-pa shook it in the air in agitation.

'My Lord Khan! My Lord Khan! The revolt has spread.' He literally forced the scroll into Kublai's hands. 'It has spread down from the east side of Lanzhou to Ju Juyan!'

Kublai seemed to awake from a sleep and he blinked, remembering something half-heard. 'You say you saw Princess Aigiarac at Nayan's camp? . . .' Then he glanced at the scroll and its seriousness jerked him fully awake. 'This is the greatest threat there has ever been to the empire. If Caidu has joined Nayan – then so have the nomad tribes!' Kublai made a great effort to throw off his lethargy. He gestured sharply to Phags-pa, 'Summon the Council! And the army command! I want them here in an hour!'

Phags-pa and Timur hurried off while Kublai picked up a map from a basket beside him. Sweeping all the papers off his desk with his arm, he unrolled the map and pored over it. Marco stood at his shoulder. Kublai laid his hand over the land mass of China, then swung it over to the West. 'The Empire. China and the East – Persia and the West.' His hand moved north. 'Nayan's territory.' He slammed his fist down in the centre of the map. 'The steppelands of Caidu!' The area covered by his hand cut him off from Russia and Persia.

Marco was amazed at the transformation. The tired, brooding old man had suddenly become an emperor ready to defend his territories with the utmost vigour. By the time the Council of barons had arrived, along with the military leaders, he had recovered his dynamic spirit. His mind was already devising strategies and drawing up battle plans.

He confronted his councillors and generals. 'Two of the largest nations in the empire are in revolt!'

Most of the councillors were alarmed. 'Do we know what they intend, Great Lord?' one asked hesitantly.

'Lord Marco?' Phags-pa brought the emissary forward.

'I believe that Nayan is worried that his people will be crushed,' Marco reported. 'He himself is a man of peace. There is still a chance of persuading him to abandon the revolt. And without him, Caidu cannot attack. But the offer *must* be made, Great Khan!'

Some of the councillors, and Timur, were impressed by the vehemence of Marco's words. Kublai was not.

'I have forgiven them too often. Ever since they grew to be men, Caidu and Nayan have led revolts. When they were put down, I have forgiven them.' His voice rose in pitch and volume. 'But this time they thought that my grief had killed my courage and my dignity. Whatever he says, Nayan is no man of peace. And this is no simple revolt for more independence.' Marco was clearly disturbed by his cold anger. Kublai pointed at him. 'Even as you talked to him, *this* was in his heart. Not independence – but a war to carve himself out a new kingdom in North China, while Caidu rouses Central Asia, cutting us off from the West and splitting the empire in two!' His voice rose in fury. 'This time there will be no forgiveness!

Nobody even dared to speak, still less to challenge what had been said. It was Timur, respectful but determined, who finally broke the silence. 'What are your orders?'

Kublai addressed a commander. 'How long would it take you to summon the garrisons of the South?'

'Thirty to forty days, Great Lord.'

'Too long,' Kublai grunted.

'However hard they ride, it will take that at least for Bayan and Nasreddin to get here,' a councillor predicted. 'Who will you appoint to lead the army?'

'I shall lead it myself!'

Kublai's announcement caused consternation. Marco shared the doubts of the others, knowing that it was almost forty years since the Khan had led soldiers into battle.

Once again, however, nobody had the courage to gainsay Kublai.

'Without Bayan's men, how will you form an army, Great Lord?' Phags-pa asked.

'The Imperial Bodyguard, the garrison of the city and any others who join us on the way. I do not need Bayan's men. Our forces will hit Nayan before he and Caidu can join forces. We must take him by surprise. Close the passes to the North so that no word of our coming can reach him. Tell the men to get ready. In less than two months, we must attack Nayan! We will give him a war that will grind him and Caidu into the dust forever! A true Mongol war!'

While the room became a cauldron of argument and speculation, Marco gazed at Kublai with an admiration not unmixed with awe. He felt as though he had seen him properly for the very first time. He comforted himself with the thought that if it turned into a Holy War, it was Nayan's doing, not the Khan's.

The hall consisted of four adjoining rooms, containing between them some five hundred golden Buddhas in a bewildering variety of poses. The effect created by a few lamps in the Hall of the Five Hundred Golden Buddhas at Cheng De was incredible. Light animated the expressions on the faces of the statues and lent them a warmth and glow that gave them a semblance of transfigured and exalted humanity. Tendrils of smoke rising from incense stick burners heightened the sense of mystical quiet evoked by the mute eloquence of the ancient statues. The wisdom of centuries seemed to hang in the air.

The figure in the dark robe stood alone in front of a giant Buddha that was armed with a sword and a stare of blank defiance. The Great Khan Kublai offered incense to the mighty Buddha before him, gazing up into the blind, all-seeing eyes.

*

Mongol drums kept up a thunderous beat as the army of the Great Khan surged forward. Kublai himself, in full armour and riding his white stallion, was at the head of his thousands, preceded by his standard-bearers who held aloft his yak-tail emblem and his great banner of the sun and moon. Behind Kublai came his senior commanders, experienced generals in armour and with full weaponry. Next came a column of standards, flags and banners, followed by Phags-pa, Marco, Timur and various dignitaries. The veteran cavalry came next and the infantry were behind them, moving at a steady jog-trot across a wide front. Because it was the duty of Mongol wives to follow their husbands to war, the empress's *yurt* was being pulled along on a huge cart by dozens of oxen. Sailing carts with supplies followed her, then came more infantry. The cavalry rearguard was made up of some of the finest horsemen in the army, who kept a constant watch on the flanks and rear.

At Gansu, they crossed the river at the ford, and Timur pointed to the mountains in the distance. Marco was waiting to cross with him. 'Beyond that range, we'll be in rebel territory.'

'Let's hope they don't know we're coming,' Marco said. A great cheer went up. 'What's that?'

'Reinforcements.' Other units had ridden up on the opposite bank to join them. 'The garrison from Shangtu.'

Their numbers swollen and their spirits lifted, the soldiers of the Khan's army began the difficult climb through the mountains. When two of Nayan's lookouts saw them, they were horrified by the size of the army and the speed and comparative silence with which it was moving. They turned to race away, but found themselves facing a detachment of Kublai's archers who had worked round behind them. A flight of arrows swept both lookouts over the precipice.

The army camped for the night in the valley beyond the mountain pass, but set off again before dawn. Burning villages soon dotted the Manchurian plain as the horde swept on, destroying all in its path with a brutality that sickened Marco. Not even the memory of the massacre on the road to Jerusalem could match the savagery and horror of the fighting.

Nightfall brought them to within a few miles of the enemy camp. Kublai summoned his commanders and gave his directions. The cavalry were ordered to dismount in order to muffle the horses' hooves and stop the jingle of harness. Infantry checked their weapons and archers their quivers. Strict orders were passed on for total silence.

In the early hours of the morning, Kublai gave the signal for the advance. His army glided forward. Black-clad soldiers were sent ahead to creep up on the guards who ringed the rebel camp and dispose of them; then the main body of warriors came up. Expertly deployed by their commanders, they waited tensely for the attack itself. The sky over the sleeping camp grew lighter, flushed with dawn.

Nayan slept soundly in his tent beside his wife, secure in the knowledge that with Bektor and Caidu supporting him, his forces could outnumber those of the Great Khan. He woke with the dawn and the first thing he heard was a soft thudding on the distant sands. He could not understand what it was until the warcries rang out.

Rushing out of his tent half-naked, he saw that the whole camp was encircled by hundreds of banners and that horsemen and infantry were pouring over the dunes all around. He had time to notice the Great Khan himself, sitting calmly on his horse on top of a large dune, directing the attack. The next instant, he was fighting for his life. The first flurry of arrows was so swift and accurate that dozens were killed in their sleep. Lances uprooted tents and brands were hurled on to them. Nayan heard his wife screaming in their burning *yurt*, but there was no chance of reaching her. There was fighting all around him and he had to wicld his sword with superhuman strength to avoid being overwhelmed.

When resistance threatened in any part of the camp,

Kublai's arm would fall and a fresh wave of troops raced to crush it. Near him, Jaimu could not hide her distress. Marco, seeing it all from the same vantage point, was appalled. Powerless to stop it, he instead tried to record some of the more horrific details on a piece of parchment so that it would never be forgotten. He saw lances thrust clean through bodies, limbs hacked off, horses blinded, men burnt alive, throats cut. At the height of the massacre, he even picked out the burly figure of a proud young man whom he had once wrestled. Kasar had unsaddled and stabbed one of the commanders, then fought off two more attackers, only to be surrounded by a dozen lances that lunged forward as one, skewering him like a wild boar.

And even when the fighting was over, the reek of it remained.

Kublai's soldiers celebrated by looting the tents that were not lying in ashes, stripping the corpses of the Crosses on their tunics and throwing them on to a growing heap. Laughter mingled with the groans of the dying and the wounded. Marco entered the camp with the Empress Jaimu, both of them unable to look at some of the sights. Eventually he found what he was searching for, Princess Aigiarac, pale and beautiful still in death, her sword in her hand, lay near the body of Kasar, whom she had tried to save.

After victory came the final humiliation of the enemy commander. Nayan, stripped and bound, was made to watch while his banner was hurled down before Kublai and all the Crosses taken from the tunics. Cheers resounded. Kublai looked down at the captured rebel leader as he was led to stand before him. 'You, Nayan, are guilty of the greatest treason that has ever been committed in the empire.'

The Empress was weeping silently, gazing at the Cross on Nayan's neck. Marco, wanting to plead for mercy on his behalf, nerved himself to speak but anything he might have said was drowned out by the rhythmic demand of the army.

'Death! Kill! Kill! Kill! Kill!'

Kublai silenced the mass-chanting with a wave of his hand, then turned to Nayan. 'Since you are of my blood and the blood of Genghis, the Kha Khan, it cannot be spilt on the ground. You will die as prescribed by our law.'

He gestured and one of the men holding the prisoner tore the Cross from Nayan's neck and hurled it to the ground. The Empress Jaimu sobbed. Marco bent to pick up the Cross, unaware that Phags-pa was watching him.

Wounded and dazed, Nayan was dragged backwards towards a carpet that had been laid out on open ground. He was rolled up tight in it and left. Kublai, his commanders, his standard-bearers and his infantry moved off without a backward glance. Marco stayed long enough to see the Mongol horsemen begin their advance towards the carpet and then he, too, moved away.

When he next looked back at the camp, the body of Nayan had been trampled into the ground.

'No! No! No!' yelled Kublai, smacking the arm of his throne.

'But I'm an old man, Great Lord,' Niccolo argued.

'Not as old as me!' Kublai snapped pettishly.

'No, Great Lord. But it is a journey that soon I will be unable to make. If I don't leave soon, I shall never see Venice and my home again.'

'You went home once,' Kublai reminded him.

'That was almost twenty years ago, Great Lord.'

Niccolo Polo could see that he was wasting his time. The Great Khan Kublai, now almost eighty, was testy, capricious, self-willed, losing his sight and racked by gout. He would never give permission for them to return to Venice. They would be kept forever in the luxurious imprisonment of the Forbidden City.

Kublai tried to justify his decision. 'No. I cannot spare you. And I will be angry if you speak of it again. You have made fortunes since you have been here.'

'True, Great Lord.'

'Whatever they are, from today they are doubled.'

'You are too kind—' Niccolo began.

'But do not ever mention leaving again!' Kublai scowled.

Niccolo bowed and left the audience room. He passed on the news to Matteo, who sighed resignedly and looked out at the high walls that enclosed them. It made him long even more to see the open skyline of Venice.

Marco Polo leaned over the parapet and gazed down upon the rooftops, temple cupolas and pagodas. Sadness weighed down his spirits and he could find nothing to relieve him of his burden. A hand, light as a leaf, brushed against his shoulder. He was surprised to find that Phags-pa had come out on the terrace behind him.

'Are you still grieving over Nayan's death, Marco?' the Lama asked, with surprising gentleness.

'I can't forget that massacre. Brother fighting brother,' Marco told him.

'I have suffered, too,' Phags-pa confided. 'I dreamed of a peace that would make all things better – even men's hearts.' He paused. 'But Nayan doesn't deserve to be mourned by you, or by Jaimu.'

'He wanted peace, too.'

'No, Marco. His pride was stronger than any other feeling. Just think – if your God really *had* been on Nayan's side, he wouldn't have allowed him to be defeated. It was only a rebel that was defeated – not your faith.' Phags-pa smiled faintly. 'If he heard me now, talking like this, the Great Khan would think that I had been converted to your Christ.'

'Have you?' Marco smiled back.

'I saw you pick up Nayan's Cross after it had been torn from his neck. I respected you for that. I said a long time ago that we should have understood each other better and been friends.' He sighed deeply. 'What great things we could have achieved together.'

'It's too late now,' Marco said with some regret. After all this time, the Head Lama and he were only just beginning to appreciate each other.

'Perhaps. Yet friendship is a bridge that can reach across space and time. Even when you are back in your homeland, in Venice . . .'

'When will that be? The Khan refuses to let us go. He is keeping us here.'

'Maybe he will change his mind,' Phags-pa suggested.

'We have asked him a hundred times. Each time he refuses even to consider the idea of releasing us. What can we do? His word is law.' He became rueful. 'And we have seen what happens to those who break that law.'

Phags-pa gazed out over the city. 'I am grateful to you for many things, Marco, and I believe in paying my debts.'

'Debts?'

'Yes.' Phags-pa tried to sound casual. 'By the way, have you heard that Princess Kokachin has arrived back?'

Marco was surprised. 'Kokachin? But she should have been in Persia by now, with her future husband, the Il-Khan, Arghun.'

'She and the Persian envoys got as far as Daciu on the edge of the Gobi desert when they were caught in a violent sandstorm and forced to turn back.'

'They should have travelled by sea. With a stout ship and expert navigators, they could have reached Persia in safety,' suggested Marco.

'I'm glad you think that,' Phags-pa murmured.

'Why?'

Phags-pa turned to face him, his eyes hooded. 'The envoys have complained that they were given poor guides. Now they're demanding the services of someone more expert.'

'Demanding? They dare to *demand* from the Khan?' Marco was surprised.

'They do it with tact and diplomacy, Marco. And since the Khan is anxious to maintain good relations with his empire in the West, he wishes the envoys to be satisfied.'

Marco frowned, 'Experienced navigators are not so easy to find, though.' He felt the beginning of excitement, having now realized what Phags-pa was telling him.

Phags-pa smiled. 'Well, I am glad we had this chance to talk. Soon I must leave Khanbalic. I will be returning to my temple in the snow.'

'Tibet?'

'I need the solitude and the purity there. Power is a poison, Marco. It corrupts everyone in time.'

'I envy you,' Marco admitted. 'I wish I was as certain as you are about what I should do.'

'Certainty is an illusion. We are all journeying towards a great unknown. The only certainty is uncertainty.'

Marco was touched. The cold, impassive, humourless Phags-pa whom he had distrusted and despised for so long had revealed himself as a warm, sensitive man with strong convictions. And he had provided Marco and the others with a faint hope of returning to Venice after all.

'Shall we go?' Phags-pa asked. 'The Great Khan is waiting . . .'

Niccolo and Matteo were waiting outside the Audience Room when they arrived, both looking rather bemused. Marco had no time to explain to them why they had been summoned, because Phags-pa conducted them straight in to see the Great Khan.

Kublai was seated on his throne, irritable, unhappy and uncomfortable at having to control himself. Below him on the dais sat Princess Kokachin, wearing her court regalia and a magnificent silver belt. Marco noted how she had matured into a beautiful young woman since he had first met her, and he also saw the air of determination about her. Clearly, she would do all she could to ensure that the arrangements for her journey to Persia were made speedily and in the proper manner.

Prince Timur was seated in Chinkin's former throne. The three Persian envoys were kneeling before the dais. The Venetians went through the ritual greetings, then knelt in front of the Khan. Marco's hopes were dampened slightly when he saw Kublai's obvious dislike of the plan that had been suggested. Old, ailing, irascible and used to having his own way in everything, Kublai was not going to agree easily to the envoys' request. 'You would first have to cross the Indian Ocean. It would be a voyage fraught with dangers.'

Ulatai, the leader of the envoys, spoke up. 'Yet Lord Marco has crossed it twice, Great Lord, as your ambassador – in perfect safety. And at this season, many traders make the journey.'

'Would it not be better to trust yourselves to one of them?' asked Kublai, sharply.

'Is the bride of the Khan of the West to be sent to him on a merchant ship?' Ulatai responded, indignantly.

Kokachin tensed and looked up at Kublai, who grimaced. 'It would not be suitable,' he muttered.

'It would be an insult!' Ulatai asserted.

Phags-pa intervened smoothly. 'You have heard the Great Khan, gentlemen. More than anyone, he appreciates that Her Royal Highness must be given a noble escort, one that will do honour to the Il-Khan and to himself.'

'Our most experienced ambassadors and ladies of our court will attend Princess Kokachin,' said Timur, speaking for the first time. 'Marco Polo, his father and his uncle have talents that are exceptional, and knowledge that is incomparable. Your master will surely be satisfied if they were to be in charge of the expedition?'

Ulatai and the other envoys kowtowed. Marco was surprised by the Prince's intervention in his favour, but Niccolo and Matteo, who had now realized what the meeting was all about, were highly excited. Kublai looked around them and saw that he was outnumbered. More annoyed and uneasy than ever, he addressed Marco. 'When would you have to leave?'

'At once, Great Lord.'

'So soon?'

'The winds are in our favour. In another month or so, they will be against us.'

'We cannot postpone any more, Great Khan,' Ulatai stressed.

'The Princess must be fearing that she will never be married,' observed Phags-pa, dryly.

This reference to Chinkin made Kublai wince with pain. The pressures on him to concede were very strong, but something in him resisted.

'What message am I to send the Il-Khan?' Ulatai asked.

Kublai made a supreme effort to control his anger and his displeasure. He knew he could not risk offending the envoys' master, Arghun. 'Make your arrangements to leave,' he muttered.

Delight made Niccolo and Matteo gasp. Kokachin was smiling and the envoys were obviously relieved. Marco looked gratefully at Phags-pa who had more than repayed any debt he owed him.

'The audience is over,' Phags-pa said, seeing that it was wise to usher everyone out.

As they all bowed and retreated to the door, Kublai pointed to Marco. 'Stay one moment.'

Marco remained on his knees. As the others filed out, he looked up at the Great Khan. Even in old age, there was still a grandeur and majesty about him. Marco might have reservations, might be appalled at the barbaric streak in him that had led him to such wholesale slaughter, but there was still much to admire and respect.

'I cannot let you go, Marco,' Kublai said.

Marco's heart lurched. 'Great Lord!' he protested.

'I cannot let you go . . . unless you promise to return.' The qualification gave Marco hope, and the Khan went on. 'I know that it is a difficult decision to make and you will need time to consider it carefully. It's a promise that should not be given lightly, but that is my wish.'

'Your wish – or your command?' Marco smiled.

Kublai gave a faint smile, a hint of his former self, so long obscured by the killings and bloodshed. 'I understood that the two were the same. Now, listen. I will write letters to the Pope and to the Kings of France, England and

Spain. These will be entrusted to you to deliver because you appreciate the importance of building those bridges between East and West, between the Mongol empire and the Christian territories.' He became more tentative. 'When you have delivered the letters and seen your homeland again . . . I would like you to return to Khanbalic.'

'I promise!' Marco said, firmly.

'No, do not rush into an answer. Allow yourself—'

'I promise, Great Lord,' Marco insisted. 'And I will try to keep that promise.'

'I know you will. If I am still alive . . .'

A few days later, early in the morning with the sky grey and overcast, Marco took his horse from its stall and led it past the guards to the Imperial stables. It was something he had not done since the days when Chinkin and he used to ride every morning with the Khan.

Ahead of him, he saw as he expected the master-of-the-horse holding the Khan's superb white stallion for Kublai to put on the saddle himself, as was the strict custom. All the grooms present had prostrated themselves. Kublai was sweating with exertion as he fastened the girths. He broke off, pleased, as Marco approached and kneeled to him. 'You have come to ride with me one last time?' he asked.

'Yes, Great Lord,' Marco told him. Now that the moment had come, Marco was deeply affected.

Moved, Kublai gestured to him to rise and turned back to finish fastening the straps. As he jerked and strained to pull them tight, he muttered, 'I would never have given my consent for you to leave, if I had known how much sorrow it would cause me.'

'It is hard for me, too, Great Lord,' Marco said, softly.

Kublai grunted. 'Well . . . Something of you will remain behind in this land, Marco Polo. As long as men have memory.'

Seeing that he could not manage to tighten the girth,

Marco glanced round to make sure that no-one was watching, took hold of the strap himself, heaved on it and clicked the buckle into position. Kublai squeezed his arm in gratitude, then dismissed the master-of-the-horse. He took hold of the saddle and, with some effort, got his foot in the stirrup. He tried to heave himself up into the saddle, but his age, his weight and failing strength were against him, and he could not do it. Distressed and anxious for him, Marco stepped nearer, but Kublai gestured to him roughly not to help. Summoning up all his strength, he tried once more and failed, hanging on to the saddle, panting, his face against the horse's flank. The effort left him exhausted and deeply ashamed.

'Caidu was right,' he muttered. 'We conquered the world on horseback – and should rule it on horseback. But now I'm too old to stay in the saddle. I'm only half a Mongol.' He was trembling, and had to catch his breath. 'Too much blood has been spilt. The gods are angry with us . . . and Timur will inherit a crumbling empire.' He made an effort to pull himself together and stand straight. 'Everything I have done was for Chinkin . . . But what I gave him was not what he wanted. He believed in the dream that China could be united.' He shook his head heavily. 'Not in his time, nor in mine. But one day . . . One day . . .'

He turned back to his horse, gathering all his strength for one last effort. Marco stepped closer, knelt and cupped his hands. Kublai reached out to touch Marco's face in a gesture of great tenderness. Then accepted. He put his foot into Marco's hands and, with his help, mounted the horse at last. Once in the saddle, he straightened and shook himself, gripping the bridle. Once again he had become an imperious and commanding figure. Kublai raised his hand in salute to Marco and wheeled his horse.

Marco watched him until he was out of sight.

Drums and trumpets sounded. Large crowds had flocked

to the quayside in Amoy to watch as the huge Imperial junk was made ready, sailors checking the rigging and swarming over the decks. Princess Kokachin was one of the first passengers aboard, with her retinue of well over fifty ladies-in-waiting. Next came a Sung princess, daughter of the King of Manzi, with an equal number of ladies in attendance. Marco, Niccolo and Matteo boarded the ship to the cheers of the well-wishers, who knew and respected the Venetians and the service they had given to the Mongol empire.

Prince Timur took the opportunity to have a last word with Marco. They had never been close and his manner was stiff and formal. 'It is a solemn day in our lives, Lord Marco.'

Marco matched his tone. 'Please convey to the Great Khan my continued loyalty, your Imperial Highness, and tell him that my final thought on leaving China was of him.'

Timur hesitated. 'Many years ago, my grandfather told me why you first came here, as envoy from your Pope. It made me suspicious of you. Your privileged position with my father, whom you saw more than I did, only made me more resentful.'

Marco was taut, but he had expected nothing more from him. 'I am sorry, Prince Timur. I loved your father very much, but I never intended to keep him from his children.'

'Do not apologize,' Timur said, with the same hint of hesitancy. 'The fault was on my side. I was too envious. Now it is all different, Lord Marco. I have come to realize why even Phags-pa honours you.'

Marco could see how embarrassed the Prince was, but he responded to the younger man's sincerity. Their relationship in the past had been strained and uneasy, and it took courage and honesty for Timur to admit that his judgement had been at fault.

'As you journey home,' Timur went on, more easily, 'you may think that your embassy to China was a failure, that you leave nothing behind you.' He took a deep breath.

'In respect for you – and in memory of my father and my grandfather – when I am Khan, I shall have a church of your faith built in Khanbalic, for those who follow you here.'

'Thank you . . .' Marco was surprised when the prince bowed to him.

'The part of you that is in our hearts will never leave China. It will be handed down from father to son, from generation to generation.'

Prince Timur held out his arms and Marco clasped them tightly. Their friendship was sealed.

When Timur had gone ashore and the last farewells had been exchanged, the ship raised anchor, turned its vast sails to catch the full strength of the wind, and began to glide out of the harbour, to the sustained cheering of the bystanders.

With Niccolo and Matteo, Marco stayed on deck until China was no more than a tiny speck off the port bow. Venetians were born to travel, and now they travelled home, taking with them a last memory as they left the harbour of an enormous brightly-coloured kite with a laughing boy perched on it, soaring high above them and waving goodbye.

An immensely long, exacting and perilous voyage lay ahead of them and they knew that there would be delays, setbacks and continual problems. But they set out with buoyant spirits, believing that one day in the distant future, whatever lay in wait, they would see the Serene Republic of Venice again, a welcoming glow on the far horizon.

It was over twenty years since Marco had first sailed out into the Adriatic with his father, uncle, Giulio, Agostino and Jacopo. His life had been an endless sequence of travels, dangers, joys, sorrows, adventures, explorations, losses, honours and unforgettable sights. It had been a journey from youth to maturity, from innocence to experience, from insignificance to distinction. He had found a father, he had found friends, he had found himself. Most of all, he had travelled through time from an old world into a new one.

Before him lay the city of his birth; behind him lay an empire that had welcomed him, taught him, and come to respect him. Though some of his memories would return to wound and harrow him, he would always have the consolation that the Khan, his court and the whole Mongol empire would remember the name of Marco Polo.

Epilogue

Christendom was ungrateful.

The young man who had once set out on a spiritual mission with the blessing of the Pope himself was now a middle-aged prisoner being interrogated by a panel of black-robed Dominican monks.

'You admit to having entered Pagan places of worship?'

'And to having taken part in magic rites and abominations?'

Captain Marco Polo looked at his questioners, wondering if any of them even wanted to hear the truth from him. Pope Gregory, who had blessed him at the start of his journey to the East, had been dead for years, or he might have vouched for him. The members of the clerical council sitting in judgement on him took such a narrow and intolerant view that he longed for some of the priests they called, in their ignorance, pagan.

His mind was drifting, as his junk had once drifted for a month with no wind to stir its sails in the Indian Ocean. Decimated by disease, the crew had been too weak to man the small boats and tow it. He thought of the long journey home, escorting Kokachin; of being trapped on Sumatra by the monsoons and having to live behind a hastily-built stockade, ever on guard against the attacks of the local cannibals with their hideously painted faces and poison darts; of the gentle sweetness of young Kokachin, who never complained of the hardships, and the deep affection that had grown between them. The tenderness of his feelings for Kokachin had healed the hurts of the past.

Their voyage lasted over two years. On their arrival at Hormuz, having lost all their escorting ships and half their men through disease and storm and pirate attacks, they learned that Arghun, Il-Khan of Persia, to whom she was pledged, had died. At the same time, they also heard that the Great Kublai had gone to his secret resting place in the Altai. Timur was now the Kha Khan. After their first grief was over, Marco remembered the excitement of realizing that Kokachin was free, and that there was nothing to stop her travelling on with him to Venice. Then the messengers had come from the regent governing Persia for Arghun's young son, Ghazan. In accordance with ancient Mongol custom, Ghazan would marry his dead father's intended bride. Kokachin would be his queen. The messengers had come to take her to him, and the few of her ladies who had survived the journey.

Barely holding back her tears, Kokachin said goodbye to Niccolo and Matteo, who had become like twin fathers to her, and finally turned to Marco. Explaining to the surprised messengers that all the gifts she had brought to reward her escort had been lost, she unclasped the silver and gold belt from her waist, the symbol of her royalty, and gave it to him as a remembrance. It carried the same message as her tears, that with her gift she gave her heart for him to keep. But she could not neglect her duty.

The Polos journeyed on, coming to Trebizond, the first Christian city they had set foot in for over twenty years. And there they were robbed of most of their remaining possessions. Fortunately, Marco wore the precious belt with his own, under his tunic, and Niccolo had advised them to adopt his old habit of travelling in their plainest clothes, carrying their riches in the form of jewels sewn into the lining. Thanks to his good advice they saved enough of their fortune to ensure a comfortable and respected future life.

When they arrived at last in Venice in their shabby clothes, the new servants at their home tried to chase them away. Uncle Zane was dead and Aunt Flora so old it took her minutes to recognize them. How sorry people had been for them, returning after all this time as paupers . . . Accepting invitations to their homecoming reception, their relations and former friends had come out of charity and found them still dressed in their worn and travel-stained clothes, only bread and thin soup on the table. When Marco, Niccolo and Matteo had ripped off their outer garments to reveal themselves in the splendid cloth of gold, silver belts and jewelled necklets of nobles of the Mongol empire, the surprise had been extreme. It was almost like a fairytale.

Marco was smiling, as he remembered. He was jolted back to the council chamber in Genoa by a voice shouting at him.

The balding, heavily-jowled monk was demanding an answer. 'Speak up! Will you now confess that most of what you have caused to be written is nothing but a tissue of lies?'

Marco decided to continue telling the truth, whatever the cost. 'I have only reported what I saw, without adding or taking anything away. My Christian conscience is one thing, my eyes are another. With regard to all the religions that I have talked about, I have learned one thing. They are good or bad according to the hearts of those that practise them.'

Murmurs of alarm and disapproval filled the council chamber. What had been said was nothing short of heresy. The monks seated at the table were shocked by the suggestion that any religion but their own could be described as good, and they were insulted to be told that their faith did not in fact bring equal blessing to all whom it touched.

Seated to one side, Master Pietro de Abano winced in anxiety. Marco was virtually condemning himself; he wished he could be more cautious in his replies. Beside de Abano sat Brother Damian, the eager young monk who had visited Marco in his cell. He, too, began to fear for the prisoner. On the bench next to him, Captain Arnolfo shifted uneasily. He had warned Messer Marco not to risk burning for a book.

'Can you still call yourself a Christian!' challenged the old monk at the centre of the table.

'Yes,' Marco replied firmly.

'When you have been in the places you have been!'

Brother Damian tried to intervene. 'Saint Paul did not hesitate to enter the temples of Pagan deities in Greece and Rome—'

'Do you dare to say that this Venetian is like the Holy Apostle?' the old monk demanded, scandalized.

'That was not my argument . . .'

'I say,' Marco interrupted, 'that I have never been so close to my God as after having known the religions of the world.'

The old monk was about to reply when he was stopped by a gesture from the emaciated man to his left. This man turned his attention to Rustichello, who was watching the proceedings with Giovanni on a bench. 'You wrote that Messer Marco Polo had found the Garden of Eden!' he accused.

'I never said that!' Marco denied.

Rustichello was hesitant and uneasy. 'Well . . . maybe I wrote it by mistake, Marco . . . when you were talking about Badakhshan.' He faced the clerical council and tried to show his readiness to oblige. 'We can cut it out . . .'

Giovanni laughed aloud, then became embarrassed as the court glared at him. He lowered his head, uneasily.

'Is it not true,' asked the old monk, returning to the attack, 'that you, Rustichello of Pisa, have written – as *he* dictated – of Oriental wives who lie with foreign men with the consent and encouragement of their husbands?'

'Messer Polo said that it was their custom . . . their way of honouring guests.' Seeing the shocked response to his remark, Rustichello tried to retrieve the situation. 'But every sailor in Pisa or Venice – and probably in Genoa, too – tells the same story.'

The emaciated monk took over. 'The fact that sin is repeated in many parts of the world, and is multiplied, does not make it less abominable! Nor less to be condemned in those who spread its stench or tolerate it! These stories that have been told – they are not fit for innocent ears!'

'Forgive me . . .' It was Giovanni, trying to catch their attention.

'Well?' the old monk asked, irritably.

'I just wanted to say, Reverend Sirs, that his tales made me homesick . . . made me long for my wife. How lucky, I thought, for me to have a married woman who lives for me, *only* for me, all her life . . .'

Giovanni's voice trailed away and it was obvious that his comment had made no impact whatsoever on the grim-faced council. It had, however, provided Brother Damian with a point which he was able to develop.

'Indeed, it is true. To a God-fearing conscience, what Marco the Venetian tells us can be a valuable lesson. By exposing sin, he exalts in contrast the true aim of man: virtue.'

The monks at the table conferred in lowered voices, some taking Brother Damian's point. There were still serious reservations, however, and these more decisive. It was the old monk who took it upon himself to voice one of the main ones.

'Your statements on the existence of groups or clusters of stars which our astronomic science does not recognize corrupt the harmonious order of creation as it appears to us, faithful servants of God and His truth.'

'Similarly subversive,' his emaciated colleague added, 'are your descriptions of countries and peoples which you claim exist in places where by certain knowledge there is nothing but howling darkness.'

De Abano shifted on his seat. The old monk noticed.

'The learned doctor, Pietro de Abano, has permission to speak.'

The old monk relaxed complacently, confident that the eminent witness would refute the scientific heresy of Marco Polo. From de Abano's severe and authoritative manner, Marco was worried.

'No astronomic map we possess includes the stars that this Venetian claims to have seen,' de Abano agreed. Marco lowered his head, disheartened. 'Yet I have come to learn that Messer Polo's observations, unlikely as they seem, have recently been confirmed by other navigators and Arab astronomers.'

'Heresy confirmed by infidels!' the old monk protested.

'And not only by them,' de Abano informed him. 'We have at long last been able to read . . .' He broke off and turned to Marco to apologize for something. 'We do not *yet* have the privilege of knowing how to reproduce books with special machinery – to print them, as your Chinese friends say – and we have to content ourselves with waiting for patient hands to transcribe copies one by one . . .'

The emaciated monk was impatient. 'The point?'

'We have at last been able to read the long report written by the Franciscan monk, Giovanni from Pian dei Carpini, on his travels beyond the borders of Mongolia . . .' de Abano could not resist a faint smile at the emaciated monk. 'Where it was certain knowledge that nothing exists but howling darkness.'

There was a ripple of suppressed laughter around the room, but the monks were only angered. Their gaunt spokesman rounded on Marco once more.

'If your life in Mongolia was so luxurious and noble, why did you wish to return to Venice?'

'My father and uncle wished to see their home again before they died. As I did. But I believe it was God's will that we should return – to show men the road to new knowledge.'

'So you continue to claim that everything in your book is true?' the old monk demanded. 'Men flying? A magical powder that sends objects hurtling through the air? A metal tube that brings stars nearer? Be warned, Messer Polo.'

'As God is my witness,' said Marco, earnestly, 'I have told less than half of all I have seen.'

'If I might comment, Reverend Brothers?' Brother Damian was given permission to speak. 'It has been confirmed by the Patriarch of Venice that Messer Polo was indeed sent as envoy by Pope Gregory to the Mongol

Khan. We can only admire the foresight of the great Pope and also Messer Polo's courage. For think, brothers, if this mission had succeeded! Think of the glory for the Church if the Khan and all the subjects of his great empire had embraced our faith!'

There was a long pause as the council considered.

Marco stood quietly, knowing his fate was being decided. He felt that it would be unjust if he were condemned simply for reporting what he had seen. And if they had read the whole of his story, why did they bother about flying men and gunpowder and telescopes? Those were minor matters. All could be explained. What could not be explained were the true miracles – the love he had shared with Monica, the peace of mind of the Immortal, the grandeur of God as revealed in a thousand varied landscapes.

His incoherent thoughts were stilled suddenly, when the judge spoke.

'It is with some reluctance that we reach our decision, Messer Polo,' the emaciated monk said sternly. 'We find that you have touched on questions beyond your understanding and steered perilously close to false doctrines against which the Holy Mother Church must be constantly on Her guard. But . . .' In the pause that followed, Marco tried hard to cling to hope. '. . . We believe that you had no intention to sin. Therefore, we order you to revise your tales and take out all dangerous statements. And may God have mercy on you and enlighten you! You are free to go.'

Giovanni, unable to believe the verdict, jumped to his feet in joy as if he was already free. Arnolfo, de Abano and Brother Damian smiled in relief. Marco bowed to all three of them in gratitude. Everyone was rising and the members of the council stalked out of the room. The one person still seated was Rustichello, flanked by guards ready to take him back to his cell.

Marco crossed to his friend. Rustichello rose and they looked at each other for a long moment.

'Enjoy your freedom, Marco. For me, also,' Rustichello said.

'For you?' Marco did not understand.

'Pisa, my country, has lost the war and cannot find peace. You Venetians are now being released. God alone knows when I will be.' He paused. 'I ask you to forgive me.'

'For what?'

'For a few inventions . . . for some background colour that my pen was allowed to scribble. When you read what I have written, you will see. Don't hate me for my little additions. I can see now that they were not needed. Yours is truly a book of wonders.'

'Ours! *Our* book, Rustichello,' Marco told him.

He reached out his hand to shake the writer's, but he was too late. The guards took Rustichello by the arms and led him back to the tower cell. Marco stood there for some time with his hand still outstretched.

Nothing had changed.

When they arrived back in Venice and saw St Mark's Square again, it looked exactly as it always had done, a cheerful mixture of splendour and squalor. There were the same shops and booths and stalls, the same entertainers competing for audiences, the same raucous noise of barter, the same shifting and self-absorbed throng of pedlars, priests, shopkeepers, merchants, sailors, nobles, housewives, prostitutes and lively children.

Marco stood on the deck with Giovanni and all the other discharged Venetian prisoners, sharing a communal emotional response that was overwhelming. Most wept, some laughed hysterically, some collapsed. They were home.

A small crowd, mostly women and children, waited on the quay with anxious joy while the vessel was moored. Giovanni at last saw something he had dreamed about every night in Genoa. A rounded, pleasant-faced, careworn woman was standing near the edge of the crowd with two small children. Giovanni turned to Marco as if to tell him something, but he could only mouth wordlessly. Grabbing his bundle, he rushed headlong towards his family. When his wife saw him, she cried out and they flung themselves into each other's arms.

Pleased for his friend's happiness, Marco turned away as Giovanni picked up his children and tried to kiss away the memory of his absence. The sight of such joy only served to remind him of his loneliness. No wife or child had come to meet him. As he gazed back across St Mark's Square, he saw that Venice was carrying on as if it had not even noticed his arrival.

He picked up his belongings and left the galley. Eager to get away from the sprawling life of the Square, he walked to a quieter part of the city in search of a particular canal. It was the place where he had once walked with Caterina and he did so again now, reliving their stroll and their talk. When he reached the spot where she had skipped over the bridge and stolen fruit from the monks' garden, he smiled and turned away.

His next visit was to the abandoned boatyard, now almost derelict, but still recognizable as the haunt of his boyhood. The laughter of his friends seemed to fill the place, as it had done in those far-off days. He could almost hear it. Then he noticed the old bench on which Giulio had liked to squat. He thought about the cane fights and street games, about the building of a boat that sank in the lagoon, about the desperate, panting, fevered friend who had died in his arms.

The murals had largely gone, yet enough remained of Bartolomeo's art to rekindle a hundred memories. As he studied some of the fabled creatures that his friend had drawn, he recalled how Bartolomeo believed they existed simply because his imagination had conjured them up. When Marco looked closely at one drawing, he was spellbound for a moment. It was a small, fish-like creature with a beautiful fluid form and a face that could bewitch and allure a saint.

It was the face of Monica.

By the time he finally put her from his mind, he found that he was in the middle of St Mark's Square once more. Life bustled on around him and he, so long absent, was totally ignored. Marco did not mind. When a small procession of Turkish noblemen marched up the Square towards the Basilica, he did not join the crowd that surged across to see what was happening. He was seeing the lines of banners of the defeated Sung, and Bayan advancing to the Great Khan. And hearing the thunder of voices.

Marco Polo stood alone in the middle of an almost empty Square. It was the place from which he had left to embark on travels that lasted almost a quarter of a century; travels that had taken him to places and peoples unheard of in the West. Part of himself had been left behind in those places. It had been buried with Giulio, betrayed by Achmet, given to Chinkin. It had been locked away in a Buddhist temple with Monica.

He was a citizen of Venice, but a son of the whole world.

Many did not believe me – many still do not believe me – but I believe it was God's will that we should return, so that men might know the things that are in the world . . . since there was never man yet, Christian or Saracen, Tartar or Pagan, who explored so much of the world as I, Messer Marco Polo, son of Messer Niccolo Polo, great and noble citizen of Venice.

Thanks be to God
Amen, Amen